D0441284

ALSO BY JIM KNIPFEL

Noogie's Time to Shine

Ruining It for Everybody

The Buzzing

Quitting the Nairobi Trio

Slackjaw

UNPLUGGING PHILCO

Jim Knipfel

SIMON & SCHUSTER
New York London Toronto Sydney

Simon & Schuster
1230 Avenue of the Americas
New York, NY 10020

First Simon & Schuster trade paperback edition April 2009

Designed by Jill Putorti

10 9 8 7 6 5 4 3 2 1

Library of Congress Cataloging-in-Publication Data

Knipfel, Jim.
Unplugging Philco / Jim Knipfel.
p. cm.
1. Brooklyn (New York, N.Y.)—Fiction. 2. National security—Social aspects—Fiction. I. Title
PS3611.N574U66 2009
813'.6—dc22 2008054134

ISBN-13: 978-1-4165-9284-6
ISBN-10: 1-4165-9284-9

For David E. Williams, a true son of liberty

When other people start thinking about you, it's to figure out how to torture you, and nothing else.

—Louis-Ferdinand Céline,
Journey to the End of the Night

ONE

There was a helidrone thumping in wide, slow circles high overhead. Apart from that, the neighborhood was silent.

Wally Philco pulled the front door closed behind him with a scrape and heavy click. It sounded final in the still morning air.

From the top of the brownstone stoop he surveyed the sidewalk below. He knew he should've done this before stepping outside, but it was too late now. He was exposed. His eyes scanned the empty concrete to his right, then his left. It seemed clear.

As he slowly began to descend the steps he saw them a full block away, silhouettes in the dim grainy light. Three of them were gathered at the corner, talking among themselves in voices far too low to hear at this distance. They were spread out across the sidewalk, making any easy passage difficult, if not impossible. Of course, trying to walk around or between them wasn't even an issue.

Wally dropped into a crouch, knees be damned, trying to hide behind the skeletal iron banister. It was useless. Hardly any cover at all. If they saw him he was doomed. His only hope was that they were too preoccupied to notice.

The trick, he'd learned through painful experience, was to get across the street before they caught a whiff of him. If he could just get across the street things should be okay.

Still crouching, briefcase in hand, he checked the road. There were no cars approaching from either direction. That was both a blessing and a curse. It meant he wouldn't have to do any risky dodging through hostile traffic (at a mildly battered and soft forty-three, he no longer dodged the way he used to), but it also meant he wouldn't be able to use the noise and moving cars for cover.

As furtively as possible he checked the three of them again. Still chatting. If they began moving his way he'd need a new plan, and quick. If only there was another pedestrian to draw their attention away from him—but there never was. Nobody else was out at this hour. It would be simple enough to change his own schedule, he sometimes thought, but he knew it would never happen.

He flexed his legs and his toes, checked the sidewalk directly below him again, then took a deep breath and willed himself into action.

As he scrambled down the stairs like a convulsive heron, Wally told himself for the thirtieth time in as many days that it was about time he picked himself up a new pair of shoes. This old pair he was wearing was simply not made for scrambling of any kind. Not with soles worn that smooth and thin.

Without pausing at the bottom to see if they'd caught sight of him, he dashed across the sidewalk, staying as low as he could manage, and ducked between two parked cars. He was breathing heavy and sweating despite the cool breeze, but at least he had some decent cover here.

Holding on to the rear bumper of a cherry red Chrysler Xanax for support, he pushed himself up just enough to peer over the trunk and down the street.

They still hadn't seen him, too engrossed as they were in their little chat.

Probably exchanging diapering tips and murder stories, he thought. He checked the street again.

There was someone at the stoplight two blocks away. He was driving one of those Dodge Dipsomatic GX Mini Forts, an enormous vehicle, almost a full lane and a half wide. It was little more than a street-modified tank, really, but they'd become quite popular lately.

Perfect, he thought. That would be his ticket across the street. Staying low between the parked cars, Wally shifted his body around to face the opposite curb, tensing himself to jump and run.

The light changed and the Mini Fort began to rumble slowly toward him.

"*Come on, come on…*" he whispered. He wanted to check over his shoulder once more but didn't dare, knowing it could throw him off. Timing was everything here.

The monstrous vehicle drew closer, and Wally prepared to dash behind it as it passed and across the street, letting the expansive bulk of the Mini Fort block their line of sight for a good eight or ten seconds at least.

Five...four... he counted down in his head.

"*GOOD MORNING GOOD MORNING GOOD MORNING, GOOD CITIZENS!*" The voice exploded in his ear.

Wally flinched hard and half stood. The driver of the approaching Mini Fort, thinking the jerkoff who'd just popped up from between the parked cars was going to dive under his wheels, leaned on his horn. He didn't need another one of those this week. The thunderous wail, like five foghorns being clubbed to death, ruptured the quiet morning. The heads of the three figures at the end of the block snapped around.

The Mini Fort screamed past him, horn still blaring, the driver yelling inaudibly. In a panic, and with that voice still bellowing in his ear, Wally bolted into the street. He normally would've aimed to dive between two more parked cars on the other side but he knew it was too late for that. They were on to him—that much was a given—and he had to get out of there fast. Lumbering and heaving, his knees screaming, he aimed for the far corner. If he could get around the corner and up the street out of view before they caught up with him, he'd be safe. He *might* be safe, anyway—there were no promises in this business. He didn't dare look over his shoulder. He didn't want to know, and he couldn't afford the break in concentration. Had to focus on that corner.

The voice was screaming in his ear.

"*...GLORIOUS DAY HERE IN NEW YORK CITY, WITH AN EXPECT—*"

With one hand in front of him, the other still clutching the flailing briefcase while trying to cover his ear, eyes wildly measuring the distance to the far curb, Wally began to giggle. It was a high-pitched, staccato giggle. A giggle of fear and panic—the kind he hadn't experienced since he was very young, and his father was chasing him down the hall and through the kitchen. He knew his father was getting closer, he knew there was no escape, and what had started as a simple game had quite suddenly become a terrifying hunt. He no longer wanted to be tickled.

This wasn't about tickling, though. It was no game at all—and nothing at all to giggle about.

His foot hit the far curb at an awkward angle and he stumbled briefly, arms swinging wide to either side, briefcase twisting his wrist, before regaining his footing. He continued running fast as he could a few more yards up the street, out of view.

Once he knew he was out of sight he slowed to a stop and leaned back against a pristine redbrick wall. Mouth open wide, eyes shut, it took a few long and painful seconds before he was able to catch his breath. His chest burned and he could feel the blood pulsing in his temples and gums.

That other voice was screaming.

"*...AMMA LEVELS AT A COMFORTABLE AND SAFE—*"

Wally reached into his pocket finally and slid his fingertip across a smooth vinyl button on his Earwig GL-70 communitainment unit. The voice in his head was abruptly silenced.

He waited, fully conscious of the new silence ringing in his ears. His teeth ached and his fingertips itched. He tasted copper. It felt like he might have bitten his tongue. He took several deep and labored breaths while snatching quick glances back toward the corner to see if they were following him.

If they were, they were taking their own sweet time about it. That was a relief. He simply couldn't run anymore.

Two minutes later, as his heart rate returned to something approaching normal, and after mopping the sweat from his eyebrows and cheeks and chin, he glanced up the street toward the avenue to make sure there weren't more of them waiting up there (sometimes there were), then continued up the narrow, uneven sidewalk. It wasn't the quickest way to the subway, but this morning it was his only choice. He hated starting every day like this, but there was no way around it. It's the way things were.

"*Stupid mothers,*" he muttered, before looking around nervously to make sure no one was within earshot.

Along the way, he kept an ear open for the squeak of unbalanced ATV wheels and the light clink of metal on metal approaching from behind. He also counted the ads on the sidewalk. He counted the ads every morning. It gave him something to focus on.

When he saw a new one, he paused and stared at the painted concrete.

It was for Flippy Bits Chips, a new algae snack Glaxxo International was putting out. The chartreuse letters of the name danced across the top of the ad. Beneath them, a bespectacled, apple-cheeked boy was grinning almost maniacally as he demanded, "Hey Ma, flip me some Flippy Bits!"

Wally smiled to himself. He'd have to remember that one.

The helidrone swooped low above the rooftops over Wally's

head. As he watched, it arced to the north and out of sight. He forgot about the ad and continued on his way to the train.

There was a sharp but hopeful beep when he swiped his identification card over the reader. He tapped the five-digit code of his intended destination onto the screen, held his briefcase up to the electronic sniffer, and stood motionless as a thin red beam pulsed over his face. When he heard another pleasant beep, he pushed his way through the turnstile.

He descended the stairs to the platform, where a guard wearing camouflaged fatigues and clutching an automatic rifle was waiting. At the man's feet sat a quivering, muscular rottweiler who stared at Wally with hopeless black eyes.

Wally flashed his card again and moved toward an empty aluminum bench. There were a handful of citizens down there already, all of them pacing, gesturing, and talking to themselves. Most of them were staring at two-inch-wide ovular minivid screens as they paced. He presumed that nearly all the screens were displaying live images of whatever happened to be directly in front of them—steel posts, benches, the gray tiled floor, other commuters. As time went on, more and more citizens were finding it impossible to interact with the world without an intervening vidscreen of some kind. It made things easier, somehow. More real.

Wally knew that within fifteen minutes the platform would be packed, so he liked to get there a little early. It gave him a chance to sit down and relax for a few minutes, which was always a relief after the morning chase.

Apart from the plasma adscreens buzzing and chirping at either end of the platform it was quiet. Things were safe down here. The other citizens had their own concerns, and he knew they wouldn't bother him.

The back of his shirt was still damp, but he'd stopped sweating. He was breathing normally again. His knees were still sore and shaky, but to be honest they were almost always sore and shaky these days.

Most people wouldn't—and didn't—give Wally Philco a second glance when they passed him on the street. Granted, most were deeply engrossed with whatever appeared on their minivids, but even if they saw him they likely wouldn't notice. He was just another citizen, nothing particularly unique or threatening about his appearance. Unremarkable tie, a jacket fraying slightly at the cuffs, permanent-press slacks, black vinyl briefcase.

If anyone looked closely enough at his skin, they might have noticed the scars left behind after an unfortunate and unholy bout of late adolescent acne. But no one to date had ever asked to closely examine his skin. Every once in a while he tried to grow a beard to cover the scars for his own sake, but it always came out thin and patchy, leaving him looking like he had the mange. The scars, he figured, were preferable.

All in all, he looked exactly as he was expected to look for a mid-level insurance company operative. It was as he preferred it. Nobody paid him any mind, and as a result his crises remained minor and private, and his evenings were mostly undisturbed.

He heard a sound echoing from deep within the subway tunnel, but it seemed to be coming from the wrong direction. It stopped him for a moment. Then he recognized what it was.

He glanced to his left, down the tracks into the darkness, and saw the dim approaching lights. He could feel his stomach tighten, and he turned his eyes away and down.

The arriving train wasn't his, wasn't anyone's. A slow, grinding yellow work train crawled out of the darkness of the tunnel, loud as a low-flying jet as it churned and squealed along the tracks. Instead of passenger cars, the engine was pulling a series of flatbeds. Some were empty, others carried wooden crates, still others were loaded with the hulks of rusting, filthy, and unrecognizable machines.

The work trains always made Wally uneasy, especially when he was more or less alone on the platform early in the morning. There was something inexorable about them, something powerful and menacing. The flat, arrhythmic clanging of the bell, the thick odor of coke dust and brimstone that always followed them like a comet's tail. No one ever seemed to be aboard. It was like they were dragging themselves deliberately and perpetually just beneath the surface world, pausing only now and then to pick up a few damned souls along the way.

We hurtle onward in the darkness, he thought, *down a million roads.* It was an old memory, a line that came to him every time one passed. He no longer remembered where he first heard it, or where it came from. Probably something he'd learned in school, but he couldn't be certain.

They moved so slowly, these trains, that every time one chugged past him, he felt the momentary urge to leap aboard one of the flatbeds himself, just to see where it would take him. He inevitably reconsidered, afraid he already knew the answer to that question.

Wally glanced up at the row of six monitors mounted above the platform. In three of them, he saw himself sitting on the bench and could watch the train passing slowly behind him.

At that moment, the train let loose with a piercing blast from its horn, and Wally's shoulders nearly came together behind his ears. In the restricted and tiled space, the blast was amplified a dozen times louder and sharper than the Mini Fort's horn had been. He should've known it was coming—they always blew the horn when they trolled through the station. Usually when they were directly behind him, too.

His shoulders gradually relaxed as the echoes faded, and he saw by the brightening beam of light spreading along the opposite wall that his own train—at least the train he'd been waiting for—was on its way.

It was either a few minutes early or a few minutes late that morning. In either case, Wally was relieved. The platform hadn't become too crowded yet, and with luck the train hadn't either.

He stood and approached the edge of the platform to wait. The other citizens were scattered evenly to either side of him, still talking to themselves, staring at their minivids, and shifting from foot to foot.

After the train hissed to a stop, the doors in front of Wally slid open silently, and from inside he heard dozens of voices, some louder than others, all speaking at once. He also caught the now familiar scent of heavy perfume. They'd started doing that on the subways a few months earlier—perfuming the cars. The transit authority thought it would make for a more pleasant trip. There had been rumors that a coalition of citizens allergic to perfume (and virtually every other chemical known to man) had attempted to file a lawsuit to block the practice but were quickly silenced and, as a group, "sent someplace where perfume wasn't an issue."

Wally stepped aboard and grabbed the empty seat to his immediate right.

Looking around, he saw that most of the plastic blue seats in that car remained empty. There were more than enough citizens to fill them, but they were opting instead to continue pacing up and down the aisle in a haphazard dance, talking to themselves and colliding with one another. No one seemed to be bothered.

Above all those voices was another, much louder than the rest. It was the same voice Wally had heard in his ear earlier that morning.

"*—anic level remains a steady vermilion... Our top story this morning: pop sensation Ambien McCorkle, winner of last month's Digipod Roundup, announced plans for her world tour today, which includes stops in war-torn Paris, the north African provinces of Raimiland and Symbionia, and of course...*"

He scanned the faces of the other passengers. Many of them he recognized from the regular morning commute, so they were okay. The ones he didn't recognize seemed okay too. Every other passenger, upon stepping aboard, had paused and made a similar scan before resuming his pacing.

When the doors opened at the next stop, another familiar face stepped aboard. Without pausing to scan the crowd he began weaving down the aisle, trying to avoid the other passengers. Wally knew his name because the man announced it every morning at the beginning of his spiel.

"Hello ladies an' gennelmen, my name is Smitty Winston," he began, trying to raise his voice above the din of the commuters and the broadcasts. "I'm *homeless*... an' I'm *hungry*. If you don't have it, I can understand that 'cause I don't have it... But if you could spare some change... a sandwich... piecea *fruit*... somethin' to *drink*... it would be greatly appreciated... Thank you."

It never changed. Every word, every beat, every intonation was exactly the same as it was every morning. Wally guessed that after spouting it hundreds of times a day over the years in crowded train after crowded train, Mr. Winston didn't even think about it anymore. Just opened his mouth and out it came. He'd almost become a strange source of comfort to Wally in the mornings. Something to count on. So long as Smitty was still making the rounds, all was right in the world.

A small security vid swiveled at either end of the car. Six different animated commercials were playing at once along the band of adscreens above the windows. There was a new one this morning, for Donkey Oaties, the breakfast cereal. There was also a public service announcement he'd never seen before. It featured a bear with the voice of Mortimer Snerd. The slogan (which the bear uttered shortly before devouring a presumably diabolical raccoon) was "Security is our biggest consumer item."

The news report continued, half buried under so many other voices. "*...within years and not decades, as previously thought... Finally, movie star Herschel Palantine has once again apologized for the June fifth comments he made regarding the nation's economy, and asks that we all forgive him. The trial is still scheduled to begin next week... And those are our top stories* *at the moment. I'm Gag Peptide, wishing you all a glorious and productive day, reminding you to be Good Citizens. Be vigilant—LWIW!"*

"*LWIW,*" Wally whispered, then closed his eyes, letting all the voices and jingles and colorful images flow over him.

Forty-five minutes later, he stopped by the coffee cart half a block away from the office. It was chillier in Manhattan than it had been in Brooklyn, though he knew it wouldn't last. A hazy brown fog obscured the upper floors of some of Midtown's taller buildings. On the street below, the early pedestrian traffic was growing thicker, as increasingly heavy clusters of citizens poured from the subways into the gray light, before scurrying to get back inside.

"Morning," Wally said, reaching into his pocket for the bill he'd set aside before leaving the house.

"Good morning, boss," replied the squat, round-faced Syrian who squinted down at Wally through the cart's square window. "How is today?"

"Guess I'll find out soon enough," Wally said, eyeing the array of donuts and bagels on display behind the glass. He was always curious and tempted but knew they were nothing but old pictures. "Large coffee please? Black?"

With the same bored, heavy sigh he offered Wally every morning, the coffee cart man grabbed a paper cup from the stack behind him, placed it beneath a polished steel spigot, and flipped a red lever. As the weak, flavorless coffee began trickling into the cup, Wally wondered once again why he stopped here every morning. The coffee, after all, was miserable and the proprietor's personality less than sparkling.

The reason was actually quite stupid. His route from the subway into the office brought him directly past the cart. No matter how crowded the sidewalk, there was no ducking past, no hiding behind a fat lady, no avoiding the coffee cart man's gaze. If Wally simply strolled past the cart—or, worse, strolled past clutching a cup from another, better vendor—he knew there would be trouble. The coffee man would track him down and confront him the following morning, demanding with tear-filled eyes and a pained voice to know why Wally would ever want to insult him and his family in such a profound manner. It was something Wally had encountered before and didn't care to encounter again.

No, there was no getting around it unless he wanted to circumnavigate the entire block and come down the other way. But that would mean passing through two more checkpoints and adding at least twenty minutes to his trip. Plus, it offered no guarantees that the Syrian wouldn't still see him trying to sneak in. So Wally gave the man his business and drank his awful coffee.

Behind Wally, a HappyCam whirred past down the sidewalk, weaving neatly in and out of the thickening foot traffic. Nobody paid it any attention. A swarm of yellow cabs packed the avenue, along with a few Mini Forts trying to crush their way uptown. Most everyone was honking their horns for no reason and less effect. Rising above the ground level fray in whatever direction you looked were the forty-foot plasma adscreens. Every morning Wally was relieved to remember that the volume on the screens wasn't turned up until eight-thirty. Things could get deafening after that.

"So how are things going?" Wally asked, if only to break the uncomfortable silence as the coffee slowly dribbled into the cup. He placed the bill on the counter next to the plastic tub of Sweetum.

"Eh, it is better like nothing," the Syrian said, snatching the bill away and tucking it into his apron. He slapped a cardboard lid on the cup, shoved the cup into a small brown paper sack, and handed it through the window to Wally without another word.

Warm paper bag in hand, Wally crossed the small cement courtyard in front of the smoked glass and steel edifice of the LifeGuard Insurance building on Second Avenue, just north of Fifty-fifth Street. At a scant twenty-eight stories, it was dwarfed by the other office towers that surrounded it but remained just as ugly.

As he approached the enormous front doors, he reached into the inside pocket of his jacket and removed the same thick rectangle of plastic that had gotten him into the subway. One side of the card contained Wally's name and photo, his address, his citizen and employee identification numbers, and a brief physical description. The other side was blank. Embedded in the card was a series of microchips, which contained all the information on the front of the card, as well as his complete medical and employment histories, a link to his bank account, ongoing purchase and travel records, and much, much more. Technically, it was known as the Single Universal Citizen Identification card, but everyone just called it the SUCKIE card.

He waved the blank side in front of a square white box mounted next to the front doors. A tiny red light near the top of the box blinked green. He grabbed hold of the door handle and pulled it open.

Inside sat Lawrence Whipple, the security guard, behind a low, lacquered black iron desk. The desk was unadorned except for a vid monitor and scanner box.

Whipple was a large man, who seemed to have expanded over time in order to perfectly fill the chair he'd been provided. Wally had seen him every morning since the day he started with the firm, and saw him again every night when he was heading home. He'd never once seen Whipple standing, and never once saw anyone else sitting in that chair. As far as Wally could figure, Whipple never left his post. Ever. Not to go home, not for lunch, not to go to the bathroom. He wondered idly sometimes if the guard was, in fact, animatronic. It certainly wasn't unheard of—and Whipple's general demeanor would seem to confirm the idea. Wally dismissed the notion eventually, concluding that no one would put the time and effort into designing an android quite that fat.

"Hi Lawrence," he said, trying to smile as he held out the SUCKIE card for inspection. After all these years, Whipple had never once called Wally by name. Never called him anything, in fact, or said a word or smiled. This morning was no different. He stared hard at the small digitized portrait on the card, then squinted up at Wally, trying to determine if it was a close enough match. The picture had been taken several years earlier, around the time Wally first started with LifeGuard. He'd had more hair back then, but he was wearing the same tie he was wearing now.

There was usually a moment every morning during this exchange when Wally, for no logical reason, feared that Whipple would deny him entry into the building. Then what would he do? But his resemblance to the photo was apparently close enough once again, as it was every weekday morning at a little before eight. The guard nodded once briefly to himself in satisfaction of a job well done, then slid the card through the scanner before handing it back to Wally and hitting a button behind the desk. There was a hum and a click, and Wally passed through a second set of smoked glass doors into the elevator lobby.

Once up on the fourteenth floor, he waved the card in front of another white box mounted next to another door and let himself into the office of the medical claims department. It was separate from the auto claims department, the home owners claims department, the life insurance department, and several others. Up on fourteen, they handled the claims of people who were dying of rare digestive ailments, or had lost a few fingers to a blender, or wanted to voluntarily commit themselves to a thirty-day drug rehab or memory adjustment clinic.

He flicked on the row of seven light switches just inside the door and the fluorescent panels overhead blinked awake with some apparent reluctance. Seen from above, the office might have looked like the world's most frustrating maze—a single entrance followed by nothing but dead ends. Dozens upon dozens of identical white cubicles filled the floor. Lining the department's four walls were the real offices, which, unlike the cubicles, came complete with windows and doors.

Wally didn't notice any of this anymore. He knew the route with his eyes closed, and simply followed his feet along the well-worn ash-colored carpet to cubicle 407-R, which corresponded to the employee number programmed into the SUCKIE card.

On his desk—more a wide shelf than an actual desk—sat his computer console, a digital telephone, and a pair of stacked plastic in/out trays. The trays were empty, as they had remained for well over three years. There simply wasn't any call for paper in the office anymore. Claims began as digital files and simply grew into more complex digital files by the time they worked their way up the ladder to him. The in/out trays, as a result, were as much a quaint anachronism as the telephone. Still, he liked keeping both around for some reason. They reminded him of something, though he couldn't remember what.

He removed the coffee from the bag and set it down next to the terminal. On the floor beside his chair sat a vinyl garbage can lined with a clear plastic bag. The smaller shelf above his desk held several boxes of long-outdated computer discs. Those were antiques, too. Utterly useless. Next to the discs squatted a green ceramic frog. It was meant to be cute, but its eyes bulged in apparent horror and its mouth gaped open in a hollow scream. His wife, Margie, had given him the frog when he'd first started in medical claims, thinking it might "brighten the place up a bit."

Wally left the frog there for Margie's sake, but in general he was content to let his cubicle be what it was, with no illusions. Unlike so many of his coworkers, he preferred not to transform his cubicle into a home away from home, or make it in any way a reflection of his personality.

He did sometimes wonder if a window might not change his outlook toward his job. A view of the Krudler Annuities Inc.

Bridge in the distance—which he still found a lovely old bridge, in spite of all the adscreens—might turn him all around on the question of his role on the LifeGuard team.

It was a pointless dream and he knew it. With his luck, if he ever did get his own office one day, he'd end up with a view of the SoniCram building next door, which essentially would amount to looking at a mirror all day.

He rolled out the chair and sat down in front of the computer, leaned forward and swiped the card just below the screen, then leaned back as the machine hummed into life. There was a quiet click and buzz from the black box on the cubicle wall to his right.

He knew no one else would show up for at least another hour. That's exactly why he came into the office when he did every morning. It gave him a chance to get a leg up on the day before the cloud of chummy and chirpy voices descended around him and scraped on his nerves. It also gave him a chance to catch up on the news for a few quiet minutes before he got down to work.

Work. It was a stupid name for what he did.

He tapped the office password, his own password, then both his employee and his citizen identification numbers onto the screen, hit the ENTER button, and waited.

Odd thing was, if pressed, he'd have a difficult time explaining what exactly it *was* he did.

More than anything else he was a proofreader and a gatekeeper. For eight hours a day, five days a week, Wally read through electronic documents passed along by people one rung below him in medical claims. They, in turn, had received the files from someone one rung below them. His job was to make sure one last time that everything had been filled out properly and that all the requisite information was in place. If any of the lines or boxes were left blank or filled out incorrectly the claim was rejected, and whoever was trying to be compensated for a debilitating thumb injury, have a new prescription covered, or receive permission for life-saving surgery had to start over again from the beginning—a process that could take months, if not years. If everything was okeydoke, he typed his initials into a small box at the bottom of the file, passed it along, and forgot about it.

He tried not to think about any of this. He tapped an icon on the screen, then a few buttons on the keypad in front of him, and the voice of Gag Peptide burst from his computer

"*—Horribleness, so be sure and wear your reflectors... Speaking of the wars, our troops in Albania have announced another glorious advance against the Horde. Force Commander General Pierce Weevil says that today's victory now means this arm of the war might well be—*"

"*Hey,* there, 407-R!"

"*Gaah!*" Wally yelped as his back muscles spasmed. He spun in his chair to find a diminutive gnome of a man in an ill-fitting short-sleeved shirt and brown clip-on tie standing at the entrance to his cubicle.

"I scare ya?" the man asked, smiling to reveal a mess of brown and crooked teeth. "I'm real sorry there." His hair was mussed, and though his face was heavily lined, it was hard to estimate his age. Probably in his mid-forties, Wally guessed, but at first glance he seemed to carry himself (even though he shouldn't) like he was twenty years younger. Wally had never seen the man before. That in itself wasn't strange, as there was a lot of turnover on fourteen. "Didn't mean to startle you. Really."

"It's okay," Wally told him, as his heart began to slow to its regular pace. "I'm—I'm just not used to other people being here so early."

That wasn't the only thing that made the encounter so odd. What was strange about this was that so few of the people in the office ever spoke to him at all.

"Yeah, well," the small man said. "I'm new, so I guess I wanted to make a good impression. Hard to do that, though, when there's nobody here, huh?" He forced a weak laugh, looking over his shoulder, then back to Wally.

"Uh-huh," Wally replied. *Great. There go my mornings, especially if he decides to be "chummy."*

"I'm 518-*D*," the man declared, putting an unusual emphasis on the "D." He thrust a meaty hand in Wally's direction. The nails were in need of trimming. "I'm over there." He jerked his head in the general direction of some other cubicle.

"407-R," Wally replied, hesitantly taking the hand. "But I guess you know that already."

"Sure do. Hey, guess what?"

"Um... what?"

"I got some coffee brewing. You want some?"

"Oh, that's... very nice, but I—I think I'll pass. Already have some." With some effort he extracted his hand from 518-*D*'s grip and gestured at the cup on his desk. "But thank you."

"You're sure? It's real good."

"I—I don't doubt it, uh, but I'm fine. All set. Really. Thank you." Wally half turned and peeled the soggy cardboard lid off the cup. If you didn't get those things off soon enough, they'd melt right into the coffee, which was bad enough as it was.

"Okay then, but if you change your mind— *Hey!*"

"*What?*" Wally said, a bit more sharply than he intended.

"You hear about that face transplant guy? Really something, ain't it?"

"I—yeah, it sure is," Wally replied, feeling the muscles around his skull tightening. He wanted to tell 518-*D* that in fact the face transplant *wasn't* that big a deal at all, but he saw no reason to diminish the troll's enthusiasm. Celebrities had been getting face transplants left and right for the past ten years, ever since the franchises began opening in New York, Galveston, and LA. Only thing that made this most recent one interesting was that twenty-two-year-old talk show host Bernie Tschungle had been given the face of a seventy-three-year-old Sri Lankan woman. Wally didn't see how that would really help anything, but then he remembered what Tschungle's real face had looked like.

Still, it wasn't that big a deal.

As abruptly as he had appeared, 518-*D* vanished again, and Wally began to relax. As he turned back to his monitor, he paused. Why hadn't he been a little friendlier? That was the first time anyone in that office had offered him coffee. He punched a few keys on the keypad and got on with the day's work, feeling mildly touched that someone finally had.

Growing up in the suburbs of Cleveland, he'd had plenty of friends. Kids from school, kids from the neighborhood. There was Narky and Spazz and Lefty and Buggy and Boner—a dozen or more of them he could still count off in his head. In the summer, they'd play baseball or football in the open and trash-strewn field down the block from his house, or get on their bikes and go throw rocks at the abandoned can factory. In the winter there were snow forts and ice fights.

There'd been scuffles with each of them along the way (usually as a result of the football or the ice fights), but they never lasted long. Wally found it very easy, for the most part, to get along with almost everyone back then. Except for that Polack kid who lived up the street. He was a moron.

Something changed when he was in his teens. He was finding that immediately after meeting someone, no matter how friendly and pleasant their conversation might have been, he would feel himself flinch and begin plotting how he might avoid ever seeing that person again. Something about talking to people began to make him nervous. He'd been that way ever since. How he and Margie ever got together—even ended up getting married—remained a bit of a mystery to him sometimes.

As it stood, he could name only three people in the world he talked to at any length with some degree of comfort—and two of them only because it was unavoidable.

He turned once again to the files he hadn't had a chance to get to on Friday. The first one to come up was from a sixty-two-year-old woman living in Albany whose doctor had prescribed a massive daily dosage of Benzedrine PM.

Shortly after nine-thirty, he heard 518-*D*'s voice from somewhere down the row of cubicles.

"*Hey* there, 419-B!" That was followed by a woman's high-pitched shriek, then the same introduction, in exactly the same words, that Wally had been offered earlier. He couldn't hear the response, but 518-*D* went on to make another futile offer of fresh coffee, and ended things with "You hear about that face transplant guy? Really something, ain't it?"

He then moved down to cubicle 418-B and began all over again. The unexpectedly warm feeling Wally had experienced ninety minutes earlier now chilled.

By eleven he had scrutinized some fifteen claims forms for everything from AIDS drugs to memory rehab to hip replacement to one poor schlub who wanted reconstructive surgery. It seems he'd permanently disfigured himself after somehow getting his penis caught in a ceiling fan. That one Wally decided to forward along to CHUCKLE immediately.

Citizen Health Universal Collection was the first stop even before LifeGuard made any final decisions regarding compensation. CHUCKLE (as it was known) in turn would pass the information on to Supreme National Information Technology Collection (SNITCH), which passed it up the line to Complete Information Analysis (CIALIS). If someone at CIALIS decided that the case required special attention in order to protect the population, or even the citizen in question from him- or herself, it was then forwarded to the offices of Federal Enforcement of Long-Term Citizen Health (FELTCH). It wasn't all that uncommon, in fact, to see a crew of armed FELTCH operatives in full HazMat gear kick their way into the home of a citizen whose medical condition had been determined to pose a potential threat.

In any case, for safekeeping in the end all the files, no matter what response they received, would eventually end up in the SUCKIE database at the Bureau of Operational Organization (BOO). Every federal, state, and city agency in the country—from the Grand Forks, North Dakota, Department of Sanitation to Florida's Fish and Wildlife Service to SNITCH—sent all of their collected data to BOO. So did every school, hospital, airline, bank, church, nonprofit organization, grocery store, library, communitainment retailer, four-way site, car dealership, and multinational corporation (well, at least a couple of the latter). Every e-mail sent, communitainment call made or received, trip taken, product purchased, and four-way site perused was registered at BOO. Apart from that, BOO was also continuously gathering similar data from other nations worldwide. All of those bits and snippets and recordings, tracking records, fingerprints, and individual genomes were cross-referenced and input to the federal SUCKIE files on every citizen, which in turn were stored on PROTEUS X, the largest and most manly database on earth.

At least that's what they said. Wally didn't think about it much. Once he tapped the SEND icon, they were out of his hands and he forgot about them.

After sending the rest of the claims files off on the next leg of their long and tortuous journey, Wally pushed himself back from his desk and headed for the bathroom. After that, he planned to step outside and get a sandwich, which he would eat at his desk. Then he'd begin work on another batch of claims.

He was fascinated by that guy who got his penis caught in the ceiling fan. It amazed him sometimes, the things people did. *I bet he hasn't even told his closest friends about that one,* it occurred to him. It was like he was in on a dirty secret.

As he approached the bathroom door, he heard a voice behind him.

"Hold on there a sec, 407-R."

Wally didn't need to turn around to know who it was. "Yes, Lou?"

Lou—*Big* Lou—was his departmental supervisor, a curly-haired man in his early fifties, so named because he weighed an estimated three hundred and twenty-five pounds. He was one of those types who announced his wacky individuality to the world by wearing a different hideous tie to the office every day. Today's atrocity involved golden pyramids, smirking pink camels, and fake hieroglyphics set against purple polyester.

Big Lou insisted that everyone call him by name, and he called everyone by his or her employee number. He once explained to Wally that because of the turnover rate, calling people by number simply made things easier for him than trying to remember all those names.

"Hey, we gotta talk about one of the claims you forwarded along this morning—"

Wally cut him off. "Yeah, sure thing, Lou. But... could it wait a minute? I'm, uh . . ." he nodded toward the bathroom door.

"Oh, God, yeah. Of course," Lou said, almost apologetically. "But listen, before you go . . ."

Lou kept talking anyway. He always did. And, as always, Wally let his mind and his eyes drift. Sometimes he looked at the people shuffling around the office, only half of whom he recognized. Sometimes he thought of a song he liked, or what he might get for lunch. Often—like today—he made up little movies in his head, most of which ended with Lou going out a window.

The growing pressure in Wally's bladder finally forced him to break both his own and Lou's trains of thought. "Look, Lou, um, if you'll excuse me, I really need to . . ."

"Oh, yeah, yeah sure," Lou said. "Sorry. But stop by my office later so we can figure out this claims thing, okay?"

After getting a sandwich at a deli a block away—the same deli he went to every day about that time—and returning to the LifeGuard building, he found himself in the elevator with Raymond Hawkey and Roger Bingham, two of the company's insurance investigators. They, and several others, worked for a private detective agency that had signed a long-term contract with LifeGuard to check into cases of suspected insurance fraud. Their job was to track down claimants to make sure they really were sick or maimed or dead before any payments were authorized. Although they were freelance contractors, they'd been with the company as long as Wally had. The thinking was that hiring a few private dicks was much cheaper in the long run compared with what LifeGuard stood to lose to insurance cheats.

Over time, Wally had come to learn their names. They, in turn, never seemed to notice him.

Hawkey was tall and rail thin, a gruesome, cadaverous fellow in his early sixties who'd been a PI for nearly four decades now. He had tiny, piercing black eyes, a massive beak, and a narrow, thin-lipped mouth drawn into a perpetual scowl. Bingham was the shorter and beefier of the two, with a shiny pink face and a fat neck. He was a loudmouth in his mid-thirties who had yet to leave his fraternity days completely behind him. Wally didn't care much for either one.

Whether they allowed the private detective racket to dictate their fashion sense or whether their inborn fashion sense pushed them toward private detection was anyone's guess. Both men wore gray fedoras desperately in need of blocking, stained trench coats regardless of the weather, rumpled brown suits with ill-knotted ties, and scuffed black wingtips.

You never saw one without the other, and in the elevator, as usual, they were trading war stories about old collars.

". . . and remember that guy—that speed freak? DeGrave was his name, right? The one who claimed he was hit by a taxi and cracked his coccyx so he couldn't work no more?" Bingham prodded his partner as the elevator ascended.

"The one we found running in the marathon. Yeah, I remember him. A real smart guy." Hawkey's voice rested somewhere between a rasp and a croak and never betrayed the slightest hint of emotion. "Smart guy" (or, as he pronounced it, "*smart-guy*") was the term he always applied to the ones they caught.

"Yeah, he was pretty stupid, huh?"

"Maybe so. But he ran a pretty good marathon."

Bingham's hooting laughter made Wally wince. He always laughed harder at these stories than was necessary. Wally wanted to grab Bingham by the hair and slam his head repeatedly against the stainless steel elevator doors, screaming "It's *not—that—funny!*" But he didn't.

• • •

After lunch, Wally glanced at the clock on the far wall. It was ten to twelve. He slid the tiny black Earwig GL-70 disc from his pocket, flipped up the minivid, and tapped a picture on the screen. Then he leaned back in his chair. A moment later he heard a woman's voice in his ear.

"*Hel-lo, Mr. Philco!*" She sounded excited about something. "*Flippy Bits Snack Chips blend the delicious flavors of cumin and apricot in a dried algae base to give you, the consumer, the kind of—*"

Crap, he thought. *I shouldn't have looked at that ad for so long. I'll be hearing this for a week now.*

"*—So the next time you're placing an order, be sure and tell the proprietor, 'Flip me some Flippy Bits!'* "

Behind the announcer the jingle kicked in. "*No matter what you pour, you'll like it even more with some Flip-py Bits! Flip me some, flip me some, flip me some Flip-py Bits!*"

This was followed by another, sterner male voice.

"*You know they're out there, Philco. We know they're out there. So as the anniversary of. . .* "

Wally sighed and looked at his computer screen, just waiting for the ad to pass. There were usually no more than two commercials—though sometimes they snuck in a third—before each call was finally put through.

The ad was followed by a short beep. Then, with some relief, Wally listened to the rhythmic buzzing on the other end. On the third ring, Margie picked up.

"Hello?" Her voice was clipped and tense.

"Hey," Wally said. The minivid screen remained blank, which meant she hadn't bothered to turn hers on.

"Hi."

He sensed immediately that this was a bad time. "I'm sorry," he said. "You sound busy."

"A little," Margie replied. "What's going on?" With Margie, he learned quickly enough, "a little" could easily be translated as "you're bothering me."

"Nothing much. Just wanted to see how things were going over there... How's that Ikons job coming?"

"Fine, but I still have a lot to do."

"I'm sorry," he said, knowing this probably wasn't the time to share the stupid story about the guy with the penis injury. "But I'm sure you'll get it done."

"Yeah," she said, her syllables growing sharper, "but it's going to be a long night. This is due tomorrow noon."

"Oh... should—should I just bring some dinner home, or... ? "

He could hear her sigh. "You do whatever you want. I'm just gonna grab something here."

"Oh... okay. Well, um, I'll let you get back to work then."

"Okay." She sounded relieved. "I'll see you later."

"I love you," he told her, but she had already hung up.

He closed his eyes for a moment wearily, then replaced the Earwig GL-70 in his pocket and headed for Big Lou's office.

Big Lou was squinting at his monitor when Wally knocked on the half-open office door.

"You wanted to talk about something?"

Big Lou looked up, surprised. "Oh, there you are 407-R. Yeah, come in. And close the door."

Wally did as he was told, then stood uncomfortably in front of the enormous man's desk. A picture frame off to the side held a portrait of Big Lou's entire Big Family.

Lou looked back at the screen and hit a few buttons in quick succession. "Jesus H. Christ, 407-R, how the heck long were you in the crapper?"

"Excuse me?"

"Did you just get out of there? You sick?"

Wally's eyes cut to the right in confusion. "Um... no? I mean, I went and got my lunch, then came back and, uh... ate it. I wasn't in there more than a minute."

"You weren't doin' anything *dirty* in there, were you? 'Cause we can't have that sorta thing. Not on *company* time." Lou let out a thick, wheezing laugh at his own joke, a light spray of spittle misting his computer screen. Even though he called people by number, Lou still wanted to be everybody's pal and thought the best way to do this was to toss around the locker room jibes—or at least as close as he was allowed anymore—whenever no women were present. In general it only made everyone a little uneasy, in part because they knew that if the wrong ears ever heard him he could be looking at some hard time.

"*No.*" Wally could feel his face growing warm.

"Oh." Lou looked more closely at the screen again, after wiping it off with his sleeve. He glanced up at 407-R as if to make sure he was still there, then back at the screen. "*Ah, frig,*" he whispered. "You know, according to this thing, you're still in the can."

“Excuse me?” Wally repeated.

“Here, look.” He spun the monitor so Wally could see. The date and his employee number were at the top of the screen, together with the same photo that appeared on his card. Below it was a neatly arranged chart.

7:47 Outer Lobby
7:49 Inner Lobby
7:52 Elevator B
7:54 14 Office
7:56 407-R Work Station
9:27 14 Restroom—M
9:31 407-R Work Station
11:03 14 Restroom—M

Beside each entry was a digitized snapshot. Wally in the building lobby. Wally on the elevator. Wally at his desk. Wally standing at a urinal. And below each picture, what appeared to be a brief description of his mental state: “Increasing Tension,” “Melancholy/Regret,” “Boredom,” “Relief,” “Nonwork Distraction.”

If he doesn’t mention it, Wally thought, *neither will I.*

The entries had stopped shortly after eleven. It was now shortly after noon, and the screen showed no record of his leaving and returning to the building and his cubicle.

“That’s very odd,” Wally said.

“Ain’t it? You didn’t drop your SUCKIE in the toilet or nothing, did you?”

Wally held out the (quite dry) plastic card. “Got it right here.”

"You're sure you didn't lend it to anybody or anything?"

Wally looked at his shoes, then held the card a little higher. "Lou, it's right here. I wouldn't've been able to get past Whipple otherwise."

Lou considered this. "Yeah, that's true." He swiveled the screen around and examined it carefully. "Damn thing," he muttered, then looked up again. "You know, these things are a dream when they work. Million times better than the old-time clocks used to be—those were before your day. Somebody hangs out at the coffee machine for twenty minutes, I got 'em by the shorties. But now there's *this*—" he swung a thick palm against the side of the computer, as if that would jar the clogged information loose. "Cripes. Now I'm gonna have to call COOTY to report this, and it'll take months before they do anything. Plus all those forms." (COOTY was the Committee for Occupational Technology. Any and all office computer trouble, no matter how minor, required COOTY notification.)

Lou noticed the concerned look on Wally's face. "I'll try and make sure you aren't docked for an hour in the can, if that's what you're worried about. I'll put it in my reports, but that might take months to recoup, too."

"Yeah, I understand," Wally said. "If you could just do what you can…Now, you said there was a problem with one of this morning's claims?"

Still slapping at the monitor, but more gently now, Lou said, "Oh, yeah. The nutty old lady looking for Benzedrine. I went over the form again, and you were right to forward it. Everything's clean. All paid up, doctor checks out."

"Oh. Okay." He wondered why he'd been called in here in the

first place but then accepted that it was just another example of Lou being his big dumb self. Friendly enough, certainly, but dumb.

"Something about it still makes me a little suspicious, but that's not your problem, 407-R. I'm gonna send a couple dicks up there, see if she's as crazy as she says she is."

If she's not now, she will be soon enough, Wally thought. As usual, he kept it to himself, saying instead, "In that case, I'll get back to work."

"Good. Yeah. And try restarting your computer. I'll see if it shows up here... LWIW."

"Yeah, LWIW," Wally said.

He returned to his desk and did as he was told.

The rest of the day was uneventful. But looking back on it, the day as a whole had been more exciting than most.

Shortly after five, he forwarded the last claim of the day to CHUCKLE, shut down the machine, and headed for the elevators.

When the doors opened, two younger men from the floor above him (automotive claims), their ties already loosened, were laughing.

"*Dentyne* said that? The chick in accounting?" one of them asked.

"It's true," the other replied with a nod and a leer.

They stopped and glanced at Wally as he stepped aboard, then remained silent as the doors closed.

As they passed the eighth floor, the one Wally took to be the older of the two spoke again. "So you goin' to the thing next week?"

"What thing's that?"

"Horribleness Day."

The younger man looked disturbed by the question. "Of *course* I am. Don't want to look like an Unmutual."

"Yeah," chuckled the other. "LWIW."

"You got that right. Flip me some Flippy Bits," the kid responded.

Back at the house, Wally knocked lightly on his wife's office door.

"Margie?... Hey, I'm back... How are things going?"

When she first began working at home, he could determine how busy she was by the clacking of her fingertips across the plastic keys. The sound really came to gnaw at him. Whenever he heard it—at the office, in an ad, on the subway—it set his teeth on edge. After she got the new system a few years back—a Kraken MD8, top of the line, a giant leap forward in home computing technology, he was informed—the clacking of keys had been replaced by what sounded like a dog playing a theremin. It wasn't long before he missed the clacking.

"*Fine*," she responded through the door.

He knew that would likely be the extent of the evening's conversation.

In the kitchen, he opened a small brown paper sack and removed the dinner he'd picked up on the way home. On a clear Lucite tray, he placed an artificial roast beef on rye (the wrapper read "Caution: May present a choking hazard. Chew thoroughly. Be sure and eat as part of a well-balanced diet, complete with vegetable matter.") and a cellophane package of GenAk Froot-Enhanced Lectoids ("Tastier Than the Real Thing!"). He carried everything into the living room and placed the tray on the coffee table. He passed a finger over the pulsing orange light in the upper left-hand corner of the wireless console beside him on the couch. The five-foot-tall four-way infotainment screen glowed into life.

"Good day, Good Citizen Philco," the faceless voice announced in relaxed and loving yet somehow hollow tones. "We trust your workday was pleasant and productive."

"Fine," he responded.

"That's very good news."

With his left hand, Wally tapped a few buttons on the console, until the newscast appeared.

"*... who, fortunately, was all dressed up in his best Sunday-goin'-to-meet-your-Maker clothes at the time...*"

The newscaster, Daniel DeLyon, was standing in front of a screen flashing dozens of images in quick succession. Some were animated, others apparently live action. A few of them seemed to be related to the story he was reporting. DeLyon wore an austere dark blue tunic and was always smiling broadly, no matter how terrible the story at hand might have been. As it was, none of the stories were too terrible—the crimes and car accidents had been shifted to the entertainment channels, leaving the official news broadcasts free to focus on celebrity gossip and occasional security updates.

Wally chewed the flavorless sandwich without much enthusiasm, his eyes fixed on the screen.

"*... host Bernie Tschungle. Many in the industry consider the* *transplant a risky move on Tschungle's part, not only because he's receiving the face of an elderly foreign woman, but also on account of the number of celebrities whose careers have faltered after the operation, leading several to commit—"*

"You're gonna get crumbs in the unit."

Wally looked up to see his wife standing in the doorway.

"Hmm?" he asked, still chewing.

"I said you're gonna get crumbs in the unit. You're making a mess."

He looked around himself but saw nothing amiss. He swallowed what he'd been chewing.

"No I won't, honey—it's supposed to be crumbless bread. That's what they told me. It's new."

He could tell she wasn't impressed by this. She hadn't seemed very impressed by much of anything he'd said or done for the past several years.

It was of course different when they were first married thirteen years earlier. But then he got stuck in a go-nowhere position in the insurance industry, and her public relations firm took off, mostly because she was willing to take on clients no one else would touch, such as corporate officials caught raping young boys in the park, or her current client the Ikons Foundation. She had a knack for making evil sound charming.

Her green eyes, made much larger behind the round glasses, stared at him. She said nothing.

Finally he offered, "I'll clean up when I'm done. Promise. Uh . . . good luck with that account."

"Yeah, thanks," she said, before returning to her office and closing the door.

He had no idea why she'd come out in the first place. He took another bite of the sandwich. *I was probably chewing too loud,* he thought.

"*Preparations are coming along for this year's Horribleness Day celebration,*" DeLyon was saying, "*the day we all pause to remember those who were lost, those who lost loved ones, and how each and every one of our lives was changed forever on that fateful afternoon. It's also a chance to say thank you to those citizens who've helped make our lives and our nation so much safer and more secure ever since... Part of this year's celebration will include not only the traditional Horribleness Mimes but music and cook-offs and a chance for you to identify—*"

Wally hit a few more buttons until he saw what appeared to be the interior of a small middle-class home.

A woman, probably in her sixties, was sitting on a greenish-brown sofa, knitting. She looked tired. Across the room, an overweight man about the same age sat in an easy chair, leaning his head in his hand. He was staring at the screen of his own four-way.

Wally hit another button and, in the window that appeared to the side of the image, he learned that it was the Mitchells—Lorraine S. and Samuel D.—from Atlanta. Both were retired, both had diabetes. No criminal record or hint of unmutualism. Good Citizens.

It was one of the most popular shows available, and it was always on.

Wally liked spinning randomly through the other reality channels of the HAWG Network. Getting a look at the lives of other people made him feel oddly better about his own.

Funny, he thought, how the only time you heard the word "reality" used anymore was in reference to a four-way genre.

At eight-thirty, after making sure he had thoroughly cleaned off the coffee table, the couch, and the control unit, he removed the VidLog, which had been clipped to his lapel since early that morning, and inserted it into a port on the side of the four-way.

He sat down on the couch again and tapped a button beneath a blinking blue light to begin downloading everything the VidLog had recorded that day.

While that was taking place, he pulled up the daily report page on the screen and typed in his Citizen ID number.

He waited until the number, the date, his name, and his address appeared on the screen.

A moment later he was staring at a live image of himself in a small box near the bottom of the screen. Above it, the words "Enter Daily Report" were flashing.

Wally cleared his throat.

Sometimes when he made these reports, he liked to adopt an intense, authoritative voice, as if he were reporting directly to the president on the results of his latest secret mission. Then he heard the sorts of things he was actually saying.

"Philco, Wallace," he stated slowly and clearly. "Citizen Identification Number NY00169765/P...Awoke at six-oh-five. Prepared for work. Left home at six-fifty-five. Arrived at Fifty-third Street subway station Manhattan at approximately seven-forty a.m. . . ."

It was difficult to gauge how many helidrones were circling overhead. Quite a few, that's for sure—six or seven at least. It was necessary, Wally supposed. Ground troops could work the periphery, but they couldn't keep an eye on everybody. There must have been at least fifteen or twenty thousand people stuffed behind the steel barricades in FumiCorp Park's One Big Area.

It had been known as "Prospect Park" until the city sold it to FumiCorp six years earlier. Once the condos were erected and the permanent ad space established, the One Big Area was the last significant patch of grass left in the park, so that's where everyone gathered at times like this.

After that morning's parade down Flatbush Avenue, the

crowd had been herded through the security checks and then into the One Big Area for the annual rally.

Each of the boroughs had its own parade and rally. That was the only way to control the throngs. In fact, as on Thanksgiving or Veterans Day, nearly every city in the country had its own parade, followed by a rally, followed by cook-outs and games. Horribleness Day had come to rival even the Holidays (as they had officially come to be known to avoid offending anyone) in terms of scope and national significance.

Wally was pressed shoulder to shoulder with a stocky Dominican named Pedro. Pedro was a nervous fellow in his late twenties, there with his wife and four kids, all of whom sported "I Can't Believe I Survived the Horribleness" T-shirts. Those had always been popular. Others were wearing shirts that marked past Horribleness Day events. Some of the designs were austere and stark, while others bordered on the shockingly graphic. Wally didn't own any T-shirts of any kind anymore. Looking around the crowd, he suddenly felt out of place because of it.

It was an overcast day. Nowadays it always seemed to be overcast. Overcast and humid, though the temperature never varied much—mostly wavering around eighty, regardless of the season.

Between the barricades and the condos, licensed vendors were selling everything from underwear and baseball caps to sno-globes, autographed celebrity photos, bobbleheads of corporate icons, toy spycams, Italian ices, and a variety of ethnic snacks, all produced by FumiCorp. Likewise, the massive adscreens that ringed the area were running commercials for various FumiCorp products: insect repellent, pharmaceuticals, GPS accessories and tunics.

A midget shoved his way through the crowd and past Wally.

"Hey!" Wally said after a tiny pointed elbow caught him hard—and perhaps deliberately—under the ribs. The midget stopped and slowly turned, silently considering him.

Below the receding hairline, his face was weathered and serious, his dark eyes set off by heavy black eyebrows. He wore a black suit, a narrow red silk bow tie, and black leather gloves. He neither smiled nor apologized. Merely scrutinized Wally for a moment, looking him up and down twice before turning and continuing to push and paw his way toward the stage.

You saw a lot more midgets around these days, Wally noted. There certainly seemed to be more since the Horribleness, anyway. He didn't know why that was and often wondered if anyone else even noticed.

A quiet August afternoon had been shattered eleven years earlier when something—no one was sure what it was initially—plummeted from the Mississippi sky like a meteor, exploding through the roof of the Crosseye Bear Grocery Store. The resulting inferno soon engulfed seventeen buildings in downtown Tupelo. At first everyone simply assumed it was a small plane. Bad news and bad aim, but not unheard of. Certainly not enough to justify a nationwide panic.

It became clear before long, however, that something else was going on. Something, well, *horrible.* Would-be rescuers arriving on the scene were dropping dead before they got close to the smoldering wreckage or any of the adjacent buildings, which were burning out of control. What's more, small bits of debris discovered early on didn't resemble anything anyone had ever seen before.

It was reported that within three hours nearly a thousand people in Tupelo had died—many of whom were nowhere near the initial carnage.

On the television, panicky and ill-prepared announcers were reporting everything from the crash of a flying saucer (undoubtedly the first of an invading alien armada), to chemical warfare, to a neutron bomb, to the coincidental emergence of a deadly new plague. More than one reporter claimed that the dead were getting up and walking around again. ("If you have a gun, shoot 'em in the head," one local announcer instructed his viewers. "That's a sure way to kill 'em.")

In the tense and distressing days that followed, millions of eyes across the country turned skyward, expecting the same thing to happen in their towns, too, but it never did. It happened only in Tupelo, which was soon deserted by the survivors, and had remained a veritable ghost town ever since. Every August the eighth, thousands of people from around the world gathered at the city limits, satisfying themselves with the offerings at the souvenir stands there. Only the hardcore Horribleness Groupies took the pilgrimage one step further, venturing deep into the desolate city to the site of the flattened Crosseye Bear Grocery to pray and collect True Relics. They never stayed long.

As it happened, there wasn't much to any of the theories the hysterical reporters had tossed out for their viewers to fret over. Whatever had killed all of those people didn't seem to be spreading. There was no obvious chemical, biological, or radiological residue to be found, and the dead weren't going anywhere. (In fact, as a direct result of that one local announcer's instructions, eighteen more names had to be added to the list of casualties.)

Of the lot, the one bit of wild conjecture that stuck around the longest was the "flying saucer" theory, as the bits of recovered wreckage really *didn't* seem to have much in common with any recognizable earthbound craft.

Wait as they might, no alien force showed up to satisfy the true believers. By early September pretty much everyone had agreed that it must have been the work of terrorists. Terrorists were easier to think about than aliens.

Right around the same time, the event came to be officially dubbed the "Horribleness." Television networks had toyed for weeks with calling it the "Hullabaloo," the "Foofarilla," and the "Big To-Do," but in the end the "Horribleness" stuck.

As for what had killed all those people, no solid conclusion was ever reached. Or if it was, it was never reported. It might have been a short-lived virus or some new, intense form of radiation. Maybe a bunch of simultaneous heart attacks. All anyone knew for sure was that two months after the Horribleness, the country had declared war on Australia. No one had been expecting that one, least of all the Australians. The assumption, of course, was that Australia had been responsible for the disaster, somehow. But the evidence for that seemed shaky—all anyone could come up with as proof seemed to be a string of semipopular "fish out of water" comedy films released by Australian directors in recent years. A presidential advisory panel decided that it was enough, however, and the bombs started falling across New South Wales.

After a while, the reasons didn't matter. As the war dragged on for two weeks, then three, all those Australians who'd had the misfortune to be in the States at the time were being rounded up, placed on school buses, and shipped to an undisclosed location in the West. Someplace in Montana or Wyoming, most likely. It was unclear what happened to them after that.

Rounding up the Australians was a tricky business. They tended to fit in pretty well, so long as they didn't talk too much. Sadly, because of their accents, thousands of Brits, Irish, South Africans, and Welsh were rounded up as well, which meant that almost overnight three-quarters of the country's bartenders were either incarcerated or on the lam. It was considered a "small price to pay" to ensure our national security.

The war quickly began to spread through Europe, into Asia and the Middle East—even poking into northern Africa, though no one seemed to notice.

Along with the war and the roundup of the Australians and suspected Australians, the day-to-day lives of regular Americans began to change as well. Quickly, too, most directly as a result of the Homeland Interior Stability Through External Ruffian Infiltration Control—HISTERIC—provisions.

The provisions, an 8,000-page document, which had somehow been conceived, written, printed, distributed, studied, debated, and voted upon in a matter of days—even hours—after the news first broke, were passed unanimously by the House and Senate, then signed into law before the end of the week.

For security reasons, the contents of HISTERIC were never released; however the public was assured that the provisions had been carefully crafted to "keep our citizens safe from terrorists," and that seemed to satisfy anyone who might've been curious.

Eleven years after the fact, long after all the initial craziness had petered out, the Horribleness was still being used as an excuse for everything from insomnia and lower back pain to joblessness, bank robberies, AIDS, higher taxes, drunk driving, and murder. Likewise, everything from icy sidewalks to earthquakes to casino bus accidents was now being cited as the work of crafty terrorists (Australian and otherwise).

The elderly woman in line in front of Wally at the grocery store earlier that week had explained to the clerk that she had to change her mind and replace nearly every product she had carried to the checkout because, as she put it, she "found it so hard to make decisions like these since, y'know, the *Horribleness.*" She spoke the word in a whisper, as if it were an obscenity or an item of filthy gossip about a mutual friend. Then, as if to emphasize this, she clucked her tongue and shook her head sadly before shuffling back to the shelves with a bottle of ketchup (her third).

Wally might have taken this as normal, if aggravating, behavior had the clerk not been a MarketMonolith automated grocery checkout system, programmed with a pleasantly supercilious female voice.

Even the soothing voice over the grocery store's public address system—the one that rattled on incessantly, encouraging you to buy things you would never, ever want or need—suggested that customers purchase as much as possible in order to "help keep the memory of the victims of the Horribleness alive."

Wally hadn't known anyone in Tupelo at the time of the Horribleness, and, living in Brooklyn as he did, likely never would, which made it difficult to keep their memories alive. He also didn't know how buying a six-pack of FlushCom Yogurt Cups would help keep those memories alive, even if he had any. It perplexed him when he first recognized this growing nationwide neurosis, but it had since become such a part of the language, of the way things were now defined, that he simply accepted it like everyone else.

And that's why everyone who was at all mobile was celebrating Horribleness Day. It had been declared a national holiday four years after the incident, and now, seven years after that, participation in Horribleness Day events was mandatory.

Wally excused himself from Pedro and began squeezing his way through the thick crowd, hoping to spot Margie. She'd said she was going to be there—it would be bad news if she wasn't—but trying to pick her out of a group of twenty thousand people was, at this point, a matter of dumb luck.

Up on the stage a hundred and fifty yards away, a twelve-piece orchestra was playing a smooth jazz medley of recent and familiar commercial jingles. Earlier, they'd performed irony-free versions of golden oldies like "Beautiful World" and "Everybody's Happy Nowadays," which the band leader introduced as "commercial jingles from yesteryear." At the front of the stage, a young man in whiteface, suspenders, and a striped leotard juggled artificial watermelons.

It wasn't long before Wally found himself pressed up against the steel barricades, inescapably hemmed in by the crush of bodies. In and among the vendors, several uniformed guards kept a close eye on the gathering, which, apart from that ornery midget, seemed perfectly well behaved.

Along with the usual Department of Dissuasion troops, Wally spotted a contingent of guards from the Crowd Observation and Control Korps, a civilian volunteer outfit whose members were handed automatic rifles to patrol public events like this. Much to his surprise, there was also at least one member of the Salacious Materials Enforcement Group (Metro Area) on patrol too. The black satin jacket emblazoned with the bright yellow SMEG/MA logo gave him away.

What are the porn cops doing here? Wally wondered. He turned back to scan the crowd, half looking for Margie, half thinking he might see a woman in a swimsuit or a low-cut Horribleness Day T-shirt. He didn't. All he saw was a big guy, over six feet tall, with a heavy flame-colored beard. He wore a white cowboy hat and yellow rain slicker, and he was smiling broadly. He had an odd skip to his step as he picked his way through the crowd, which left Wally wondering if he was crippled, somehow.

The man turned, saw Wally staring at him, and gave him a friendly wave. Wally quickly looked the other way.

Leaning back against the barricade, his mind began to wander.

Okay guys, if we get enough of us together, we can crash outa this joint tonight. Are you with me? There are only so many of them, so if we all go over the wall at once we have a fighting chance. Sure, they might pick off a few of us, but they'll never get us all. C'mon! Follow me!

He felt his hands tighten on the steel bars behind him as he unconsciously began raising his right leg. Then he remembered the scar on his wrist. He stopped himself and lowered the leg, looking around nervously to make sure none of the guards had noticed.

"*Helloooo, Brooklyn!*" a voice boomed from the stage. "*And welcome to FumiCorp Park and the Eleventh Annual Horribleness Day Celebration!*"

Every voice in the crowd cheered and whooped.

That's not exactly right, Wally thought as he cheered and whooped with the rest of them. *It's really only the seventh.* He knew it was an irrelevant point, and so did anyone else who noticed. They also knew that it was a point no one dared bring up aloud.

As they all quieted down the emcee continued.

"*This year's celebration is being brought to you by Buzz's Chateau Maison, on Atlantic Avenue... Buzz's—where good eatin' is good fun!*"

The crowd roared once again.

"*And by Majestic Information Systems. Data collection fit for a king!*"

Everyone seemed very happy about that too.

"*And of course none of this would be possible without the kind and generous support of FumiCorp and FumiCorp Park, where vicious rapes and murders are a thing of the past!*"

Wally remembered when Margie was working on the Fumi-

Corp ad campaign after it had first acquired the park. She was mighty proud of that one. It did the trick.

"*You've been entertained for the last hour or so by the Weintraub Synchopators, featuring the juggling pyrotechnics of Pyrex Frenzy!*"

The applause was growing slightly more spotty.

Wally still applauded. He didn't dare not to with those guards standing a few yards away. He also stopped leaning on the barricade and stood up straight, facing in the general direction of the stage. Having been to enough of these over the years, he knew what was expected, and what was coming next. He'd have to find Margie later.

"*So now, ladies and gentlemen, Good Citizens of all ages, as two-eighteen approaches, I ask you to stand near the ones you love and bow your heads for the traditional five minutes of silent contemplation and thankfulness for having survived the events of that terrible day... Remember how very lucky you are to live in safety and security, knowing your loved ones are being protected...*"

The few quiet murmurs in the crowd fell silent. Wally bowed his head and clasped his hands behind him. Apart from the helidrones overhead and the slight breeze in his ears, the park was as quiet as he'd ever heard it. They'd even turned down the volume on the adscreens.

Then Wally felt something bump his calves from behind. He opened his eyes only briefly, before closing them tight. He didn't move.

The bump came again, more insistent this time. He didn't dare look. Just an accident.

A moment later it wasn't a bump, nor was it an accidental jostle, but a solid, malicious ramming just above the Achilles' tendons of both legs, nearly dropping him to his knees. He stumbled forward a few steps, colliding with the two citizens in front of him.

"*Ow!* Hey!"

He whirled and found himself staring into the cold razor eyes of a pinch-faced woman, her lips pursed tight in disgust, her knuckles white around the handle of the stroller.

"*C'mon,* lady," he snapped, "Do you *mind*? This is not the time."

He had tried to whisper, but when he closed his mouth Wally could still hear the echo of his own voice drifting away over the bowed heads of the solemn and silent masses. Several hundred heads rose slowly and turned to stare. He then noticed the triangular patch on the woman's blazer—the silhouette of a perambulator above two crossed and bloody swords. Immediately he recognized the horrifying depth of his mistake. He'd not only interrupted the National Moment of Silence—he'd snapped aloud at a member of the Stroller Brigade.

"Look, lady—I... I'm real—I didn't mean—"

There was nowhere to move, no place for him to hide or even step away. She pulled the stroller back a foot and slammed it into his shins.

"*Ow!*"

He looked down in the stroller and saw a round, butter-fed three-year-old, sleeping peacefully in spite of the cramped quarters.

All those mornings when he was alone on the sidewalks,

that was one thing. He was, after all, living in the middle of one of the city's eight officially designated breeding zones. But to go after him here, in the middle of a crowd of thousands, at a Horribleness Day rally? That was cheap.

He saw the guards approaching fast, guns at the ready, and didn't try to run. He closed his eyes and stood still as he heard them clambering over the barricades.

The first guard grabbed his left arm and wrenched it roughly behind his back. Wally felt the handcuff click tight around his wrist. He didn't resist as they cuffed his right hand as well.

He heard a sharp beep in his ear, followed by a man's voice.

"*. . . better than any other Soylent product you've come across. Yes, citizens, you're sure to ask for seconds after you try—*"

Nausea swept over Wally. His brain could form no words. He wanted to fall to his knees and empty his guts on the thinning brown grass, but now four hands were holding him upright.

"*And now the Horribleness Day Singers, brought to you by Our Lady of the Stereotypes Church, located on—*"

The whole world had gone a blurry, trembling green. He shook his head in an effort to make it stop. "You will come with us, please, sir," instructed a black-clad Department of Dissuasion officer in a quiet monotone. "You don't want to appear more unmutual than you already do. Trust me."

Wally offered a weak, nearly imperceptible nod but said nothing. He couldn't have said anything if he'd wanted to. He could no longer feel his legs. With a guard on either side of him and one behind, they half walked, half carried him through an opening in the barricades and toward a DOD van, parked on the torn lawn several yards away.

He didn't want to fall. He knew he couldn't. If he did, it would be a sign of resistance, and he'd be facing even more dire consequences than he already was. Behind him, Wally heard the emcee getting on with the show.

"*...After their set, our first speakers this afternoon will be a pair of Good Citizens who actually knew people living near Tupelo at the time of the Horribleness...*"

The throng began cheering once again.

"*These two are true heroes, ladies and gentlemen, who have done so much these past eleven years to help design a proper and lasting memorial here in New York for those who were lost that fateful day...and we're all hoping to see a design we can agree upon soon.*"

The interior of the van was brightly lit. The walls were lined with dozens of digital monitors and other equipment Wally couldn't comprehend. He'd been dropped into a gray metal chair beside a compact workstation. The right cuff had been removed from his wrist so that it could be locked around an arm of the chair. The chair itself was bolted to the floor of the van.

Before locking him in the chair, one of the guards was kind enough to punch him in the thigh, disconnecting, if only momentarily, his Earwig unit, silencing the voice in his head.

Staring at him from the other side of the workstation was an unsmiling DOD captain with a graying mustache. A scarlet patch over the left pocket of his uniform read "Hauk." Wally remembered hearing once that you had to be at least a captain before your actual name was used. Normally—as with the guards outside—they stuck with numbers or nothing at all.

The guards who had delivered him had returned to their

posts by the barricades to continue looking for troublemakers, roustabouts, and blasphemers.

The captain, a taut, thick-jawed figure of about fifty, said nothing for a long time. He merely stared at Wally with clear, unimpressed eyes.

Finally he said, "SUCKIE card."

With some effort, Wally reached gingerly into his pocket with his free hand, removed the card, and handed it over. He knew now was not the time to begin protesting his innocence.

The captain waved the card over the scanner and waited for Wally's file to appear on the screen. He did not return the card. The only sound in the room was the restrained whirrings and clicks of the machines, and he could still hear the muffled shouts of the enthusiastic crowd outside the van.

Wally knew he was going to die. That's all there was to it. They were going to execute him. Maybe not right here, but someplace, and soon. His gums hurt.

"By my assessment, NY00169765/P," Captain Hauk began in steady, aloof tones, "we have you on five counts, from disrupting the solemnity of Horribleness Day, to denigrating a member of the Stroller Brigade, to—"

Wally finally found his voice. Unfortunately, his timing was very poor.

"*Denigrating*? But she was—"

"*Six* counts," the captain corrected, hitting a single key on his console. He turned back to Wally. "May I ask you, NY00169765/P, why you aren't wearing an official Horribleness Day T-shirt?"

Wally's eyes darted around the cramped interior. "I… I don't have one," he finally offered, his voice weak.

"Mmm-hmm." The captain punched a few more keys. "Why don't you buy one? There are a number of vendors around the city—even right here in the park today. We're at *war,* in case you've forgotten."

Wally could feel the sweat collecting on his upper lip but didn't dare wipe it away. "I'm... I guess... I guess I would rath—" He stopped himself. He couldn't make it an issue of choice, and didn't dare reveal that he found most of the designs tasteless. "It's a money issue, I guess." Then he added, "Sir."

Captain Hauk glanced at the screen. "Not according to your file, it's not. I also notice here that you have no children." He stared hard at Wally. "What are you, some kind of *terrorist*?"

"Of *course* not—" Wally protested. "That's ridic—" He stopped himself again as he saw the anticipatory twinkle sneak into the corner of Captain Hauk's eye. "It's just, sir, that my wife and I . . ." He wasn't exactly sure how to go on from there.

"Yes, I know. Which, I'm presuming, is why you weren't celebrating together today... Am I correct?"

"We were supposed to. I mean, she was... she said she was going to meet me here."

"Mmm-hmm," the captain said again. He punched a few more buttons and suddenly all the vidscreens in the van were displaying what was apparently live footage of Margie shot from multiple angles. She was near the front of the stage, whistling and applauding wildly.

"Your... *wife*... clearly understands and appreciates the importance of Horribleness Day. What it means to all of us, and how we must use it to prove to the terrorists that they haven't won. While *you,* on the other hand . . ." He hit a few more keys, and now the screens were filled with shots of Wally himself, leaning back against the barricade, looking by all accounts to be awfully bored.

Captain Hauk gave Wally a moment to register what he was seeing. "It doesn't look to me like you're terribly excited by the proceedings, NY00169765/P, which once again sets off that *potential terrorist* bell in the back of my mind."

"But sir—no. Please. I'm not in any way—"

"No children, no passion for or apparent understanding of what your country has been through, no official T-shirt," the captain interrupted. "Add it up."

Wally wasn't exactly sure how to respond to that.

The captain glanced at the monitor again. "And I haven't even gotten to the most serious charge yet."

If it was possible at this point, Wally's stomach sank even further.

"You not only denigrated a member of the Stroller Brigade. In doing so, you also used a hate word."

Wally went cold. A hate word conviction meant hard time. *Then* execution. His mind raced back, trying to remember everything he'd said, but he couldn't think of anything. He'd raised his voice, yes, but he hadn't used any hate words. They weren't even a part of his vocabulary. Once something was banned, he simply erased it from his consciousness. Even if he still accidentally thought one here and there, they would never, ever come out of his mouth.

"Ummm. . . ? " he offered, helplessly raising his right hand in a futile gesture.

"You don't even remember."

Wally paused, still thinking, terrified, then shook his head. His eyes were wide. He was going to die. It was useless.

On the screens around him, he now saw the back of his own head. It flinched, then turned, staring into the vid.

"*C'mon, lady. Do you mind?*" the images said. "*This is not the time.*"

The scene backed up and played again, then a third time.

"Got it yet?"

Wally stared at the image. Clearly it had been filmed by the woman pushing the stroller. It almost looked like she'd targeted him specifically. Still, for having heard it three times, he was unable to pick out any hate words. Even putting parts of the words he'd uttered together in different ways, he couldn't come up with any hate words. He looked to Captain Hauk and bit his lip.

The captain, noting the fear and confusion, shook his head. "You didn't read today's bulletin."

Wally dropped his eyes. "I guess I—I didn't see it this morning, no sir... Not yet."

"Obviously not, because if you had, you might not have been so foolish as to refer to an esteemed member of our social community as"—he dropped his voice, "*lady.*"

Looking up again, Wally asked, "*Lady*?" He was even more confused.

"As of ten-twenty-three last evening, 'lady' is now considered a hate word. Article two-two-seven-nine of the Post Horribleness Language Intolerance Code."

"But what's wrong with 'lady'?"

"If you had read the bulletin, as is expected of all citizens, you would know that it's considered an offensive, antagonistic word that often makes the victims to whom it is directed feel old. The Language Council had received the requisite five complaints over the past three years, so now it's the law."

"Oh," Wally said.

"Punishable by up to eight years at an Unmutual Rehabilitation Center. Together with the multiple other charges, you're looking at a minimum—a *minimum,* mind you—of twenty."

Wally's throat grew dry and tight. He could feel the hot tears welling up in his eyes as the blood rushed from his face. He was dizzy. *She targeted me. This is her fault.* But he knew he dare not open his mouth.

"*But,*" the captain said, "you have been a Good Citizen by all other accounts. Your file is clean, trouble with the wife and your wardrobe aside... But you need to keep up with these things if you want to get along. So tomorrow morning at ten a.m. you will report to Behavior and Language Adjustment, in Resident Control. If for some reason you cannot make this appointment, all six charges will be filed against you, and you will be found guilty. You will be labeled an Unmutual and you will face the harshest penalties allowed by law. Remember, we know where you live. And what you had for lunch. But you were aware of that already."

Wally wasn't immediately clear on where that left him at this particular moment.

"So... I'm free to go?" He prayed it wasn't the wrong question—second-guessing a DOD officer was also a punishable offense.

"You can go, yes," Captain Hauk said. "And finish celebrating

Horribleness Day in a manner befitting a proper Good Citizen. Remember that those people died for *you.*"

"I... I certainly will... And thank you, sir." He began to stand, but then paused.

The captain, who had turned away, turned back. "What is it?"

Wally's voice was meek. "I'm still chained to the chair, sir."

Outside the van, at least thirty people were waiting in line, handcuffed, single file, heads down in a narrow, newly assembled barricade. A few of them were bleeding.

Wally saw how lucky he'd been. Somehow he could tell just by looking at their faces, the fear and guilt in their eyes, that most of these people—men, women, and children as young as eight or nine—would never be heard from again.

"You see?" one of the Crowd Observation guards was saying to a recent volunteer as Wally passed. "Law enforcement can be fun!"

Resident Control, a one-stop shopping complex for all your social order needs, was housed in an imposing, forty-seven-story steel and concrete structure at the corner of Forty-second Street and Fifth Avenue. Along with the Behavior and Language Adjustment Bureau, it also housed the city's central DNA collection facility, administrative offices, several Unmutual Detention Units, and the offices of at least eight other local and federal agencies, including the Operation RAT (Resident Alertness Team) command center. Nobody was sure what was happening on the top five floors, but rumor had it that's where the headquarters for SPOOK (Secret Pervasive Observation of Kriminals) were hiding. The ground floor offered a tourist information booth, a collection of charming shops and boutiques, and a very nice snack bar.

The broad cement courtyard outside the main entrance was dotted with dozens of squat bomb-thwarting fortifications disguised as modern sculpture. As he attempted to squeeze between two such contrivances on his way to the building's front doors, Wally found his path blocked by one of the many HappyCams that patrolled the area.

"Good morning good morning, Good Citizen," the device sang in a voice programmed to sound warm and friendly. "Is there anything I can help you with today?"

HappyCams stood just over four feet tall and rolled about the city on octagonal, six-wheeled bases. They were dubbed "HappyCams" on account of the round yellow smiley faces affixed to the top of each. Their primary function was to operate as surrogate Officer Friendlies, offering directions, travel and weather advisories, restaurant recommendations, personal advice, and even the occasional joke, all in an effort to make each citizen's day a little brighter and a little safer.

It was generally accepted, however, that they were in reality wandering surveillance units, scanning random faces and biometric data in the ongoing search for potential unmutualism. And most of the jokes were just plain awful.

"I have an appointment inside," Wally told the HappyCam, "with Behavior and Language."

"Really?" the android responded, sounding genuinely interested. "For what?"

Wally looked around nervously and swallowed. "Vocabulary adjustment."

"*What?*" the device shouted. "Speak up!"

Wally closed his eyes and took a breath. There were so many people around. If a HappyCam stopped you for too long, people got nervous. "Vocabulary...adjustment," he said, forcing the words out.

The HappyCam emitted a mechanical chortle. "Ooohhh, look at you—NY00169765/P said a bad word!"

"Yes, well." He checked the time. "If you'll kindly excuse me, I don't want to be late."

"You were *naughty*!"

As it spoke, Wally could sense the pinpoint video lens scanning his face. He tried to step around the device but it rolled to block his path. "Hey!" it said, the voice more hostile. "I'm not finished here."

"Please," Wally said, trying to step around the other side. "Please—I'll be late, and then I'll be in worse trouble—"

"Not until you hear today's joke." It moved to block his path again, but Wally stepped back through the fortifications and jogged a wide arc around the HappyCam toward the front doors.

A glance over his shoulder revealed the machine already moving in to corner another flawed citizen on her way inside. He pushed open one of the massive iron lobby doors. A slow puff of heavy, stale air hit his face.

Inside the sprawling and cavernous lobby, Wally stepped to his right and joined the security check line.

Ten minutes later, when it was at last his turn, he presented his SUCKIE card, removed his shoes and belt, emptied his pockets onto a flat green plastic tray, pulled the pockets themselves inside out, and untucked his shirt. As two guards sorted through his personal effects deciding what they wanted to keep, Wally stepped into the ScanRite pod for the full body screening. When the results came out clear—no guns, bombs, mysterious powders, or hidden contraband—he stepped out of the pod and over to the retinal scan. When that was complete, he stepped to the third desk, where he opened his mouth wide for a DNA swab conducted by a sleepy female guard with a tongue depressor and a toothpick. He was then handed his shoes, belt, cards, and what little was left of his loose change, before being directed toward an obese man in a blue uniform sitting behind a gray steel desk identical to Whipple's. Wally didn't have much choice in the matter.

"SUCKIE number," the man behind the desk wheezed as Wally approached. He was clearly both bored and ill.

"NY00169765/P," Wally recited, holding out his card. The man took it in his broad fingers and inserted it into a rectangular reader, which had been covered with small round stickers, each featuring a colorful drawing of a flower.

"Reason for visit," the guard droned.

"Vocabulary adjustment?" Wally checked the time once more. He was afraid he was going to be late. That wouldn't look good.

"Time of appointment," the guard sighed.

"Ten o'clock."

The guard glanced at his watch and Wally saw his eyebrows jump slightly. Then he yawned, removed Wally's card from the reader, and returned it to him. "Through the turnstiles to the registration desk," he said. "They'll tell you where to go from there."

At the turnstiles, Wally waved his card again and stood still for an iris scan. Then he pushed through a polished metal door to the interior lobby.

A line of well over a hundred people snaked back from the wide registration desk, behind which sat a single Resident Control representative. Wally checked the time. It was ten minutes to ten. He considered the line with despair, then dutifully took his spot at the end.

For all the people standing around in there, the lobby was unusually quiet. The only voices Wally heard were coming from the HappyCams trolling the line like smiling electric armadillos and the two wall-sized liquid monitors to his right and left.

On the monitor to his right, a face some twenty feet tall—Wally assumed it belonged to a Resident Control greeter—was welcoming the masses and outlining certain behavioral expectations. To his left, a series of "actual citizens" were offering their own heartfelt testimonials, thanking Resident Control and its employees for helping to keep them on the straight and narrow. Most also thanked Resident Control for going above and beyond the call when it came to protecting the citizens of New York and the neighboring regions from the ever present terrorist threat. At the end of the testimonials, each citizen held up and endorsed consumer products, including UniCam Cola-Flavored Water ("Keep an eye on your waistline!") and Joyce's Own Fingerprint Enhancement Cream ("Got nothing to hide? Then prove it!"). They all seemed quite sincere.

The line moved slowly but no one complained. Ten o'clock

came and went, but Wally took some comfort at least in knowing that the records would indicate that he had been in the outer lobby and sent on to the inner lobby long before that.

The Earwig beeped in his ear. He reached in his pocket and flipped open the minivid, then sat through two commercials before finding out who was calling him.

Before the second commercial was finished, Wally noticed several people looking at him with fear in their eyes, shaking their heads insistently. One pointed to the screen where the giant face was gently reminding everyone that communitainment devices were to remain silent at all times while in Resident Control.

"With the exception," she said, "of those of you already registered with CHUCKLE as suffering from communitainment-related neurological overadaptation." (This was an increasingly common ailment in New York, affecting nearly thirty percent of the population. Constant use of communitainment systems of various kinds—especially implants like Wally's—had resulted in a physical rearrangement of the neural cells in the temporal lobe, making it impossible to function normally without an electronically modulated voice in one's ear.)

Lou's face filled the minivid screen.

"Heya, 407-R—"

"*Lou,*" Wally whispered sharply, "I'm in Resident Control. Gotta go. See you tomorrow."

He held up the screen and flashed it around the room so Lou could see he was telling the truth. Without another word he flipped the screen down and replaced it in his pocket, offering an apologetic shrug to the people who were still staring.

"My boss," he said, by way of explanation.

One hour and forty-nine minutes later, Wally heard the three tones that gave him clearance to approach the registration desk. There he was met by a perky young woman wearing a neon yellow tunic and an impossibly bright smile.

"Good morning, good morning, good *morning,* Good Citizen!" she chirped at him. "Before we get started, I would just like to let you know that this conversation will be recorded."

"Sure," Wally said, in an effort to be friendly in spite of having spent two hours in line. "For quality assurance, right?"

The woman's eyes flickered in momentary confusion. "No . . . no, not particularly. Now, please insert your SUCKIE card into the reader and place your right hand on the scanner. Then we can begin. I just need to ask you a few questions."

By "a few" she meant seventy-eight questions, and when he reached the twenty-ninth floor an hour later, he was already drained, knowing full well that he hadn't even begun yet. It was almost one o'clock.

Behind the door of the Behavior and Language Adjustment Bureau, Wally found himself in yet another enormous sterile, fluorescent-lit room. There were no shadows and no windows. The white tiled floor had been trod a light gray, detailed with black fishhook scuff marks and old coffee spills. The fifty molded plastic chairs scattered haphazardly around the waiting room were filled mostly with despondent citizens staring at their hands or into their laps.

Several of the people in the room, Wally noted, apparently had reason to be there. One man in a deeply stained Horribleness Day T-shirt stood in a corner, lightly knocking his forehead repeatedly against the chalk white wall. Another was pretending to smoke a large cigar, though what he held between his fingers was in fact the cardboard tube from an empty roll of toilet paper.

"Ah, there's nothin' like a ten-cent cigar!" he'd announce after blowing another cloud of imaginary tobacco smoke toward the bank of lights above him.

A black woman in a faded green housecoat was shuffling the perimeter of the room, pausing to give the finger to each of the wall-mounted vids.

Why haven't some of these people been locked up yet? Wally thought as he picked his way through the chairs toward the booth at the front of the room. Behind the bulletproof glass sat an unusually well-dressed man with thickly mascaraed eyes.

"Hello, ah," Wally began. "I had a ten o'clock appointment for, uh . . ."—he dropped his voice to a whisper—"uh, language adjustment?"

"Yes," was all the man said.

Wally waited a moment for some hint, some clue as to what he should do at this point. "I'm real sorry I'm late," he said, reaching for his card. "I checked in downstairs just before ten and didn't realize—"

"We saw you," the man said.

"Oh... well . . ." Wally held his card out to the man, who made no move to take it.

"We have all your information on hand already, NY00169765/P. Just take a seat, and when your number is called one of our case workers will see what we can do about that stuttering problem."

"Oh—no—" Wally said. "No, I'm afraid you're mistaken. I'm not here for a stuttering problem. You see, it was all a simple—"

"Yes I'm sure," the man said. "In fact . . ." Then he stood and walked away.

Wally waited a few minutes, expecting the well-dressed man to return and finish his sentence.

When he didn't return, Wally shrugged to the empty window and began looking for an unoccupied chair, hoping he wouldn't end up sitting near one of the crazy people. You never knew what they might do.

There were a few small and colorful posters on the otherwise bare walls. They featured photographs of kittens, puppies, and flowers, with inspirational slogans like "Mutuality is the way to go" and "How well do you know your neighbors?" The old woman in the housecoat gave each of those the finger too.

He found a seat between an elderly Asian man who was snoring quietly and a woman of about thirty with long blonde curls and clothes that seemed to be from another time. From the look on her face, he could tell she was irritated by the whole situation.

Wally sat down with a sigh and commenced staring at his hands. It seemed the thing to do.

"So what are you in for?" the woman whispered.

He looked up, not sure whether she'd been speaking to him. She was staring straight ahead and seemed to be addressing the air in front of her. More likely it was a communitainer call.

"Me?" he asked anyway.

"I wasn't talking to the sleeping guy."

Wally glanced at the man next to him. "Oh. Well, I guess I'd really rather not say. It's... I'm ashamed."

She looked at him quickly, then continued gazing straight ahead. "You might want to look straight ahead or down," she said quietly. "They don't like us speaking to one another in here."

"Oh," Wally said. "Okay." He returned to looking at his hands. That was an odd thing, he thought, asking him a question then telling him not to talk.

A minute passed in silence.

"So?" she asked finally. "What was it?"

He looked at her again.

"*Stop that,*" she whispered sharply. Then she sighed. "We can talk—we just can't *look* like we're talking, understand? The vids in here are old models—they don't pick up sound too well."

"Oh," Wally said again, looking quickly back at his hands. "Well, like I said, I'd rather not say. I said something I shouldn't have said to someone I shouldn't have said it... um... to."

"HappyCam?" she asked.

Wally shook his head. "Uh-uh. Stroller Brigade."

The woman let go a harsh laugh she tried to disguise as a sneeze. "One of *those* cows? Trust me, no matter what it was, it wouldn't've been bad enough for me. At least if she's still alive."

Wally was stunned. He'd never heard anyone use language like that in reference to the Brigade before. If anyone else had heard her, she could easily find herself upstairs in an Unmutual Unit.

"*Shhh,*" he wheezed.

"Oh shhh yourself," she whispered back. "Look at this." Pretending to scratch her ankle, she pulled up her flower-print pant leg a few inches to reveal a patchwork of wicked, criss-crossed scars.

"My God," Wally whispered "They did that to you? I mean, they've left me with a few nicks and scrapes but nothing like that."

"In my neighborhood some of them trick out the strollers with razor blades. Guess I'm one of their favorite targets."

"Wha'd you do?"

"Nothing, really. They tend to be a bit more barbarous with their own gender," she said. "Especially those of us who don't stop and coo over their ugly spawn for ten minutes. I guess we make them feel bad about themselves."

It was odd. Wally had been through more than his share of confrontations with the Brigade on the sidewalk—it was almost as if they could smell childlessness on him—but he'd never heard Margie complain about them, and she was just as childless as he was. She wasn't exactly the cooing type either.

"That's terrible," Wally offered.

"Yeah, you see? So whatever it was you said that got you sent here, it's okay with me."

Wally considered for a moment, then confessed, "I called one of them *lady*."

She pretended to sneeze again. "So in other words, you lied in public, and they sent you here."

He shook his head. "No, 'lady' was banned the night before. I missed the bulletin."

She shook her head. "Unbelievable."

"Yeah, that's kinda what I thought at the time," Wally said. Then he figured he'd take a chance. "So... why are you in here? Trouble with the Brigade?"

"Nope," she said with mock penitence. "Far worse than that, I'm afraid."

Given what she'd told him so far, he couldn't imagine what could be worse. Well, he could, but they take people away for those things. They don't send them to BLAB.

"What?" he whispered, almost afraid to know the answer.

"Well," she sighed, "I don't own a communitainer."

Wally looked at her involuntarily, assuming it was a joke. That didn't even make any sense. "No *communitainer*?" he asked. It seemed too improbable. "I mean, you're joking, right? How could you get along?" He was no fan of his, but still.

She clucked her tongue. "I have a *phone*. I just don't have one of those." Her eyes darted to the scar above his left ear. "And I seem to get along just fine, thank you."

"But what if there's an emergency? Another attack or something? I mean, that's why they want us all to have one, right? In case there's an emergency or we need to report something?"

She rolled her eyes. "Well, then, I guess I'll just deal... What is it with people always turning novelties and gadgets into necessities? I've been through emergencies before without one, and it seems I'm still here."

Wally was still having trouble accepting the idea. He'd never met someone without a communitainer before. It was just a given. She must've been one of those... He racked his brain for the old term but couldn't come up with it. The clothes were part of it too.

"I don't have one of those either," she added, with a nod toward Wally's lap. He felt his face growing warm.

"I…um, I kind of . . ."

She smirked. "I mean *that,*" she said, pointing at the scar on his wrist.

"But I thought those were mandatory."

"They are. But they haven't gotten everybody yet. I'm betting they'll be bringing that up today, too, along with the usual counseling."

Wally was beginning to realize that he might be getting off easy here, in comparison. This woman wasn't just unmutual, she seemed to almost revel in the fact. Just the kind of person they were told to report. Terrorists might've been responsible for the Horribleness, but Unmutuals would pave the way for the next attack.

Still, though, there was something about her. A liveliness and fearlessness that Wally admired, but that terrified him at the same time—though he would never dare admit the former. Plus there was the fact that she was young and attractive. He couldn't believe the way they'd been speaking together, right there in the middle of Resident Control.

"My name's Carlotta, by the way," she said. "Carlotta Bain. I'd shake your hand but that would give us away, and then we'd both be in it."

"Of course, I understand," he said, still looking at his hands, the scar on his wrist left by the GPS chip.

"And you are…? " she asked expectantly.

"Oh, um . . . " He began reaching into his pocket reflexively. "N-Y-zero-zero-one—" He caught himself. "Um, Wally. Wallace. No, Wally Philco…Funny how you forget sometimes."

"More sad, really."

A garbled voice came over the PA system. Wally listened hard but the only number he could positively identify was a six, which meant it might or might not have been his.

“That’s me,” Carlotta whispered, standing. “Wish me luck.”

She left without looking back and disappeared through the door next to the still-empty glass booth.

THREE

"This is what you wear?"

These were the first words out of the language counselor's mouth when Wally was ushered to her cubicle.

He remembered looking down at himself, not seeing much of anything out of sorts. His shirt wasn't stained. His fly was zipped. His tie was knotted neatly. The shoes needed replacing, but she couldn't see those.

"Never mind," she said, turning her attention back to the monitor on her desk. "Take a seat. Though we may need to discuss your wardrobe at some future date."

The lacquered black name plate on her desk read "NY71237001/J." She was dressed in an extravagant lavender chiffon evening gown, and as he listened to her over the hours that followed Wally noticed that every object on her desk, from the monitor to the coffee cup emblazoned with her citizen number to the stapler—even the staples themselves—was Armani.

At some point during the previous decade, Fashionism had become not just a way of life but a powerful and legitimate political lobby in New York. The Fashionist Party, like the Corporatists before them, had infiltrated nearly every government agency, which is why Wally wasn't surprised to see it had a major foothold within the ranks of BLAB, given that BLAB created and enforced the rules of public behavior. Poor and sloppy dress came to be considered a quality of life issue, and so designer apparel—preferably in the current season's style—was stressed and, in some extreme cases, administered.

Sitting on the train back to Brooklyn after three hours of browbeating regarding his flagrant and abusive use of banned words (as well as his failure to abide by the daily bulletins), Wally thought that the counselor might have carried a bit more credibility had she not been hampered by such a serious glottal stop.

Still, after all that, he wasn't quite finished. In his briefcase were five different forms that needed to be filled out in full and returned to the BLAB office no later than Monday, at which point he would be given two more follow-up forms to complete. Of all the hundreds of city agencies and bureaus, those associated with Resident Control remained the only ones that still relied on physical pieces of printed paper. No one could say why, though it was assumed to be a way of reminding citizens who was in charge.

Beyond the forms, for the next six weeks Wally was also expected to read aloud a prepared statement confessing his guilt and enduring shame at the beginning of his nightly reports.

All in all, he'd gotten off easy, considering his childlessness, his less than eye-catching fashion sense, and his outrageous use of hate words. Fortunately for him, he had an otherwise stellar record of mutuality and Good Citizenship.

After being excused from the language counselor's cubicle, Wally had paused to ask her what her name was. She merely pointed at the black name plate.

"No, not your number," he said. "I mean your name."

She raised a long red fingernail to the corner of her mouth and scratched at it lightly. She looked concerned. He couldn't tell if she was unsure of her name or unsure whether or not she should divulge it to someone with the fashion sense of a Croatian leper.

"Why do you want to know?" she asked, clearly dubious.

"Just curious," he said. "I'm curious about names."

She still seemed doubtful, but finally said "Jones."

"Is that your first name or your last name?"

"Last name," she said. "First name's Lavoris."

Wally saw something nearly human creep onto her features. It didn't last long.

"Lavoris Jones," he mused as he stood to leave. "I think that's an awfully pretty name. Thank you, and I thank you for your help here today, uh, Ms. Jones. I promise you my language skills will be better in the future... LWIW." He held out his hand.

"LWIW," she replied absently, ignoring his hand, already preparing herself for the next linguistic transgressor on her docket.

Wally slid his hand into his pocket, turned the corner, and headed back toward the waiting room. As he did, Ms. Lavoris Jones added one more flag to his file.

• • •

He'd been half hoping that Carlotta might be waiting for him when he left the counselor, but she was nowhere to be seen. That was to be expected, he guessed. He knew trying to ask someone about her would be foolishness. It was bad for him to even think such a thing, and if the monitors detected any hesitation or undue inquisitiveness on his part, it was possible he'd be stopped again before he left the premises.

LWIW, he thought. The original slogan, "If It Looks Weird, It Is Weird," had been part of a nationwide public service ad campaign that appeared three weeks after the Horribleness as a reminder to all citizens to keep their eyes open for potential terrorists. The ads were inescapable—they appeared on adscreens, four-ways, subways, sidewalks, radios—the jingle blasting into millions of ears at least twenty or thirty times a day. The jingle itself reached number one on the charts. It became such a part of the national consciousness and language that it was eventually condensed to "Looks Weird, Is Weird" (or, as some of the Fashionists preferred, "Looking Weird Is Weird") before becoming acronized and, in time, entirely replacing "good-bye" as a standard salutation.

After the briefest, futile glance around the waiting room, Wally put his head down and headed for the elevators.

Back in Brooklyn he felt a growing heaviness as he approached his house. Margie would be there, and he had no idea what sort of ugliness awaited him. If it was going to be anything like the previous night, he might as well let himself in, drop his briefcase on the table, then lock himself in the bathroom until morning. In spite of his dread, and while trying to keep an eye out for any roaming Brigade patrols, he forced a smile onto his face and a pleasant squint in his eye as he passed his neighbors. It didn't matter. Those who were outside were pacing in tight circles on the sidewalk, talking to themselves. None of them seemed to notice as he stepped around them. Just like no one noticed the flags anymore.

Apart from the heavy Brigade presence (he didn't dare call them a "menace" aloud—he'd learned his lesson that afternoon), the neighborhood was a quiet one. It had changed considerably since Thor Communications bought it up five years earlier. Yet even after all the trees came down and the adscreens went up, Wally still thought it was a decent place to live. Other citizens seemed to think so too. It surprised him that there was such a heavy turnover rate—houses were opening up all the time.

He noticed that another house had just been put up for sale three doors away from his. He'd actually sort of known that guy but had no idea he was thinking of moving. Now it looked like he was gone already. The curtains had been taken off the windows and, from what Wally could see, the place was completely empty. He'd been a teacher or something, Wally remembered. Nice guy.

He paused when he reached his own house, a three-story brownstone nearly identical to all the others along his block. Trying to steel himself, he straightened his spine, flexed his neck, tensed and relaxed his stomach muscles. This wasn't going to be good. He decided to use the ground-floor entrance tonight. If nothing else it would offer him at least a few extra moments of peace before he got upstairs to Margie.

After pushing through the knee-high wrought-iron gate, he heard a voice to his left.

"Hey, Philco! Check it out!"

Wally's head snapped around, expecting to see one of those new armor-plated double strollers from Munich bearing down on him.

Instead, he was honestly relieved (perhaps for the first time) to see that it was only his neighbor, an energetic sort named Whittaker Chambers, who'd been doing some gardening in his minuscule front yard.

"Hey, Whit," Wally offered with a small wave. "What goes on?"

"Hey," Chambers said, brushing the dirt from his knees as he approached, a dangerous-looking set of shears still clutched in his gloved hand. "Check it out, huh?" He gestured at his chest with the shears.

Wally looked but didn't see anything out of the ordinary. Chambers—a stocky, dark-haired man about Wally's age whose eyebrows actually did meet above his nose—was wearing the same Operation RAT T-shirt he always seemed to be wearing.

Below the logo was a cartoon of a smiling, winking rat in a DOD cap and trench coat, holding up a coin.

"Yeah?" Wally asked. "What, did you wash it?"

"Nah, man," Chambers said. "It's *new.*"

"You got another one?"

"Number thirty-seven," Chambers said proudly, puffing out his chest. He stepped over the front gate and leaned against the stoop.

"Wow," Wally said. "You sure got a nose for sniffing out potentials."

"Yeah, y'know, it's a gift. When they came by this time, they told me I was one of the best. Don't have the record yet, but I'm gettin' there."

"Wow," Wally repeated. "That's really great. You ever thought of, y'know, joining the DOD or something? That way you'd get paid for it."

Chambers shook his head. "Nah, man—but thanks. I guess I prefer to work independent... Besides, I just look at it as my duty as a citizen. And this here"—he pulled the shirt away from his belly—"this is payment enough. That and knowing that my wife an' kids are a little bit safer."

"Yeah, well," Wally said, struggling to keep the enthusiasm up, "you have my and Margie's thanks too. Living next to you is like... well, you just keep this whole neighborhood more secure."

Whittaker beamed and rocked back on his heels slightly.

"So who was it this time?"

"*Ah,*" Chambers barked. "That's the kicker. You remember that faggot?" He jerked his thumb over his shoulder toward the newly vacant house. "Said he was a teacher or something?"

"Of course—his name's Tim, I think. I was just noticing his house was up for sale. I never heard him mention that he was thinking of moving. Not that we talked all that much."

"Yeah, well," Chambers said with a quick bounce of the eyebrow, "let's just say he wasn't exactly planning on it."

"My God, so . . ." Wally stopped for just a second. "He always seemed like a nice guy—wha'd he do?"

"Wha'd he *do*?" Chambers threw his hands in the air and Wally ducked to avoid the shears. "Apart from being a faggot? It's more like, what *didn't* he do? And what was he gonna do next? I'd been keeping my eye on him for a while now, see. There was just something about him that wasn't right."

"Ahh," Wally said. "Gotcha... Well, that's too bad."

Chambers's smile dimmed slightly and he fell silent. He squinted at Wally. "Whaddya mean by that?"

"By what?"

"By saying 'that's too bad.'"

Oh, God.

"No... Whit, no. Don't take that the wrong way... I was just saying that he always seemed like such a nice guy. I mean, he—he was always just real nice to me, is all... Y'know, it's just that it was too bad he turned out to be a terrorist, because, you know, if he *weren't* a terrorist..." Wally knew he shouldn't be getting nervous like this. Not in front of Whit. It would only make things worse. "Just that... if he *weren't* a terrorist... he would've been a nice guy. Is all."

He knew it was time to get out of there before he said anything else that might imply complicity. It had been a long day as it was, it was probably going to be a long night, and the last thing he needed in between was a neighbor deciding that he was a terrorist. "Hey," he said. "None of it matters, though. He was a terrorist, and you did the right thing." He clapped Chambers on the shoulder in what he hoped would be taken as an open, neighborly, unterroristic gesture. "We're all grateful—you have our thanks. But right now, I should get inside. I'm sure Margie's wondering what happened to me."

"No she's not," Chambers said. "She keeps peeking out the window up there." He pointed above Wally's shoulder. "She knows where you are. But I should get back to these begonias anyway. Hey, though, it's good talkin' to you, citizen. EOFTB, huh?"

Wally had already begun to turn away but stopped. "Pardon?"

"What?" Chambers asked.

"That acronym—I'm afraid I don't . . ."

"Oh, yeah. Sorry. Sometimes I forget. You haven't earned any T-shirts at all, have you? It's just something we ratters say. EOFTB—Eyes Open for the Baddies."

"Oh, yeah, sure," Wally said, attempting to summon up a chuckle. "Yeah. Do that."

As Whit turned away, Wally saw the printing on the back of his T-shirt. A paraphrase from the HISTERIC provisions, in blood-red block letters:

> REMEMBER
> Any Citizen who hinders the arrest of, does not report, or does not testify against an accused terrorist will himself be considered a TERRORIST.

When he got up to the second floor, he was surprised to find Margie in the kitchen. She appeared to be putting some sort of meal together.

This is new, Wally thought.

"Hey," he said.

She glanced over her shoulder briefly. "Hi."

The word most often used to describe the kitchen was "efficient." An electric oven, an aluminum sink, a narrow countertop, a bar fridge. In that, it was identical to nearly every other kitchen in the new and renovated buildings throughout the city. Given the ongoing rationing and the growing list of banned foods, it was all the kitchen anybody really needed.

"What's that I smell?" he asked. He couldn't remember the last time he'd come home to dinner cooking. At least he hoped it was dinner.

"Soy roast," she said flatly. "Genetically enhanced. New formula. The Chevrix people will be putting it out, and I might be working their campaign, so I thought I'd try it . . . Part of the job is coming up with what to call it."

He set the briefcase full of BLAB forms on the compact end table, loosened his tie, and took a seat. "So it's experimental?" He was wondering what sort of felonious hoodoo Chevrix was involved in that would make them turn to Margie.

"Sort of. It hits the market next year. S'posed to be okay." She was wearing a black silk blouse and charcoal coolie pants, which had become quite fashionable in recent months. It struck Wally as a bit fancier than necessary for the kitchen, but he figured it best not to bring it up. He also figured it was best not to ask how many subjects had died or were disfigured during the testing phase of the soy roast.

"Well, I can't wait to try it," he said, trying to sound sincere. He glanced out the small window above the fridge at the brick wall of the neighboring building. He sighed. He was very tired.

She continued chopping something by the sink. "I see Whit cornered you again."

"Yeah, he had me out there for a while."

"He show you his new shirt?"

"Number thirty-seven, I think it was. Thirty-six or thirty-seven." Sometimes he wished she'd at least turn around to talk to him.

Using the blade of the knife, she scraped what he finally recognized as diced red peppers into the palm of her hand, opened the oven door, and tossed them in with the roast. "They suggest you cook it with something so that it'll have any flavor at all...I'm trying peppers. They're as artificial as the roast but I figured it was worth a shot."

"Good," Wally said. This was all very strange. He could tell by the clipped quaver in her voice and the sharpness of her movements that it would be best to keep his mouth shut as much as possible. There was an anger in there she was trying to keep down, and one wrong word from him was certain to detonate it. He had to admit, though, that she was making a yeoman's effort at civility. That was the strange thing about the whole scene. Why was she bothering?

"He tell you what he got Tim for?" Margie asked, scrubbing the artificial pepper oil from her hands under a weak trickle of tepid water in the sink.

"No, not exactly. Doesn't really matter, I guess."

"Smoking," she said.

"Really?" That caught Wally by surprise. "He sure didn't seem like the type...I mean, I didn't know him all that well, but still, he didn't strike me as the type with connections like that."

"Maybe he was smoking, maybe he wasn't. He might've been searing some meat. Whit never actually saw him with a cigarette. Just smelled the smoke."

"Either case he's guilty, I guess."

"Right. And Whit says he wasn't at any of the Horribleness Day events either. That just doesn't look good, especially when you start adding things up. So Whit made a call last night, swore on the flag there was no personal enmity with the accused, got a new T-shirt this morning, and Tim's doing twenty at an Unmutual Rehab."

"System works," Wally said. He kept watching Margie, who wouldn't stop moving, apparently trying to avoid any eye contact. Wiping down the counter, straightening some napkins, checking the roast. Checking the roast again. "Why don't you sit down and relax a minute?" he finally suggested. It was against his better judgment, but he felt he had to say something. Might as well get it over with. Better than letting it simmer. Let it simmer, it'll only get worse, and come out later. He was beat as it was and didn't feel much like dealing with it at two in the morning.

"In a minute," she said, opening the refrigerator and pretending to count something.

He leaned back in his chair. "I liked Tim," he said. "Sometimes I think it would be nice to get to know some of the neighbors a little better before, y'know, Whit turns them in... I'm surprised sometimes he hasn't turned *us* in yet."

Margie slammed the refrigerator door and whirled on him, her eyes blazing. *Here we go,* he thought.

"*Shhh!*" Margie hissed. "Don't even *think* something like that. It's talk like that that *will* get us turned in. You know how something like that'll be taken."

"I didn't say we were doing anything—I just meant that—"

"*Stop* it, would you? Just shut up? Aren't you in enough trouble already?" She crossed her arms and shook her head. "That's your problem, you can't keep your mouth shut. You should never have said anything at the park. And to a member of the Brigade? I mean, what were you thinking?"

They'd been through it all the night before, and it was exactly the conversation Wally was hoping to avoid tonight. No wonder she never asked him how things had gone at BLAB.

"Margie," he pleaded, "I told you what happened. She was ramming me with her . . ." He swallowed what he wanted to say. ". . . with her stroller. I told you that. I'm just supposed to let her?"

"That doesn't matter. You *know* that. And now I'm the one who's married to an Unmutual who was picked up for disrupting Horribleness Day. That makes me suspect too. Did you stop for a second to think of what it would do to my business?"

He had to admit it hadn't been tops on his list while armed DOD troops were dragging him to the van.

If the opportunity presented itself, he thought, he would begin sliding gradually and silently off his chair and under the table as she spoke. Then he'd slither across the floor to the fridge, out the window, down the side of the building, and away.

"I'm . . . I'm sorry," he said. He felt his stomach begin to cramp up, "But hey, look—" He spread his arms. "I'm home, right? I couldn't've been *that* bad. I just have some forms to fill out and a report addendum. That's it. Everything's fine. They aren't sending me away."

He thought he smelled the roast burning, but he couldn't be certain. He decided not to say anything. A little charring might help.

"Everything's *fine,*" she spat. "We'll see how fine things are. At least if you'd been sent away, you wouldn't be—"

"Margie, c'mon," he cut her off. He didn't want to know where she was going with that one.

She closed her mouth. He saw her take a breath. Then, finally, she took a seat at the table across from him.

"I just think it's best you not talk about it at all," she said. "You should maybe just keep your...mouth shut. Especially around here. You don't want to end up saying something you'll regret." Her eyes darted to the clock on the wall, then back to him. Her voice was back under control. They didn't like it when you yelled. "And if you do have to say anything, you'd be better off to talk about the good things. Nice things." In case he hadn't caught that first glance, she nodded toward the clock again. They both knew one of the spyvids was up there. There's always one in the kitchen clock, you could be sure of it. They weren't so sure where the others were, though. Could be anywhere. Enough to cover every corner of the house.

"Yeah, you're right," he said. She was, too. "I'm sorry." He stood and walked casually into the next room, where he turned on the radio. He tuned in one of the three remaining music stations (they were all pretty much the same), cranked up the volume, and returned to the kitchen. A light jazz combo was playing an upbeat if sterile rendition of the *Peter Gunn* theme.

"I'll just try and keep my mouth shut," he said. "And my mind focused. It's best for everyone." He looked down at his folded hands, then remembered Carlotta.

Hippie. That's the old word I was looking for. She must've been a hippie.

He looked back at Margie. "I didn't tell anybody where I was today, you know," he said quietly, almost helplessly. "For what that's worth. I mean, I had to tell Lou why I wouldn't be in, but he would've received a report about it anyway. And I think I can trust him to keep it to himself." They both knew full well that it was chemically impossible for Lou to keep anything to himself. "But Whit didn't know when I talked to him. Didn't seem to, anyway. That's a good thing, right?"

"Whit's a *ratter,*" she said, "If he doesn't know now, I'm sure he'll get the news within the hour. You think you need to *tell* anybody? That you could keep it a secret? No. There are no secrets... and if we want to be safe, that's the way it should be."

"You think so?" he asked, not wanting to bring up the little fact that she made a good living helping hide the dark secrets of powerful and sinister people.

Margie stared at him the same way Whit had earlier. "That's a very unmutual thing to say," she told him. "You know as well as I do that we're at war. And we're at war with people who'll stop at nothing to destroy us and our freedom."

"Who, the Australians?" Wally asked. His voice was incredulous. He knew he was pushing it, that he was saying things he shouldn't be saying, that he should just shut up while he still could, but he was tired, and for some reason he suddenly didn't care what he said. Margie, fortunately, took it as another one of his bonehead questions.

"Everybody," she said. "That's why all this is necessary." She pointed at the clock. "To keep us safe."

Wally took a deep breath. For the first time, this was all beginning to sound patently absurd. He felt his stomach relax. He felt his whole body begin to relax. He smiled and leaned forward. "Fine, sure... But wouldn't it be nice," he said, "to—just once—be able to do something without being watched? Walk around naked or eat a steak? Read an old book, whatever?" Despite his newfound boldness, he kept his voice low, in the hopes the mics wouldn't pick it up below the music.

"That's what the terrorists want. To hide. To work out their plans in secret."

"Terrorists like Tim."

"Yes, maybe. Look, if you're not doing anything wrong, then what's the big deal?"

The soy roast was most definitely burning now. The air in the kitchen was growing hazy with smoke.

"I know that's how they try to justify it," Wally said, "but doesn't it feel sometimes like they're protecting us by taking away everything that needs protecting? What about all those Belgians who ended up in the Detention Camps? They weren't doing anything but talking funny. I wasn't doing anything wrong yesterday but look what happened." He tried to control his rising voice. "I'm not doing anything wrong. You know that."

"You're talking like an Unmutual. That's something." Margie pushed her chair away from the table, stood, and grabbed an oven mitt. "Let me put it this way," she said. "By talking the way you are, you've placed us both in serious danger. You put us both in danger at the park too. You're putting the whole country in danger. I... just don't know what's been happening with you. I don't care what you do to yourself, but you're dragging me along, and I want nothing to do with it."

Wally had wondered when she'd finally say as much. It had

been coming for a long time. By saying the incident at the park was his fault, she had the viable excuse she was looking for. He had to admit that he never would've guessed that this would be the excuse she'd grab, when there were so many others handy.

"I understand," he said quietly. "Fine." The music was starting to get on his nerves, but he made no move to turn it down. A different light jazz combo was now playing an uptempo version of "Over the Rainbow." In a way, he thought, it was providing a ridiculous soundtrack for a ridiculous conversation. "All I ask is that you not report me yourself. Do that much for me."

She opened the oven door and pulled out the pan, in which sat a gray, two-pound blob of genetically enhanced bean curd, flecked with fake peppers and patches of black crust.

"I wouldn't do that," she promised. Her voice was laced with both regret and relief.

As she began cutting the roast into rubbery slabs, an abrasive voice leaped into Wally's ear.

"*Good news, Good Citizen Philco! You have a call! And this call is being brought to you by Acriphonex, the pill that won't let go . . .*"

As the Acriphonex jingle played itself out, Wally closed his eyes and waited. He sure wished there was a way to turn these things off. He reached for the minivid, opened the screen, and set it on the table.

"Hey 407-R." The phlegmy voice was unmistakable long before the face came into focus.

"Hello there, Lou."

"Hey, hey, am I bleedin'?" The image on the small screen tilted its head back to expose the third chin. Lou sometimes had problems with unexpected bleeding.

Wally opened his eyes. "Doesn't look like it from here, Lou, no... Um, is that why you called?" He closed his eyes again.

"Naw, not really—just noticed it. Just wanna make sure, though. You ain't in a camp, are ya? One o' those rehab camps?"

"Not exactly, Lou, no."

"But you got out okay, then, right? You're back home?"

"Yeah, that I am, Lou." His voice was flat.

"And you'll be back in here tomorrow."

"Bright and early."

"Great. Give my best to Mrs. 407-R and I'll see you then. LWIW—get it?"

Wally's eyes were still closed. Under the table, his fists were clenched.

"Yeah. I get it, Lou. LWIW."

The noise in his ear went silent. He opened his eyes to see Margie approaching the table with two sad plates in her hands.

They ate in silence, and Wally began wondering how, exactly, he was going to explain the previous half hour in that night's report. Whatever he came up with, the VidLog account sure wouldn't help his case any.

FOUR

Shortly before six a.m., as he did every morning, Whit Chambers put on his thin maroon bathrobe, set a pot of coffee brewing, then crept down to the basement, trying to avoid the creaky fifth step. His wife and daughters were still asleep, and he preferred it that way. This was his time.

Upon hearing the first burbles of coffee dripping into the stained glass pot across the room, a pair of oversized, triangular bat ears emerged from a tattered gray pillow in the corner and twitched. The Chambers's Chihuahua knew that if somebody—anybody—was moving around, there would be more food in his bowl soon. He hopped lightly from the pillow and clicked briskly down the stairs after Whit.

In the basement, Chambers settled in at his desk and passed

a finger over a pulsing light on the console before him. At once, an array of six video monitors hummed awake.

Half an hour later Judy Chambers, awakened by her husband's shouts and the incessant, frantic barking of the dog, dragged herself reluctantly out of bed and headed downstairs.

As she drew closer to the basement door, she could tell finally that what she was hearing—apart from the barking—was maniacal laughter, not the screams of distress that had been part of her dream. She should've known better. It was the same every morning. Before venturing into the basement, she poured herself a cup of coffee. She considered pouring one for Whit, but it sounded like he'd had enough as it was.

As she approached the basement door, past a sink still filled with dirty dishes, a disheveled red and white checkered tablecloth, dirty clothes hanging from the backs of chairs, and a textured linoleum floor littered with yesterday's toys, the cackling became almost coherent.

"*Run, you homo, run!*"

She closed her eyes and tried to gather all her patience together into one cool ball, then stepped to the basement door.

"Whit?" she asked the darkened stairwell. "You okay?"

"Oh—God, yeah. Honey, c'mere, you gotta see this. This is classic." He was still laughing, the dog was still yipping. Wrapping both hands around the warm mug, she descended the chipped and worn wooden steps with no little skepticism.

The basement was a cold and empty cement box. There was no carpeting, no furniture. Just a few warped cardboard boxes stacked against the wall. It was, in a word, uninviting—but that's the way Whit wanted it. He didn't want the girls playing down there, he didn't want company going down there. They might start messing around in his corner. He called it his office, which consisted of a chair, a folding card table, his control console, and those six monitors, each fed by the high-rez security vids Whit had installed around the exterior of their house.

She crossed the cold and dusty floor in her bare feet and stood behind him, staring at the monitors.

Across all six screens she saw their neighbor Wally Philco being chased down the sidewalk by three women pushing strollers. He seemed genuinely terrified.

"You see the look on that guy's face?" Whit asked, clutching his own coffee cup, not daring to move his eyes from the screens. "God," he said, "they've been after him for ten minutes now…used a classic pincer movement, and he walked right into it…What a homo."

The Chihuahua, apparently all yipped out, trotted back upstairs to his pillow in the corner.

Chambers at last acknowledged his wife's presence. "Are Buick and Coors up yet?" he asked over his shoulder.

"They will be soon if you keep yelling like that," Judy replied. "Do you need to do this *every* morning? I'm just saying, I could use an extra hour's sleep now and then. I'm the one who has to go to work, remember?"

"Hey," Chambers said, "and miss this? This is a hell of a lot better than any of those four-way shows."

Chambers took another swallow of his lukewarm coffee, and for just a second Judy contemplated pouring the contents of her still-steaming cup down his back. It was the same conversation every morning.

Once Wally Philco was no longer visible on any of the monitors, she asked hesitantly, "So... do you think you're gonna look for work today?"

Relenting, Chambers turned away from the screens, all the laughter gone from him now. "How many times do I have to tell you? This *is* my job."

"Whit," she began patiently, wondering why she even bothered explaining it to him anymore, "we can't pay the electric bill with T-shirts."

Chambers had been through this exchange more times than he cared to remember. "Look," he said, "let me try to explain it to you again. If we had better security in this city—at the ports, on the streets, in the buildings—then maybe I wouldn't have to do this all day and all night. But since we're livin' in a town that's wide open, that's just *askin'—beggin'*—to be attacked again, then it's my duty, hear me? My *duty* to do what I can to protect you, and the kids, and my neighborhood."

Judy knew it was best not to remind him that the Horribleness took place in Tupelo. That got her smacked once.

"I can't do this all by myself," he went on. "For god sakes, I'm only *one man.*Once everyone else gets on the stick and starts doin' their part, then, maybe, I'll have the time to go look for a job. But baby, until then, your safety and the girls' safety is resting squarely on my shoulders. You have no idea what kind of responsibility that is. But don't you worry, I'm not about to let you down."

"I know... I know that, Whit. But do you think there'll ever come a time when you might start getting paid in something other than T-shirts?"

• • •

In the days and weeks that followed what he came to think of as the "Soy Roast Blowout," Wally went about his daily routine: dodging the morning Brigade patrols, going to work, coming home, filing his reports (complete with shame addendum). He was, if anything, doubly vigilant in his citizenship, always aware that at any moment the DOD might grab him off the street or raid the office or kick in his front door while he was in the bathroom.

But it never happened. No one seemed to be following him. No one said a word about it. He received no vaguely threatening messages via the Earwig, there were no postscripts on the daily bulletins.

This left him even more apprehensive and suspicious. The only thing he was certain of was that he hadn't gotten away with anything.

It was too reminiscent of when he was a kid. His parents were the camera-happy types, long after a time when cameras were considered a mere suburban luxury, and long before everything was recorded digitally as a matter of course. They didn't just snap pictures of vacations and birthday parties and Christmases but candid shots around the house as well. Hundreds of them. There were weekly trips to the drugstore to drop off a new roll.

As a result, they had pictures of a young Wally crying on the toilet, being chased by a goat at a petting zoo, and far too many, he felt, of that unfortunate week when he was seven and had decided he wanted to be a ballet dancer. All of these photos were arranged with loving care by his mother in a series of fat, faux leather bound photo albums.

Whenever Wally brought friends over—especially new ones—his parents would drag the albums out and everyone would get a good laugh. He never heard the end of it in school. Even people who'd never seen the pictures made fun of him. It reached the point where he simply stopped inviting friends over. Or, if they did stop by, he'd spend the entire afternoon distracted and sweating, his guts in an uproar, waiting for one or the other of his parents to head for the bookshelf. He knew they would eventually.

"If you don't like it," his mom had told him once when he asked them to please stop embarrassing him that way, "you shouldn't have done those things."

As Wally fretted over his impending arrest, Margie was hired by a Costa Rican pharmaceutical company anxious to make some inroads into the local marketplace.

"Cartel, company, what's the difference?" she'd replied when he asked why they hired her specifically. In any case, it meant that she was now spending seventeen or eighteen hours a day locked in her office. For some reason, it also meant that whenever she made or received a call she'd suddenly begun talking much louder and faster than usual.

She had an actual office with actual employees in Midtown but had decided two years earlier it would be easier and more efficient if she worked at home. She had everything she needed there and, given the hours she tended to put in, it saved her all that wasted commuting time.

After the tofu confrontation, she didn't bother making any

more dinners, so Wally stopped at the deli on the way home every night, picking up the same artificial roast beef on crumbless bread. His digestion was suffering for it, but he considered that a small price to pay.

It was Wednesday, September sixteenth, about a month after he'd shot his mouth off to Margie. Wally cleaned up after finishing his sandwich, returned to the living room, and continued flipping idly through the four-way sites.

"*Despite initial reports, authorities are now saying that the cyclone which killed over twenty-five hundred people in Bangladesh was not the work of terrorists. There are still skeptics, however, who argue—*"

"*...outbreaks in New East Germany and the Netherlands now have medical officials at FELTCH convinced the SuperVirus will reach the East Coast by the spring... In other medical news, popular talk show host Bernie Tschungle suffered a temporary set—*"

"*—ilitary officials around the globe promise it to be the biggest pay-per-view event in history!*"

"*...some Flip-py Bits!*"

"*Who will survive the new season of the nation's most popular reality game show,* Concentration Camp*?*"

"*—inor infection will keep him in the hospital for at least another week—*"

"*Let 'em know where you've been when you eat at Belchin' Waffles, New York's only—*"

"*...Do people call you a jerk? Obnoxious? Inconsiderate or rude? Chances are good you suffer from a form of autism known as McBragg Syndrome. And you know what that means? No mat-*

ter how bad your behavior, it's not your fault—you can't help it since you have McBragg Syndrome!"

"*...Now enriched with more Brown-twenty-five than ever before!"*

"*—three-year history course in just three minutes!"*

"*Compliance currently stands at eighty-nine percent, and Resident Control hopes to get that number up to one hundred percent by year's end. If you ask me, it only makes sense..."*

In frustration, Wally switched over to the Crime Network.

On the screen, a group of eight chubby youngsters, boys and girls alike, most of them in their early teens, descended upon an elderly woman outside an upscale hotel in lower Manhattan. Wally recognized the hotel. Chevrix owned it, if he remembered correctly.

Over the course of the next two minutes, he watched as they pummeled her senseless and bloody with meat tenderizing hammers, a coffeepot, a cheese grater, a pair of egg beaters, and an old-fashioned wooden juicer. Wally averted his eyes when one boy, with a devilish grin, slid a turkey baster out from beneath his apron. He'd seen it once, and he didn't care to see it again. Turning his eyes away didn't help. The cartoon sound effects told him all he needed to know.

The Kitchen Magicians were considered the nation's most vicious street gang. Given that, they were always a big draw whenever they appeared on the Crime Network's *Random Street Crime Cavalcade.*

The Kitchen Magicians had formed originally in New Orleans but soon had chapters in every major city across the country, with an estimated membership of close to a hundred thousand. Given the unavailability of guns to anyone not affiliated with a recognized security force, the Kitchen Magicians had armed themselves with every cooking utensil and kitchen gadget they could get their pudgy little hands on, from the aforementioned cheese graters and juicers to teapots, cleavers, apple corers, and tongs. Anything that could inflict some damage. They even discovered potential treachery in the most benign of implements, such as ice cube trays. They attacked randomly but tended to focus on targets who were elderly, crippled, or much smaller than themselves.

There was something that always fascinated Wally about the shows on the Crime Network. Even though all the incidents chosen for broadcast were recorded by the nationwide grid of enhanced security vids—the ones programmed to "film only crime"—the production values were unusually high. He also wondered how a single security vid mounted above a doorway or on a lamppost could capture all those different angles and close-ups.

He'd often suspected that quite a bit of the footage had been shot by the minivids and VidLogs carried by members of the crowd who often gathered to watch the carnage firsthand. The news programs admitted as much about their own footage. Not the Crime Network. Perhaps, Wally thought, they didn't care to reveal that there were so many Good Citizens out there not only willing to stand around watching an old woman beaten by a mob—but also willing to film it and sell it to a four-way network.

He preferred not to think about it too much. He watched another twenty minutes of beatings, stabbings, and attempted drownings before clicking the screen off.

He stared at the silent dark Plexiglas for a long time.

The following morning, Wally was surprised to find that the Brigade patrol wasn't waiting to pounce on him. He did catch sight of them as he was crossing the street, but they were operating a block to the west, down on the avenue, well out of range. Feeling inexplicably snubbed, he continued on his unmolested way to the subway station.

Two blocks later he heard a voice from the opposite corner.

"*Greetings from a dead man, pardner!*" it shouted.

Wally looked. It took him a second to recognize the figure waving at him. Red beard, cowboy hat, yellow slicker in spite of the weather.

Yes, it was the guy he'd seen briefly at the Horribleness Day celebration—the one who'd waved at him a few minutes before the trouble began.

Wally looked around, praying there was someone else nearby, someone who knew this insane man enough to acknowledge such a greeting. Anyone but him. There of course wasn't anybody matching that description.

Wally looked back and, uncertain of what else to do, offered a vague wave.

The large man smiled through his beard, then continued down the sidewalk with that odd half-skipping gait. Wally watched him for a moment, relieved the man hadn't crossed the street to talk to him. He put his head down again and continued on his own way, now feeling both snubbed by three women who wanted to kill him and unnerved by friendly greetings from a dead man.

He had the sense already that this would not be an easy day.

"You remember 328-A?" Lou asked.

"Not offhand, Lou, no, can't say as I do," Wally admitted after Lou called him into his office to discuss a few of that morning's files. "Why do you ask?"

"Really?" Lou seemed honestly surprised that 407-R and 328-A weren't better acquainted. "You don't know her? Hot little tomato, she was—short chick, tiny thing, but I'll tell you . . ." He began to make nebulous but decidedly obscene gestures with both hands. "You really don't, uh...?" He fell silent and his eyes seemed to stare through the wall, his hands still performing a disturbing dance in the air.

Wally waited to make sure Lou was finished. "Why are you asking me this, uh, Lou?"

"Oh. Yeah." His boss seemed to physically shake himself back into focus. "Well... doesn't matter, I guess. I had to let her go. I hate having to do that. And it was worse this time, because Resident Control had to get involved."

"That's awful," Wally said. Then, remembering that weird encounter with Whit a few weeks earlier, he wondered if it would be better not to express any sympathy. Lou, however, didn't seem to notice. "Wha'd she do?"

Lou shook his head. "Bad news. We caught her shopping during work hours."

That didn't seem terribly awful. In fact, it was usually encouraged. In some offices it was even required. "So what's wrong with that?"

"In most cases, nothing, right? I mean, you hear a commercial, you get a jingle stuck in your head, what can you do? But in this case . . ." He let out a heavy, disbelieving breath. "In this case she was shopping for seditious materials."

"Really?" Wally asked. "Right here in the office? That takes some guts." *Never tell this guy anything,* he thought. Not that he needed to remind himself at this point, but it couldn't hurt.

"Yeah. Pretty amazing, right? How could anyone be that stupid? Who knows, maybe she was suicidal or something. In any case, it's something Resident Control needs to handle, one way or another."

Wally remembered his own day there and felt sorry for 328-A, no matter what she'd been thinking.

As usual, Lou had called him in to discuss a very important matter regarding some claims, then had apparently completely forgotten what the problem was (if anything at all) by the time Wally showed up.

"How'd you catch her?" Wally asked. Lou was in his usual blabbing mood, so he might as well find out what he could. "If I might ask. COOTY or DEVOUR get in touch?"

Lou shook his head again and glanced at his screen. "Nah, that would've taken months. And by then who knows what might've happened. No, as it turns out, I got a tip from 518-*D*. You know him, right?"

Wally started to say no, but the strange accent Lou had placed on the "D" gave him the clue he needed.

"Oh yeah—the mousy little guy. Makes the coffee, doesn't seem to do much else."

"*That's* the one," Lou said, pointing a confirmatory finger at Wally. "He just marched right in yesterday morning and told me about it. He'd been talking to 328-A and right there on her screen, plain as day. Sedition."

"Really?"

"Yup. So I pulled up her workstation's log for the last twenty-four hours"—he patted his monitor affectionately—"and there it was."

"I'll be... Bomb-making plans or something?"

Lou snorted. "Worse." He leaned in close and dropped his voice. "Australian cookbooks."

"Holy crap," Wally whispered back. "Right out there for 518-*D* to see? How could—I mean, how was the site still accessible?"

"Ah," Lou said. "You know how these terrorists work. They can sneak their way around anything, the conniving bastards. I still can't believe someone like that was working here."

"It still seems strange, doing that right in the office."

"Whether or not she wanted 518-*D* to see it is something for Resident Control to figure out. Too bad, though, tomatoes like that." He sighed. "But I'll tell you, that little squirrel's more than paid for himself."

Wally was confused. "Um... which little squirrel's that?'

"518-*D*. Let you in on a secret." Lou leaned back in his protesting chair and folded his hands behind his neck, causing his belly to bulge over the edge of the desk. For a second, Wally thought Lou was going to spill over backward, and he took a cautionary step closer to the door. "LifeGuard brass sent him down here a while ago—over a month now—just to be an extra set of eyes around the office. Sure a hell of a lot quicker to have a handy snitch on the premises than to wait for everything to get up to PROTEUS X, analyzed, and back down here again."

Wally felt a light sheen of sweat begin to form under his arms. "Sure," he said, trying to recall whether he'd said or done anything in the little troll's presence that might end up in the wrong ears. He couldn't think of anything. He knew he hadn't been to any seditious sites—he wouldn't have been able to find them if he wanted to. Apart from checking the news in the morning (via respectable authorized outlets), when he was in the office he worked. But still.

When Wally was nine years old, his father, who worked a split shift at the local paper mill, suggested in no uncertain terms that finding a job of some kind during the holiday break might be good experience for the boy. Child labor laws being what they were at the time, however, the employment opportunities available to a preadolescent were severely limited.

The factories weren't hiring and there were no farms within walking distance, so Wally did the next best thing—one day after school he went to the mall.

Even in those days before the explosion in the midget population, the waiting list of people hoping to be department store elves was over two years long. Nobody would even consider him as a salesman, and he was still too short to run a cash register without standing on a chair.

It was looking hopeless and he was beginning to fear the

inevitable wrath of his father when he came home jobless yet again. It was already mid-November, and if he didn't find something by Thanksgiving he knew he wouldn't find anything at all. He'd be reduced to shoveling driveways at five in the morning—but even that, he knew, had become a vicious racket controlled by the local twelve- and thirteen-year-olds.

Finally, just two days before Thanksgiving, the manager of a small gift shop specializing in handmade Norwegian tchotchkes suffered a flash of brilliance and hired Wally part-time (and off the books) to be the store's first-ever undercover retail theft prevention specialist.

That meant that four days a week—Thursday, Friday, Saturday, and Sunday—Wally would casually wander into the little shop shortly after it opened and pretend to be a customer. In reality, however, he was keeping a careful eye on the actual customers, to make sure none of them slipped a pair of wooden shoes or a set of hand-carved elves or a "Kiss Me, I'm Norwegian" coffee mug into their bag.

"No matter what they're looking at," his new boss, Mr. Erickson, instructed him, "no matter what they might be saying, no matter what else about them might distract you, always watch their hands. That's where the action is. You understand?"

"Yes sir," Wally nodded. "Always watch the hands."

Norway or the Highway—the only store in all of Cleveland specializing in handmade Norwegian tchotchkes—was tucked away into a distant back corner of the mall's second level, snuggled between a plus-size dress shop and the public restrooms. As a result, no matter how crowded the mall itself might be, not too many people ever made it back that way. Most of the shop's customers were simply killing time while a friend or spouse or child was in the bathroom.

Still, since Wally was undercover, he was expected to stay in the store all day long, pretending to be a customer. He was not allowed to remove his heavy winter coat, was not allowed to talk to any of the employees unless it was to ask a customer-type question, was not allowed to step into the office to sit down for a few minutes.

Whenever a customer entered the store Wally, pretending always to be very interested in the soaps and plush elk toys and silk tulips and miniature windmills, would maneuver himself into position next to them, keeping a close eye on what they were doing with their hands. Every time someone stepped away from a display, he'd move in fast and take a quick inventory to make sure nothing was missing.

Given how few customers the store had at any given time, this was not very subtle. And sometimes Wally wondered if people who came in more than once ever noticed that he never seemed to leave.

He went home every night with numb legs, a sore back, and a terrible headache from the scented Norwegian candles—sandalwood, boysenberry, and lutefisk—whose collective odor worked its way into his nostrils and refused to leave. He'd also, he found, lost close to ten pounds, mostly from sweating all day in that damn winter coat.

Still, come New Year's Eve, he was proud to report that nothing had been stolen during his watch. Not that he was aware of, anyway. And true to his word, Mr. Erickson—a delicate blond man in his forties—handed Wally a plain envelope containing one hundred and fifty dollars in cash, which was far more money than he'd ever held in his hands before. Best of all, he came away from his month at Norway or the Highway with a newfound appreciation for the handicrafts of northern Europe.

As he walked home from the mall that last time, he couldn't help but feel disappointed. For all the aches and pains, the sweating, the boredom, there had been something exciting about the job. At any moment of any day he could've seen someone slip something into a pocket, and then it would've been his job to tackle them before they got away. There might've been some gunplay, or a razor fight.

He'd fought off the daily boredom, in fact, by imagining scenario after scenario in which he captured all manner of thieves, from top-hatted Snidely Whiplash–types to innocent-looking old ladies who secretly ran drug rings out of their nursing homes.

None of it came to pass, of course. The real thieves were too busy casing the electronics stores or stealing tennis shoes to concern themselves with ashtrays from Oslo. It was too bad. But still he had to wonder how many potential thieves had been thwarted by his mere presence (or the fact that he was always staring pointedly at their hands). Nobody'd said anything about it, but what could they have said to a nine-year-old with such an intense, unhealthy interest in Norwegian handicrafts?

During the subway ride back to Brooklyn that night, Wally stood in the aisle, clinging tight to a slick mirrored pole for support and performing an ungainly dance to avoid the shuffling, mumbling rush hour crowd.

As he rocked along with the train and gyrated with the conflicting tide of commuters, he recalled not only that afternoon's conversation with Lou but another, equally curious conversation that had taken place nearly eight years earlier, shortly after he'd been transferred up to the fourteenth floor.

Being new to Big Lou's team, he was still trying to make a good impression. Not that he was a kid by any means, but back then he believed that upward mobility was still within his reach.

The Random Stops & Searches—or RSSs, as they were called—had recently begun across the city. Nobody was complaining about this. They were merely the latest means to assure an antsy public that no cleverly disguised terrorists were lurking about in their midst.

Wally had stopped by Lou's office to explain that he was late getting back from lunch because he'd been stopped by three DOD agents on RSS patrol. As one pawed through the bag containing his lunch, another scanned his SUCKIE card and made him empty his pockets, and a third ran the Threat Detection Wand up his front and down his back. It was the only time before or since he had been stopped for RSS.

"I don't blame them," Lou told him. "I mean, *look* at you."

Given that humor had all but evaporated in New York a few years earlier, Wally was no longer accustomed to ironic wisecracks.

"I'm *kidding,* 407-R," Lou chided him after noting the sickly horror on Wally's face. "It's no big deal. Relax."

"Sorry," Wally said. "Guess being stopped by DOD threw me a little bit."

"Aah," Lou said, "guess it's the way things are gonna be."

At the time, people were still getting used to the growing and evolving list of citywide security measures. It was all still new enough that people could remember what life had been like before the Horribleness. Now, he thought, it seemed that things were as they always had been. There was no longer any "past" without VidLogs and armed guards in the streets. The pre-Horribleness world was nothing but a fairy tale used to frighten small children.

Lou had invited Wally to have a seat before getting back to work. "I know it's weird," he said. "Out there, I mean. But it can be a little easier if you try and look at things like I do—like a businessman." (Lou had weighed only about two hundred and thirty pounds at the time and hadn't yet discovered the joys of the tacky tie, making it easier to accept the idea that he was some kind of "businessman.")

Wally leaned slightly forward in his chair and made eye contact in an effort to look like he cared deeply about the drops of wisdom his new boss was about to pass along.

"From a businessman's perspective, see?" Lou went on. "There's money to be made in a little overreaction. Potentially *lots* of it. Think about it, 407-R—whenever someone from CIALIS or BOO or one of the newscasters, whoever, tells everyone that they should be frightened, the security industry stands to make a healthy profit. Not just the big guys with the government contracts. I'm talking about the little guys too. Locksmiths, home security systems, personal spy cams. The independent geomappers or the shops that'll armor-plate anything you give 'em. All of 'em go through the roof." He looked over Wally's shoulder into the office beyond, then leaned closer. "You know, 407-R, between you and me, I'm thinking sometimes that *that's* the industry to get into. That or right here in insurance. Because it's not gonna end, see? And you can sell people all *sorts* of crap if you tell 'em it'll keep 'em safe. Let's face it, a terrorist threat is good for the economy."

It was the first and last time, up until he met Carlotta in the BLAB waiting room, that Wally had heard Lou or anyone else express even a hint of cynicism about what was taking place. Eight years ago it was shocking to hear, and for the briefest of moments Wally had even struggled with the question of whether or not his new boss's comments should be reported. That's what the public service ads had been telling him to do. Considering that it would either earn him a promotion or get him fired, Wally decided to err on the side of economic security, and soon he forgot about it. Until now on the train back to Brooklyn.

That night while flipping hopelessly through sites on the four-way, Wally heard an administrator from one bureau or another say, "If we don't continue living our lives the way we always have, then the terrorists have won."

Wally got a mighty chuckle out of that one but turned his face away from the screen so that his reaction wouldn't be considered unmutual.

Yeah, he thought, *we're living like we always have. That's why I have a neighbor turning in all my other neighbors as soon as they move in, and a hot tomato is facing time in Unmutual Rehab for trying to figure out how to cook a platypus.*

People loved the lie too much to let go of it at this point, he thought, but he was getting pretty darn sick of it himself. Sick of being watched in his own house, sick of being cataloged and analyzed and scared.

The idea was beginning to fester in his brain. He felt he had to do something, but he had no idea what that might be. Something, though.

There was no point in protesting it publicly. No one would dare join him, and he'd simply be taken away. Probably be sentenced to life in Terminal Five—supposedly the worst of the Unmutual Rehabs. Even if thirty thousand people joined him, he somehow had the impression that a few rousing choruses of "We Shall Overcome" wouldn't exactly lead a bunch of teary-eyed BOO officials to say, "Oh, goodness—what were we thinking?" No. He and those thirty thousand people would get together, sing a few songs, then go home. Nothing at all would change, except that most of those people would be arrested, one by one, over the following weeks—that is, if they weren't all simply gassed in the middle of "Give Peace a Chance."

Part of him could understand that too.

Voting wasn't exactly an option anymore either. Not since Skull and Bones and the Bohemian Grove set pooled their resources and became a franchise operation.

No, this wasn't something for the masses. It would never happen that way. It was something he'd have to do alone. He just wanted to disappear, to become a shadow. Wally Philco, Citizen NY00169765/P, wanted to delete himself from the vids and the databases and the files. He didn't want to deal with any more computers gauging his emotional state, or adscreens calling him by name, or communitainer implants screaming in his ear, or global positioning gimcracks following him to the deli. He didn't want to make any more nightly reports in which he was forced to grovel about things he didn't feel that bad about. He was sick of celebrity news on the four-way, and SUCKIE cards, and iris scans to get on the subway, and accusatory smart-aleck robots, and neighbors just itching to report him as an Unmutual.

This was no longer his world, his city—even his house—and he wanted no part of any of it anymore. No part of *nothing,* except for Wally Philco, going about his daily business the way he saw fit. In short, he wanted to be left alone.

In his mind's eye, he was taking a casual stroll up Broadway toward Vigilante Infotonics Square. The streets were packed as always, but no one paid any attention to him. What made it different was that now they paid no attention to him because they couldn't see him. Not just the other citizens either—no vids could record his image, no scanners could detect his presence in any way. He was invisible. The only one who could see him was Carlotta, and she could see him because she was invisible too. And she was wearing a red dress—

He stopped himself. He shouldn't be thinking that way. It was just a chance encounter. She'd probably forgotten about him the minute she turned her back. It didn't matter. He knew what he had to do.

And man, he didn't even want to think about what Margie would say when he told her.

FIVE

It would take time, he knew that. It would take a lot of planning. So many things to consider. He had to do it right. If he screwed up, if the plan gestating in his brain ever became known, he was dead.

On his morning commute into the office, he still scanned all the faces around him as soon as he boarded the train, just as he'd been instructed. Now, however, he found he was scanning those faces in a different way. Instead of asking himself, "Which of these citizens is a potential terrorist?" he asked himself, "Who are the snitches?"

All of them, probably, he concluded. Or most of them, anyway. They weren't after him, not personally. He wasn't that paranoid. These people were after one another. All of them aching to get their hands on one of those T-shirts.

Still, he thought, at least by scanning the faces like he was supposed to, he was taking a few steps to protect himself. It was the people who didn't scan the other passengers you had to watch out for. That's what the commercials said. It meant they were either tourists or terrorists, with the odds weighing heavily toward the latter.

It was a Thursday morning less than two weeks after Wally had made his decision to erase himself. The train was crowded, and he was sitting crushed between a businessman with a shaved head and a digestion problem and a woman who had chosen to wear an outrageously wide-brimmed Easter bonnet festooned with ostrich plumes to work that day. He tried to relax as best he could, eyes closed, finger poised for the moment when an unexpected jostle or bump would set off his communitainer. Every few seconds, he had to blow the tickling feathers out of his face.

The door at the far end of the car slid open and, like clockwork, in walked Smitty Winston, making his morning rounds.

"Hello ladies an' gennelmen, my name is Smitty Winston . . ."

Moments after Smitty stepped off the train at the next stop, a haggard bum with watery eyes and a week's growth of beard stepped aboard. He wore a crusty knitted cap and a ripped down-filled jacket that left a loose trail of tiny white feathers behind him as he began making his way through the crowd.

Smitty had always spoken loud enough to be heard, but he always came off as polite and humble. This guy, his eyes swinging from commuter to commuter, wasn't trying to disguise the bubbling rage in his voice.

"They won't let me get a job...They don't *want* me to get a job because it's in their own best interest that I *don't,*" he grumbled. "But where does that leave me?"

A few heads turned, but not many. As he drew closer Wally was beginning to catch his first whiffs of the man.

The bum grabbed hold of a pole and stopped, blocking the path of the pacers. He lowered his voice an octave. The bitter anger of seconds earlier was suddenly weary, and dark, and frightened. "I've been out here three days now...I've been trying. I don't know why this happened to me...If I don't get a place tonight, you know what'll happen—you all *know* what'll happen. *Please.* You know what they do to people...Is there anyone here who can help?...C'mon people—get the chips outta your head and *listen*!"

As if on cue, all those people who seemed be paying no attention at all stopped talking and were staring at the man in the cap and torn jacket. Several were already scrambling for their minivids and tapping furiously away at the keypads. Others were whispering desperately.

"Please," the bum was saying. "I'm no threat to you or anyone...I—I just need to get off the street by tonight or I'll be—"

A young man in a charcoal pinstripe suit and a prim-looking woman in her sixties grabbed him, one going high, the other low.

"*You gotta listen to me!*" the bum screamed. "*This ain't how we—!*"

Half a dozen other commuters closed in, kicking the man to

the floor, clawing at his face, dragging him toward the nearest door. Apart from heavy breathing, the shuffling of feet, and the man's screams, the scene was eerily quiet.

Wally remained motionless in his seat. He'd seen it too many times before and knew that if he made any move to interfere, if he even let the horror creep into his features, he'd be facing the same fate.

As the train pulled into the Second Avenue station, he could see the platform was already crowded with a contingent of armed DOD troops, poised and waiting.

Sitting in his cubicle later that day, Wally briefly considered faking his own death and creating a new identity. It might save him a few steps and a lot of work. He could even afford one of the discount face transplants if he wanted to go that far. He'd seen a movie like that once when he was a kid, one with Rock Hudson. Then he remembered how that one turned out. The final sound. He shuddered. Maybe it wasn't that hot an idea.

The real thing standing in the way of a faked death scheme was the Coffin Cam. The EternaLife Corporation's Coffin Cams were touted as a way for loved ones to preserve the deceased's memory long after death. ("With closed-circuit monitors in the bedroom, at the kitchen table, wherever you like, it's as if they've never left!") It was also a convenient way to alleviate the fear of premature burial much more effectively than a bell and string.

At heart, Wally realized, it was just a way to keep an eye on you, make sure you weren't up to any postmortem unmutualism.

What would a new identity get him, anyway? A new set of

files, a new SUCKIE card. The world he lived in wouldn't have changed a bit. He would still be watched, he would still be scanned and searched. Plus there was the whole biometrics issue to get around. How could he change his irises, or DNA, or fingerprints? It was pointless.

"*... Golden Orb SuperVirus, for which there is no known cure, has already taken the lives of an estimated nine people in Ghana, Morocco, and Denmark. While there have been no known cases as of yet here at home, officials at FELTCH warn that it's only a matter of time... Someone or something carrying the SuperVirus might well be on a plane or a boat heading our way this very instant. All citizens, therefore, are encouraged to take any and all necessary precautions.*"

The vid cut to a female newsanchor wearing a surgical mask and rubber gloves. "Thank you for that report, Nick. Tell us, do authorities believe that terrorists are behind the SuperVirus?"

The picture switched to another anchor in a white HazMat suit. The face was barely visible through the tinted plastic faceplate. "Not certain yet, Diane," a muffled voice replied, "though they certainly suspect some terrorist connection will become apparent in the days to come."

"That's terrifying news, Nick—thank you. And now a public service message for all you proud parents out there."

Under the delicate strains of a richly orchestrated rendition of an Eldon Hoke song, the camera panned slowly across the faces of eight men and women of a carefully selected ethnic cross section, all of them smiling.

"*We all know that it takes a lot of citizens to make a nation great,*" an announcer intoned.

The camera pulled back to reveal that the eight people were, in fact, four couples, each clutching one or more infants, and each standing behind a massive double stroller.

"*You've certainly done your part, and we're all proud of you.*"

The intense, almost painful colors of the opening shot faded to a grainy black and white and the music turned ominous. The scene shifted to a garbage-strewn alleyway, where a seedy-looking character, unshaven and wearing a wrinkled trench coat, was leaning against the filthy brick wall, his eyes narrowed. He was clearly up to no good.

"*But do you know someone—a neighbor, a friend, a coworker—who hasn't yet performed his or her civic duty by having one or more children? We all know what those people are like.*"

The camera cut from the alley to a grimy street, where one of the couples from the opening shot was pushing a stroller, still smiling. The sidewalk in front of them was grainy black and white, but as they passed with the stroller the world behind them erupted into a glorious sea of red roses, green grass, and azure sky. The music took on a more hopeful tone. The couple stopped at the entrance to the shadowed alley.

"*Why not encourage them to step up to the plate? Show them what a joy children can be, and remind them that it's not just for the strength of the nation—it's for their own good.*"

The woman reached into the stroller and cuddled the blanketed infant to her chest. The father put his arm around her and gave her a squeeze. They both smiled even more broadly as rose petals began falling from the sky.

A close-up of the seedy thug's face as he stared at the loving family revealed a brief flash of understanding, before his scowl returned and he began walking away.

Ingrid Ogami, founder and president of the Stroller Brigade, appeared on the screen. Wally had never been able to identify her age or ethnicity under all that makeup.

"*Remember,*" she said, her voice both shrill and hoarse, "*it's the duty of all Good Citizens to do whatever it takes.*" Her eyes narrowed. "*Whatever... it... takes.*"

In the final shot the couple—their smiles twisted into hideous screams, their eyes filled with savage bloodlust—chased the unmutual hoodlum deeper into the alley with their stroller. It was clear there was no escape. The music swelled to a triumphant crescendo before the scene dissolved and the screen was filled with the crossed swords and perambulator of the Brigade.

As Wally sneered at his four-way from the couch, a wave of thick static crept across the screen.

That's never happened before, he thought.

As he stood to see if there was anything wrong with the connection, he could hear what sounded like a distant voice creeping through the white noise.

"*Hellooooo Everybooooddyyy,*" he thought he heard, "*This... is the 'Transparent World'... with your host Sid Powell.*"

Wally sat down again. He'd heard the name before. Sid Powell had been a controversial radio talk show host based in Texas whose show had been abruptly and unexpectedly yanked off the air two days before the Horribleness. Nobody would say why, and Powell himself had apparently disappeared.

He'd been one of those abrasive, paranoid conspiracy nuts, always going on about secret government plots, aliens, and John von Neumann. His syndicated show was incredibly popular, but Wally had never listened to it. Didn't interest him. He'd heard about the show's cancellation only because it made the news. Then the Horribleness happened and people had other things to think about.

Meanwhile, Powell's hardcore fans began circulating conspiracy theories of their own concerning his disappearance. Some said he'd been kidnapped by the very aliens who crashed in Tupelo, others that he'd been silenced because he knew too much. The only thing they did agree upon was that somehow Powell had escaped a terrible fate and had gone underground, setting up a pirate broadcast station at a secret location, determined to hack into the federal signal.

No one had any solid evidence of this, but eleven years after the fact the dwindling community of obsessive Sid Powell fans still believed deep in their hearts that he'd be back to lay it all out for them.

Wally had paid little or no attention to any of those stories and didn't believe what he did hear. Yet he could swear he heard the distant voice on the four-way say "transparent world," which had been the name of Powell's radio show.

Curious, he leaned in closer to the screen, concentrating hard on the voice leaking through the static hiss. In spite of the white noise, what came through was a piercing nasal drawl. He could see why this Powell character annoyed people.

"*You think you're safe because you're not doing anything wrong?*" the man he now assumed was Powell asked. "*Well I got news for you, brothers and sisters—you may have even... to worry...*"

That's what I was telling Margie, Wally thought. He squinted at the screen. There was definitely something there behind the snow—a shape, a figure of some kind—shattered and rippling and without any detail. If you weren't looking for it, you might not even notice.

"*There are real people behind these things. That's... worries me... Real stupid people, who can't spell names, who... numbers, who misinterpret jokes. That's... problem. If it were... ly machines, it would be another sto... Not that machines... perfect, given... doing what real stupid... programmed them to do.*"

The voice was beginning to break up, drowning beneath the increasing sonic turbulence. Wally punched up the volume thinking it might help. There were only peeps and pops and staccato bursts of noise behind the buzz now, no recognizable words. As long as the static was there, though, it meant someone was still interrupting the federal signal.

Then it came back, startlingly clear, for just a moment.

"*—rick Henry? And what about all those 'Live Free or Die' tattoos? Didn't they mean anything? If—*"

The signal was abruptly blasted off the air, replaced with a commercial for the new FELTCH chip implant, which fed directly into their database.

Fumbling over the control unit, Wally snapped the volume back to a comfortable level, hoping Margie was too wrapped up in her work to come out and complain.

He sat back on the couch staring, not quite stunned but certainly surprised.

Powell, he thought. *He'd done it.*

On the screen, a black-clad paramedic at the scene of a bloody automobile wreck was screaming into his wrist: "*I need the file for Harry Kneale of Raleigh, North Carolina, stat!*" A second later, a comfortable-looking young FELTCH operator was replying that Mr. Kneale was allergic to peanuts and, according to his personal genome, would develop pancreatic cancer at age fifty-three.

Powell was out there, Wally thought, living under the radar and spreading the word. The gospel, even. If he could track him down, maybe talk to him. Find out how he did it.

Even if he couldn't find him, Powell's very existence was still proof that Wally wasn't insane. There were others out there. It could be done.

Something else swelled up in him. An odd and alien bravado.

He didn't need to track Powell down. He'd have to disappear first anyway before he could do that. No, this was his plan, his idea, and he'd do it his own way.

It was pretty fortuitous to stumble across that broadcast right now, though, he had to reluctantly admit. It was also a strange comfort.

It wasn't just a matter of ducking a few vids, after all. This could turn into a real pickle—one that not only could get him sent away if he was caught but, even if he wasn't caught, would profoundly affect his marriage, his job, everything he had. If he wanted to take this all the way (and there was no other way to do it), he wouldn't even be able to travel anymore.

He remembered when he first moved to New York, long before the SUCKIE cards were introduced. You wanted to ride the subway, all you needed was a token—a small metal coin you dropped into a slot to get through the turnstile. That was all you needed, and with it you could go anywhere. Nobody else had to know where you were going or why.

Then, not long before the Horribleness, the city began experimenting with flexible plastic travel cards. A magnetic strip on the back of the card kept track of how many fares you had left. Slide it through a reader, another fare would be removed, and off you went.

What transportation officials hadn't mentioned was that those little magnetic strips also encoded your location every time you used it. If the cops wanted to know where you'd been, all they'd needed to do was download the information off your card. It wasn't exact, but it did narrow things down considerably.

Then after the Horribleness came the national SUCKIE cards. They worked in much the same way but were a thousand times more precise, given that all you needed to do was walk past one of the one-point-five-million public readers installed around the city to have your exact location duly registered. And that was just the beginning. The SUCKIE cards weren't just for travel but for shopping, work, banking, doctor's visits. Having it lost or stolen was simply out of the question—it was impossible to function without it. It meant throwing your life away.

No, it was worse than that. It meant handing a near complete record of your life to a stranger—in all likelihood a terrorist, who could do all sorts of dastardly things for which you would be blamed.

The SUCKIE card, he decided, would have to wait until the very end.

That Saturday afternoon, Wally removed the small toolbox from the closet near the bathroom. Not being a handy sort, he didn't have many tools, and most had never been used. He had a couple of screwdrivers, a claw hammer, needle-nose pliers, and a socket wrench (he wasn't even sure what a socket wrench was used for, but it had seemed like something he should have). Apart from these, the toolbox contained a jumble of nails and screws and nuts and washers. Merely opening the box made him feel inadequate most of the time.

That afternoon he knew what he was doing.

He grabbed a chair from the kitchen table, dragged it over near the wall, and took a seat, the toolbox on the floor beside him.

Screwed into the wall at eye level in front of him was a four-square-inch beige plastic box. Along the bottom of the box was a row of three buttons. It wasn't much but it was another step forward. He assessed the situation, took a breath, and reached into the toolbox for his Phillips head screwdriver.

He didn't hear the door to Margie's office open. Intent as he was on the job before him, he didn't even notice her standing behind him, arms folded. The look on her face was half amused, half confused. Once or twice a week for the past five years, she'd found herself presented with still more evidence that her husband was a boob.

When he had removed the sixth and final screw and began tugging vainly at the device, she finally spoke.

"What, may I ask—"

Wally yelped loudly and spun, wild-eyed, screwdriver in hand.

"—are you trying to do?"

Upon realizing it was only Margie, he leaned his forehead against the wall and tried to breathe normally.

"I'm disconnecting the buzzer," he said, trying to make it sound as casual as possible, like this was something he did every day.

"I see," she said, arms still folded. "May I, uh, ask you why, exactly?"

He didn't turn to look at her. Still tugging at the box, which had apparently been painted to the wall, he said, "It's just a nuisance, is all. And besides, people don't need to know whether we're here or not. If we don't know they're coming, then I'm not sure I want to see them. That's all."

This, Margie had to admit, was certainly an interesting twist. She retrieved another chair from the kitchen table, dragged it next to his, and sat down. "I see," she said, watching him. He was now using the screwdriver to try and pry the buzzer away from the wall. It wasn't working. "Had you considered, Wally, that no one ever stops by unannounced? That buzzer hasn't made a noise in years."

"It's the principle," he said, still not daring to look at her.

She thought she was beginning to understand now.

"Is this connected to some of those things you were saying that night?" Even though "that night" had been nearly two months earlier, they both knew what she was talking about.

He made a noise deep in his throat, then dropped the screwdriver and reached for the hammer.

"Has it occurred to you," she asked, really trying to be helpful here in spite of herself, "that clipping those wires might well send a signal to Resident Control?" She tried to keep her voice as low as possible. "They installed it."

"In that case," Wally said, his lips tight, "when they show up, we won't know they're downstairs because the buzzer'll be disconnected."

Even Margie had to admit it was a logic that almost made sense.

There was an unpleasant crunch as the leverage of the hammer's claw ripped the plastic housing away from the wall, revealing a nest of blue and red wires.

His face exhibiting no expression, he plucked the pliers out of the toolbox and began snipping the hair-thin wires one by one.

She continued to stare at him. The amused and confused look had left her face, but she was doing quite a bit of blinking. "Maybe you should take a pill," she suggested. "I have a couple bottles of Acriphonex in my office. I could—"

"Don't want a pill," he said, snipping away. "Don't need one."

Margie sighed. "Wally, what are you afraid of? You don't *do* anything. If anyone out there does take any sort of personal interest in you, I mean, it won't be long before they just get bored and start watching someone else."

He snipped the last wire, then finally turned to look at his wife.

"You don't get it, Margie. Fear is not the issue. I'm not being paranoid. If I were paranoid I would think they were after me personally, but I don't. They're after *everyone.* And what I'm doing is simply trying to cling tight to whatever vestiges of privacy and dignity and humanity we have left. Maybe you can't understand that."

It occurred to her that they were both sitting there facing the wall like punished children. She pushed herself back a few inches.

"I'm pretty sure I get it," she said, only mildly insulted by his tone. "I just think you're taking things too far. I mean, what does disconnecting a door buzzer have to do with it?"

He didn't say anything. He didn't dare tell her that this was just the beginning, barely a baby step compared to what he had in mind.

She looked at his face. For the first time, there in his eyes and the way his mouth was set, she saw something that resembled defiance.

"Nothing ever bothered you before," she said quietly. "Nothing at all."

"Maybe things did, but I just kept my mouth shut about it."

"Did you? I mean, was that the case? Were things bothering you?"

He shook his head. "No, not really. But these past few months, the insanity of it all—like that business at Resident Control—it's just crazy, all of it. That we allow ourselves to live this way"—he nodded toward the clock—"is nutso."

She thought about this as he began replacing the tools in the gray metal box. It seemed he intended to leave the jagged, gaping new hole in the wall.

"By the way," he said, "don't be surprised when you look in the cupboards or the fridge."

This worried her. "What else did you do?"

"I just transferred everything out of its original packaging. Everything's in jars and bowls now. Whatever worked best. It may be a little harder to, y'know, find things, but it's safer that way."

She didn't want to ask, but he knew an answer was necessary.

"RFID tags," he explained. "They already know everything we bought. They don't need to know where we store it, too, or how long we keep it around...Speaking of which, you might want to go through your wardrobe. Anything you've bought in the last six years is being tracked."

Only then did she notice the neat empty square that had been clipped out of the shoulder of his shirt, revealing the smooth, pale skin beneath.

"You're *sure* you don't want a pill?" she asked. "Maybe you should at least take a nap or something." She glanced again at the hole in the wall. "I'll clean this up."

"What do you mean 'no, we can't'? Yes we *can*. You're not making any sense."

"Okay then, Lou, let me put it another way. 'No, I won't.'"

"All you need to do is pee in a cup, see?" Lou's nervous half-smile belied the deep confoundment that now led him to describe the most fundamental activities with a childlike simplicity. "Then they take it away and you're all done. You've done it every month for the past, what... well, however long you've been here."

"Yeah, that's true, Lou, and because of that I think Life-Guard has enough of my urine already. And enough of my DNA too. Believe me, my DNA hasn't changed, and it won't be changing any time soon."

They were back in Lou's office yet again. It struck Wally that in recent weeks he'd been spending more pointless time in Lou's office than he was in his own cubicle. Difference was, this time there were two other men in the office with them. Wally didn't recognize them and presumed they were LifeGuard security officers. In any case, he wasn't terribly comfortable discussing urination in front of them.

"What the hell's wrong with you, 407-R?" Lou asked. "You sick?" There was honest concern on his face, as if only some kind of brain fever could explain 407-R's inexplicable burst of uncooperativeness.

"No, Lou," Wally was suddenly feeling weary. He'd known this scene was coming, and he'd been dreading it. "No, I'm not sick. I just don't want to. Not now, or ever again."

Lou had never run into anything like this before, and was having trouble comprehending what was happening or what was expected of him. He certainly hadn't been expecting anything like this from a team player like 407-R. Nobody else on fourteen had said a word. Just peed in the cup and that was that. "I don't get it, then. What's the problem?"

Wally shot a nervous glance at the two strangers. He was well aware of all the recording and transmission devices around the office. Still, the idea of talking about this in front of real people made him even more uneasy. He turned back to Lou. "Is there any way that we could discuss this privately? There'll still be a record of everything I say, right?"

"It's protocol," one of the men said. They were dressed in identical charcoal gray suits. Wally didn't think he'd ever be able to recognize either one of them if he encountered him on the street or in the elevator. They were like mannequins—their faces so emotionless and unmarked they were almost completely invisible. Yet maybe because of that, Wally found he was painfully aware of their presence.

Lou looked from the guards to 407-R. He hated making decisions like this. He hated making decisions, period.

"Look, fellas," he said, "would you mind stepping outside for a minute? Just outside the door? It might make things easier."

As if they were being controlled by a single puppeteer, both men reached into their breast pockets, flipped open their identical communitainer units, lightly tapped three buttons, then closed them again. Without another word they both stepped outside.

This wasn't going nearly as well as Wally had hoped. He knew he was coming off like an Unmutual. That was bad. The presence of the guards threw him. It never used to. Doing what he was told used to be so easy. Lou would hand him the cup, he'd go over to the corner and pee in it, then hand it to one of the guards. Then he would open his mouth while the other guard unwrapped a sterile toothpick and took a cheek scraping. He'd return to his cubicle and continue with his work.

Now he was sweating.

When the door closed, Wally looked to Lou and mouthed the word "android."

"Not sure," Lou said. "Still trying to figure that one out myself. But about this piss business—they'll be back in here in"—he glanced at his screen—"three minutes and counting." He began talking more rapidly than usual. "You remember you signed an agreement when you first started here. Every employee will provide monthly urine and DNA samples. It's routine. Every company in the city does it. You work in a deli, you'd be doing the same thing."

"I guess I rescind that. Or my agreeing to that. You know what I mean."

Lou's confusion was starting to give him a headache. "Rescind? That doesn't even make any sense. You *can't.*"

Somewhere in the back of his mind, Wally had vaguely hoped that Lou might remember that conversation they'd had eight years ago, extrapolate from it a bit, and almost understand Wally's position. Apparently that wasn't happening. And given how badly this was going, he didn't think it would be wise to mention to Lou—especially with prying android ears around—that he could no longer send the private health files of citizens on to security and intelligence agencies. What business was it of theirs if some poor sap had an ear infection or genital warts? What he'd been doing for the past week was simply sending the files to Lou, but nowhere else. He knew full well that, unless there was a problem, Lou wouldn't do a damn thing with them.

"I'm afraid I have to, Lou."

Lou, bless him, was still trying. "Is it a religious thing? Is that it? You turned all Buddhist or something? I'm not big into my Eastern religions, there, but if there's something in the teachings of the Buddha against peeing in a cup, I mean, we can make provisions for that."

Wally found himself beginning to feel sorry for the big lug. "No, Lou, it's—I mean, I am starting to get rid of a lot of clutter, but it's not a Buddhist thing."

Crap—that might've been my chance and I blew it.

He knew he couldn't lay it all out. Not here, and certainly not with the security guards waiting outside the door.

"So what are you afraid of?"

Wally was getting the sense that this was a question he was going to be asked more and more often as his plan moved ahead. At least if anyone noticed, and he prayed they wouldn't. That was the whole idea, that he'd be noticed less and less. Already, though, having heard it only twice, the question dug at him.

I bet Sid Powell never pees in cups.

"I'm not afraid of anything, Lou. Okay? Nothing. That's not the point. I just think I've been here long enough, I've proven my value as an employee, you know you can trust me, and you don't need any more of my urine."

With that same nervous half-smile, Lou raised his hands. "All right, calm down there, Buddha-boy. Look—these guys are going to be coming back in here in"—he glanced at his screen again—"about thirty seconds." He suddenly looked uncomfortable and serious. "I like you, 407-R. I think you're an asset to the LifeGuard team. But this ain't my choice, and these two here will remind me of that." He nodded toward the door, which was going to open again in a few seconds. "You don't provide monthly samples, you can't work here. That was all in the agreement you signed. Whatever secret, weird reasons you might have, you should keep them to yourself. But please—"

The door opened and the two stony-faced security officers reappeared. Both Lou and Wally glanced at them but said nothing as they reassumed their position side by side against the wall.

"So—" Lou went on. He seemed more saddened than confused now. "Unless you change your mind... *soon* . . ." He was almost pleading. "I'm afraid... I'm afraid we're gonna have to let you go, 407-R. Effective immediately."

After stuffing the ceramic frog into his briefcase, he set about deleting all the information stored on his computer. Every last record, every stored file from the past eight years. Assuming an armed squadron of DOD agents would be waiting for him downstairs, he knew their next step after arresting him would be to come up to fourteen to seize his computer. Well, he wasn't going to make it easy for them. He knew deleting all these files would be bad news for the poor suckers trying to get their mounting medical bills taken care of, but somewhere deep in his brain Wally felt that erasing their records along with his own would be better for them in the long run. Morally, anyway.

He hit all the necessary delete buttons in the proper sequence but nothing happened. He stared at the static, humming screen for a moment, waiting for something to happen. Then he tried again. This time, a rectangular window appeared, bold white letters in a black box. In the window were four words:

Don't

Even

Think It

The black box on the cubicle wall began to whir. Wally gave it the finger, grabbed his briefcase, and fled the office without saying another word to anyone.

In the elevator he began to panic. What would he do when the doors opened and the guards were waiting? Try to shove through them and make a dash for it? Run a serpentine pattern to avoid the bullets aimed at his back? Or should he just surrender peacefully, knowing it was a lost cause? That had worked in the park. But could he hope for a second reprieve, being let off with nothing more than another visit to Resident Control?

I could tell them I wasn't feeling well, that I had a fever and that explains everything. Some kind of infection or something that left me a little loopy. No, they'd just check my records...In that case I could tell them that I hadn't seen a doctor about it yet...But then the biometrics would give me away. Crap. Maybe—

The elevator stopped on the ground floor, and as the doors began to open Wally threw himself to one side, hunched his shoulders, squeezed his eyes shut, and held his briefcase in front of his face, waiting for the inevitable.

When there was no shouting and no gunfire, he gently lowered the briefcase and opened his eyes. The woman who had stepped aboard the elevator was staring at him. Wally straightened himself.

"Excuse me," he said, then stepped out.

Apart from what appeared to be a small handful of Life-Guard employees, the lobby was empty. He peered through the two sets of smoked glass doors to the courtyard but saw no waiting agents out there either. He couldn't imagine them hiding in wait, ready to pounce on him the moment he stepped outside. DOD was rarely that subtle.

With an almost imperceptible shrug, he pushed through the first set of doors into the outer lobby.

Still unsure, still looking around, he stepped over to Whipple's desk and handed over his SUCKIE card.

Whipple, exhibiting more verve than Wally had ever seen before, placed a black box atop his desk, inserted Wally's card, tapped a button, consulted his screen, removed the card, and handed it back.

"You are no longer 407-R," he said.

In spite of his lingering fear, Wally couldn't help but smile. "Those are the kindest words you've ever said to me, Mr. Whipple. Thank you."

Whipple was silent, replacing the box under his desk.

Wally slid the card into his pocket and walked out the front doors, feeling lighter with the knowledge he would never walk through them again.

Once outside, he took a wary look around. There were a few guards around, as usual, but none of them seemed to be interested in him.

"That Lou's a good egg," he whispered to himself, wondering what kind of story his ex–boss might've concocted to keep him in the clear.

Across the street from the LifeGuard building, a new adscreen had been switched on in front of the VeeboCorp building.

Get ready for the latest SUCKIE upgrade!, it screamed. *Now with more information than mankind ever thought possible!*

The words morphed into a cartoon of a man in a suit literally climbing inside a SUCKIE card, before the card was picked up by a giant hand, which we learn belongs to—surprise!—the same man.

Without Your New SUCKIE, Life Itself Will be Impossible!

"Bet they mean it, too," Wally said.

As he turned and headed home from work for the last time, he noticed that the entire neighborhood smelled of scorched coffee.

That night his plan was to destroy his travel and shopping cards. With SUCKIE, they were mostly superfluous and outdated anyway. After that, he would have to start thinking of alternative ways to get his groceries. Maybe after figuring out how best to handle groceries, he'd set his mind to figuring out how best to explain to Margie that their household income had suddenly been reduced by one-quarter.

The next morning, not yet having worked up the nerve to tell her, Wally got himself together and dressed like he would on any other weekday morning, then left the house as if he were headed to the office. She looked at him funny as he left, but in recent days she'd been looking at him funny most of the time.

Outside, that same helidrone was circling in the gray morning sky. At least he thought it was the same one. Hard to tell.

Instead of heading to the subway after evading the Brigade trio, he walked eight blocks in the opposite direction, past all the children's boutiques, Tibetan spas, nail salons, and communitainment outlets. He stopped into a simulated diner and had a cup of weak coffee, pretending to be deeply engrossed, like everyone else, in the display on his minivid. At nine o'clock, he closed the minivid, shoved it in his pocket, and headed for the bank.

Wally hadn't dealt with an actual human bank teller in more than seven years. Most citizens hadn't. It simply wasn't necessary anymore.

He had always tried to keep a few of the old-fashioned paper bills around—most places still accepted them with only minor grumbling—but most people chose not to bother. Cards were so much easier.

There was only one live, bored teller on duty, and he seemed shocked to see Wally snaking his way through the maze of ropes and stantions toward his window.

As Wally drew closer, the teller, Norman Caul, grew more anxious. He couldn't remember the last time he had had to deal with an actual customer standing in front of him.

"Um," he said. "Can we help you?"

Wally, not wanting to give anything away, smiled and said simply, "I would like to close out my account, please."

There was a time when that request would have been the teller's cue to plead and weep and beg the customer to reconsider, to let the bank do what it could to make him comfortable and resolve any difficulties he might be having with the way they did business. But given that all the banks in the country were now subsidiaries of the Bilderberg Corporation, having your money in one bank was the same as having it in any other. Even the account number would stay the same. All that changed was the bank logo on the screen when you were checking your account.

Norman's face brightened with relief. This he could handle. "All right, sir... um... if you could just give us your SUCKIE card and let us know into which bank you'd like us to transfer your money, this'll just take a second."

Wally produced the card and slid it beneath the window, explaining, "No—I don't want it transferred anywhere. I would just like to close down all my accounts and get the money in cash, please."

"Oh," Norman said, his eyes darting to the right. This was something he'd been trained for, he knew that. But to date he'd never been called upon to actually do it. "I'm... afraid that's a bit more complicated then." He took Wally's card and waved it over a gray plastic box with a glowing laser scanner in the lid. The screen next to him flashed Wally's account. "Um," Norman said as he perused the screen. "You say you want, ah, cash?" He was no longer exuding the professional confidence of a few seconds earlier. "All right, um... I guess we could simply transfer the amount onto your card, sir, but that of course would—"

"I don't *want* it on my card. I mean *cash* cash," Wally insisted. "Bills. Smackeroos. You know."

Norman was puzzled. Nobody got *cash* cash. It didn't make any sense. At nineteen, he was aware of cash (it had been part of his History of Banking class), but he couldn't remember a time when anyone actually used it for much of anything. Apart from what was in the ATMs, he wasn't even sure they had any on the premises. "I must tell you, sir, that's, uh, *extremely* unorthodox. If I may, sir, it's like asking that the amount be paid to you in muskrat skins or something."

"Fine," Wally said. "I realize that, but it's what I want." Then just to be on the safe side, he clarified, "Not the muskrat skins, but you know. The cash."

Norman began wondering if he should call a manager in on this one. They'd probably just tell him the guy was crazy, and that it didn't make any sense. Besides, he was the only one in the building, so it was up to him.

He'd been taught that if confronted with irrational or even borderline unmutual behavior, just play along and hope that they went away peacefully. Then call in the authorities. "All right then, sir," he said. "We'll see what we can do." He briefly considered summoning DOD but chose to wait and see how things went first.

Norman waved a finger over a button next to him and the bulletproof window slid up. He then reached below the counter and returned holding a rectangular device, approximately eight by twelve inches and half an inch thick. The top was a translucent sheet of Plexiglas. He blew the dust off and placed it on the counter in front of Wally.

"First," he said, "we'll need a hand scan."

"*What?*"

"A handprint, sir. We need a handprint."

"Well you can't have one," Wally said, slipping his hands into his pockets.

"I'm sorry?" Norman asked. This wasn't looking good.

"*No.*" Wally took a step back from the window. "My entire account record is right there," he said, nodding at the screen. "If you'll just give me my money, please. There's no need for a handprint."

"Sir," Norman said. The frustration was edging into his voice.

He didn't need this. But he could handle it. It was his job. "Sir, *please.* We can't process this any further without a handprint for verification."

"Verification? Verify it against *what*? You don't even have my handprint on file."

"Yes we do, sir."

"But I never gave you one."

"We still have one. Look." He tapped a few buttons and a scan of Wally's right hand appeared on the screen.

"Where did you get that?"

Norman shrugged. "I'm afraid I don't know, sir. All I can tell you is that the biotechnicians working for Bilderberg are top-notch. Leave a fingerprint on a screen in here and there you go… I saw them do it once. Takes about a minute." Norman had been extremely impressed by that, but his customer today seemed less so.

Wally stared at the machine. He wouldn't feed them anymore. "I won't do it," he said. "Sorry."

Norman was becoming seriously fed up with this. It was way too early in the morning, and they didn't pay him enough anyway.

"C'mon, buddy," he begged. "Don't be a jerk. Just give me the handprint, okay?"

He lunged through the window and grabbed Wally by the right arm, yanking his hand from his pocket and dragging it toward the scanner.

"Hey!" Wally shouted, snapping his arm free from Norman's grasp. "Stop that!"

"Sorry," Norman apologized sheepishly. He pulled himself

back through the window as Wally made a show of brushing himself off and straightening his jacket.

"You have my card," Wally said. "Everything's on it. I don't see why you need anything else on top of it. Except maybe a signature. I'll give you that. That used to be enough."

"Can't say I know when that was, but whenever it was, it was a long time ago, *sir,*" Norman said, deciding to try reasoning one last time. If this didn't work, he'd call in DOD. "Sir—" he took a breath. "Withdrawals or transfers of fifteen thousand dollars or more require that a report—several actually—be filed with CIALIS, and BOO, and SNITCH. And they all require handprint verification."

Wally considered this.

"What about less than that?" he asked.

"Well, um," Norman said. "Everything's recorded, of course... but there are no special reports filed, no."

Wally crossed his arms. He looked at his feet and thought about it.

"And if you aren't filing the reports you don't need the handprint."

"Well, no, sir. We don't. Technically."

Wally thought some more.

"All right, then," he said. "I would like to withdraw fourteen thousand, nine hundred and ninety-nine dollars from my account. In cash. *Please.*"

Norman wanted to punch him. He knew he should've called in DOD the minute this guy walked in. He could've claimed it was an attempted robbery, and they'd believe him. But at this point he'd had enough. This was the last time he was going to volunteer for the morning shift. "Fine, then," he said bitterly. "But you can kiss your credit rating good-bye."

"Thank god for that," Wally replied.

"No," Norman said, knowing he would have the last laugh here. "Perhaps you don't understand me, sir. Only terrorists have any need for that amount of cash these days. Have you seen the commercials? There's that song about dirty money and dirty ideas? I'm just warning you—if you go ahead and do this, you'll no longer be considered a Good Citizen as far as the Bilderberg Corporation is concerned."

Wally let himself back into the house shortly after eleven that morning. Packed neatly in his briefcase was something just shy of fifteen thousand dollars in limp, faded greenbacks.

"Margie!" he shouted up the stairs as he closed and locked the door behind him. "Could I talk to you for a minute?"

SIX

Wally was mildly shocked by how calmly he reacted when Margie told him she was moving out. It had been coming for such a long time that actually hearing her say it was, more than anything, a relief to both of them. They could finally stop anticipating the inevitability of it all. Most indicative, the first thought that came to mind when she told him was, *Well, there's one less set of eyes I'll have to worry about.*

It was true. As his plan quietly unfolded, he'd done what he could to work around her. He didn't touch the four-way, or her computer, or anything else in the house she might use. He didn't even touch the kitchen clock. It didn't leave him with much to work with. Now, with her out of the picture, his plan could at last get fully under way.

Her last words to him had been "Could you at least save some of the cables? I might be able to use them."

He agreed, then closed and locked the front door behind her. Returning upstairs, he went into the living room, plopped himself on the couch, and turned on the four-way. A little distraction now seemed like an appropriate gesture.

He began flipping randomly through the channels and sites. Celebrity news. Celebrity news. Commercials. Horribleness footage. A mugging. A warehouse fire. An encore showing of episode six of *Concentration Camp.* More celebrity news. The Classic Commercial Channel. More Horribleness footage. Old celebrity news.

"*Coming soon to New Madison Square Garden—It's Autism Under the Big Top!*"

He hit the button again, switching to the HAWG network. His finger froze.

He was staring at a photograph of himself sitting in his old LifeGuard cubicle. Next to the picture was the following legend.

> Hi! My name is Wallace Philco, SUCKIE No. NY00169765/P
> I am a male, 43 years of age
> I live in Brooklyn, New York, with my Lovely Wife Margie. We hope to be expecting children soon!
> I am employed by LifeGuard Insurance Corp., where I am a medical claims scrutinizer. I have been there

for 11 years!
Flippy Bits are my favorite snack
For more information about me, including hilarious vid moments click here

In the upper left-hand corner of the screen was the animated HAWG logo. In the upper right-hand corner was a six-inch-square vid insert, which, at the moment, was playing footage of his encounter with the bank teller.

Wally stared at the screen without emotion for a long time before his finger found the power button at the top of the control unit.

He stood and quietly walked into the kitchen, where he opened the bar fridge, pulled out the pitcher of fortified guava juice, and poured himself a glass. As he sipped it he began thinking.

He wasn't sure what sort of self-protection mechanisms he might encounter as he worked his way around the house. There were only a few things that still needed to be plugged into the wall sockets, but it might be wise to have the electricity shut off. After that, the communitainer.

He emptied his glass and poured himself another. He hated guava juice.

He carried the glass into the front room and poured the contents onto the four-way control unit.

Gotta be cool, he thought. *Don't give anything away. They're still watching.*

"Whoops," he said aloud.

He gently lifted the dripping control unit off the couch, examined it for a minute, then hurled it into the middle of the four-way's massive screen.

With a hollow *thunk*, it bounced uselessly off the Plexi screen and clattered to the floor, two or three small pieces snapping off and skittering across the parquet.

Wally stared at the undamaged unit, then up at the screen, his heart sinking. He strode across the room, twisting himself between the four-way and the wall, bending down to unplug it from the socket. He knew it wouldn't do much—most of the machine's operations were wireless—but it was something.

Still squeezed behind the four-way, he braced his back against the wall, raised his left knee, and shoved. The screen tipped forward. For a moment Wally was afraid it would swing back and smack him in the head, but gravity took hold and pulled the four-way over onto the floor with a satisfying crack and splinter.

"Whoops," he said again. "Clumsy."

Staring at the ruined apparatus at his feet with triumph in his eyes, he reached up to his lapel and plucked off the VidLog.

He tossed it to the floor in front of him, raised his foot, and brought his heel down on top of it with all the force he could muster.

A spear of pain shot through his foot, his ankle, and up his leg. Wally winced and bit his tongue, limping in wild circles about the room, emitting a string of squeaking grunts until the pain had subsided enough for him to open his watering eyes again. When he looked down, the square black VidLog was unharmed.

"Ahh, *crap.*" Why was it that when you didn't want something to break it fell to pieces, but when you *did* it became indestructible?

He'd gone this far and he wasn't stopping now. Not when he was on a roll. With a growing fury in his chest, he marched to the closet, yanked out his toolbox, and returned to the front room. Snatching up the claw hammer and kneeling on the hardwood floor, he raised it over his head and brought it down square on the VidLog again and again, not stopping until the exploded bits of reinforced plastic and tiny vid chips had scattered across the room.

Still clutching the hammer, he stormed into Margie's office—what had been Margie's office, anyway. It was empty, save for Wally's own computer, which sat on a table in the corner. He had barely touched it in months, using it only to pay bills and check the bank account. It was almost two years old now, which meant it was all but utterly useless. It was nothing but a giant eye staring at him from the gloom.

He yanked the cables out of three different sockets and sent the computer toppling to the floor. There was a crash and a tinkle of glass. A series of hissing sparks danced through the cracked casing, and a thin wisp of white smoke curled slowly toward the ceiling. Then it was still. He raised the hammer again, but then paused. He didn't care if the internal vids were still functional at this point, so long as they were staring at the floorboards. They'd all be out of there soon enough.

Keep an eye on that parquet, you sonsabitches, he thought.

He glared around the room like a beast in a snare, hammer in hand, his breathing ragged. What was next? What was left?

He scanned the walls. Those would come soon enough. They'd have to. But first the satellite radio. It was just a wireless attachment of the demolished four-way, but it was designed to listen as well as play. Yes, that was next. He reached up and wiped away that sweat gathering on his upper lip.

Later that evening, he tapped the screen of his minivid three times, then sat back on the couch.

It took him nearly forty-five minutes to hack his way through the tree of computer-generated faces, each asking a series of increasingly specific questions, before he found himself facing what at least appeared to be an actual human operator.

"Octopoda Hybrid Electric customer service," the young woman with tousled blonde hair said. "I'm operator B-thirteen-twenty-seven, and I don't need to remind you that this conversation is being monitored. Citizen number, please."

Wally bit his tongue and recited his number.

"Customer identification number?"

He gave her that too.

"Security code?"

Wally typed it in.

"Mother's occupation, dress size, and favorite singer?"

"Waitress, six, Ed Ames."

This went on for quite some time before Wally was allowed to explain that he was calling to have his power shut off.

He was well aware that the vids and various transmission devices hidden throughout the house weren't electric in nature, but the utility companies, archaic as they were, kept records just as extensive as CHUCKLE. They knew what he used, when he used it, and what he used it for. Plus the billing records were a means of following him. The only way to cut off that trail was to cut off the power.

"May I ask why you wish to do this, Citizen... Philco?" Her pitch dropped noticeably when she spoke his name, which she pronounced in three syllables. He also noticed that she never looked directly at the screen.

"I'm... going away," Wally said. He should've been expecting that question.

"Moving? Well, certainly. If you'll give me your new address, I can simply have the account transferred, so the power will go on at your new residence the moment it's disconnected at your current one, and you won't waste a single watt."

"No—I'm sorry," he said. "It's not that I'm moving... it's just that I'll be traveling. For a long time... A long, *long* time. And I just think it would be safer to simply shut the power off here while I'm away. Then, uh, before I come back, I'll call again and have it turned back... on."

I'll be damned—that was thinking on my feet.

"Actually, Citizen... Philco, it's not quite that simple. You see, we require—"

Wally stopped her, trying to maintain a friendly demeanor. Things seemed to work better that way. No hint of unmutuality. "Wait—" he said. "I understand it may not be quite that simple. But since I'm leaving here almost immediately, I'd rather deal with the other side of things when I get to that point. Right now, I'd just like to have things shut off."

"You realize, Citizen... Philco, that without power, your

house is much more vulnerable to invasion by terrorist and other unmutual elements."

"You don't know my neighbor," he said.

"Mr.... Whittaker Chambers?" the operator asked, before rattling off his address.

"Okay, fine. You know my neighbors. Let's just say I'd rather not be responsible for a bill when I'm going to be away for a long... *long* time."

"Our billing system," the operator said, her tone insistent but upbeat, "is among the most convenient in the nation, and can be accessed anywhere in the world via your communitainer. Payment may be submitted through the four-way, through the communitainer—even through the MarketMonolith of any nearby grocery store wherever you happen to be—"

"*Look*—please—I'd just rather not pay for something while I'm not using it."

The operator's face seemed to go fuzzy for just an instant before snapping back into hard focus.

"If you're having trouble paying your bills, please contact—"

That's when he realized that he was dealing with another virtual operator, and one he was apparently confusing something awful. With each answer, he was being channeled into a different response loop.

One way or another, he was going to end up without power that night. The question was, under what circumstances? If they cut the lights out of spite, which was not unheard of, they'd begin hounding him the next day for the bills he was refusing to pay. He didn't need that. Best way out of it now was to start acting like a simpleton. They seemed to understand that better.

"Hello!" Wally told the image. Then in a nasal voice, he began, "I am...go...on a happy trip. A far-away one!"

Half an hour later, after establishing that there was no bill discrepancy, that he was simply a customer who needed to "go away for a long, long time," the lights in Wally Philco's house went dark.

"Hey, what goes on here?"

Wally had just spent the better part of an hour dragging and thumping the remains of his four-way down the stairs, out the front door, and over to the curb to drop it on the remains of his computer, radio, VidLog, and every other machine with meddling capabilities he could find in the house. According to the recycling schedule, Friday was Digital Refuse Day.

He was sore and exhausted and sweaty, and the last thing he was in the mood for was Whit asking a bunch of snoopy questions.

"Oh—hey, Whit," he said, drawing his arm across his forehead in an exaggerated gesture. "Had a little accident a few days ago. Just getting it cleaned up now."

Chambers scanned the pile of technological mayhem on the sidewalk. "A little accident? Looks like more than that to me."

Best thing to do, Wally figured, was give him something almost legitimate to work with. Make it seem like he's revealing a secret. He'd find out soon enough anyway, and if Wally told him first all the better for everyone.

"Well, if you must know...Margie moved out a few days ago. I guess I got a little upset."

Chambers took a few steps to inspect the pile more closely. "Sure looks like it," he said. "Jeeze, Philco, I didn't know you had it in you."

"Yeah, well." He tried the forearm gesture again,

"Did you just smash the computers? That's a little dangerous, ain't it? Plates and dishes would've been easier, don't you think?"

"Believe me, I broke a bunch of other stuff too. Lost my head."

Chambers squinted at the area around the broken machines. "I don't see anything else here."

"No, of course not," Wally explained. "I'll be dragging all that out later—on Ceramic Refuse Day and Glass Refuse Day... Don't wanna get a fine for misrecycling, y'know."

This was already going on longer and growing more complicated than he liked.

"Whatever, fine," Chambers said, dismissing Wally's excuse. "But all of these things here," he gestured, "these are *necessary.* You can't be a Good Citizen without them. I mean, how are you gonna read the daily bulletins?"

"I'll replace them. It'll be okay."

"Uh-huh." Chambers gave him that squinty look that said he smelled something he didn't quite like. "Between now and when you do, what about your nightly reports?"

"These were strange circumstances, Whit. I'll get caught up."

Chambers bent down, shoved a few things out of the way, and picked something up. He considered it, then turned back to Wally. "How do you intend to do that accurately without your VidLog?" He held out a few pieces of the shattered black box.

Crap crap crap.

Wally's brain began racing around for an excuse. Something plausible. Or at least something Chambers would buy, even if it wasn't exactly plausible. He and Chambers both knew that VidLogs were more mandatory than pants. "I…I have another one. You know…a backup."

It was time to change the subject before Whit asked to see it. Wally dropped his eyes to Whit's chest. "Say—that a new T-shirt?"

"Uh-huh," Chambers said, scrutinizing the pile again. "Number forty." Behind him in the distance, Wally saw a woman with an oversized jet-black stroller turn the corner. She was walking beside it, pushing it with one hand, while using her free hand to tap at her minivid. She began moving in their direction but as yet hadn't taken on the deliberate intensity of a shark closing in on a blood spoor. He knew that would change the moment she spotted him, Chambers or no Chambers.

"Look, Whit," he said, "I gotta get inside. Brigade's coming."

Chambers looked over his shoulder and smiled coldly. "Yeah, you got nothin' but women troubles these days, don'cha, buddy? Well you go on ahead and run inside. But take my advice and get these things replaced pronto. Today, even. You don't wanna be living in a blind spot."

"Sure thing…uh, Whit," he said, already edging toward his front door, not turning his eyes away from the approaching stroller. She was beginning to pick up speed.

"*Hey, Philco!*" Whit shouted after him. Wally turned, his eyes growing more frantic. "When you do replace these things, you might wanna consider an upgrade—this four-way's at least six months old. I get a new one every month. You wouldn't believe what these babies can do now."

"Yeah, I would," Wally replied. With the stroller bearing down on him fast he broke for the door, feverishly punching his twelve-digit code into the electronic lock.

Safely inside his dim and silent house, he dropped himself on the couch, breathing hard and sweating anew, his mind churning.

Damn that Whit. Why did I say anything at all to him? I have to stop talking to people, period. At least so far as anything personal's concerned. Never tell anyone anything. Just agree with them. That's what I'll do. Someone says something, I'll smile and nod. Then what argument could they have? I'm just pleasant and agreeable. That's the way to be invisible… Unless they try to get me to agree to something subversive. They could be setting me up. That's what Whit's always trying. Why do I even talk to him?… He corners me, that's why. If I say nothing, it'll just make it worse. He's trouble, and it'll only get ugly—if it's not already too late… There's just too much. The spyvids saw everything in here, passed it along.

There may be too much for me to completely clean away, but there's too much for them to keep track of, too. There's always that. Just gotta stop talking.

The following morning he stopped shaving. The water was still a problem. He hadn't had the water shut off, so there would still be that record. If he kept his use to a minimum it might be okay. He wasn't yet ready to start peeing in jars. He'd still have to take the occasional shower; if he didn't the smell would be noticeable. He'd always had a bit of an odor problem. And if he was ever caught on the street smelling that way, they'd assume he was homeless. He didn't want to think about what would happen then.

Water wasn't the only reason he skipped shaving. He was thinking in terms of altering his appearance. Even if the beard was sparse and patchy, it might still work as a disguise. Enough to throw off the face recognition vids, anyway.

He went into the bedroom and opened the closet. In the middle of the clothing rack hung the seven or eight shirts he'd always worn regularly. They were nearly identical except for the color, which ranged from white to light blue. Squeezed to either side of his usual shirts were the shirts he never wore for one reason or another. They didn't fit very well, the fabric wasn't comfortable, they were missing buttons. Whatever the reason, he'd shoved them to the side, meaning to throw them out one of these days. Now he was glad he hadn't. Same with the pants. He'd gladly wear ill-fitting pants if they helped him look like someone other than the guy who wore the same damn clothes all the time.

Granted, the clothes he hadn't worn weren't all that different in color or style from the ones he had, but in a city as obsessively fashion conscious as New York, the switch was likely more than enough to turn him into someone else.

Christ, that woman—what was her stupid name? Wearing an evening gown to the office. That's just dumb.

The clothes—the appearance in general—would be an issue when he went outside. He should try to avoid that as much as possible. In the house he was more or less safe. At least after he tracked down the spyvids. He knew his parameters. The GPS satellites could do a lot of things, but they still couldn't see into houses. At least not after he took care of the implant. And the satellite infrared scans, so far as he knew, could penetrate only the top floor, so he'd have to limit his activities to the first two floors and the basement.

But there was still outside. Outside there were too many factors to consider. Not just the vids and the GPS but the people. The real spies and the amateurs, all of them watching, minivids at the ready.

Should I go to different places all the time, or the same places? If I go to different places all the time, they'd never be able to establish a pattern in my movements. If I went to the same places, they'd see me all the time, but I wouldn't stand out like someone different would. They'd be more likely to ignore me. On the other hand, if they start thinking of me as a regular, they might start getting all chatty. That could be dangerous. Unless I just agree with everything. Smile and nod and don't say much. Plus if I were a regular, they'd have no reason to suspect me of anything—and they wouldn't want to lose a good customer. Maybe that's the way to go. You see a new face, you're gonna notice it and follow it.

God, I hate chatty clerks.

Then there's the grocery issue. Does the store even accept cash anymore? It's been so long since I've tried. But that's the only way, cash... And how long will it last? Fifteen thousand isn't much at all. Maybe I could call and have them delivered—one of the last public phones in the city is only about eight blocks away. If it still worked anymore . . .

There was a shrill whistling in his ear, followed by a voice he knew all too well.

"*Hel-lo, Mr. Philco! I'm pleased to report that you have an incoming call. I'll put that call through right after these messages.*"

Wally banged his head on the kitchen table until the ads were finished. He was so sick of that Flippy Bits tune. The minivid was across the room on the end table, but he didn't bother to go get it.

"Wally?"

He wasn't sure who he'd expected to hear from, but it certainly wasn't Margie.

"Oh. Yeah. Hello," he said, sitting up straight. "Um... what's up?"

"I was just calling to ask you the same question."

"Oh. Well... everything's fine here, gotta say. I was just, you know, going through the... Well, things... Everything's fine."

"Really?"

"Yup."

"That's not what Whit said."

Wally squeezed his eyes shut. Should've kept his damn mouth shut. He was going to blow it. "And what does Whit say?" His voice was flat.

"He says you dragged all sorts of things out to the trash—that they were all smashed."

That rotten little worm. He has to snitch on someone at least once a day or he can't sleep.

"I had an accident," Wally said. "I tripped... that's all. You know Whit."

"Yeah, I know," Margie said, "but he said your VidLog was all smashed up too—like you'd jumped up and down on it."

"These things happen. It was just an accident. Really." She knew he was an oaf, that a clumsy accident was absolutely plausible.

"But you're okay?"

"I'm *fine.* Yourself?" He needed to change the subject. He didn't want to be discussing his broken VidLog. Especially not over the communitainer. He crossed the room and grabbed the unit off the table but didn't open the screen.

"I'm doing okay."

"New place okay?"

"It's a little small, but you know what these new places are like."

"Yeah," he said.

There was a long silence.

"Look," he said finally. "I was just in the middle of cleaning here, so...I guess I should get back to it."

"Oh," she said, sounding surprised and a little hurt. "All right then."

"But thanks for calling. I'm glad you're doing well."

"Yeah, you too...Please be careful."

"Oh, I will," he said. "LWIW." Before she could respond he hit the disconnect button.

Once he was sure she was gone, he grabbed the minivid, flipped up the screen, and tapped the icon that put him in touch with Earwig customer service.

As he expected, having his communitainer service discontinued was much more difficult than disconnecting his electricity.

It took close to five hours and he had to put up with an inordinate amount of accusatory verbal abuse and name-calling on the part of several (possibly real, possibly virtual) customer service representatives, middle managers, company spokespeople, and even Denny, the animated company mascot, who called Wally a "fart face."

"You really aren't doing much to encourage my company loyalty here," Wally said finally, after a manager of some kind called him a "thimblehead."

Through it all he remained calm but insistent, and at the end of that five hours—perhaps out of sheer frustration—someone in the customer service center (located in Jakarta, he learned along the way) agreed to disconnect him. There was an immediate, shrieking pulse, which drilled straight through Wally's ear and deep into his brain, throwing him out of his chair and onto the floor.

"Take *that,* you ugly pig!" someone screamed. The pulse ricocheted through his head once again before there was silence. Wally slowly, cautiously opened his eyes. He was still on the floor. His head echoed with pain, like the dry flapping of wings in a dusty room, but it was fading.

Although the house was without question a far safer place to be, Wally tried to make a point of getting outside at least once a day, if only briefly. It was probably foolishness on his part, taking a risk like that, but he wasn't going to make himself a prisoner. That wasn't the idea. The idea was to swoop below the radar and live the way he wanted, unmolested. To justify stepping outside he made a job of it, strolling casually (yet purposefully) around the neighborhood, ticking off each outdoor vid he spotted. Some were easy—there were three on every stoplight and every other lamppost. He was obviously aware of the vids planted around Whit's house, though he was unclear on exactly how many there were—at least five, but if he knew Whit there were no doubt far more than that. Most of the other houses had at least one, usually mounted above the front door. Then there were the stores and other businesses. That would take time, spending long enough in each place to pinpoint the security bubbles in the ceiling. Most of the ads on the sidewalk, too, contained a recording vid chip, to keep a record of how long people stopped to pay attention. It all went on and on—and this was just in a five-block radius of his house. He didn't dare go any farther than that. You end up in a residential neighborhood outside your own, there could be trouble. That's why he stuck to familiar streets.

Every time he ventured out he changed his clothes. The beard was coming in scruffy, as usual, but it was enough to obscure his features and bone structure.

He wished he had a notebook or something in which to jot down the locations of each vid, but notebooks weren't sold anymore (terrorists could avoid electronic and verbal communication if they had access to pens and notebooks). He'd simply have to memorize them all. Maybe it was for the best. Computer records are one thing—if there was a search and they found a notebook on him or on his premises he was screwed.

By his count there were at least two hundred and thirty public vids within his range. And that's not counting the helidrones or GPS. Plus he hadn't even started going into the stores yet.

What struck him more than anything was the lack of Brigade trouble he'd been having of late. They had their own schedules and, as much as possible, Wally worked around them. Between eleven and one things were pretty quiet.

It was about twelve-forty-five on a Monday afternoon in (so far as he could tell) mid-November. Wally was approaching his house when his steps slowed.

Then he picked up the pace again, trying to appear jaunty.

Be agreeable, he told himself, *but say nothing.*

"Hello there, citizens," he said, raising his hand in a brief wave. Then, turning from one to the other, "Mr. Hawkey, Mr. Bingham."

The insurance dicks who'd never spoken a word to him were now standing on the sidewalk in front of his house.

"How'd you know our names?" Hawkey demanded, his features stiff.

"Yeah," Bingham added. "And what's that on your face?" He glanced down at the photo he was holding.

Wally cut his eyes to the right and sighed. Ignoring Bingham's comment, he explained, "We rode the elevator together at least twice a day at LifeGuard for eight years. Remember?"

"I don't recall anything like that," Hawkey said, narrowing his suspicious eyes.

"Me either," added Bingham, scrunching his eyebrows in a failed effort to look menacing.

"Well, I wouldn't be too surprised by that...So how can I be of help to you gentlemen?" He didn't offer to bring them inside to discuss things more comfortably and had no intention of doing so.

"We've been watching you, 407-R."

Friendly and agreeable. "Well, that's certainly very interesting. Might I ask why, or is that against policy?"

Somehow after riding the elevator with them for so long, he had a difficult time accepting them as a serious threat, at least not in comparison with the others he was facing. It did worry him that he hadn't noticed them before now. "By the way, 407-R was my employee number. As you probably know, I'm no longer employed there."

"Yeah, we know all about that, 407-R. That's part of the reason we're here."

"Please—you can call me Wally." It was sort of fun, he had to admit, watching these two in action after hearing all those stories. Of course after hearing all those stories, he also had a sense of how they operated. Bingham probably wouldn't say much until the beating began.

"Don't be a *smart*guy," "Hawkey sneered. "We just want to know why you left the firm. Why'd you walk?"

"Yeah, why'd you walk?" Bingham echoed in his trademark whine.

Wally rolled his eyes in a way he hoped would seem more amiable than irked.

"Gentlemen, I'm sorry, someone, somewhere must be confused. I didn't walk. I was fired."

Hawkey looked at him closely, his thin lizard lips tight. "You sure about that?"

"As sure as the day is long. Go ask Big Lou on fourteen,"

Wally said. "They just up and fired me. I never would've left a swell job like that on my own."

"Oh," Hawkey said. It clearly wasn't the answer he was expecting. "So... you didn't go to another firm?"

"You two are awfully good at what you do. Trained professionals. So I'm guessing you already know the answer to that one."

"Doesn't seem like you have, no... We just need to make sure."

Wally raised his eyebrows, hoping again it appeared friendly. "If I were at another firm, I don't think I'd be out here right now."

"No, I... yeah, it checks," Hawkey said, clearly more confounded by this than he preferred to be. "So what are you doing?"

Wally glanced at Hawkey's watch. The next Brigade patrol would be starting in a few minutes, and he didn't want to have to run for the door again. That wouldn't look good right now. "Not a whole lot at present... I'm sorry."

The two detectives glanced at each other and shrugged.

"All right, then," Hawkey said, pretending to have the situation well in hand, "you can carry on."

"Thank you. You two have a very nice day."

The pair began walking away, murmuring to each other as they went. Wally watched them go.

So much for the beard and new clothes idea, he thought.

Before they reached the end of the block, Hawkey whipped out his hand and smacked Bingham hard on the back of the head.

Wally headed for his front door but paused at the rusted

mailbox. Surprised he hadn't thought of it earlier, he peeled off the "Philco" sticker and rolled it between his fingertips.

The next morning, after another dark and soundless evening filled with space for nothing but thought, Wally got up and ate two pieces of bread. There weren't many left, and he noticed a few flecks of pale green mold on one of them. Just because it was crumbless didn't mean it wouldn't get moldy. He was starting to miss the niceties, like coffee and refrigeration.

He'd noticed that strings of red and blue and green Holiday lights were beginning to grow like unchecked vines around the doors and windows of most of the houses in the neighborhood. Drooping inflatable Santas and snowmen were wobbling drunkenly in a few of the front yards. Time was he would've worried about winter without any power, but he didn't figure it to be much of a problem this year. And this year, too, he wouldn't be drowned in Holiday carols, Holiday-themed commercials, Holiday specials on the four-way, miserable Holiday parties at the office, endless reminders wherever he went, so long as he stayed inside. That was a relief.

There were still so many things to do—and from this point on they only became more difficult.

He brushed off his hands and opened the knife drawer. He tested each blade for sharpness and each handle for comfort and control. Satisfied he had the best one for his purposes, he walked into the bathroom.

It was too dark in there. He'd need light for this. He returned to the kitchen and stood next to the sink. The light coming through the small window would have to do.

He considered a chair but figured standing would be easier. He bent slightly and leaned his left arm over the edge of the sink. More calmly than he ever would have imagined at any previous time, he took the knife in his right hand—it was a small paring knife with a surprisingly sharp blade—and drew it along the scar on his left wrist. He was glad it wasn't the other way around, him being right-handed.

That first cut left little more than a scratch, slowly dotting with blood. He knew he had to be careful to avoid any major blood vessels down there, so he'd take it slow.

He drew the point of the blade along the inch-long scar again, trying to follow the path of the first cut. He couldn't remember whether reopening scar tissue was supposed to be easier or tougher than opening a fresh wound. One of the two. Whichever. It had to be done.

Within a few minutes the cut was beginning to burn. The dotted blood had merged into a single red line. He gripped the knife again and, steeling himself, applied more pressure to the tip of the blade. This wasn't nearly as easy as he thought it would be. The first drop of bright blood gathered in the split flesh, quivered, then rolled down his wrist, hanging there for a second before plinking into the empty aluminum sink. Wally sure hoped he finished this before he got too light-headed.

The deeper he dug into his wrist, the more the skin separated, the more it burned. It wasn't a screaming pain—more a dull ache—but it throbbed, leaving his stomach tight and his knees weak. He forced himself to stay upright. Maybe a chair would've been the way to go, but it was too late now.

Half an hour later, the bottom of the sink was a lacework of red spatters, melting together, his forearm a map of tributaries erupting from a single source. A few were beginning to dry and turn brown along the edges, others were still bright and fresh. They had all formed slowly enough that he was certain he hadn't struck anything major. That was good. There was no way he could go to a hospital.

Then, with another quick flick of the blade tip (he was going to have to wash the whole knife soon—it was becoming too slick to handle), he heard a different sound. Something small and solid had clattered into the sink. He sure hoped it wasn't a bone chip—he'd scraped what he was sure was bone a couple times already.

He turned his eyes away from the garish hole in his arm and peered into the sink. He didn't see anything at first.

He set the knife on the counter beside him and, making sure his left arm remained poised over the sink, dipped the fingers of his right hand into the sticky, dark blood-spattered basin and began swirling them around like fingerpaints, hoping to feel something that wasn't blood.

He found it near the drain. It was hard and thin and rectangular. That was no bone chip.

He turned the water on just a trickle (which is about all he could get out of that faucet anyway) to rinse the blood off the chip and take a closer look.

That was it all right—the GPS microchip they'd implanted four years earlier when, by law, everyone in New York was instructed to line up at the makeshift "hospital tents" that had appeared overnight throughout the city. He brought it closer to his eyes. It didn't look like he'd left any of it in his arm.

Wally wanted to laugh, to cheer, but he knew he had to take care of this arm first. He set the chip next to the knife on the counter and headed for the bathroom.

It was horrifying to consider that this was the easy one.

If he left them in, he would need to get them upgraded in a few months anyway. It would cost thousands of dollars and wouldn't be any prettier or less painful than this had been. The upgrades, it was reported, would be coming more and more frequently in years to come. And if you opted not to get an upgrade, both chips would begin emitting shrill, ear-piercing whistles until you relented.

After washing out the wound the best he could (it was already beginning to clot), he smeared it with antibiotics, laid four square bandages on top of it, and wrapped the entire wrist in gauze.

When he was finished he flexed his hand. All of his fingers seemed to be operating normally, though he could feel something small tugging inside his arm when he wiggled his index finger. He tapped each fingertip against his left thumb in turn. They could move, and they had feeling. Good, that meant there'd been no serious nerve damage.

Okay, then.

He returned to the kitchen, washed the knife thoroughly, then washed all the blood down the drain. He now wished he'd washed the knife before he started, but it was too late for that. He moved the chip to the kitchen table, placing it in a small cup so he wouldn't lose it.

Now the tough part. Although a good mirror and direct light would be a help, he couldn't think of any way to arrange it. The kitchen sink wouldn't do either.

He brought the knife into the bathroom, removed his clothes, and crawled into the tub.

With his back pressed against the cool tiled wall and his knees up against his chest, Wally reached up to feel for the lump above his ear. He took a deep breath.

"You been watching this guy?"

"Which guy's that?"

"NY00169765/P." The man with close-cropped dark hair pointed at the screen in front of him.

"Send it over here."

Sergeants Victor Argerlick and Logan Swanson, both wearing identical black tunics, were seated in a cramped and dim monitoring bunker three hundred feet below street level, in the bowels of DOD headquarters, located on the site of the old Empire State Building. (The Empire State, it was argued, provided too obvious a target for terrorists, so in a preemptive move it was taken down in a controlled demolition and replaced with the featureless and impregnable DOD HQ.)

The Outer Band Individuated Teletracer room in which the two were seated was identical to nearly two hundred others honeycombed beneath Manhattan. Each was staffed by two DOD operatives, and each contained three hundred monitor screens and an array of computer equipment. Each bunker had immediate video access to eight thousand citizens.

When NY00169765/P appeared on Swanson's screen, he asked, "What's that he's doing? . . . What is that thing?"

"It's a lock," Argerlick explained. "And if you ask me, it looks like he's installing it . . . or trying to."

"Don't look like any kind of lock I've ever seen. Not in a long time, anyway."

Argerlick tapped a few buttons to enlarge the image. He peered closely at the screen. "I think it's called a deadbolt, if I remember my history . . . something like that. Maybe it makes sense, what he's doing. Nobody knows how to pick those anymore. It's a lost art."

On the screen, Wally Philco was crouched on a wooden chair in front of an open door, a small toolbox at his feet. He had a bandage wrapped around his head just above the ear, and his left wrist was heavily wrapped as well.

"He must know that it's illegal for citizens to make their own home modifications," Swanson said.

"No doubt he does," Argerlick agreed. "You want to fill out the report?"

"Yeah, okay, maybe not," Swanson said. Then his eyes blinked in recognition. "Wait—ain't this the guy from the other day? The guy in the kitchen?"

"You bet," Argerlick grinned.

"Yeah, what the hell was that all about?"

"Swanson, son, I've seen it before," said Argerlick, who'd been with DOD two years longer than his younger counterpart. "I figure it was just a little healthy self-mutilation. You'll see it every now and again. Relieves stress. In this case, the guy lost his job and his wife left him a few days later. He seems to have gone a little bonkers."

Sgt. Swanson, in the meantime, had pulled up NY00169765/P's video file. As he scanned through it, he couldn't believe what he was reading.

"My God—he's disconnected his communitainment unit, disconnected his electricity, knocked over his four-way... This guy's had trouble with BLAB, there's a report here about his fashion sense, he's got a 932/V, a 4501/M, a 1730/M, a 701, and a 0816/B... He's been antagonistic toward the Brigade, and he hasn't made a nightly report in almost three weeks now. No job, no children. Why haven't we brought this guy in yet?"

"He closed his bank account too. I've gone through the file."

On a screen to Argerlick's right, a middle-aged man was savagely beating a child with a table lamp. Below that, an elderly woman was standing on a chair in front of an open window, looking down.

"So? This guy's been quoted on numerous occasions making unmutualistic remarks. Why hasn't he been arrested?" Swanson was genuinely upset at this obvious lack of vigilance.

"His wife—well, ex-wife, soon enough—has been brought in for questioning about him. Hot little number that one." He paused a moment. "Anyway, she says he's harmless. More pathetic than anything. Just look at him."

On the screen, Wally was banging the handle of the screwdriver viciously against the door.

"If you ask me, Sergeant, I think he should be given his own channel. Watch him long enough, you'll see. This guy's a real hoot. Hey—you need another drink?" Argerlick kicked his chair back from the console and it rolled across the narrow room to where a fully stocked bar had been set up.

• • •

Wally froze as he was leaving one of the few drugstores in the neighborhood that still accepted cash without any dirty looks. In his hand was a bag full of assorted bandages and a new economy-sized tube of antibiotic. He stared at the woman on the corner. It couldn't be. No, it probably wasn't.

He'd never been able to shake his memories of Carlotta Bain, regardless of how brief and odd their single meeting had been. Even if the idea had begun forming in his mind before he'd met her, it was that encounter, her attitude, her almost joyous unmutuality, that finally solidified things.

So much about the woman on the corner said it wasn't her—the expensive red dress, the high heels, the hair. Yet something drew him closer. He couldn't see her face. He'd try sneaking up beside her, pretend he was waiting to cross the street, and take a furtive look.

He couldn't help himself—as he drew closer he finally said aloud, "Carlotta?"

She turned. Her face was suspicious. Even seeing her face now he wasn't sure. The makeup, the lipstick. *Jesus, maybe it's not her. But she turned.*

"Carlotta Bain?" he asked, drawing closer.

"Yes?" she said, looking him up and down with some vague distaste, as if she'd just bitten into a hunk of gristle.

Hearing that voice, even that single syllable, now he was sure. He stopped in front of her, his eyes wide. "I'm…I—you may not, um…We've met before." *God, that was smooth.*

"Yes?" she said again, curious perhaps but hardly convinced.

"At Resident Control. Some months ago. Right after this past Horribleness Day? We sat next to each other."

"Oh yes," she said, her expression unchanging. "Now I remember."

He smiled, thankful that she remembered him. "Well how—how have you been? To be honest, I...didn't think I'd ever see you again after that."

"I'm fine," she said. "They were very kind. And...you?" She asked the question as if it were a formality and nothing else.

Other pedestrians stepped around them, many clucking their tongues in annoyance, others too preoccupied to notice. Three yellow cabs and an armored DOD vehicle were waiting for the light to change.

"Oh gee," Wally began, "I don't...even know where to begin...But you look so different, just the way you dress and...well, anyway, it's been crazy. I gotta say, though, right after I talked to you that day, I decided—"

"Oh," she interrupted. "I have a call coming in."

Wally began to feel the queasiness sneak up on him as Carlotta, apparently being transmitted a commercial she particularly liked, closed her eyes and bobbed her head along with the jingle. She reached up a hand to brush the hair out of her eyes and, in so doing, revealed the small pink scar above her left ear. He looked to her hand and, sure enough, spotted another scar on her thin, pale wrist.

Suddenly he knew that they would have nothing else to say to each other. As she began mumbling to herself, her back half turned to him, he excused himself, his nausea growing, and headed home with his new bandages.

She was the only one, he thought as his feet dragged him up the sidewalk. *Can't talk to anyone, ever. No one. About anything.*

There was one thing left to do.

No, two things.

Okay, maybe even a few more than that if he wanted to be completist about it and look at things on a grand scale, but first things first.

He was proud of the fact that over these past weeks he'd become so much handier with his tools.

After putting the bandages away in the unlit bathroom, he returned to the closet where he kept his toolbox. Ignoring the toolbox this time, he felt around in a back corner of the closet until, with relief, his fingers found what they were looking for.

Sure am glad the electricity's off, he thought as he pulled the crowbar out of the closet and weighed it in his hands. *That'll make things easier.*

SEVEN

In the dream, Wally was at an elegant cocktail party in a lavish, sprawling mansion. There must have been fifty people in attendance, all dressed much better than he was and laughing among themselves. He didn't know a single one of them. Even though he wasn't talking to anyone, he became deeply offended by something someone said and began screaming at them, calling an end to the party and forcing them all out of the house. Only after they were gone did he remember that it was neither his party nor his house, and so not exactly his place to go throwing everyone out. Everyone, it seems, including the actual host. He felt bad about that but decided to stay anyway.

He went upstairs, entered a room, and walked to a window that overlooked the skyline of a city he didn't recognize. It might have been New York, but if it was someone had rearranged all the buildings.

He was still trying to make sense of the skyline when he noticed something else. As he watched in horror, a giant eyeball, at least six or seven feet in diameter, rose like a heavy, untethered balloon outside the window. It paused, looking in at him.

The deep blue eye was mapped with a web of delicate crimson veins. It stared at him for well over a minute. Then it blinked.

It was odd that it could blink, he thought, since it had no eyelid. But it had most definitely blinked. He reached down, picked up a plunger, and began poking at the giant eyeball hoping to make it go away. The eye dodged to the left, then floated backward a few feet, just out of reach.

Wally caught his own dim reflection in the glass and saw that he was dressed like a fireman.

When he awoke exhausted the next morning, the sky was its usual dull gray. He heard the helidrone in the distance.

After getting dressed and making himself a glass of powdered milk, he crunched back through the thick white dust and broken plaster that covered the floor of the front room and looked out the window. Parked across the street was a black van he'd never seen before. It was one of the newer models, complete with its own satellite dish. Stenciled on the side panel was "Rollin' Snake Eyes Mobile Ophthalmology."

"*God!*" he erupted in high-pitched and angry disbelief. "That's only *sort of* clever! What kind of *moron* do they think they're dealing with?" For an instant he considered marching outside and confronting them, whoever they were, but then he realized what a terrible idea that was. Instead, he closed the blinds and twisted them shut. Then he worked his way around the house, closing *all* the blinds. Having nothing but darkness and silence in the house between five p.m. and seven a.m. was bad enough. Having it all day long might be too much, but it was necessary at the moment. Once he was certain they were gone, he'd allow the listless gray light back in.

He sat on the couch and stared across the room to the empty spot where the four-way once stood. He could wait them out. He'd been up against worse. There was still work to do in the basement, but he'd wait right here, sit perfectly still, until they gave up and went away.

This creature is sly, he thought.

Shortly before noon he pulled the blinds aside half an inch and peered outside. The van was gone.

That was a relief, not because he was worried about the van so much but because he wanted to step outside. He needed a little fresh air, or what passed for it these days. He had no idea what the gamma levels might be, but he'd find out once he got outside. Being cooped up in the house for almost a week now, while safe, had left him feeling tight and jittery.

He changed into a dark blue shirt he'd never worn before. He then checked his face as best he could in the bathroom mirror, deciding that the new beard was coming in well enough. It might not have fooled Hawkey and Bingham, and it might not really fool any of the face readers either, but it was enough to sneak past most everyone else.

He tested the new keys in all the new locks again and they

seemed to be working just fine. Good thing, too—those locks had cost him a bundle. The old man at the antiques shop kept them hidden in a back room with the canned meats and Horde memorabilia. You had to ask for them special. When Wally made an offer to buy the entire stock, the old man didn't give him a second look, and never asked to see a SUCKIE card. The wad of bills in Wally's hand was identification enough.

Wally snatched up the "VidLog" from the end table and clipped it to his pocket. He knew to avoid suspicion he'd need something that at least looked like a VidLog when he went out, so after smashing his minivid he had glued the shell back together and begun wearing that. It seemed to be doing the job, so long as no one looked too closely.

Seconds before bringing the hammer down on the minivid he had seen the product warning on the back. He'd never noticed it before, printed in microscopic ashen lettering across the lightweight black plastic.

> *WARNING: Unauthorized attempts to modify or disconnect this unit may result in criminal prosecution, serious personal injury, or death.*

As he headed up the hill toward the One Big Area, Wally hoped the park's only bench would be open. He hadn't been there since the Horribleness Day incident—had no desire to go back there after that—but today it seemed like just the thing. In spite of everything that came with it, a little space and a little greenery might do him good.

Passing through the requisite gauntlet of adscreens before entering the One Big Area, Wally was comforted, somehow, to note that only one of them (for Chrysler's new Mini Fort, the Abomination DRI) addressed him by name. Maybe he was getting there.

He strode quickly past the screens and followed the black-topped path as it curved between two condos and into the openness of the One Big Area. The twisted and sickly trees were leafless and gray, and the grass was brown and dead, most of it stomped into the dirt by the estimated half a million citizens who passed through every weekend.

FumiCorp officials didn't like the idea of citizens loitering in the park, so they did what they could to encourage visitors to move along. The more people moved, the more ads they saw, and the more room they made for other people to see those same ads. One way to ensure citizen flow (and thus increased ad dissemination) was to remove most of the park benches. All but one, in fact. Benches encouraged slothfulness. The single remaining bench had been positioned with its back to a sparse grove of frail trees and facing an intentionally abrasive ad for the Whispering Trestles Development Corporation.

There were surprisingly few citizens around that afternoon. Some were walking their dogs. Two elderly couples were hobbling along the path on walkers. At the south end—too far away for him to see clearly—four armed guards milled about. He couldn't tell if they were DOD or FumiCorp security. He guessed the latter.

As he approached the bench Wally saw with disappointment that it was occupied. Another midget, hunched over on the far end of the bench, his legs dangling a foot shy of the ground.

He seemed completely absorbed in his minivid or some other handheld device, not paying the least attention to the natural wonders around him. Maybe he wouldn't mind, then, if Wally sat at the other end.

Wally had to admit that he never fully understood how to use his communitainer except to make calls and listen to the news whether he wanted to or not. These people who were so consumed by them, who knew everything about them, every possibility and permutation, who made every use of every application—they were exactly the kind of . . .

He let the thought trail off as he stared at the midget's back. The small man was wearing a crisp black suit. Too heavy, it seemed, for weather this mild. He must be sweating.

"Excuse me, Good Citizen," he said, remembering the etiquette lesson Lavoris Jones had provided. "I'm . . . sorry to interrupt your concentration. Would, ah, would you mind if I sat on this end of the bench?"

The man turned his head slowly, as if it required some massive isometric effort to pull his attention away from the device in his hands. Only then did Wally notice the black gloves and the red tie. His face was haggard and serious, his eyes piercing. It took Wally a few moments to put it all together and recognize him as the same midget who'd elbowed him on Horribleness Day.

The midget said nothing upon seeing Wally. He merely slid off the bench, making the short hop to the ground. Then he walked away across the dead grass toward one of the condos, head down over the console again, stubby fingers dancing with unexpected grace over the miniature controls. Wally watched him go.

Well, he's got the right idea, Wally thought. *Never open your mouth.*

He took a seat and closed his eyes. For some reason he thought it would drown out the dozen or more voices streaming from the nearby adscreens and the roar of traffic on the avenue some fifty yards behind him. It didn't. But at least with his eyes closed he could ignore—just for a few minutes—the ring of vids. They were on every lamppost, every adscreen, every building, and nestled in most of the trees. It was still good to be out of the house, even if it meant revealing himself briefly.

"Hey, *buddy,*" someone said. Wally felt something nudging his ankles. "No sleepin' in the park." At first he thought it was the midget again.

He half-raised his eyelids to see Whit Chambers grinning down at him. He felt the muscles in his neck contract. "Hey Whit—what a surprise."

"Hey, yeah, ain't seen you in a while. And ain't never seen you out here before." The loose wooden slats of the bench bucked and creaked as he took a seat next to Wally. Chambers was clutching a pink leash of braided nylon.

"Decided to get some air," Wally said, trying to bury his discomfort. "I, uh... didn't know you came up here."

"Oh, yeah, every day. Gotta walk this damn thing." He tugged on the pink leash and a transparently mortified Chihuahua poked its head from beneath the bench, staring up at Wally with bulbous pleading eyes.

Chambers turned his head and spat. "Don't worry, though—I'm still keeping an eye on things." He pulled a minivid from his pocket. "I can punch into anything I want. But I needed to take Miguel here for his walk."

"I see," Wally said. "I never knew you guys had a dog."

"Aww, yeah. We got it for Buick and Coors. Teach 'em responsibility, right? But guess who gets to take care of it."

"That's always the way, isn't it?"

Be pleasant and agreeable.

Chambers tipped his head slightly to one side as his eyes focused on a spot above Wally's ear. "So what's with the bandage?"

"Oh, this?" Wally reached up and felt the adhesive strip. He was hoping nobody would notice it the way they'd noticed the thick gauze headband that had wrapped his skull for two weeks. "Guess I'd almost forgotten about that... It should come off in a day or two. No big deal."

"Yeah, but what happened?"

"Just a little accident. Been doing some work on the house."

Whit's heavy eyebrows went up. "Another one? You been havin' a lotta those lately. Accidents, I mean."

"Yeah, I guess." He tried to avoid drawing any attention to his wrist, where another adhesive strip covered the slowly healing hole in his arm. At least on his wrist he didn't have to worry about hair so much.

"I can imagine...'specially after having your wife walk out on you like that... She used to keep an eye on you, I bet."

I bet she did. Wally felt the bitterness growing. He fought back the urge to tell Whit to mind his own business. "She sure did," he said.

"She probably wouldn't've let you try an' grow that beard, either."

"Uh-huh." He jaw tightened. He hoped the beard helped disguise it.

Whit's eyes shifted to an austere, nattily dressed woman coming down the path. She was walking a sprightly cocker spaniel who bounced along on wide, flat paws, its woolly ears nearly dragging on the ground. Wally was half expecting Whit's dog to start yapping wildly, since that's what small dogs always did. Instead, it remained cowering under the bench, even backing a few steps deeper into the shadows.

Chambers leaned over to Wally and whispered, "Hey, Philco—get a loada this homo dog comin' here." He gestured with his head.

Wally looked. "What, the cocker spaniel?"

"Yeah—the homo dog."

"You know the owner?"

He shook his head. "Never saw her before in my life."

"Then... what do you mean the dog's a homo?"

"I mean the dog's a *homo.* Just that."

Wally looked again at the approaching dog, who had paused to snuffle around the edges of the blacktopped path with some enthusiasm. He turned back to Chambers. "Really... um... how can you tell?"

Whit pursed his lips in disgust. "Just look at it. Damn thing *looks* like a homo."

They both fell silent but smiled pleasantly to the woman as she and her dog passed.

As she continued out of earshot, Wally whispered, "I dunno, looks like any other cocker spaniel to me."

"Yeah? That's because they're *all* homos."

"But," Wally began, having no idea why he was pursuing this but happy to have something else to talk about, "what about girl cocker spaniels?"

"Then she'd look like a transvestite homo. Look, that dog's just queer by nature. All of 'em. Buncha homos."

Wally followed the leash in Chambers's hand, which trailed down to the ground and beneath the bench where Miguel cowered.

"I see," Wally said.

They sat in silence. Miguel took a few quiet steps toward Wally's leg, where it leaned against his calf and continued to shiver. Normally Wally might have bent down to pet the creature, but he was growing tense. This was hardly the relaxing visit to the park he'd been hoping for. He just wanted to get home and lock the door behind him.

"So . . ." Chambers said, breaking the uncomfortable silence, "you take care of all the Housing and Urban Renovation Tracking permits you need for this work you're doing?"

Wally shook his head lightly. "It's not renovations, really. I'm just fixing a few things that needed fixing. I don't think I need to go to HURT for that."

"Well, normally, no, you could take care of it through the four-way. But given that you don't have a new four-way yet, it might be a good idea. Y'know, just to make sure you're doing this by the book."

Wally tasted something cold and sour at the back of his throat. *How does he know I didn't get a new four-way yet?*

He began pushing himself to his feet. "Yeah, you're right," he said. "That's what I'll do...Now, if you'll excuse me, I should probably get going. Didn't mean to stay here this long anyway… Good talking to you, though—and thanks for the tip… I'll—I'll take care of those forms right away." Wally offered a brief wave and pained smile. "LWIW." He had turned to walk away when he heard the bench creak.

"*Hey!*" Chambers shouted.

Oh, God. He didn't want to turn around but knew he had to. Summoning all the will available to him, he paused and tried to force his voice into "neighborly" mode. "Yeah?"

Whit trotted a few steps toward him, dragging an unwilling Miguel behind. "Looks like you might need a little help over there, way you keep having accidents. You know, I'm pretty handy. A real Mr. Fix-it. We could go back to your place, I could take a look around, see what's what and then when you get the permits—"

"*No,*" Wally snapped, much more sharply than he ever would have intended. He knew he'd just blown it. "I'm… I'm fine, Whit. Really. These were just stupid accidents." He had to backtrack. He didn't want to look at Chambers, knowing his fear would be evident, knowing his neighbor would be staring at him with that smug, accusatory smirk. He dared to take a peek anyway and found he was right. "But… but maybe when I get the permits, we'll see if, if, if I think I need any help. If I do, you'll sure be the first to know."

"All right, buddy," Chambers said, that awful smile creeping into the corners of his mouth. "No need to be so touchy."

"I'm not touchy," Wally said. "I'm just . . ." *God, why couldn't I be like that midget? Just keep my trap shut. And of all people to talk to.*

He continued walking back down the path toward the ad gauntlet and the street.

"Hey, hold on there a sec," Chambers shouted after him. "You just don't jump up and run away when I'm trying to have a friendly chat, offer you a little help." He jogged up behind Wally, who didn't stop this time.

"I really gotta go," Wally mumbled, head down.

Chambers grabbed his arm and spun him around. "I'm talkin' to you. You hear me?"

"Yeah. I...yeah. I just need to—"

"Need to what? Go hide in that house some more?"

Wally looked up at him helplessly, then around at the cameras, all of which suddenly seemed to focus on him.

"Yeah, I know all about that. I know a lot of things, Philco." Chambers lowered his head and glared at Wally from beneath his heavy brow. "No wonder you don't want me to come inside an' help you out."

"No, that's not—"

Just don't say anything.

"Not *what*?" Chambers asked, finally releasing Wally's arm. "What've you got going on in there?"

Wally said nothing, pressing his lips together and biting the inside of his cheek to remind himself not to open his mouth. *Where were the guards?* Then he realized the foolishness of the thought. If the guards did show up, they'd grab him, Wally, not the guy in the Operation RAT shirt.

Chambers breathed heavily through his nose. He looked down at Miguel, who was tugging at the leash, trying to get away from the scene.

Wally knew that if he didn't defuse this somehow the DOD would be kicking in his door later that night and Chambers would be getting a new T-shirt in the morning. He also knew if he said anything at all at this point, it would only bury him deeper. He bit the inside of his cheek again until he tasted blood but didn't make a sound.

"*Answer* me," Chambers demanded. "What's going on in there? Your wife, y'know, is worried about what you're up to."

Wally looked down toward his shoes. He had never gotten himself that new pair he'd been needing. These were splitting in a few places and were coated with plaster dust. He remained silent.

Miguel was still trying to pull away, to escape back to the safety beneath the bench. Chambers looked at the desperate dog and gave the leash a sharp snap with his wrist, yanking Miguel off his feet briefly, before tumbling back toward Whit. "None of this," he said, "I'll warn you, is gonna look too good in your SUCKIE file." Chambers glowered at Wally as he waited for a response, his face growing tight.

He reached out, grabbed Wally's chin, and tipped his head up. "You don't wanna answer me? Or you can't? Either way, buddy, you're showing some pretty obvious signs of unmutuality... and I know them all. If you don't care about that, *that's* unmutual too. And I'm not about to stand around and do nothing if there's an Unmutual living next door to my wife and daughters."

Wally glared back at him, paralyzed, not knowing what to do. If he runs, he's dead. If he remains silent, he's dead. If he speaks, he's dead.

"Look, Philco, don't push me here. I'm only trying to help you."

"*Help* me?" Wally blurted, his fists tightening involuntarily. "You know how you could *help* me? By keeping your damn nose out of my damn business, *that's* how!"

Oh, that really wasn't the thing to—

Chambers's fist, wrapped with the pink nylon leash, shot up, simultaneously yanking Miguel off his feet again and clocking Wally in the jaw.

Wally found himself on his back, staring at the sky.

"People like you," Chambers sneered at his prone neighbor, "are the reason we need people like me. So don't *you* tell *me* what is and isn't my business." Then after a pause, he snarled, "*LW...IW.*"

With that, he turned and stomped away across the One Big Area, dragging his protesting Chihuahua behind him.

Maybe Carlotta had the right idea, Wally thought. *Giving in that way. It's so much easier.*

At least he'd fallen on the grass. What was left of the grass, anyway. The dirt. It was still better than the pavement. It felt good down there in the dirt. He closed his eyes, thinking he might well take a nap while he was down there.

He heard footsteps approaching, then Chambers's voice above him.

"And if I may offer one more bit of neighborly advice? You better start wearing a real VidLog, and soon, my friend... Y'know, just a suggestion." The footsteps withdrew once again.

Slowly, carefully, Wally worked his jaw back and forth to make sure it still functioned. He didn't hear any grinding bone, so that was good, he guessed. No stabbing pain either. Prodding each of his teeth in turn with his tongue, none of them seemed terribly loose. He opened his eyes and groaned but made no effort yet to stand. Apart from the aching face, it was sort of nice staring up at the gray sky. From this angle he couldn't see the adscreens or the condos. It was pleasant. Besides, he wasn't sure his legs would hold him if he tried to stand quite yet—they felt half liquid.

He should get up, he thought, knowing that if he didn't, somebody—FumiCorp security or DOD—would nab him as a vagrant.

It was strange. He couldn't remember if he'd ever been punched in the jaw before. You always heard about it but it rarely seemed to happen. Like quicksand.

He heard more footsteps approaching across the grass. He didn't want to look. It was Chambers, he suspected, returning to level a few kicks at his skull. He rolled onto his belly, covered his head with his hands, closed his eyes, and waited.

The footsteps stopped and the voice above him this time most definitely did not belong to Chambers.

"Well, land o' goshen... if *that* ain't a pretty picture then I'm the Durango Kid."

It was an accent like no other he had ever heard before, from some uncomfortable verbal territory lost somewhere between Copenhagen and San Antonio.

"Got to dustin' up with the wrong polecat, looks like to me."

Wally opened his eyes. Now he knew for sure it wasn't Chambers. Looking straight ahead from where he lay, he saw the narrow toes of two mud-spattered leather cowboy boots.

That wasn't Whit's footwear of choice either. *Dirty dead man's shoes,* he thought. And where was the dog? Poor thing.

Wally let his eyes move up the legs until they hit the bottom edge of a bright yellow rain slicker.

Oh, God.

His eyes trailed still farther upward until he found himself staring into the round face of a hefty man with a thick red beard and a white cowboy hat, smiling down at him.

"I think I've had just about enough of all this," Wally groaned.

"Y'ain't eatin' dirt yet, my unmutual *amigo,*" the man said. He bent slightly and extended an enormous, callused hand. "C'mon, can't be lyin' 'round here all day like that. There's doin's afoot."

Against his better judgment Wally took the hand, having completely forgotten about the jaw, and the man in the cowboy hat yanked him to his feet like he was six.

"Thank you," Wally said, brushing the dirt and dead grass from his shirt with both hands, "though I'm afraid you have me confused with someone else."

One of the man's red eyebrows arched upward in amusement. "How you reckon?"

"I'm... I'm not an Unmutual... I'm citizen number NY0—"

The cowboy raised his hand. "Oh, now, there's no use in tryin' to hornswaggle me with that routine. I know plenty well enough what I'm sayin' an' who I'm sayin' it to."

Wally was suddenly very frightened. He wanted to turn and run but knew if he did he might well get shot in the back by Wyatt Earp here. Then again, the way things were going it seemed that inevitably someone would be shooting him in the back by day's end.

"I'm not an Unmutual," he insisted, though with his voice kept low. "I don't bother anybody. So please . . ."

The cowboy smiled again. "Walk down the yeller line too long, a truck's gonna hit you."

Wally looked around to see if there were any DOD agents closing in on him. He saw nothing.

"I'm . . . really not sure what you're talking about."

The man looked away for a moment, as if giving a reaction shot to an invisible audience. He lowered his voice to a calm whisper. "Listen, buckaroo, so you're unmutual, so what? It ain't like you're on the high and lonesome."

The more he spoke, the more Wally was beginning to detect the northern European accent overtaking the heavy cowboy twang he was clearly adopting. It was confusing in the end, given how terrible his cowboy impression was. Wally couldn't remember, even when he was a kid, having heard anyone in a cowboy movie call someone "buckaroo."

"C'mon," the stranger said, gesturing, "let's mosey on a ways, we'll jaw awhile." He turned and began walking away but Wally stood where he was, thinking now might be the time to make a break for the street in the opposite direction.

The moment he decided yes, that was exactly what he was going to do, the Swedish, or Danish, or Norwegian cowboy—whatever the hell he was—stopped and turned back. "You got potatoes in your ears?" he asked, his voice louder now. "I *said* let's mosey. I reckon you'll be plumb tickled you did."

Wally was frozen to the spot. There was no way he was going

anywhere with a stranger in a cowboy hat and a raincoat. If he was another ratter, he sure wasn't a very subtle one. If he wasn't a ratter, then he was insane. Either way it was bad news. Wally sighed. Why had he ever left the house? First he gets punched by a snitch, and now this guy.

"Git on along," the man insisted. "I ain't gonna bushwhack you. Though it might be smart to vamoose these here parts. In all of Brooklyn, 'tain't no place with more of the highfalutin' look-see... the *trees,* y'know."

Wally looked at the gnarled and dead oak not ten feet from him and stepped away from it. Then after staring a moment at the stranger dumbfounded, he asked, quite simply, "What?"

The cowboy rolled his eyes, then translated slowly and deliberately. "I think you might want to get out of here, as no single location in Brooklyn is more heavily wired."

"Oh," Wally said. "Thank you."

"You're welcome," the cowboy said. "You should get to know your culture better. Now... why don't we mosey?"

Figuring his options were limited at this point, Wally reluctantly joined the stranger. Anyone who warned him away from the park couldn't be a ratter. Maybe he'd walk with him for a few blocks, then make some excuse and head home. It couldn't hurt, he supposed. He wouldn't know what the guy was saying anyway.

The two of them began walking back toward the park entrance. Wally didn't want to argue with a guy who could and might punch him eight times harder than Whit had. He didn't want to say anything at all. That had been his mistake with Whit.

As they were about to turn the corner and enter the ad-screen gauntlet, Wally heard a frantic, shrill scream some distance behind them.

"*Miguel! Miguelll!!*"

He whirled and saw Whit fifty yards away, sprinting across the One Big Area. His arms were outstretched and he was gazing up into the sky as he screamed.

"Well, wouldja lookee yonder," the cowboy said, pointing.

Silhouetted against the gray clouds just before it vanished beyond the roof of a twenty-three-story luxury apartment complex, Wally saw Miguel the Chihuahua, held fast in the talons of a red-tailed hawk, the bird's wings flapping wildly.

"*Miguel!*" Chambers screamed again, still running, the pink leash trailing in the dirt and tangling in his feet.

"Gotta say," the cowboy offered calmly, "that surely ain't somethin' you see every day."

"No," Wally said, unsure where his sympathies lay at the moment. "No, it sure isn't."

They turned and continued walking, while behind them Whittaker Chambers kept screaming "*Miguel!*" long after the dog had vanished over the rooftops.

EIGHT

They were walking through what had been known in another life as Grand Army Plaza. Now it was home to one of New York's thirty-two extant Horribleness memorials (none of them official). This particular memorial was a massive concrete cube, sixteen by sixteen feet, which squatted grotesquely in the middle of the open and gray cement plaza. Each of the four visible sides of the cube featured a vidscreen, each of which replayed a different network's live coverage of the events of that day, complete with commercial breaks, in an endless loop.

"Done found yourself at the little end of the horn, huh?" the cowboy asked. "Bet you got yourself a real tear squeezer. Most of 'em do."

Looking at his feet as he walked, Wally said, "I still can't understand a word you're saying."

The cowboy sighed. "I'm just trying to say that I sympathize."

That peculiar gait of his made walking next to him awkward, but Wally did his best. "Sympathizing with someone in cowboy lingo doesn't . . . count," he said. "And besides, there's nothing to sympathize with. I'm doing fine. Just minding my own business. I'm happy as a—"

"Sure," the stranger interrupted. "Look, I know where we can go. We'll be safe there." Then he stopped abruptly and placed his hand on Wally's chest. "Get back," he said sharply.

"What?"

"Get *back*!" He grabbed Wally by the arm and shoved him bluntly against the memorial. Wally slammed against one of the screens, just as a mob of at least a dozen teenagers came boiling across the street, whooping and screaming around the memorial. Some were waving rolling pins, others corkscrews and muffin tins. At least one was waving a meat cleaver. They were dressed in the unmistakable uniform of the Kitchen Magicians.

The mob roared past Wally and the cowboy without paying them the slightest attention and charged on toward the park, their feet pounding on the pavement, their sharp young voices ripping the air.

Two armored DOD cruisers were parked in their path, but the agents inside made no move to stop them, merely watching with amused interest as the gang bounced over their hoods and trunks before continuing on into the park.

Staring after them in astonishment, Wally said, "The DOD didn't do a thing to stop them."

"And why would they?" the cowboy asked. "Would you have stopped Hank Williams from singin' about a broken heart? If them cops'd stopped 'em, they'da found themselves wastin' shoe leather in Bed-Stuy faster'n you can spit. The show must go on."

Wally shook his head. "Should've figured." At least he was beginning to understand what this cowboy was saying. "Well, thanks for pulling me out of the way of greatness."

The cowboy pinched the brim of his hat between his thumb and forefinger and nodded. "That's twice now you're obliged, as I figure. So why don't you and I hash it out over a little cactus juice?"

"Fine," Wally said. Even if it wasn't the most attractive offer he'd heard all day, he was too deep in it now. "So long as you promise to stop talking like that."

"By the way," the cowboy said, apparently ignoring Wally's request. "If you're of such a mind, you can call me Faro Jack."

"Feral Jack?" *Oh, man.*

"No, not feral—I wouldn't get very far with that, now would I? Nossir, it's *faro*—F-A-R-O."

"Oh," Wally said. "I've never heard that name before. Is it, uh...Dutch?"

"Ah," Faro Jack said with a dismissive wave, "Not Dutch. You people *really* don't know your own history, do you? Well, no matter, I reckon—it's not worth explaining."

"Oh," Wally said, a little confused. "Um...pleased to meet you."

"Likewise, much obliged to make your acquaintance, Mr. Philco."

Wally was not the least surprised that this Faro Jack character knew his name already. It had been that kind of a day.

They continued walking, then stopped at a corner with eight or ten others waiting for the pictogram to change.

Why am I following this man? Wally thought as he waited.

As ever, it was too late. They crossed the street and continued nosing their way through the crowds of the plaza, turning onto the even more crowded sidewalks of Flatbush Avenue. Wally had no idea where they might be headed, but from the looks of things, it was downtown.

As he tried to keep his bearings straight, his traveling companion, out of nowhere, began singing—no surprise here—a cowboy song.

Will you come with me, my Phyllis
dear, to yon blue mountain free?
Where the blossoms smell the sweetest,
come rove along with meee

The moment Jack burst into song Wally, not expecting this, panicked and tried to bolt. Without missing a beat, Jack reached out and wrapped a heavy arm around Wally's neck, drawing him close, releasing him only when he was convinced there would be no more such foolishness.

As Faro Jack sang, Wally dodged oblivious pedestrians and fretted. He fretted about where he was headed, and about who he was headed there with. He fretted about encountering a

HappyCam (there weren't many in Brooklyn yet, but there were a few). He fretted that a large man with a bright red beard and a cowboy hat singing at the top of his lungs in public might draw undue attention. He fretted most of all, however, about running into a pack of Stroller Brigadoons. He wasn't terribly familiar with this neighborhood and didn't know how they operated over here. Carlotta had run into razor blades.

As he was about to begin the final chorus, Jack stopped singing. "What in tarnation are you lookin' for?" he asked.

"Who, me?" Wally glanced up at him, startled. "Oh...um, Brigade."

"Ahh," Jack said, patting Wally on the shoulder. "Don't you worry none. Those varmints won't raise no sand so long as you're with me...Always on the prod, that bunch, ain't they?"

"Yeah," Wally agreed. He wasn't sure if he should be comforted by this or convinced he was going to die.

The farther they moved away from his house, the more uncomfortable Wally became. As everywhere else, adscreens lined the streets, blasting out slogans and jingles and warnings. But the buildings they were passing alternated between lavish glass high-rises and crumbled, fire-savaged ruins. Every month there were a few more suspicious fires along both sides of that broad and hectic avenue, a few more demolitions, and a few more new luxury complexes going up.

The traffic grew heavier and slower the closer they came to the Brooklyn Bridge. Cars had to get through three checkpoints before crossing the bridge, so things always moved more slowly over there. At least it made crossing the street easier.

"We're not...we're not walking over the bridge, are we?

Because, to be honest, I'm not sure I—these shoes . . ." Wally began.

"Oh, no, no, no," Jack said. "In fact, here we are." He stopped walking and Wally looked up. They were standing in front of one of the ugliest storefronts he had ever seen in his life—and things in New York could get mighty ugly.

It was painted in alternating shades of salmon and turquoise, with a wide black and white checkerboard stripe above the entrance. The glowing pink neon sign read SEAMUS MCWINGWANG'S.

"Um?" Wally said.

"Yup," Faro Jack affirmed with a nod, reaching for the door. "It's a saloon."

"But those—"

"All right, then," Jack said patiently. "If you're gonna be all technical, it's a speakeasy. But I prefer saloon."

As Jack began pulling the door open, Wally grabbed his sleeve. "Oh, hold on—no . . . I think I'm in enough trouble as it is. I don't need to go asking for more."

Jack reluctantly let go of the handle and turned. "You really don't need to worry. Nobody cares. They banned the booze, yeah, but that don't mean they don't want you to drink. They *do.* Desperately. They encourage it, even. They just want you to be scared when you do it. So c'mon. We gotta lot to talk about."

He yanked the door open and stepped inside. Wally looked behind him in a panic—at the vid boxes, at all the pedestrians, at all those slow moving cars. Being seen was bad enough, but being seen entering an illegal establishment was a death sentence. Still, he thought, entering one had to be better than pacing in nervous circles outside of one. Taking a deep breath, Wally followed, once again kicking himself for having ever stepped outside the house.

Historically, most speakeasies by nature tried to remain as inconspicuous as possible. Unmarked doors, whispered passwords, peepholes. Not Seamus McWingWang's.

Compared with the interior of McWingWang's, the exterior was as unassuming and restrained as a Cézanne watercolor. The floor was patterned in red and black tile. The lime-green walls were zigzagged in silver and adorned with adamantly kitschy knickknacks—stuffed rhinoceros and goat heads wearing straw hats and heart-shaped sunglasses, novelty license plates, and clusters of oversized plastic fruit. Inspirational posters similar to those Wally had seen in the BLAB waiting room were ornately framed, but artistically defaced and hung upside down. Stuffed animals, rubber brains, and antique record albums dangled from the ceiling.

The top of the bar was a thick slab of clear Lucite illuminated from within by red and blue neon tubing. Neon, in fact, seemed to be the sole lighting source throughout McWingWang's.

The bright orange bar stools were in the shape of giant hands—you sat in the palm and the fingers curled up behind you. German electronic music filled the air and a four-way screen buzzed in a corner above the bar.

Wally hadn't been in a bar since Neo-Prohibition went into effect, and already his head was starting to hurt.

"*Hey hey!*" the bartender roared upon seeing Faro Jack. "You're just in time, Jacko—it's Failure Night here at Seamus McWingWang's, an' I'm gonna show ya how to fail!"

He was a squat, potbellied man with a squashed face. More than anything, with his wide, flat lips and bulging eyes under heavy lids, he resembled a toad. His shaved head offset the wiry beard that ringed his jawline. He was wearing a pristine white apron over a profoundly stained T-shirt.

"Howdy, Ivan," Jack said with a jovial tip of the hat. Then, jerking his thumb over his shoulder, "This here's Wally Philco, of Brooklyn. Wally Philco, this here's Ivan Johnson, your blind tiger this afternoon."

"Pleased to meet you," Wally said, leaning uncertainly over the glowing bar to shake the squat man's thick hand.

"Yeah," Ivan said, barely looking at him.

"Belly on up," Jack told Wally, "an' set yourself a spell."

As the two men took seats in the immense orange hands, Ivan made a series of quick and complex hand gestures in Jack's direction, an enigmatic twirling and snapping and tapping of fingers.

Wally looked to Faro Jack in hopes of an explanation, before remembering that he didn't understand what Jack was saying most of the time anyway.

Jack leaned over and whispered, "Don't be buffaloed. Sometimes reality is too complex for oral communication. Ivan's just telling me that the crowd in attendance includes one smoke cop, three DOD horse thieves, and one agent from SPOOK. We only have to worry about that last one, but Ivan'll let us know when she leaves. The others are just here to get drunk."

Wally took a surreptitious glance around at the rest of the bar. There were only six other customers in there as it was. The smoke cop was obvious enough—he was the one with the full ashtray in front of him, puffing away furiously at a hand-rolled cigarette. The trick was identifying the one who *wasn't* a security agent. He didn't like his odds.

Wally began sliding out of his chair, hoping to make a dive for the door. Before his feet hit the ground, Jack had that arm wrapped around his neck again, pulling him back into the seat.

"Whoa, reign back there, pardner," he whispered. "They're more likely to let you roam if y'don't go buckin' around."

Not understanding a word, but understanding the tone and the arm around his throat perfectly, he quietly settled into the orange hand again.

"All right, gentlemen," Ivan said, "I'm afraid your choices today are limited to beer and…beer. I still got a bottle of that Anti-Gin back here, but to be honest I really wouldn't recommend it."

"Ivan," Jack said, "when in tarnation're you finally gonna get some genuine hootch in this dump?"

Tossing a soiled bar rag over his shoulder, Ivan planted both hands on the bar and leaned his nose in two inches shy of Jack's. "Now you listen here, *cowboy,*" he hissed. "I serves what my suppliers supplies. You got a problem with that, I suggest you take it up with them…And for the record they're much bigger than you."

Jack, to Wally's surprise, backed off. "Right as rain, then," he said. "Make it two beers. That's all right with you, ain't it?" he turned to Wally.

"Yeah…sure…It's been a while, though."

"*Has* it, then?" Jack laughed. "Yeah, you're a trip, *amigo.*"

It was unclear to Wally what was so funny. The only thing

that *was* clear at the moment was that this foreign singing cowboy had brought him to an illegal speakeasy filled with law-enforcement agents and that he had to find a way out.

The beers arrived in dirty, mismatched glasses and Jack slid a SUCKIE card across the bar to Ivan, facedown. Ivan plucked it from the glowing Lucite, examined the name and picture, shook his head, and ran it through the scanner. "Better dump this one soon or they're gonna be down on you," he whispered as he handed it back.

Faro Jack flashed a grin that seemed to say, I can't say as I much give a damn, and replaced the card in his pocket. He took a sip, then turned back to Wally, continuing where he'd left off. "And by that, I'm sayin' you used to be such a Good Citizen. *Now* survey the landscape." With a slow sweep of the arm, Jack indicated the room.

Smelling a hamfisted setup if ever there was one, Wally nevertheless took a sip from the dirty glass and nearly gagged. The "beer" tasted like a blend of kerosene, Sweetum, and fermented tires. Until he could get out of this place, however, he'd try to play it cool. "I still don't understand what you're saying."

"Really?" Jack asked. "I thought that was pretty clear. My apologies. I'll try again—"

"No," Wally said. "I understood you. And I appreciate your helping me earlier, but I don't understand the assumptions you're making. I'm just a Good Citizen trying to mind his own business."

"Ah, see?" Jack said, poking a friendly finger into Wally's shoulder. "That's it right there—you just showed your hand. Good Citizens *don't* mind their own business... like your friend back in the park. You, on the other hand, are a Johnson." He glanced at the bartender. "I don't mean like Ivan—I mean the good kind."

Wally considered the predicament he was in, and he didn't like it. His options seemed to be shrinking by the second. He could try to run again, but that seemed futile with Jack next to him and DOD agents between him and the door. He could give up, as Carlotta apparently had. Admit to everything, beg forgiveness, then sit back and accept the lobotomy. That would be easy, he supposed, unless they decided to send him to Unmutual Rehab for his crimes, which seemed likely. Or he could fight back. He decided to give the latter a shot. He'd come too far in the past months to roll over.

Wally took another sip of the thick, foul bathtub lager in front of him. "I don't know what you're up to, or who you work for," he said. "But whatever you think you have on me, I have twice as much on you." He prayed it would work. It might, if this guy was as paranoid as everyone else.

Jack leaned back in his seat and barked out another harsh laugh, slapping his thigh. "Hoo, *nellie!*" he said, as he leaned forward again. "You surely are a pip, I'll give you that, *amigo*... Okay, deal. I'll play. An' tell you what—I'll even make things easy on you. I'll lay my hand first."

"Fine," Wally said, hoping he sounded assured. "But in English, if you don't mind."

"Deal," Jack said, still chuckling to himself. He cleared his throat. "Now, let's see... Not to go all Sherlock Holmes here, but—" He held up his right index finger. "The attempted beard and the ill-fitting clothes say that you're either trying to create a new fashion trend that's doomed to failure or trying to change your appearance." He held up a second finger. "Your daily schedule has changed dramatically, which indicates you're not only no longer employed but not eagerly seeking new employment neither." The third finger went up. "You have a whole lotta people watching you, whether you know it or not, and, let's see...oh yeah—" Up went the pinkie and thumb. "Those carefully placed bandages would seem to correspond with the former locations of your communitainment and GPS implants. Strangely enough. And one of the best ratters in the city fetched you a sockdologer in the jaw earlier today."

"A what?"

"He flattened you. And that says something." His left index finger went up. "And last but not least there's your, um, 'VidLog.' Nice try on that one." He lowered his hands. "See? It wasn't real hard to put the pieces together. Not just that a Good Citizen is flirting with some serious unmutualism, but that you've also taken a few steps toward unplugging. I didn't even mention the plaster dust. You, *amigo,* are now officially an outlaw." He spoke the word with undisguised admiration.

Wally nearly choked—not only on the awful beer but also at realizing how very obvious he'd been. He'd been trying so hard to be invisible. Oh, he was an idiot. Margie was right.

"You've also been talking too much," Faro Jack added. "And...you want I should go on? I could. You've been a bad boy." His eyes shifted to Wally's shirt. "That VidLog's really a doozy, gotta say."

He was clearly relishing this. He was keeping his voice low, yet there was something less than menacing about it, as if it really were nothing but a game to him. Still, Wally's eyes darted around the bar in fear. "Shouldn't you, maybe, not be talking about this out in the open?" he whispered. He noticed for the first time that Jack wasn't wearing a VidLog himself.

"Out in the open's best place for it. Especially in here."

"But what about . . . ?" Wally tipped his head toward the occupied tables behind them.

"Who, them?" Jack jerked his head over his shoulder. "They can't hear us. The acoustics in this place are a nightmare for eavesdroppers. It was designed that way. You could step three feet away, and even if I talked in a normal voice you wouldn't be able to hear me. Damnedest thing, really. Besides, they haven't dug out their communitainment implants like someone I know." As Wally looked around again he saw that all the people in the bar were, in fact, talking to themselves.

"This is a free zone," Jack explained, lowering his hands. "One of the few left in the city. That's the understanding, even if they don't publicize it. What happens here, as they say, stays here. In fact, so far as they know, we're one of them. Or two of them . . . Now, your turn. What are you holding on me?"

Wally looked down at the glowing bar, his empty hands, knowing he was beaten. "Nothing," he admitted.

On the four-way screen hanging in the corner, Gag Peptide's newscast was on.

"*. . . Officials from CIALIS, citing a recent PROTEUS X analysis report, have announced a nationwide ban on gumball machines, fearing they might provide an easy invitation to terrorists to either spread poison among the nation's young citizens or perhaps make them explode in some way . . . In related news, CIALIS officials also report that terrorists may currently be concealing guns,* *flamethrowers, and even small nuclear devices in fig bars, ordinary shirt buttons, toothbrushes, and hand towels. Therefore all citizens are hereby...*"

"So what are you gonna do to me?" Wally asked, his voice lifeless. Only an agent from DOD or SPOOK could get away with not wearing a VidLog. Why had he ever left the house? If by some chance he got back there alive again he'd lock the door for good.

Jack leaned in close, and Wally shied away, not wanting to hear the answer. He could smell the rancid alcohol on Jack's breath. "Philco, ya coot, you gotta start coppering your bets. You give up too easy. If I were one of them, you think I'd waste my time on you this long? Buy you a beer? Did John Wayne sit down for a beer with the injuns?"

It was obvious this cowboy was after something, though Wally still wasn't sure what.

"Guy in your position," Jack was saying, "you can't trust nobody, right? There are folks doing life in stir for less than what you've done. Wrong move on your part, wrong word in the wrong place, you'll be right there with 'em, or worse."

Wally nodded.

"But it's CIALIS, it's DOD, it's this guy here," pointing at the image of a grinning Gag Peptide, "telling the rest of them not to trust nobody. You're doing what you're doing, ultimately, because you *want* to trust someone. You don't want to be like them anymore. And that's why you came along with me today instead of walking away, like any Good Citizen woulda done. Am I right?" He didn't wait for an answer. "Point being, there are people out there, other people around New York, who are doing the same as you."

"*...In other news, that epidemic we've been telling you about for weeks now has apparently jumped the Atlantic Ocean, as a case of human transference of the Golden Orb SuperVirus has been confirmed in Quebec, Canada. Meanwhile researchers here continue to work around the clock in search of a vaccine, so far without success. With that in mind, citizens are strongly urged to avoid physical contact of any kind with...*"

Wally had always hated being psychoanalyzed by strangers, and he hated it for two reasons. First, because it seemed to happen far too often and, second, because they were almost always right. This time at least he wouldn't dignify the cowboy's presumption with a response.

He looked over Jack's shoulder toward the screen. That's when he noticed the black vid box pointed directly at him. *Christ,* he thought, *it was a setup after all.* And just when he was starting to think this guy—presumptuous or not—might be in the clear.

He spun his chair away from the vid. It was too late. "You said this place was safe," he said. "I should've known."

Ivan, who was nearby washing a dirty glass with his even dirtier towel, glanced at the vid. "You mean that fuckin' thing?"

"Wh—?" Wally said, half-turning to the bar. It was the first time in years he'd heard someone curse so casually and publicly, and it caught him off guard. He knew the word, of course, but it had been banned so long ago that it sounded archaic to his ears. "Um...yeah," he said.

"It's nothing," Ivan assured him, returning to his drying. "It was installed by the Anti Gin people. See the logo? They wanna see what sorta douchebags drink their shit. Better focus their marketing that way, not that it matters."

"And if I'm not drinking it?"

"Then they don't care about you."

Faro Jack raised his glass to the vid. "And we don't care about them either... You know, technology has a way of warping reality."

"Oh, sweet Jesus, here he goes," Ivan said to Wally. "He gets some in 'im, he starts pontificating." He jerked a thumb over his shoulder. "I'll be over there washing glasses if you need me to punch him."

Wally wasn't sure what he meant. Then, as Ivan walked out of earshot, Jack went on, and Wally found out.

"Once you add technology—especially a vid—to a situation, all relationships change. It becomes a trap. It's like Schrödinger's cat—or rather the box containing the cat. You know about Schrödinger's cat?"

"Yeah," Wally said, though he never would've been able to explain it if called upon to do so. "Sure."

"You put a vid on somebody, they're gonna act different. They'll be self-conscious... There was a guy—a writer back when books were still around—named Burroughs, who said you could destroy a business simply by recording the sounds around it, taking pictures of the place, filming it, then playing them back at the business, like a weapon. He says you do that, the joint'll go under in a matter of months."

Wally squinted at him. The beer was beginning to seep into his blood. He didn't know what to think anymore. Was the beer just a ploy to loosen his tongue and make him susceptible? Well, whatever. He was just glad this guy was speaking normal English, even if the accent was kind of funny. "I don't get it," he admitted.

"Yeah, that's okay," Jack said, dismissing him with a wave of the hand. "The point is, the same thing works with people. Long time ago, when video technology—nothing like we know today, I mean *primitive* stuff with big tapes—once that started getting real cheap and ending up in every household in the country, things really started going to hell. You need another beer?" He looked at Wally's glass. "No, you're fine. I do, though." He waved at Ivan, then turned back to Wally. "You know all the surveillance shows on the four-way nowadays—almost everything you can find there, right? Well, those existed in some form even back when we had televisions, except it was people taping each other, not DOD or SNITCH feeds. If Burroughs is right, it may help explain why we're in the shape we're in today—our own lives are being used against us like weapons."

"*... Although no premiere date has yet been chosen for the upcoming pay-per-view Megawar event, organizers say they are currently trying to choose between April third and June second of next year... The multinational extravaganza will bring together combatants in small wars, revolutions, and border skirmishes currently raging on five continents and is expected to be experienced in one way or another by nearly seven billion people. There'll be plenty of celebrities on hand, of course, and all proceeds will go to benefit the Chevrix Corporation... Chevrix—making the world a better place for people like us.*"

I wonder if Margie came up with that one, Wally thought.

Ivan showed up with Jack's beer. As he set it down atop a damp, torn napkin he whispered, "Our friend from SPOOK is on her way out—I don't know if that's good news or bad—you were kinda loud."

Wally turned to look but Jack grabbed his arm. "*Don't* turn around. That may be all the evidence she needs."

He heard the door squeal open, letting a burst of daylight and street noise rush into McWingWang's for an instant before it slammed shut again.

Jack seemed to relax slightly after the door closed. Then he squinted and bit his lip.

"No," he said as he looked down at the new glass. His Dutch or Norwegian or Swedish accent was seeping out a little more as the bootleg beer did its work. "I was wrong when I said that's why we're in the state we're in today. It's just a symptom."

Ivan groaned and walked away again.

Before Wally could duck, Jack wrapped that big arm around his shoulders and began gesturing with his full glass.

"You go back to John Adams and his Alien and Sedition Acts, Lincoln hiring Pinkerton and doing away with habeas corpus, the first Red Scare, Japanese internment camps, then the second Red Scare, McCarthy, HUAC. The Cold War. Then Nixon... the Deadbeat Dad law—such an ugly fraud." He paused to take a drink, his arm still around Wally's shoulders. "The business with the Mexicans... Then HISTERIC. At any given moment in the history of this country we were bein' told to spy on one another, to squeal on each other, to be afraid and suspicious of each other... and people have been more than happy to oblige. But I'll tell ya"—he splashed some beer on the bar—"nobody, an' I mean *no-body,* likes a tattletale."

Wally thought of Whit's T-shirt collection. He almost said something but felt it safer to let this guy do all the talking. He didn't understand most of the references anyway. He didn't want to look like an idiot, and he also didn't want to give Jack an opening. So far as he was aware, he hadn't incriminated himself in any way all afternoon. Apart from sitting in an illegal bar drinking illegal liquor while wearing a fake VidLog, that is.

This guy was sounding more and more like Sid Powell. But given the surroundings and the fact that Wally was getting a bit dizzy-headed, the cowboy suddenly seemed more appropriate. He was certainly preferable to this history lecture.

Wally was finding no comfort in talking with someone of like mind, quite probably because he had been hoping to talk to someone who wasn't insane. Plus, the more time he spent on his own working out his own plan, the less desire he had to commingle with anyone, like-minded or otherwise. He didn't care about history. He was only concerned with now, and now all he wanted was to be left alone.

Which again forces me to ask myself, Why am I sitting here?

"Ah, you *see*?" Jack spurted, getting louder. "Amateur spies are the most dangerous of all. Orwell wrote that. They're also the *stupidest*."

In spite of everything, Wally had no argument with that.

"And here's another thing to consider. The Horribleness killed... How many people were killed in the Horribleness? And I mean as a result of the event itself, not those people who shot firemen thinkin' they were zombies."

Wally puffed out his cheeks and looked toward the ceiling. "I think it was... after they got everything sorted out, wasn't it something like eighty?"

"*Eighty*. Right." He clapped Wally hard on the shoulder. "And look at what happened to the rest of us on accounta all that nonsense. Absolute hokum. You know...you know how many people in this town landed in Boot Hill yesterday alone? More'n eighty, ain't that the truth. And what happens to 'em? The footage goes up on the four-way with a laugh track."

Wally began wondering if Jack invited him here to have an audience. Maybe no one else would listen to him.

"I can tell by the look on your face that you're still not sure why I invited you out here," Jack said suddenly, his eyes bleary. "Lookin' like you's all rode hard an' put away wet...You still think I'm a spy, maybe. Makes sense, I s'pose...numbera rustlers in these parts."

Hearing the cowboy crawl back into his voice gradually, Wally began wondering if maybe he was dealing with one of those multiple-personality cases.

"Well, I'm not, I can tell you that." Jack slapped the top of the bar, shaking Wally's glass. "I'm *not.* An' Ivan here'll testament...testify...he'll tell you I'm not a spy. Not the kind you're thinkin' of anyway. Look, *amigo,* here's the deal." He paused and gave a surreptitious glance over his shoulder to make sure everyone else in the bar was still preoccupied. He turned back to Wally and dropped his voice. "Look, it's not goin' so well, is it? The unplugging, I mean? And don't say you don't know what I'm talkin' about, 'cause y'do."

Wally couldn't help but smirk. Maybe it was the beer. "Is that what you call it? Unplugging? You got that from an old movie, didn't you?"

Jack shook his head. " 'Been around a lot longer 'an whatever ol' movie you're thinkin' of. But you know what I'm talking about—tryin' to find the blind spot."

"Everything's fine," Wally said.

"Trust me, *amigo,*—if amateur spies are punchin' you in public on accounta it, it *ain't* goin' fine."

Wally suddenly began wondering if there were DOD agents in his house at that very moment. Jesus—what was Whit gonna do to him? With luck, maybe he'd be too wrapped up in trying to retrieve his dog to remember. Unless there was a way he could accuse Wally of sending the hawk in too.

He responded with a simple shrug.

Jack sighed deeply. "Believe it or not, I'm here to help. An' you can help me too."

This time his reaction was immediate. "Oh, no. No. You've done enough, thanks." He placed his glass down on the slick Lucite bar and slid out of the orange hand. The minute a stranger says he's there to help you, there's trouble. The only smart thing to do before things got any weirder was what he wanted to do from the moment they stopped out front. With Jack getting sloppy, he might actually have a chance this time.

"I'm sorry," he said, stepping away from the bar and out of reach. "Thank you for everything, Jack, I do appreciate it, but... I've got to go now."

He excused himself and headed for the door. This time Jack didn't make a move to stop him.

Wally needed to get out to the store. Some store. Any store. He'd been locked in the house for nearly a week since he'd made the mistake of thinking a nice stroll to the park would do him good. He'd spent his days working around the house and waiting for the heavily armed cadre of DOD troops to kick through his door. If they were coming for him, they were taking their own brutal time about it. Now he was all but out of food. All he had left were a few stale pumice crackers and a can of dangerous-looking soup. He'd had quite enough cold, dangerous-looking soup over the past few days.

He was no longer sure what day it was. There used to be a guy who had a vegetable stand up on the avenue two blocks away, but that was only on Sundays. He accepted cash, that much he knew. There was still plenty of cash left. Maybe he could go back to the drugstore. That place was okay, and he was sure it'd have something—maybe those little chalky mints you can't dig out of your teeth afterward. If they hadn't been banned, that is.

Which reminded him—once he headed outside he wasn't going to follow any cowboys to any bars. That was first and foremost. He also couldn't say a word. Not one word. He might say something wrong. They might have banned the word "mints," even if they hadn't banned the mints themselves. That sounded like the kind of thing they'd do. He'd just point at whatever he wanted. That would do it.

He shuffled through the grit and broken plaster into what had been Margie's old office. He pried up a narrow floorboard, reached into the hollow beneath, and pulled out three bills. It should be more than enough. He dropped the board, tapped it back into place with his shoe, then folded the bills and slid them into his pocket.

How long would it be before someone noticed the state his house was in? The darkened windows, the lack of activity. They could come and take it away from him if they wanted. Drag him out, resell it, demolish it, whatever. It was an extension of the eminent domain laws. They could take your house away, even if it was all paid for, if they decided it wasn't presentable enough.

Maybe he should do something about that. Keep up the exterior. But that would mean spending more time than he wanted outside.

Well, he'd think about that later. Right now he needed something to eat.

He went down to the ground floor and opened the side door just a crack. He didn't want to go down the front steps. Too vulnerable. The front steps made him a target.

He peered through the crack. He wasn't sure what time it was but it looked like late afternoon or early evening. That was good. It wasn't too cold out either.

He squeezed himself through the smallest space he could manage, then slammed the door closed behind him, eyes darting around as he checked the locks. Then he headed for the sidewalk.

He'd gotten only two and a half blocks—there were three blocks to go before he reached the drugstore—when he ran into it. He hadn't even noticed until he was almost upon it.

Arranged in a mobile, undulating line across the sidewalk in front of him were two women, each pushing a double stroller, four free-range children roughly five or six years of age running around and between the women like erratic electrons and two remote-controlled wagons scooting back and forth across the sidewalk in front of them. One of the wagons held a tiny, apparently empty knapsack, the other a smiling stuffed weasel of some sort. The lot of them were inching down the sidewalk away from him very, very slowly. While the children certainly had the energy to move faster than that, they were spending it running random crisscross patterns around the women and the strollers. All of them—mothers and children alike—were muttering into their communitainers.

There was no getting around them without taking the chance of colliding with one of the children, and that was the last thing he needed. He didn't want to call attention to himself in any way. Especially not in some way that would result in his arrest.

Goddamn Chinese field trip, he thought. Neither the women nor the children were Asian; "Chinese field trip" was simply the term Wally had given this situation, after once being similarly trapped behind a slow-moving Chinese elementary school field trip in midtown.

"Amex! Google!" one of the mothers said in a cloying, sing-song voice, "be careful with those autowagons now. Don't let them get so close to the street."

While giving no indication that they had heard her, two of the children (presumably Amex and Google) each tapped some-thing on their minivids, and both autowagons veered sharply toward the curb, bouncing wickedly off a parked car.

On the bright side, he could tell immediately by the dress and demeanor of the mothers that they weren't Brigade members. If they had been, they would've smelled him already. Non-Brigadoons were becoming increasingly rare in this area. In the whole city, actually. Most people considered it a civic duty to run down the childless and took on the job with fanatical gusto.

The other thing that was rare about this group currently blocking the sidewalk was that you didn't often see self-propelled children of this age outside anymore. Most every kid over the age of five was plugged so deeply into four-way game addiction that few of them left the house.

In recent years, all school-sponsored competitive activities, from football to chess, had been banned out of fear they would foster countermutualist attitudes and potentially damage the self-esteem of the loser children. To combat this, the city began providing each child, upon his or her fourth birthday, with a new video game system (provided by WTF Industries, which had an exclusive city contract). That the systems were programmed to be dangerously addictive was well documented, though generally not discussed.

So the children sat in their rooms playing games of slaughter, all the while growing larger and softer. Before you knew it, by the time most of them were twelve they were too big to get outside the house and too weak-kneed to stand on their own. Their parents, meanwhile, nourished the development of their children's delicate selfhood with endless helpings of ego-boosting platitudes and snack cakes.

The only youngsters, it seems, who did get outside anymore were the gang members, many of whom had obtained the latest generation of game implants, which flashed a score across their retinas after every robbery, beating, or murder.

"Remember what Edmondo the Aardvark taught you!" the second mother called out to the rampaging toddlers.

"*I'm the best me that I can be expected to be!*" all four children chanted back in unison. "*The world is mine and mine alone!*"

Wally tried to make a move around to the right, but a small blonde girl in a blue dress darted into his path. He tried swinging back around to the left, but one of the remote-controlled wagons made a run for his shins, forcing him to back off again. The two mothers trod on ponderously, either unaware of his presence or deliberately ignoring it.

He slowed his steps and looked across the street. He considered a run to the opposite sidewalk but the cars were packed three deep and too tightly. There was no way to get across without crawling over the cars themselves. That would mean setting off alarms, which would trigger all the local vids to swing in his direction. Besides, he knew from experience that escaping from behind one Chinese field trip meant inevitably becoming trapped behind another, slower one.

He looked around some more and made another dash when he saw a narrow opening to the left, only to be thwarted by a young boy who made it clear he knew exactly what he was doing. It was like being stuck behind a sentient, completely unpredictable, malevolent miniature golf obstacle. He couldn't even say "excuse me" and hope they would step aside. That could be considered "Interfering with Perambulation in Progress" (IPIP) and would bring DOD around.

He tried to slow his steps as much as possible while still moving forward in the hopes of opening up a little space between him and the field trip. That way, at least he would have the illusion of forward momentum once he started walking again. But they were moving far too slowly for that to be effective. The more he tried to get around them, the more his path was blocked and the more ensnared he became.

All he could do at this point was stop completely. Then he turned and began walking home again. It was pointless.

As he rounded the corner onto the final block, hungry, frustrated, and dejected, one of the adscreens he passed caught the signal from his SUCKIE card—the last remaining bit of identification in his possession.

"*Hello, Mr. Philco! Our records indicate that you're a man of distinction, a man who enjoys a good cracker—*"

God, he thought, *will you please just shut the hell up!*

Immediately unsure if he'd only thought it or actually yelled it aloud, he covered his ears and began jogging back to his dark house as night fell around him.

He'd torn the couch and the bed apart in his search for hidden microphones and vid chips and so now was forced to sleep on a blanket he'd spread out on the floor. It wasn't so bad. It was cool down there on the floor. And there was enough stuffing from the couch and the mattress mixed in with the plaster chunks that things were almost comfortable. One of these days, though, he knew he would have to sweep.

It had been worth all the muscle-tearing effort and ensuing discomfort. In tearing out the walls and ripping open nearly everything else in the house, he'd discovered nineteen vids (not counting the obvious one in the kitchen clock) and twenty-two hi-rez audio transmitters, all of which he'd soaked in a bucket of bleach before smashing them with the hammer.

He knew he wasn't completely finished yet, but for now he would have to make do. At least as far as the house went, it was clean. It was dirty, but it was clean.

Which reminded him. One more thing. He reached into his pocket and drew out the SUCKIE card.

Keeping it around this long had been foolish and dangerous. But he'd take care of it now.

Sitting on the floor, he put his hand out in the darkness and felt for the toolbox. Inside, his fingers carefully picked over the hammer, the screwdrivers, the nails until he found the long and narrow hacksaw blade. It wasn't terribly sharp and he'd have to be careful but it would do the job.

He got to his hands and knees and brushed the dust and plaster away to clear a spot on the wooden floor. Propping the card on its edge and holding it steady between two fingers, he took the blade in his other hand and began sawing a slice no more than a quarter inch wide off the end. He knew he had to be careful when he got close to the chips—some were designed to explode at the first indication of tampering, others simply sent out a silent distress signal to DOD. He'd have to work as quickly as possible. He kept the hammer within easy reach.

Fifteen minutes later, the card had been shredded as well as one could shred something with a hacksaw blade, and Wally, with a victorious grunt, brought the hammer down repeatedly on the three chips until they were shattered to the molecular level. He set the tools down and leaned back against the wall. He was exhausted, he was famished, but at least he hadn't heard any sirens.

He crawled over to the blanket in the corner and curled up on his side.

Well, that's it. They can't see me. They really can't see me anymore. At least when I'm in here. In here I'm safe.

He was content for the first time in a very long time. The house was in ruins and he was desperately hungry, but he could relax.

Then an odd look crossed his face in the darkness.

So...what do I do now?

He reached out, pulled his knees closer to his chest, and waited. He closed his eyes.

Then his eyes opened. He'd heard something. He didn't move.

He heard it again. Somebody was knocking on his front door. They'd come for him after all. Fucking chips. When he was cutting up the card, that must've been it. One of them must've sent out a tampering signal. He didn't know what to do. He was paralyzed. When they kicked their way in and saw what he'd been doing they would kill him. This time there was no question of it. They had the authority and the justification.

He reached out and grabbed the hammer. He wasn't going to go down without at least the semblance of a fight, even if it wasn't much of one.

The knock came again. But it was odd. It was almost...gentle. Like a normal, polite knock on the door. He had no idea what time it was. If it was DOD, they would've pounded a few times, then smashed the door down. Plus he hadn't heard any sirens, and there was no helidrone hovering overhead. This wasn't ordinary. They always put on a big production as a warning to the neighbors.

Then he heard a muffled voice shouting through the door: "*All hail King Ludd!*"

NINE

"Looks like you're settin' a bear trap to catch a skunk," was the way Faro Jack put it as he took a look around the house, kicking the occasional plaster chunk aside with a cowboy boot.

Wally had no idea why he'd answered the door. He also had no idea why he'd agreed to let Faro Jack into his house when he found the smiling cowboy waiting on his top step. Most pressing at the moment, however, he had absolutely no idea why he'd agreed to let Faro Jack take him out to introduce him to a few friends of his—"fellow Unpluggers," as he called them.

"You're more than an outlaw, you're a freedom fighter," Jack had told him as the pair sat in the darkness of Wally's kitchen.

"But I'm *not* a freedom fighter," Wally had insisted, shaking his head. "Just a free man who wants to stay that way." He was shocked to hear something so overdramatic and pretentious coming out of his own mouth.

"That's pretty much what I'm sayin'."

"No," Wally explained. "To me, 'freedom fighter' implies someone who does things. I don't wanna do anything. I just want to be left alone."

"So you're no different from the rest of us—we all wanna be left alone. You think we'd hang out together if we didn't need to? *Hell* no...But sometimes you have to stand an' fight for the right to be left alone. Listen, *amigo,* I told you that you ain't the only one, and I weren't just jawin' about my own self out there ridin' the whirlwind."

Jesus.

"There are a lot of us Unpluggers scattered all over the place. There's a bunch holed up right here in New York, livin' and workin' together. We can circle the wagons that way, watch each other's back."

It struck Wally that Jack's use of cowboy vernacular became clumsier the longer they spoke, as if he'd memorized one Zane Grey novel or a couple Roy Rogers movies and had difficulty adapting the dialogue to new situations.

Still far from enticed by the prospect, Wally said, "What I did—am doing—I'm doing for my own reasons...I'm afraid I'm not interested in joining some commune with a bunch of militiamen or whatever the hell you are."

"We're not militiamen. We're not a posse. It's just folks like you an' me who've had enough—"

"Look," Wally cut him off, surprised at how adamant he

was being with a man twice his size. Being hungry and cranky might have something to do with it. "Whatever you want to call yourselves...I'm just not interested. I've never been much for joining things." Then, not wanting to appear completely rude—after all, Jack had been nice to him—he added, "But thanks for the invitation. It's just not for me."

He realized why talking to people about this made him uncomfortable. Fear of exposure was one thing, yes, but deeper than that, talking about these things with other people, be it Carlotta, Margie, even Chambers, left him feeling like some conspiracy nut or kneejerk. And here Jack was asking him to join up with some band of outlaws. It wasn't politics that drove Wally the way it apparently drove Jack. It wasn't an agenda of any kind. It wasn't even paranoia. All he wanted was to be free of it. And hanging out in some commune or hideout or compound with a bunch of paranoid nutjobs wasn't being left alone.

When they stepped off the train, Jack scanned the platform in both directions. "Good," he said. "Nobody else got off."

Wally looked at him. He was feeling more strongly than ever that this simply wasn't going to end well. "No," he said, "why would they? This is a dead station. I'm amazed the train even stopped."

As the train pulled away, Jack tapped the brim of his hat back away from his eyes. "What I'm saying is, no one's on our trail."

"Would they even need to be? Nothing else comes through here. And all the exits were sealed years ago."

Jack smiled again. He always seemed to be smiling at something, like a walrus with a secret. "You're right about the exits, I reckon, but as for nothin' else comin' through here, well . . ." He looked at his watch. "We'll just have a look-see." Wally noted the watch was an antique—one of those old models with hands, the kind that needed to be wound once a day.

"So tell me again," Wally queried, "exactly how was it you got us both through the turnstiles back there without getting scanned?"

"Never mind now," Jack said, peering down the tracks. "It's somethin' you'll pick up."

He stepped behind a pillar, leaned back, and put his hands in the pockets of his rain slicker.

"So now what?" Wally asked.

"Now we wait for the train."

This was crazy. The train they just got off of was the only train that came through this station anymore, and it usually didn't stop. "So where are these people? I thought we were going to meet them here."

Jack shook his head. "Not here. They'd surely never take that risk. We have a little ways to go yet."

"Then why didn't we just stay on the train?"

"*Because—*" Jack rolled his eyes. "That train don't take us there. Next train will... and the next train don't carry no liars." He looked Wally up and down. "By the way how are your legs?"

Wally was about to tell him about his knee trouble when Jack raised his hand and *shhhed* him. He leaned around the pillar slowly and looked down the tunnel.

Wally looked too and saw the dim, wavering light in the distance. He also heard the unmistakable grinding and squealing.

"Okay," Jack said, throwing his back against the pillar again. "Stand close to me, as close as you can. Stay out of sight. There's usually no one aboard but, if there is, we gotta lay low an' let it pass. It wouldn't do us no good if they saw us."

"What are you talking about?"

"Just get ready to jump."

"Jump where? Why?" The panic was overtaking the confusion in his voice.

Jack was peering around the pillar again. "Half the trouble's in the askin'. Just get ready to jump."

As the yellow work train pulled into view, Wally felt his sphincter constrict. His face went numb as all the old anxieties came back to him.

Oh god—why did I ever leave the house?

He caught his first whiff of coke dust and brimstone and he thought for a moment he was going to puke.

I'll let him go first... let him go first, then I'll just stay here. I'll wait for the next real train. The last one stopped, so the next one will too. Then I'll take it a stop and transfer, then go back home and stay there.

"No one's aboard," Jack shouted over the metallic scrape of the wheels as the engine rocked past. "We're all clear. You ready?"

"*No!*" Wally squeaked when Jack grabbed him firmly by the elbow. As Wally screamed, the two men half leaped, half tumbled into an empty but filthy flat car. His eyes closed tight waiting for the crushing pain as his legs were sliced off. Wally stumbled and fell hard on his side, the dual vectors of his momentum rolling him toward the far edge of the car and the void beyond. He felt Jack's enormous hands slap down on his back, slamming him flat on his belly.

There was pain but not the kind of agonizing pain he expected. He could feel that he was still moving—but it wasn't him, it was the train beneath him. After all those years of thinking about it, he had finally jumped aboard a passing work train. He cautiously opened his eyes. Only then did he notice how hard Jack—who was sitting beside him—was laughing.

"Hoo-boy," Faro Jack said between gasps, taking his hat off to wipe his brow. "Nijinsky you ain't. First time jumpin' a train, I reckon?"

Wally pushed himself up on his arms and looked around. They were on a work train, all right. The flat bed—and, as a result, his clothing—was gritty and black with oily soot.

They were entering the solid darkness of the tunnel now, and what little he could see he caught in the strobe flashes from the dim work lights mounted on the walls at regular intervals to either side of them. For what it was worth, Jack's timing had been good. The flatbeds in front and behind them were both loaded with the rusting hulks of ancient and deadly machines. If he'd stumbled the same way he had onto either of those cars, he likely would have been impaled.

"Shit," Wally said. He was getting used to cursing again. It felt good after all these years.

"Don't worry," Jack said. "You'll get better with practice. But for now I might suggest layin' as flat as you can. We roll through a few live stations before we get where we're goin', an' it's best to duck peepin' eyes if at all possible. I don't think we'd likely pass for track workers."

Avoid being seen? Wally thought. *You're the one in the cowboy hat and yellow slicker.*

But he took Jack's advice—he really didn't dare do anything else at this point—and lay flat on his back.

He had no idea where he was headed, or why, what lay an hour ahead of him or five minutes from now.

Next to him in the darkness he heard Jack begin to hum. A second later he burst out singing again.

Out in the wild and wooded prairie
With snow piled high upon the ground

In spite of the irresistible toe-tapping nature of the song, Wally was having yet further second thoughts.

I don't even know his real name. But he seems to know an awful lot about me. Too much. And these so-called Unpluggers of his. What has he really told me about them? Christ, it's probably a terrorist cell. Suicide bombers. They're gonna lock an explosive belt around my neck and send me to a day care center—

He smiled slightly to himself, as he watched the work lights flash overhead.

I could just jump off at the next station. It's moving slow enough. Just jump off and find a way home. Right. Without a SUCKIE card that would be more than a little tricky. End up at a camp for the next twenty years. Look what they did to Carlotta. Ruined her. She was something, even if she was kind of a hippie. Oh God, these people are probably hippies. Look at this guy. Buncha hippies trying to set up a collective farm or a... what did they call those things?... hell, I don't know. I'd probably end up handling forms anyway. All I know how to do. Mid-level bureaucrat on a collective farm.

The wheels squealed beneath him, bumping erratically along the tracks. The vibrations ricocheted through the length of his body. It was a world of darkness, intermittent brown light, mind-numbing noise, and an inescapable industrial stench. In that way, he thought, it wasn't that much different from Manhattan, but without all the other citizens.

Probably gonna take me to some abandoned building and kill me… rape me, then kill me. Or vice versa. But why even go to the trouble of dragging me to a building? He has me in the middle of the tunnel. He could kill me right here, roll me off the train, and be done with it.

Wally opened his eyes a crack. Faro Jack was sitting a few feet away, alert, staring ahead into the darkness, still humming the same tune.

Should've searched him. Probably carrying a knife. Those Kitchen Magicians went right past him that day… Of course they went right past me, too… This is all just too weird. He's probably gonna take me to an empty room. I bet that's it… I bet there are no Unpluggers at all, just this guy's imaginary friends. I'm gonna die. 'Course if he was gonna kill me he could've done it by now. Probably would have. And that platform was empty and sealed. Would've been a lot easier there than on a moving train. Nah, if there are people at the end of the ride they'll probably be hippies…

Whatever it was, whatever waited for him at the end of the ride, he knew it wouldn't be good. That much was given. Then again, he figured, it would be better than nothing.

Wally had no idea, no way of gauging, how long they'd been

on the train. He'd simply been watching the lights and staying low, like Faro Jack said. The next thing he knew a light hand was jostling his shoulder.

"Wally—hey, *amigo,*" Jack was saying.

"What?" Wally asked, opening his eyes.

"I had no idea these trains were so comfy."

"Hmm?"

"You were snoring. C'mon, sit up. We gotta jump again in a sec. We're almost there."

"Almost there" was stretching it a bit, Wally felt, as he had been following Faro Jack far too long now through the putrid, unlit maze of side tunnels snaking away from the platform. Without the aid of flashlights or emergency illumination of any kind, Wally's eyes strained to follow the surefooted dim yellow slicker in front of him, his hands outstretched to feel his way clear of the twisted girders and greasy stone outcroppings, which narrowed the tunnel's width at times to two feet or less. Occasionally the sound of traffic, buses and trucks mostly, leaked down from above them along with the brown water, which collected in fetid puddles between the ties. The air smelled of oil, urine, and decomposing fish. The stench made Wally's head hurt, and it seemed to grow worse the farther they went.

"Look," he said, his breath thick and heavy in the rank, humid atmosphere, "could you tell me where we're going?"

"Not exactly, no," Jack replied, his steps unfaltering. "Not yet anyway. We're headin' east, though, if that's any help. You'll know soon enough."

Oh, I'm an idiot, Wally thought, bumbling ahead. *He really is going to kill me. We're gonna reach some place that'll be full of bodies—corpses piled everywhere. And then mine'll be there with them when he goes out to look for another victim.*

"So tell me, Jack," Wally said, trying to lighten his sense of impending doom. "You ever think of getting yourself a horse?"

"Had a horse," Jack said, not looking back. "When I was a boy. A real beaut... called her Charlotte."

"Oh," Wally said. "That's a... very pretty name. What happened to her?"

"She died. Now hush. And get a move on—we're hellbent for leather here." He picked up the pace for a few strides, then stopped so suddenly that Wally nearly ran headlong into him. "I'm sorry," he said. "I don't mean to be short. It's just that security, our own kind of security—security from security, you might say—is mighty important down here. It's the only way we can function. If they find out about us, well, you can rightly imagine that we'd be pretty fucked."

Wally barely heard what he was saying, relieved at last to have a moment to catch his breath. He heard a dry scuttling beside his foot and jumped back. He looked down to see the black silhouette of a hefty rat waddling unconcernedly in the opposite direction.

"Just a rat," Jack said, as unperturbed as the rat. "Nothing to worry about. We'd better keep moving." Once again he began marching through the darkness. "I'm sorry to be movin' so fast," he said over his shoulder. "We had to take the long way 'round—there's easier ways to get here but we got some reports of unexpected C.H.U.D. activity in some of those other tunnels.

Rats are nothing. C.H.U.D.s, though...well, let's just say they generally don't ramble past and keep goin'."

Wally didn't know if he was joking or not. Ever since he was a kid he'd been hearing about the C.H.U.D.s—Cannibalistic Humanoid Underground Dwellers—in the subways and the sewers. "C.H.U.D." was the first acronym he could remember learning. But like everyone else he always likened them to the old albino alligator stories. Just another urban legend.

Then again, people still referred to the alligators as an urban legend even after that nest was uncovered. Close to thirty of them under Yankee Stadium, some as long as sixteen feet. It had been in the news for only a day—live coverage as they were dragged to the surface along with the bones of nearly ninety citizens. Then nothing more was said about it and it became a legend again. He tried as best he could to pull a little closer to the yellow slicker in front of him.

A few minutes later, just as he was about to ask Jack to tell him more about his background, Wally heard a voice from several yards ahead of them. "Hold it there." It sounded like it belonged to a nervous fifteen-year-old boy. Wally could see nothing but moved in close behind Jack and froze. "Do C.H.U.D.s speak English?" he whispered.

Jack didn't respond but raised a hand and announced loudly, "It's just me, Shep."

"Oh," the voice said. "Hey, Faro Jack. Sorry. It's been a while since you've come through this way."

Wally could hear the voice relax, and so he did the same, peeking around Jack down the narrow tunnel. A pale, twitchy young man, probably in his late teens or early twenties and wearing a sleeveless T-shirt, was standing against the wall. A red bandanna was knotted around his head. As they came more fully into view he lowered the rifle he'd apparently been training on them.

"Not a problem," Jack said, walking toward the young man. "You're just doin' your job. Now, Shep, I'd like you make the acquaintance of Wally Philco here."

Wally, still not exactly sure he liked the idea of dealing with someone who'd been holding a gun on him, took a hesitant step from behind Jack. "Hello," he said.

"Hey."

"Wally could be very important to the movement, so I want you to remember his face. We don't need any more accidents."

"Sure thing," Shep said. He leaned his rifle against the damp wall next to a skateboard, pulled a halogen flashlight out of his belt, and flicked it on, shining it directly into Wally's eyes as he moved in to take a better look.

Accidents? Wally thought, closing his eyes tight against the intensely painful beam.

"Been much action in these parts lately?" Jack asked Shep.

"Not around here, no," Shep said, still scrutinizing Wally's scrubby beard and acne scars. "Been quiet. But I heard the guys in sector nine have been dealing with a few more C.H.U.D.s than usual."

"Yeah," Jack said, "that's why we're comin' through here today. Okay, I think you've taken a good enough look. No need to blind him." Jack reached out a hand and lowered the flashlight.

"From here on in to the Hub things should be clear," he told Wally.

Another enormous rat scampered across Wally's feet and he tried not to jump. *Jack lied,* he thought. *These guys are a bunch of paramilitary nuts. Living down here with the rats and C.H.U.D.s and guns… This is supposed to be better?*

"C'mon, mount up," Jack said, tapping Wally on the shoulder. He'd been looking back the way they'd come, letting his eyes readjust and hoping he might catch the glimmer of some distant light, no matter how faint, that could lead him out.

"Wally, c'mon. I want you to meet the rest and take a look around our little sanctuary."

Wally nodded in what he hoped would be interpreted as something approximating eagerness as he stepped around Shep, who'd retrieved his rifle and was again standing at attention.

The tunnel ahead, though still damp and rank and mined with rotting wood and twisted metal, was lit with a makeshift string of spiral fluorescent bulbs. Now able to concentrate on more than following the murky yellow expanse of Jack's raincoat, Wally finally found the strength to speak up again, once he was certain Shep could no longer hear them.

"You told me this wasn't a militia," he said, apropos of nothing.

"Excuse me?" Jack asked, pausing.

"I thought you said these Unpluggers of yours weren't some crazy militia outfit."

"Did I say that?" The fact that Jack was always smiling was really starting to irritate Wally.

"Yes, you did."

They'd both come to a halt now, inches apart, facing each other in a particularly narrow stretch of tunnel. It made the exchange seem much more confrontational than Wally was hoping for.

"Well," Jack began, in a voice Wally was ready to read as smug and condescending, "what gives you the impression that they are?"

Wally gestured back down the tunnel toward Shep. "The armed guards, for one. You never mentioned anything about guns."

Jack closed his eyes slowly. He now had a beatific smirk on his face, which bugged Wally even more. "That's my mistake," he said. "I shoulda warned you." Then he sighed. "This is all a bit more than I'd really like to get into right here," he said, tapping the wall behind him, "but I shoulda told you earlier...Okay, the gun, first off, was a toy. It was taken off the market back in the 1990s because it looked too real. Parents were getting antsy and overprotective back then. Nothing compared to nowadays, but enough. They no longer wanted their kids playing with anything that looked like a real firearm. They reckoned it was a bad lesson. Plus, too many kids were getting shot by cops who either couldn't tell the difference themselves or felt they were nipping a future problem in the bud. Shep's gun back there couldn't fire *caps,*" he gestured. "It's not even a water gun. It's just an...object."

"Fooled me."

"Good. Let's hope it'll fool any stranger comin' down into these parts uninvited too. In fact, I'm hopin' it even fools Shep."

Wally started. "He doesn't know?"

"If it were real, he might hurt somebody—prob'ly himself—and we wouldn't want that."

Jack seemed to be making less sense as time went on. "But

there was all that talk about the C.H.U.D.s. What if they come along? They'd kill him, wouldn't they?"

"Excuse me," Jack said, as he squeezed out from between Wally and the wall and stepped into a more spacious section of the tunnel. The bulb dangling a foot above his cowboy hat cast a deep shadow across his face, leaving him looking like some kind of phantom of the Old West. "That's better. Now let me tell you a little something about the C.H.U.D.s, and it's best I get this out of the way too. Some of the people down here may have escaped the paranoia of the surface, but they cling tight to their fear of the C.H.U.D.s. I guess that just goes to show. Wherever you are, fear gives people purpose in life. Anyway, here's the deal." He shifted his weight and took a breath. "The C.H.U.D.s are real, believe me, and they're down here. More o' them than us. An' they can be *mean* as all get out."

Wally instinctively began looking around and took a step closer to Jack.

"*But,*" he went on. Another truck rumbled above them and Wally raised his eyes upward helplessly. The dangling bulb rocked gently, swinging shadows across Jack's face. Once it had passed he continued. "But their beef is with the subway itself. The trains keep 'em up at night, the workers destroy their living areas... it's a quality of life issue with them. If you ever been stuck on a train for two hours on accounta some so-called sick passenger or debris on the tracks, or a transformer fire, you can pretty well bet it was the C.H.U.D.s at work again."

Wally had to admit, thinking back on all those trains that stalled for no apparent reason, that the excuses had seemed awfully flimsy sometimes.

"They don't have a beef with us. Not really. There were a few scuffles when we first set up down here but we worked out a deal. We got no beef with them, they got none with us. You let them go about monkeywrenching the subways, they'll let us go about monkeywrenching the surface. It works out just fine, so long as you stay outa their way."

"I see," Wally said. This was all nearly beyond his comprehension.

"Good," Jack said before Wally had a chance to ask any follow-up questions. "Then let's get a move on. We're just up around the next bend here."

As Jack skipped on ahead Wally paused to read something spray-painted on the wall. It was faded and spotted from age and the constant dripping but still legible. In thick white block letters that wrapped around the rough-hewn stone someone had written

> All things Weird are Normal in this
> Whore of Cities.

"Ain't it the truth," Wally whispered to himself.

Wally was convinced when they turned the next corner he was going to find himself standing in a cave illuminated by two or three campfires. Maybe some torches or a few dozen candles stuck to the walls. People in rags living in the rusted, gutted hulks of abandoned subway cars. Prematurely old faces smudged with soot, wide, moist eyes staring at him hopelessly over tin cups full of thin broth. People looking like Dickens characters or post-nuke refugees. Either that or a bunch of beefy, grunting men in camouflage fatigues with oiled torsos, shaved heads, and real guns. But when he turned that last corner behind Jack he stopped.

If you could ignore the smell and the constant chugging of generators, Wally thought, it really wasn't that bad. It was shockingly modern, even. He had no idea how they'd done it.

The cavernous room was at least, by Wally's uneducated estimation, three hundred feet in diameter, with a ceiling that ranged from twenty to sixty feet in height, though it was difficult to tell exactly. Dozens of bright billiard lamps dangled from the roof of the cavern. Below them, the space was lit brilliantly and evenly, but above them the heavy darkness gathered and hung like low clouds. The painted concrete floor was smooth and gray, marked with colored arrows, which pointed toward the tunnels that spiraled out from the central room.

Above the grinding of the generators, Wally heard music, though he couldn't tell where it was coming from. It was unlike anything he'd heard since he was quite young. There'd certainly been nothing like it performed publicly in recent years. It was sinister and driving, the vocalist sliding between a hiss, a snarl, and a bark. It wasn't what he would call "pleasant."

"What the hell are we hearing?" Wally asked.

Jack raised an eyebrow. "You like it? Not my cuppa shine, but it ain't been heard aboveground in over ten years. Some o' these folks seem to like it okay." He paused and listened. "This song here, in fact, is about Tupelo and so was banned nationwide three days after the Horribleness."

And with good reason, Wally thought but said nothing.

While leading Wally around the Hub, as he called it, Jack explained that most of the tunnels had been further excavated and renovated into office space, cooking areas, storage rooms, and a number of private living quarters. Wally stared around the Hub in what could only be called wonder. Faro Jack paused beside him, clearly proud of the effect it was having.

"I can see by the look in your eye that you're no longer so convinced I'm gonna plug you one and dump your carcass on the tracks somewheres."

"What?" Wally spat, shaking his attention back to his guide. "I—I never thought—"

"Oh, yes you did," Jack said. "But it's okay. It's understandable. Took some guts to come down here thinking that way, 'specially when you have a perfectly good bunker of your own up there."

"Yeah," Wally said, "but this down here—this—"

About a dozen people of various ages, sizes, and ethnic backgrounds were sitting at desks arranged neatly around the Hub, some working on computers, others using pencil and paper, still others bent, tools in hand, over discarded pieces of machinery. Another group in a far corner seemed to be building something that looked, from his vantage point, like an oversized refrigerator.

"Where," Wally asked, his eyes still trying to register everything, "I mean how... did you do this?"

"Well," Jack said, "you remember those old plans for a Second Avenue subway? Went on for decades, people talkin' an talkin' about it."

"Vaguely."

"City started talking about it, oh, 1912 or thereabouts. Then over the next hundred years they kept startin' an' stoppin' like a buncha stubborn mules. Dig a little bit, then crap out. Few years later, dig a little more. Right now you're under East Twenty-third Street—this was supposed to be a major hub for at least five lines. They got farther along than most people realize before the Horribleness made 'em ditch the whole project. Terrorists, don't you know." He paused a moment, looking around the room. "And I guess they were right. At least in their definition. Don't let their looks fool you. These Unpluggers are a far bigger threat to their control systems than any Australians in a fake flying saucer."

"But," Wally said, "how—how did you get this so... like this? It's almost... nice."

Jack laughed. "After we uncovered it and"—he paused, looking for the right word—"appropriated it, it didn't take as much as you'd reckon. Little spit an' polish, is all. An' a few generators. Rest came natural."

Wally followed as Jack, with that weird half-skip of his, began walking toward a cluster of desks.

"One thing I don't get," Wally said, still amazed by what he was seeing.

"What's that?"

"These people call themselves Unpluggers, but most all of them seem plugged in. You have electricity, lights, computers." He spotted a screen in the corner. "Even a four-way. I mean, how is this any different from up there, except that down here it's smellier and you have C.H.U.D.s?"

With a small grunt, Jack bent over and flipped the top off a green plastic cooler filled with ice. He plunged a meaty hand into the half-melted cubes and thrashed it about briefly before yanking it free again, now clutching two brown bottles between his knuckles. He held one out to Wally. "Want one?"

"What is it?"

"It's a beer. A damn sight bettern' that swill at McWing-Wang's too."

Wally took the bottle and considered it. There was no label. "You're serious? How'd you manage that?"

"We got a few chemists down here. A monk or two. It's not that tough. But in answer to your question, yeah we have computers. And electricity. But that four-way over there?" he nodded at the screen, upon which a smiling woman in an apron was whipping a giant ant for some reason (Wally recognized it as an ad for the Phase IV oil refinery). "It's really a one-way—we grab the signal, the signal comes in, but nothing goes back out. Same with the computers. Some of the tech boys down here rigged up a firewall ten years ahead of anything they've got up there."

"That's great, but I still don't get it. I thought you all came down here to get away from all that...I mean...I was expecting, I dunno, campfires and raggedy clothes. A collective farm or something. Lots of beets."

"Give it time," Jack said, twisting the cap off his bottle and dropping it with a plink into a nearby can. "That's sort of the goal. That's why we're here. But there's a lot of work to do first. And if you count dumpster diving and hydroponics, we got a little collective farming going on here already. But remember, *amigo,* there's nothing all that terrible about computers, per se. Very useful machines, sometimes. It's all a question of how they're bein' used and who's doin' the using. Like anything. Like hammers. Or guns."

He took a drink of his beer as Wally tried in vain to unscrew the cap. "So yeah, right now we got computers and lights. But if you take a look 'round, you'll see there ain't no communitainers, no minivids, no GPS chips on anyone. No VidLogs." He paused. "No, that ain't completely true, we do have a few down here but they're bein' retrofitted to become jamming devices."

"Wow," Wally said, finally getting the cap off his bottle, taking a few shreds of skin with it.

"Yeah, they're somethin'... or will be. Should have some more prototypes soon. We may not have much by way of rules down here—too many rules'll suck you dry—but nobody gets down here with any kind of electronics in their pockets or under their skins. A single GPS or minivid grab and they could geomap this place down to the square centimeter in a flash. If someone up there"—he pointed upward—"knew what they were looking for. We don't know that they do but it's a chance best left untaken."

Jack drained the bottle and cast it without looking over his shoulder. Much to Wally's amazement, the bottle arced through the air and clinked off the wall fifteen feet away, bouncing unbroken into a fifty-five-gallon barrel full of other empty bottles. Jack wiped his mouth with his sleeve.

"As for the four-way screen," he said, "it's very important, given what's goin' on down here, that we keep track of what's goin' on up there. Some o' these hombres ain't been aboveground since we came down here. If we didn't stay in touch, we might as well be C.H.U.D.s." He stopped and looked off toward a distant tunnel entrance. "An' who knows? Things don't change, a few generations down the line we may be, riding them gators around like slow, flat broncos. C'mon, lemme introduce you around to some o' these folk. they're . . ." His voice trailed off.

The broadcast had returned to the news and, though the volume was low, as they passed Wally could hear the anchor say, "*Talk show host Bernie Tschungle died this morning after plunging from a tenth-floor window at General Dynamics Memorial hospital in Los Angeles, less than a day before his scheduled release... Already thousands of mourning fans are gathering to leave teddy bears and candles in front of...*"

Jack stopped at a cluttered desk where a man in a plaid short-sleeved shirt was tapping furiously at a computer keyboard. Wally couldn't help but notice that the computer didn't seem to be on.

"Drew?" Jack asked gently. The man stiffened and spun in his chair, grabbing an empty coffee mug and clutching it to his chest as he did so. "What? What do you want?" His wide eyes were huge behind thick lenses.

"Drew, it's okay—I just wanted to introduce you to Wally Philco. He may be joining us."

Jack, Wally noticed, was suddenly articulating his words distinctly, even formally.

Drew looked Wally up and down suspiciously, then turned to Jack. "You sure he's... you know?"

"Yes, Drew," Jack said, sounding tired. "He's human." He

turned to Wally. "See, Drew has had some trouble with alien abduction in the past."

"Really," Wally said, trying to sound earnest. "I've... I've never met an abductee before. That's very interesting."

Apparently this was all the encouragement Drew needed. Jack tapped Wally on the shoulder and whispered, "I'm gonna go get another beer yonder. I'll be back in... a while."

Wally wasn't sure he liked the sound of that.

Drew, meanwhile, had turned back to his keyboard and blank screen and once more began typing. "Many years ago," he said, his voice flat as he stared down at the keys, "I started noticing that I was losing bits of... *time.* Sometimes an hour or two, sometimes whole days. Over the months it began to happen with greater frequency, and—and I had no idea what was going on. What's more, every time I came to, I was in my bed again. I had a splitting headache and I was nauseous. Plus there were empty liquor bottles all over the floor. All kinds. Gin, bourbon, wine. I had no idea where they'd come from. I went to see a few doctors, but they were all *quacks* and *liars,* you understand? They all had their own ridiculous theories concerning my condition, but I knew they were wrong. All wrong. So I did some research and it soon became patently obvious to me that I was being *abducted for alien experimentation.*"

Oh, my.

Drew stopped typing only long enough to glance over his shoulder to make sure Wally was still there and not making faces at him like those others had. Satisfied, he began typing and talking again. "The aliens spirited me away whenever they pleased—any time of the day or night. Then they would conduct their experiments on me and drink my alcohol. They live on methanol, you know. It's the only way they can breathe in our atmosphere."

"I...didn't know that," Wally said, trying to be polite and wondering why in the hell Jack had left him alone with this man. "So . . ." He wasn't sure if he should ask how the aliens managed when Neo-Prohibition kicked in. "Has moving down here helped?"

"For a while it did, yes," Drew said, the disappointment evident. "But they seem to have found me again." Wally glanced over at the barrel of empties, then down at the bottle he was holding, then began nervously looking for Jack. The yellow slicker and cowboy hat weren't hard to spot. He was crouching next to a woman and they appeared to be in the midst of a very serious discussion. Still, desperate to get away from the alien abductee, Wally wished Drew well, excused himself, and began carefully weaving his way through the desks toward Jack. He couldn't tell what these people were working on but they all seemed quite focused, whatever it was. Several of them, he noticed, had books on their desks. That in itself was odd. What was even more peculiar was that it was the same book—something called *The Capital of Pain.*

That sure doesn't sound good, he thought. It occurred to him again, looking at all the Unpluggers around the room, that if he were to remain here, it was entirely possible he'd end up in middle management.

At least they don't have cubicles, he thought.

"*Enough!*" a voice erupted from the far side of the Hub. "I call this meeting to order!"

A man in a black turtleneck and a thin-lapeled black jacket leaped from his chair and began pointing savagely at the screen in front of him. "*Look* at them!" he shouted "Brainwashed *imbeciles.* Can you laugh? Can you cry? Can you *think*? Is this—is *this* what they did to you? Is *this* how they tried to break you? In your heads must still be the remnants of a brain, in your hearts must still be the desire to be a human being again!"

He then returned to his seat and was silent. Wally, who had not moved from the moment the man began screaming, found Jack standing next to him.

"Don't mind him," he said. "He says his name's John Drake, but we're not sure if it is. Don't really matter, if that's what he wants. That's just a speech from an old television show. Pretty much everything he says comes from that show. Gotta say, though, of all his routines that one's pretty much my favorite." He paused and looked across the room to where Drake was now working peacefully. "I don't think we've gotten everything out of him yet—he used to be with CIALIS. He knows quite a bit he's not telling us. But he will."

It was beginning to dawn on Wally that, impressive a setup as it was, this Unplugger hideout might not be the place for him.

"Are you...are you sure this isn't just some kind of...madhouse?" he asked.

Jack gave him a comforting pat on the shoulder (though it was no comfort at all) and shook his head. "No, believe you me, that guy there—Drake—he's invaluable to us down here. Or will be. An' Drew over there, despite all appearances, is a brilliant engineer."

"With a serious drinking problem, it seems."

"Don't seem to affect his engineering skills none...maybe his social skills a little." He looked around the room. "There are more people here I want you to meet—especially Angelika—but I reckon you'll meet them in time. Not all these folks are moonpies." He paused. "Well, except maybe him."

Wally followed Jack's gaze to a far corner, where a man stood dressed head to toe in what appeared to be a skin-tight rubber suit. Gloves, boots, even his entire head was wrapped in black latex. His eyes were barely visible through hooded lenses and a long corrugated plastic breathing tube emerged from the middle of his face.

"His name's John Pye," Jack whispered. "You may or may not recognize it. Anyway, he won't touch anything with his bare skin. He's determined to prevent any of his DNA from getting away from him and landing on someone's database. He's never provided a sample to anyone, and never will. It's all trapped in there."

"What's he doing just standing there in the corner?" Wally wondered.

"Matter of courtesy. He hasn't bathed in four years—doesn't want his DNA goin' down the drain where it'd be free for the grabbin'. So as you can imagine . . ."

"I thought that smell was coming from the sewer."

Jack shook his head. "Sewer's got nothin' on John Pye. Now c'mon, we'll go to my quarters an' I'll lay out the whole shebang for you."

Wally was still thinking about John Pye. That was hardcore—far beyond anything he'd done, or even considered. "But," Wally asked, as Jack began walking away, "where does he, um...? "

Jack paused and looked back. "Shit, you mean? The less you know about it, the better. You'll find out when the time comes."

As they stepped around a pair of midgets (both of whom greeted Jack with smiles) and headed toward one of the side passages, Wally heard Drake shout behind them, "*Be seeing you!*"

Wally stopped and turned, half-waving out of reflex.

"Don't bother," Jack told him. "He doesn't really mean it." He stopped abruptly as they were passing a table where a young dark-haired woman in a red T-shirt was manipulating the innards of a dismantled minivid. "Oh," he said, a thought occurring to him. "Penelope here's an interesting case." Penelope stopped her work and looked up. Wally wasn't sure he liked the fact that Jack called her a "case."

"Penelope," Jack said, "this is Wally Philco. He may be joining us."

"Pleased to meet you," she said, reaching out to shake his hand. She seemed, by all initial appearances, to be the most normal person Wally had met since hopping the work train with Jack.

"Penelope here used to work for SoniCram Communications, in the R and D wing. She's been spearheading our communitainment signal jamming efforts." He turned to Wally. "Some of our early prototypes were a little too . . ."

"Intense," Penelope suggested.

"That's a good word for it, yeah," Jack said. "There were a few unavoidable accidents. So now Penelope's working on something a touch...milder. But still effective."

"Let's hope so," she said.

Wally considered the array of tiny minivid components spread across the table. There was that word "accidents" again.

"She's also a fugitive from justice."

"You all seem to be," Wally pointed out.

Jack gave him a look. "I guess you're right there, yeah."

"How I ended up here I don't exactly recall," Penelope said, gesturing with her microlaser soldering gun.

"Ah, but it's a good thing she did," Jack interjected. "She's been invaluable. Everyone here has been."

It was beginning to sound like a self-esteem camp for defectives, Wally thought. And again he wondered if, at least in part, that's exactly what it was.

The tunnel was unlike the one that brought them to the Unpluggers headquarters originally. The walls and floor were smooth and clean and white. Halogen panels installed overhead left it bright and untreacherous. Every few yards to either side of them were doors, which presumably opened on to private rooms. It was silent except for the humming of the lights and the occasional, distant rumbling of a vehicle aboveground.

"See?" Jack said as they walked. "A lot of these people are perfectly normal. They just found themselves in the kind of trouble that forced them to recognize how fucked up things had become, and that they had to get away. A lot of 'em might seem a touch... off, yeah. But they all got one thing in common. They're people who're determined to hold on to their lives, their personalities. Their freedoms. They've become, in one way or another, allergic to the twenty-first century."

Then, before Wally could respond, he launched into what sounded like a spiel as well rehearsed as Smitty Winston's.

"A lot of these people were activists, revolutionaries, whatall, holding protest marches back when they were still legal, speaking out against this or that war or bit of legislation. Mostly things that didn't affect them at all. We also have some people from the other end of the spectrum—tax protesters, libertarians, survivalists, folks from various domestic militia groups."

Wally looked at him but said nothing.

"After the Horribleness, when everything up there started goin' to hell, well, for a while none of 'em did anything. They believed what they were told—that the vids, the SUCKIE cards, the databases were for their own good. They were as scared as everyone else. When it started affecting them directly, though—when friends and neighbors began disappearing—a lot of them ended up down here, mostly to save their own hides. But that's normal. That's honest enough. You, though, Wally, you're a different breed. Different animal altogether. You believed too, I'm guessin'. But you have no background in this. You ain't a professional. You're a . . ."—he paused, trying to get the words just right—"an improvisational revolutionary. You're doin' this on accounta you really *believe* it, not 'cause you're supposed to. That's what makes you so important to the movement."

"Movement?"

"Whatever you wanna call it. Struggle, club, league, gang. Crew. Team. I don't care—you know what I mean."

There was an obvious question here that had remained unanswered. "What about you? Why are you down here? You get into some kind of trouble?"

"Me?" Jack asked, sounding surprised that someone had asked. "To be honest, I'm mostly in it for the revolutionary pussy."

Wally looked behind them. He could no longer see the tunnel entrance. Looking ahead, it seemed to continue on forever.

Jack stopped in front of a door and pushed it open, ducked his head to avoid knocking off his hat, and switched on the lights. Wally followed.

The room was bare except for two straight-backed chairs and a small wooden desk. The walls were white and featureless but for a framed photograph of a bald man with a tight, dour, birdlike face. He wore a pair of round, thick spectacles. Wally got the bad feeling again. He should've run when he had the chance, but when was that? And where would he run?

"Is…this my cell?" he asked, afraid he already knew the answer.

"*Hah!*" Jack bellowed, loud enough in the stark room to make Wally wince. "You still don't believe it, do you? You gotta get over that, *amigo.* You ain't been listenin'."

"I've got my doubts," Wally admitted.

"Yeah, well," Jack said, "as you'll note, there ain't no lock on the door. Ain't no locks anywhere. You wanna vamoose, go ahead. If you do, all I ask is that you don't report us. We're all in this together, see? And we're all after the same thing you are, however you care to chase it down." He cast his eyes to the floor and shook his head, still chuckling. "*Cell.*" He looked at Wally again, who seemed less than convinced. "No, this is not your cell. It's my room."

Wally looked around the barren space. "Not very comfy."

"I didn't come down here for comfy. I left all that behind a long time ago."

"Yeah, but," Wally asked, ignoring a clear opening to learn something about Faro Jack's story, "where do you sleep?" The room featured nothing even approaching a bed—no blanket on the floor, nothing.

"Oh. Well." Jack began fishing around in the pocket of his slicker. "I haven't slept in almost two years now."

Wally squinted at him. "You're making that up."

Jack pulled a small green bottle from his pocket and tossed it to Wally, who scrambled and nearly fell but caught it. "You ain't never heard of Orexamyaphin?"

Wally examined the bottle. The label told him little he could understand, but inside was a dry, flaky yellow substance.

"Without getting too technical, it's a powdered form of a brain chemical that regulates sleep. Snorta that and I'm fine for three days."

"Yeah," Wally said slowly, still examining the bottle. "I think I remember the ads for this now." Actually what he remembered was the jingle, "Sleep Is for Squares," which somehow found a rhyme for "Orexamyaphin." "But wasn't it pulled off the market a few years ago? They said it was dangerous and addictive. People were going insane." He gingerly handed the bottle back to Jack, who shrugged.

"I don't know 'bout any of that. All I know is that I snagged a buncha caseloads back when it came out, an' I ain't slept a wink since. Feel dandy too. Besides, you think about it, everything up there's dangerous and addictive, ain't it? Food. Words. Hell, *air* is dangerous and addictive. You should give it a try," he said, popping the plastic lid and tapping a few flakes onto the back of his dirty wrist. He held it out to Wally.

"Oh, no—no thank you," Wally said, raising a hand. "I actually look forward to sleeping whenever I can." Which reminded him that he'd barely slept in the past couple of days himself.

"All right, then," Jack said, sounding unsure, as if Wally were making a terrible and foolish mistake. "All the more for me." He held his wrist up to his nostrils and snorted sharply. He wiped his nose and checked his mustache to make sure he hadn't wasted any.

"All right, then, yes. Now... there. Take a seat." Jack pointed at one of the chairs while taking a seat himself and crossing his legs. "I'm gonna fill you in on what goes on here."

His voice, Wally noted, was suddenly a few octaves higher than it had been, and his accent, whatever it was, had grown thicker. His *r*'s were much more pronounced. The fake cowboy lingo had been fading away from the moment they'd arrived in the Hub.

"I still can't believe you thought this was your cell," Jack said as Wally lowered himself into the uncomfortable wooden chair. "*Hoo*-boy, that's a doozy."

Great. If he starts blabbing it to everyone, it'll be like high school all over again.

He turned his attention back to Jack, who seemed to be waiting for him to finish his thought.

Satisfied that Wally was refocused on the matter at hand, he began. "Unpluggers like these out here have been with us for a long time—at least since the eighteenth century, from the earliest days of the industrial revolution . . ."

As Jack provided a detailed and interminable history of various antitechnology movements through the ages, Wally let his mind wander. He liked diners an awful lot. He wished there was a diner down here. One of the old silver trailers, with a chrome and Formica counter and red leatherette stools and a can of Raid next to the ketchup. Waitresses named Flo and Rosie.

Several minutes into a mental tour of some of his favorite diners, he noticed that Jack wasn't talking anymore. In fact, he was staring at Wally, arms crossed, his expression both annoyed and hurt, like a middle school teacher who's had just about enough of the whispering and note passing.

"Well, I thought you'd be interested in knowing the background," Jack said, sounding just as hurt as he looked. "It's important. But since you obviously don't care, I won't waste your time anymore and cut to the chase."

Thank God.

"If only five or ten percent of the population started doing the same thing you did," Jack surmised, "they could take it all back. The whole fucking culture. But it looks like the situation up there"—he pointed toward the ceiling—"is what most people want. They wanna be told they're safe. They wanna be told what to do. If they wanted to get away from it, they could. Like you did. But they don't."

This was cutting to the chase? "Maybe they're afraid," Wally offered. "I was afraid the whole time. Terrified, even."

"Of *course* they're afraid. They're afraid because they've been told to be afraid. *But,*" Jack went on, "a few of us broke away."

Yeah, the crazy ones.

Jack uncrossed his legs and put his hands on his knees. "And together we can do something."

Still not terribly interested in anything calling itself a "movement," let alone one with a silly name, Wally figured he should at least be polite while he was here. "Okay," he asked, "so answer me this. Unpluggers—what's in it for me? I mean, I was perfectly happy alone in my house. What would make me want to give that up?"

"Food, maybe, for one," Jack offered. "Here, you wanna Slim Jim?" He reached into his shirt pocket and pulled out something that looked like a desiccated cigar wrapped in plastic. He held it out to Wally. "These haven't been on the market in years, but they're still really good."

Wally reached for it instinctively. He was awfully hungry. "What is it?"

"It's almost real meat. Try it."

Suspicious as he still was about this whole arrangement, Wally nevertheless took the Slim Jim, unwrapped it, and, with some effort, tore off a hunk of the withered brown stick with his teeth. He began chewing. He hadn't had real meat in years, and although this wasn't even close to what he remembered it was still something. Hell of a lot better than soy roast.

"Apart from that," Jack said, "we do have certain connections. If you decide you wanna continue living on the surface, we could arrange to get you a new SUCKIE card, modify your irises and fingerprints to scan different—even arrange for a face transplant, if you were interested in goin' that far. It would cost you, but you'd have a completely different identity. Meantime, your old identity would fade away."

Wally continued chewing that first hunk of the Slim Jim. "I already thought of that. New identity or not, I'd still be dealing with everything I was trying to get away from, right? I mean, PROTEUS X would open a new SUCKIE file for this new identity."

"Pretty much, yeah. Plus you'd hafta memorize a new SUCKIE number."

Wally grimaced, in part from the prospect, but also on account of his jaw muscles, which were growing sore. "Took me almost four years to get it down last time."

"On the bright side," Jack said, "it would take a little while before PROTEUS X started to get a bead on you, and in the meantime you could be much more careful with the information you handed out. Look," he said, "I'm not tryin' to edge you one way or a'tother here. Just layin' out the realities. None of this'll be easy."

"No, then," Wally shook his head. "That's exactly what I was trying to escape, all that. I don't want to worry about who's watching me, or why. I just want to be able to go about my business in my own way."

Jack took a deep breath and recrossed his legs. "All right, fair enough. Understandable. You wanna get out of the city? We can help with that too. We've had pretty fair luck with the old PATH tunnels. Getcha into Jersey, anyway. After that, you'd have to take it from there on your own."

Wally shook his head again. "Getting out of here just to go to Jersey? I don't think so . . . I'm guessing driving or flying would be out of the question."

"'Less you wanna new file started. You'd pretty much hafta hoof it, yeah."

Wally thought about this. "Are things out there really any better than they are here?"

Jack shrugged. "Can't honestly say, but I got my doubts. Mostly just highways, chain stores, and DOD checkpoints. It would mean spending the rest of your life duckin' and runnin', in hopes you'd find somethin' better. Maybe in the woods, if you can find 'em. Or what's left of the desert."

"Which I'd be doing here anyway." He had no interest in living in the woods or the desert.

"Aboveground, yeah. 'Fraid so."

Wally looked at the framed picture of the bald man, then back to Jack, who stared at him calmly, waiting. "I think I'll stay in town, then. My memory of this place before the Horribleness may be getting as fuzzy as everyone's but I do have scraps. I know it was better. And despite all that's happened, as rotten as things have become, I still love it here. For some godforsaken reason." He let out a heavy breath. "If those are my only options, then I guess I'm left with a choice of going back to my house and making a go of it there—"

"You realize, of course," Jack interrupted, "that everything you tore out of the walls there has prob'ly been replaced already."

Wally's shoulders dropped. "You're kidding." That had taken weeks, and he couldn't imagine doing it again.

"Nossir. They keep mighty good files, as you know. They know when somethin's gone a little cattywampus."

It was sounding more and more hopeless. "Aw, hell," he said.

"Yup. 'Sides, let's be honest, you go back up there, it's only a mattera time before you get caught and sent to a camp. One way or another, they're gonna getcha. You know that."

Wally did know that, though until now he'd refused to admit it to himself. As he sat there, something else was beginning to occur to him. Something he hadn't paused long enough to notice before, confounded as he was by this underground world. Apart from the hum of the lights, the chugging of the generators, and the occasional distant rumblings from the traffic above, it was *quiet* down here. With the exception of one or two of them, the people spoke in normal tones—and to each other. They didn't interact with the world through an intermediary vidscreen of some kind. Best of all, there were no advertisements exploding in his head every twenty minutes, or screaming at him as he walked down the street. He could actually think normally down here without having to anticipate when the next ad for an antiseptic gel or a software upgrade was going to crop up.

And there were no strollers.

Maybe it wasn't such a bad option after all.

"You know, I've been thinking," Jack said, breaking into Wally's surprisingly comforting musings. "Surveillance is just a form of intimidation. Even a fake vid can be as effective as—"

Oh, here we go again. Where's Ivan when I need him? "Look," Wally said, trying to head off another history lecture, "you've hinted that you have some sort of plan or project or something going on down here. What's that all about?"

"Does this mean you're considerin' signin' on?"

Wally offered an uncertain frown. "Can't say yet, really. But my options anyplace else seem mighty limited. And doomed."

Jack smiled and stood. "I'm tickled to hear you say that. I mean, not the 'doomed' part, o' course, but that you might consider stayin'. We could really use you. I mean really, *really* use you. An' I'll tell you why... an' I'll answer your question. C'mon, let's go back to the Hub. Watch your head." Jack ducked through the doorway back out into the tunnel. Wally, who had no need to duck, followed. He was not looking forward to another long walk. More than anything, he wished he could take a nap. Just a quick one. He tore off another bit of the Slim Jim.

"Now," Jack said, as they headed back the way they had come, "our mission is very simple. This"—he spread his arms—"is no way for people to live. It just ain't *natural.* Who wants to live with C.H.U.D.s, right? Better'n most folks up there, maybe, but still. They're C.H.U.D.s. Only way you'd end up down here is if there's been some horrible disaster up there."

"There has," Wally reminded him. They were walking slowly.

"Well, yeah, exactly, which is why we're down here. But unlike, oh, a nuke or a plague or a massive chemical attack—or maybe an alien invasion or somethin'—this is a problem that can be easily solved."

Wally glanced at him. "Easily?" Getting that implant out of his scalp hadn't exactly been a walk in the park. And neither had that walk in the park.

"Okay," Jack admitted. "Maybe *easily* is pushin' it some. Ain't gonna be easy. Way we see things, we got two choices. We can hide down here, worryin' about the C.H.U.D.s, worryin' about bein' found out. Cowerin' like whipped hounds. Or we can fight back."

"So... you've chosen the latter, I take it." *I am doomed wherever I go,* he thought.

"Our goal is to move back up there, yeah. But we'll only do that after the machine's been busted up but good, the power structure brought down completely. When CIALIS an' DOD're gone."

Wally rolled his eyes. "And your group here is planning on doing that."

"Yup," Jack said, his tone almost glib. "We're taking the surface back. We're gonna roll back the clock a little bit."

Right, Wally thought. *The headlines'll read Lunatic Fringe Commandos Conquer City. Yeah, good luck to you there, chum.*

He stopped. "Forgive me there, Jack, but don't you think that's a little . . . much? I mean . . . you've been up there. And these people down here . . . Drew? Or that other one? They're . . ." He didn't want to say anything rude, but *damn.*

Jack nodded his head sadly. "I know. And for years it's been clear it was just a pipe dream, somethin' to keep our lips flappin'. But now things're different."

"Jack," Wally said, figuring the best way to say it was to just say it. "I think the idea of this group trying to fight what's up there is really stupid, I don't care what your plan is. I'm sorry. It's delusional. It's suicidal."

Jack kept walking, head down, looking at his feet. "Could be you're right. But tell me this—is it any stupider or more delusional than destroying your own house to get away from them?"

He might've had a point there.

"Down here at least you'll have friends who'll keep an eye out for you. You'll have food and you'll have a place to wash your clothes."

Wally looked down at himself. His shirt and pants were still filthy from the train ride. He hadn't even had a chance to wash his hands.

They continued walking back to the Hub, which still seemed to be some ways away. After a minute of silence, Wally finally asked, "So... what... *is*... this secret weapon of yours?"

"Oh." Jack said, apparently having been distracted. "Sorry. It's *you.*"

Figuring he couldn't have heard that correctly, Wally kept walking but said nothing, hoping Jack would go on to explain what *ewe* or *Yoo* or *U* stood for. Or maybe that was it—maybe Yoo was the name of some Asian Unplugger he hadn't met yet.

After another five steps without further explanation, Wally decided to risk it, hoping beyond hope that his guess was right.

"So who is this Yoo? Some kind of scientist or something?"

" 'Fraid not," Jack said. "Unless you have a degree I don't know about. See, we've been talking about this for years. We had this setup down here but nothin' more. Just idle talk like you find in any revolutionary group. Commies, white supremacists, black militants, whatever—talk, talk talk. Big plans that never get realized. But you, *amigo,* you may not believe it, but you're the leader they've all been waitin' on."

Now he knew for certain that Jack was psycho.

"Excuse me?"

"Yup. I knew you wouldn't believe it."

"No, no, no, no, no—it's not a matter of not believing it... it's a matter of it being really *dumb.* I mean, I don't even know what you're talking about. I thought you were the leader."

"Me?" Jack asked, surprised himself. "Hell no, nothing' like it. I'm just a recruiter. Bit of an organizer. Supply manager. Jack-of-all-trades. You're the guy we've been looking for. The one who had the guts to do it alone, for your own reasons. Because you *believed.* Keeper of the flame."

Wally had stopped walking. He didn't know what this was supposed to be, but whatever it was he sure didn't like it.

"No, uh-uh. I don't have any flame. This ain't—"

"You're their hero, Wally," Jack cut in, stepping closer. "And there's nothing you can do about that. Accept it. You've taken it further than anybody—and you could do the same for all of us." He paused. "I couldn't tell you any of this, understand, until I was sure you were stayin' on."

"But what about Pye? He's a lot crazier than I ever was. The man, for godsakes, has saved all his DNA!"

"Oh, he's good, sure," Jack agreed, trying to coax Wally to continue walking, "but to be honest, he's kinda self-righteous, and a little short on people skills. Plus he smells really, really bad."

Up ahead, Wally—whose brain at this point had gone all fuzzy—heard John Drake's voice shouting at his invisible oppressors again.

"*Why don't you put us all into solitary confinement and you'll get what you're after and be done with it?*"

Wally started to say something, started to protest the insanity—no, the sheer mind-numbing idiocy—of the proposal before him. He was about to remind Jack how badly he'd bungled it up there (by Jack's own admission) but stopped. Instead, he popped the remaining hunk of the leathery Slim Jim into his mouth and slowly began to chew.

TEN

Margie felt a warm and comforting twitter in her left ear, the sound of a dozen chickadees in springtime harmony. Every time a call or an ad came in, she was reminded of Wally. Not that she was hoping to hear from him. She wasn't. Instead, she was reminded that no matter how many times she explained it to him, he stubbornly refused to learn how to turn the volume of his Earwig down to a comfortable level. It was almost as if he was looking for an excuse to jump and yelp every time it went off. The silly ass was like that with so many devices, always refusing to learn how to use machines to their full potential. Instead he'd shake his head and complain that they had already overcomplicated the simplest tasks.

She flipped up the minivid and read the message.

Contact Unknown
Image Unavailable

"Oh no," she groaned quietly, convinced it was him, finally. Except for that one call, she hadn't spoken to him since she'd left, and according to Whit things weren't going very well at the house. She sure wasn't in any mood to talk to him now. As the commercials played through, she began concocting excuses that would allow her to disconnect as quickly as possible. Having no image connection was a help that way—she could be anywhere other than where she was—namely, sitting on the couch in her Gravesend apartment, making video doodles.

"Yes?" she said, as the closing notes to the Takanawa Transportation Imperative's theme faded to silence. She could hear her own hesitation.

"Ms. Philco?" asked a man who didn't sound a thing like Wally.

Oh God, they found his body.

"Not exactly, but... yes?"

"Very good then. Ms. Philco, we've been having a difficult time reaching your husband Wallace, and we were wondering if you could help us."

That's odd. So they haven't found the body yet.

"I'm sorry. I'm not exactly sure where you'd find him right now." No need to get too personal, especially when you have no idea who you're talking to. "May I ask why you're trying to find him?"

"That's not important," the man said tersely. "Would you happen to know why he wouldn't be responding to his communitainment implant?"

"I . . ." she began, "really can't say. Wally—Mr. Philco—has never been terribly adept with machines. Certainly not upgrades. Perhaps his is due."

"Please, Ms. Philco," the man said, his voice growing more insistent, "do you have any way of contacting him yourself? It's imperative that we reach him."

"If you could give me some idea what this is all about . . ."

"No, that's not important," he said. "But we do need to reach him."

The dread began to creep into her chest. Not a terrible dread. Just the usual "oh what has that big dummy done this time?" dread.

"I'm sorry, but I really can't help you. To be honest, I'm not sure where he is myself."

The voice in her ear began sliding from insistent to threatening. "Ms. Philco, it's worth noting that a Good Citizen would tell us what he or she knows in the case of an urgent matter like this. Anything else might be considered complicity."

Margie didn't like the implications of that one bit. "I'm *sorry,*" she repeated. "If I knew anything, I would tell you. But I don't. Like I said, if I knew why you were looking for him I might possibly be able to make a guess, but I honestly don't know. I haven't spoken to him in weeks now." Figuring things would be easier if she laid it out, she said, "We . . . no longer live together."

There was a long silence. Long enough for Margie to start worrying what kind of trouble she herself might be getting into.

She listened closely and could still hear the man breathing on the other end, and the light tapping of fingertips on plastic keys.

"All right, yes," he said at last. "That checks out. But I do need to ask you—should you have any contact with him in the near future, please tell him that it is urgent he contact us immediately."

"Should I hear from him, yes, I will," Margie said. "But... who should I tell him to call, and how can he reach you?"

"I cannot divulge those specifics, ma'am, I'm sorry."

"You—" she began, then stopped. "Okay."

"In the meantime, Ms. Philco, I was wondering if I might be able to interest you in a new time-share condo development near Boca Raton? If I do say so myself, the resort is really quite spectacular—trees, sunshine—and let me emphasize that all the stories you may have been hearing about the chemical waste treatment plant down there are completely unfounded."

It was late. Or early. One of the two—Wally had no idea which. Realizing that he needed a little time to seriously consider whether or not he could commit to leading a ragtag army of revolutionary Luddite nerds in a life-or-death struggle against the forces of evil (even thinking that phrase made Wally feel stupid), Jack had suggested that he return aboveground for a while, see if there was anything he wanted to pick up in his house, then return if he decided he was up to the task.

Before leaving the Hub he was able to wash his clothes, get a half-decent meal, and take a nap.

The original route he'd been shown to the Unpluggers' hide-out had been more ruse than anything, a means of keeping any unexpected intruders away and of confounding any visitors who chose not to join up. When it came time to leave, Jack led Wally through the Unpluggers' secret exit—a hole cut through the floor of an abandoned warehouse along the FDR Drive. Then he sneaked him back on a train to Brooklyn.

"As Davy Crockett said," Jack counseled before sending him on his way, "just be sure you're right—then go ahead on."

Wally dodged from shadow to shadow back to his house, hoping to avoid any unexpected DOD patrols, neighbors, and, if possible, Whit's vids. Nobody was outside, which made things easier.

Keeping a wary eye over his shoulder, Wally reached into his pocket and pulled out his keys. Trying to minimize the jingling, he slid one into the lock, turned it slowly, and let himself inside.

He moved silently up the darkened stairs. He couldn't think of anything he might need from the house, especially given the shape it was in, but he still felt it was best to look around. It was his house, after all.

As he reached the top of the stairs, he removed the flash-light dangling from his belt and switched it on. It was an old-fashioned battery-operated model Jack had lent him and the beam was weak. Even as he watched, it began its dispirited fade from white to yellow to dull brown. He switched it off again.

No matter, he figured. He knew the house well enough. He could just spend the night there and take a look around in the morning when daylight was on his side. He wasn't sure what else he might want, but he thought he'd definitely grab the blanket. You never know when you might need a blanket. He'd certainly also grab the cash from under the floorboards.

Why was he even thinking this way already? This was his home—he'd worked hard for it. Worked hard to clean it out too. He didn't just want to abandon it. And lord knows he wasn't about to lead anyone—ragtag or otherwise—into any sort of battle. That was crazy talk. He didn't know anything about these people, except that most of them were whackjobs. Jack made a lot of speeches but in the end he was still talking about alien abductees and a guy in a rubber suit.

He never wanted to be part of any group. He knew that from the start. The Math Club fiasco in tenth grade had taught him that much. Joining a movement or gang or whatever it was down there wouldn't be all that different from being out here—people around you all the time. There'd probably be office politics to deal with. Who needs that? This was his home. This was the life he'd chosen. Hero or no hero.

He didn't know what the hell he wanted to do.

As he crunched across the plaster-strewn floor, he heard something—something that didn't belong there. He stopped, heart suddenly racing.

He touched the ergonomic vinyl button on the flashlight's long handle but didn't press it.

"Hello?" he whispered. There was no response. Whatever it was he'd heard wasn't there anymore.

The streetlights outside the windows in the front room provided enough illumination for Wally to take at least a cursory look around.

There was something in the corner. The shadow of some lumpy object that hadn't been there when he'd left.

He pointed the flashlight and pressed the button with no idea what to expect, and not really ready for anything.

The face revealed by the beam was pale and bloated, lolling to the right shoulder, eyes closed, mouth half open. It was wearing a hat.

"Bingham?" Wally said aloud.

He quickly swung the dying beam around the room to look for Hawkey. Finding nothing, he swung it back to Bingham's still body.

He took a few steps forward. His knees were growing weak and his hands were beginning to tingle and sweat. This didn't look good at all. He couldn't see any blood but that didn't mean anything. "Bingham?" he asked again. This was the last thing he was expecting, and the last thing he needed. He couldn't call the hospital. Couldn't call DOD. Couldn't call anybody. Couldn't leave the body here either. Maybe he could drag him outside and throw him in Whit's garden. But the vids would see him, and it would all be over. Maybe the basement. Yeah, that might do. Dig a hole, get some quicklime.

He felt like he was gonna puke. Jack might know how to deal with something like this—he seemed the type. And Margie, well... no, he probably shouldn't call Margie. Some of the people she worked for, though, they'd know what to do. Their annual budgets probably set aside ten percent for body disposal.

"*Bingham*?" he repeated, trying not to panic.

He nudged one of the insurance dick's legs with his shoe and the corpse snorted once, shook his head, and opened his eyes. Both men screamed, Wally jumping backward and Bingham trying to push himself through the wall, knocking his hat to the ground in the process.

"*Bingham*?" Wally asked, his voice now awfully high-pitched.

It took Bingham a second to focus his bleary eyes on the shadowed figure on the other side of the dark room. "Philco?" he asked uncertainly, his voice thick. "That you?"

In an instant Wally's terror had shifted to anger. Suddenly he found himself regretting that the fat tub o' lard wasn't a corpse after all. "Don't you guys ever give up? First you follow me around, then you break into my *house*?"

Bingham was still confused. This was no way to wake up. "Didn't break in," he said, trying and failing to stifle a yawn, which left his words unintelligible.

"What?" Wally asked.

"I didn't break in," he said, pulling his knees up against his belly before letting his legs slide out in front of him again.

"What are you talking about?" Wally fumed. "You're sitting in my—" Then he remembered something. He looked around the room again. "Where's Hawkey?"

Bingham, who was stifling another yawn, didn't answer immediately, and Wally yelled again, "Where's Hawkey?" He turned and charged into the kitchen, thinking he'd find him in there or in the bedroom but, after colliding with the kitchen table in the darkness and nearly flipping over it, he stopped, groaning and sucking air through his teeth.

Brushing the plaster dust from his jacket and pants, Bingham entered the kitchen to find Wally bent over the table. "Dude," he said. "You okay? You gotta be more careful."

Wally groaned again.

"Look, if you'd given me a sec to answer, I coulda told you Ray's not here. He quit. He quit, then I got fired."

"I find that," Wally said through gritted teeth as he attempted to push himself upright, "very hard to believe."

"Your neighbor let me in," Bingham said after both men decided it would be more civilized to sit at the kitchen table to try to figure out between them just what the hell was going on.

Wally was no longer as shocked or dismayed by the situation as he could—or perhaps even should—have been. Given the state of things, he had to admit he wasn't that surprised at all to find someone in his house. That it turned out to be a sleeping Bingham was almost a comfort.

Still, though.

"You're saying *Whit* let you into my house? How the hell'd he do that?"

Bingham was looking around the kitchen, squinting through the darkness. He seemed nervous and distracted. "Your place wired?" he asked, leaning in close.

"To be honest," Wally confessed, "I don't know anymore."

"In that case, I don't think I should say any more here. You know a clean place? I mean someplace you're sure is clean?"

The first thing that came to mind was the Hub. But he didn't think it would be wise to bring a sort-of detective down there. Then he thought of Seamus McWingWang's. With all that was said there, the place had to be clean like Jack promised.

"Yeah," he said, "but I'm not sure when they open. I don't even know what time it is." He glanced up at the wall. The clock hadn't been replaced yet, but that didn't necessarily mean anything.

Bingham shifted over to one haunch, pulled his communitainer out of his pocket, flipped up the screen, and tapped a few buttons. "It's almost six-thirty now," he said.

Wally didn't like the idea of having a communitainer in the house, but he guessed it was useful in this case. "A.m. or p.m.?"

"It's morning," Bingham said, closing it and shoving it back in his pocket. "That help?"

"Some," Wally said, not wanting to mention McWingWang's by name, just in case. "I think we have a few hours yet."

As he sat there, no longer upset by the intrusion, but not understanding it either, Wally felt the fatigue of the past few days—maybe it had been only one day—catching up with him. Tromping through tunnels, hopping on trains, finding people in his house. It was all too much. Adrenaline was a remarkable drug, but now he needed some rest. That nap at the Unpluggers' hideout had been nice but not enough.

Hideout, he thought. *I now know people with a hideout.*

"All right," he told the chubby man across from him. "You're free to stay. In fact, I wish you would, because I need some answers. But right now I'm gonna get some rest. The water still works, sort of."

"Thanks, I know," Bingham said.

Wally pushed himself back from the table and headed into the front room, where he hoped Bingham hadn't been making a mess of his blanket.

• • •

"Naw, believe me, your neighbor's a good egg," Bingham was saying after the two of them had settled in at a table at McWing-Wang's. The walk over had been uneventful, the streets crowded enough that even in their unfashionable attire nobody had given them a second look.

Bingham had a double bourbon (or something approximating bourbon) in front of him. Wally, who was feeling a little shaky still, had decided to stick with water. "He told me you'd moved out."

"Well, I hadn't."

"Yeah, obviously—I'm just telling you what he told me. What I was working with."

It was shortly after noon, and McWingWang's was jumping—at least as much as a dozen people in suits and tunics staring into small screens and mumbling to themselves could constitute "jumping." Behind the glowing bar, Ivan was pouring a river of illicit alcohol.

"You still haven't told me how he got into my place and, more importantly, why you wanted to get in there yourself. I thought you guys had enough to get LifeGuard off my back."

On the four-way in the corner, the announcer was saying, "*... starlet Ovaltine Sanchez died of a brain hemorrhage earlier this morning after a freak signal surge caused her communitainment implant to explode. This is the twelfth such incident in recent weeks, but by far the most tragic, as the seven-year-old was about to—*"

Bingham took a sip and screwed up his face. With eyes squeezed shut he gasped, "We did. Pretty much, anyway... *whew,* that stuff's *harsh.* Been a while." He took another small sip and set the glass down. “We filed our report, then out of the blue Ray decides to walk.”

“So then they asked you to trail him,” Wally guessed, but Bingham shook his head.

“No, to be honest I think they were glad to be rid of him. And that’s why I was canned a few days later. See, they got this new thing. Each new policyholder gets a chip. Not just a GPS chip but one that collects biodata too—heart rate, blood pressure, muscle exertion, EEG, all that. About forty, fifty different things. Richter Dynamics is putting it out.”

Should’ve seen it coming, Wally thought.

“And that pretty much does away with any need for us. They keep track of the data, they can see right there whether a claimant’s faking it or not. They also found out it was cheaper and easier—and, to be honest, more reliable—to arrange for access to SUCKIE files and VidLog entries whenever there’s any question.”

“What a glorious time to be alive,” Wally murmured. Then, looking up at Bingham, “So what’s Hawkey doing these days? You in touch?”

“Yeah,” Bingham said, contemplating the glass. “That’s the kicker, see? After all these years tracking down insurance cheats, learning all their tricks, he decided he’d be able to make a killing in the insurance fraud racket.”

“Wow,” Wally said, impressed.

Outside, a DOD armored personnel carrier screamed past, sirens blaring. Everyone in the bar froze, poised to bolt if the vehicle stopped outside. Once the siren faded they relaxed.

“Back to the matter at hand,” Wally continued. “You’re out of a job. You're not following me. So how is it you managed to get my neighbor to let you into my house?"

Bingham looked at his bourbon for a moment. "Ah, that," he said, embarrassed, as if he'd been asked where the faded tattoo on his neck had come from. "That's a pretty funny story, actually. See, that job was *everything* to me. I don't have a wife or kids or anything, and after they canned me I wasn't in the mood to start looking for work right away. Unmutual attitude, maybe, but I couldn't help it. Wish I'd known about this place. This is great." He looked around at the crap on the walls. "So I just start walking around all over the place. Just walking. And then one day I find myself in your neighborhood. Not sure why, really—maybe it was nostalgia or something. Scene of the last case, y'know? And so I'm walking around and your neighbor—"

"Whit Chambers."

"Yeah, Whit. He stops me, 'cause he's seen me around the neighborhood but he knows I don't live there. He was suspicious at first, I guess, but we start chatting. He turns out to be a friendly sort. Plus he's the first person, really, that I talked to since getting fired, so I give him the whole story. And he's real excited, see, to find out I was a detective, 'cause I guess he always wanted to be something like that."

"Something like that, yeah," Wally interjected without elaborating.

Bingham rolled on, oblivious to the sneer in Wally's tone. "So we're standing in his front yard for a long time, and he tells me how you moved out and the place was empty. I mean, I know now it wasn't, but that's what he told me. And he says that he'd been letting himself in to set up some equipment—security equipment—to keep an eye on his wife."

"Whoa, wait a second," Wally interrupted, nearly doing a spit take. "Did he say...how *long* he'd been doing this?"

Bingham shrugged. "Uh-uh, just that you'd moved out a week or two ago, and when it didn't look like anyone else was moving right in he decided to set up a little station in there."

"I see," Wally said, glad now that he hadn't been drinking. Still, he could feel the nausea working again. He hadn't seen or heard anything, but Jesus, it looked like his decision to stay in the house or return to the Unpluggers was being made for him. Or maybe he didn't have to return down there. Maybe he could find another place—like that warehouse.

Behind him, he heard the front door creak open and the unmistakable clink of metal and bump of small rubber wheels across the threshold.

"*Raus!*" Ivan roared from behind the bar. Wally's head snapped around to see the bartender pointing to the open door, his stubby finger trembling with rage. "We don't need you in here."

Wally turned further, in time to see the front half of the stroller being pulled back outside before the door slammed shut.

He'd never seen anything like that before—especially not in Brooklyn. It was astonishing, really, and it filled his heart with hope. He'd never seen strollers prevented from entering any establishment. Nobody told the Brigade where they could or couldn't go. Hell, maybe he could just stay here in McWing-Wang's. Set up a cot in the back or something.

"Yeah, so anyway," Bingham was saying, though Wally was suddenly finding it difficult to concentrate. "It started getting dark, and with the curfew I said I wasn't sure if I was gonna get home in time—"

That caught Wally's attention. "Curfew?"

"Yeah." Bingham said, looking mildly surprised. "Didn't you get the bulletin a couple days ago? Curfew at sundown. Come to think of it, I knew there was something weird about you showing up last night. You didn't know about this?"

"Nope," Wally said. "But that's not a big issue. So it's sundown and you don't know whether you'll get home."

"Right," Bingham said, before draining his glass. The naturally rosy glow in his cheeks had spread to the rest of his face. "So I say this to Whit, and he suggests I crash at your place. Not knowing, of course, that it was still your place. He seemed hurt, by the way, that you left without saying good-bye."

"That's because I never left."

Bingham's eyes were slightly glazed. "Oh yeah," he said. "Anyway, so he let me in and there you go. I'm not homeless, but I didn't want to be mistaken for one, y'know? They'd send me off to Giants Stadium and lock me in with the rest of 'em... I hear stories. They're eating each other in there now. That's what I hear, anyway."

There was a moment of silence between them, though they were surrounded by muttering and the endless newscast on the four-way. At last Wally said, "That wasn't a very funny story."

Bingham looked hurt. "Yeah, well...these've been kinda rough days. You take what you can get."

There was something about him, something at once pathetic and unexpectedly earnest. More pathetic, though. He was waiting for the tears to well up in the ex–detective's eyes. For a moment Wally wondered if there might not be a place for him underground. Then he changed his mind.

Another DOD personnel carrier screamed past outside, heading in the same direction as the first.

"Can I ask you a question, Philco?"

"I guess," Wally said.

"I believe that a man's business is his business," Bingham said, momentarily forgetting what he had done for a living, "but I gotta ask. Your house, what happened there? It's in some…well, I mean, you know. Now I can see why you didn't invite us in that day."

Even though bringing him to McWingWang's might've been tip-off enough, Wally wasn't about to start laying it all out now. He'd just say he was making some renovations and hope this whole thing wouldn't lead up to Bingham asking if he could move in for a while. Maybe he'd buy him another drink first and duck out when Bingham's head hit the table. Wait—no, that wouldn't work—

Hearing the door open behind him again, Wally prepared to dive under the table, convinced for a moment it was the Brigadoon back in search of vengeance. Before hitting the floor he turned and looked just as Carlotta Bain walked into the bar. Behind her through the closing door, he saw eight DOD operatives jog past in full riot gear, rottweilers and rifles at the ready.

He snapped back around in his chair, eyes wide.

"What, the troops?"

"No," Wally said tightly.

Bingham, unable to ignore the look on Wally's face, glanced toward the bar. "You know her?"

"Not anymore," Wally said.

"Oh, man, is that your ex?"

"No, I—wait, did I ever tell you I was married?"

Bingham merely scratched his ear, then tapped the brim of his hat.

"Oh…right." Wally's eyes darted toward Carlotta, who was standing at the bar. He was wondering how to do this subtly. "Can I get you another drink?" he asked Bingham.

"Oh, I'll go," Bingham said, beginning to push himself to his feet. Wally reached out and grabbed his wrist.

"*No.*" Then, regaining his composure, "No…it's okay, really. You got that first round." Before Bingham could object he grabbed both glasses (coming dangerously close to dropping them) and carried them to the bar, next to where Carlotta stood.

He set the glasses down and paused, trying to work up his nerve. Gone was the Fashionist garb she'd been wearing the last time he saw her. She was once again wearing a baggy brown sweater, psychedelic flower print pants, and sandals.

"Um, miss?" he ventured.

"Yes?" she asked absently, not turning around. She was trying to catch Ivan's eye and wasn't terribly curious about some cretin trying out his bar moves.

"Carlotta?"

"*Yes?*" she repeated, mildly perturbed, but turning to look at him. It took a moment to register, but when it did her eyes widened. "Barry!" she erupted, wrapping him in a sudden and fierce bear hug.

"*Wally,*" he gasped into her shoulder, his hands floating just shy of her back, unsure whether or not he should touch her.

"Wally!" she corrected herself, pulling away, still holding him by both arms and beaming. "It's so good to see you."

"I...um," he said, not expecting that at all. He'd only wanted to apologize for bothering her on the street corner, but *this*...In the back of his mind he regretted not having taken a big whiff of her hair when he had the chance.

"My God," she said, "this is such good fortune. You've got to stay a minute, can you? Have a drink with me. Are you here alone?"

It was all quite surprising. He looked back to the table where Bingham sat, staring, waiting for his drink. "Um, no. No, not really," he said. He turned to face the bar and slid onto one of the hand-shaped stools. Her hand was still on his shoulder as she did the same. When Ivan noticed them at last, Carlotta held up two fingers but said nothing. He nodded and began pouring two beers.

"I've been hoping to run into you ever since that day on the corner," she said.

"Yeah, uh," Wally said, embarrassed, his eyes downcast, "I'm sorry about that. I want to apologize, see, I—"

She was already waving a hand at him. "No, I'm the one who should apologize. I wanted to talk to you. I really did. But I couldn't."

"I understand," Wally said. He was used to people being too busy to talk to him.

"No, I'm not sure you do. It's a long story. Just accept my apology and know I'm very happy to see you now."

Wally could feel himself blush and looked down at the glowing Lucite bar. As he did, his eyes drifted over her wrist. The scar was gone.

Carlotta noticed him noticing. She leaned in toward his ear and whispered, "It was makeup. Look." She tilted her head away and pulled the blonde strands back from her ear. That scar was gone too. She let the hair fall back into place and winked. "Shhh," she said. "Special effects."

Ivan appeared in front of them, setting two tall beers on the bar. This time the glasses matched, even if they weren't exactly clean. "Carlotta, my sweet," he said. "A pleasure as always." Then turning to Wally, "And you... yes, you're getting there."

Unsure what to make of that, Wally thanked him and began reaching for his pocket, where he had a few bills left.

" 'S'on her," Ivan said, nodding at Carlotta and returning to the far end of the bar, where a swarthy character in a black satin SMEG/MA jacket was waiting.

"I'm guessing," Carlotta said while waiting for the foam on her beer to settle, "that if you're here, then you've met Faro Jack."

Wally wasn't sure if that made perfect sense or not, but by now very little surprised him anymore (except Carlotta walking into that particular speakeasy at that particular moment). He cast a quick glance around the bar. Apart from the SMEG/MA officer, he couldn't tell who was official and who wasn't. Most of them were wearing severe professional darks.

"Are you saying that all these people," he gestured, "are friends of Jack's?"

"Oh, no, of course not—"

"Yeah, I hope not," Wally said. "There was a SPOOK agent in here the other day—Ivan pointed her out. All sorts of security types. If they were friends of Jack's too, I wouldn't know what to . . ." For all his suspicions of everyone else, and even his suspicions about Jack, he'd still said way too much to someone he hardly knew. But Jack, he had to admit, had so far done everything he said he was going to do, and Wally hadn't been arrested. Here he sat with Carlotta, so there you go. Maybe things were looking up.

"This sort of crowd's what you'd expect in here," Carlotta said. "But they're not concerned about what goes on. This place is off-limits. Anyway, I'm talking about you—someone like you, from what I saw at BLAB. A Good Citizen, no offense. Pretty much the only way for a regular Good Citizen to end up in here would be through Faro Jack." She winked at him again. "And by the time they end up here, they wouldn't be such Good Citizens anymore."

Wally felt like he'd just been dumped into the middle of a conversation between two people he only sort of knew, talking about something he didn't understand at all. Plasma physics or macroeconomics. "Wait," he said. "Y'know, I don't really know that much about Faro Jack. Like, what's the deal with the cowboy act?" It was at least a place to start. "Did he have a stroke?"

"Not that I know of," Carlotta said. "It's my understanding it's pretty common among the Europeans. Not as common as it is with the Japanese, but you know them. As far as Europeans go—Jack's from The Hague—I suspect it has something to do with their Viking heritage." She paused. "In his case specifically, he started talking that way after they began rounding up Australians. He was scared, like all of us, and thought his accent would get him arrested. I think this was his way of trying to fit in." She smiled to herself. "There was a while there, in fact, when he was a superpatriot—again, just trying to disguise himself. Didn't last. But now he can't shake the cowboy thing. It comes and goes."

"I've noticed."

"We mostly just accept it. If he's having fun, let him have fun."

"Fair enough, I guess," Wally said, trying to control the stuttering he knew would kick in sooner or later. At forty-three, he was still nervous talking to girls. "So...w-what about you? I know even less about you than I do about him...That's why I was so excited to see you on the street that day...The way you were talking at BLAB, I'd never heard anyone talk that way before, and I . . ." He stopped. "When they took you in there, I—I was worried they were going to send you away."

She laid a hand on his leg and put her lips close to his ear. "Here's a little secret. They did."

"Oh no."

She nodded, leaning in again. "In fact, if the wrong people happen to be here, and they find out who I am? Chances are good this place wouldn't be so off-limits anymore."

Who were these people he'd gotten wrapped up with? Revolutionary cowboys, ex–detective squatters, and now, well, Carlotta. People like this weren't supposed to exist anymore. Not in this country, anyway.

"When I saw you on the street, that's what I was afraid of. I thought they'd rehabbed you."

"Adjusted me? They might have. I'm sure they wanted to, but they didn't have the chance. I got away intact." She paused. "More than intact. I know what goes on at the Unmutual camps now, and we're going—" she stopped herself to take a drink and a furtive glance around at the company. She set the glass down. "I need to tell you later. Now's not the time or place, I'm afraid."

"But—"

"Later. Soon," she promised.

As he stared at Carlotta, Wally felt a thick hand plant itself across his forearm. He looked up suddenly into Ivan's swollen toad eyes. He hadn't even heard him approach.

"Your friend's leaving."

Wally spun in his stool just in time to see Bingham pushing open the door, but not before pausing long enough to cast Wally a hurt and reproachful look.

"Oh... shit," Wally sighed, turning back. "He's not really my friend," he explained. "He's just a guy who crashes at my house sometimes." Then, as an afterthought, "Though I'm guessing it's his house now."

"What do you mean?" Carlotta asked.

He tried to smile. "I don't think I can go back there again."

"I'm sorry to hear that, but I think I understand," she said, sounding sincere and touching his arm lightly. All this touching—especially from a woman—was something new to Wally. At least as far as the last ten years were concerned. "But you know Jack."

"Yeah... that I do."

"Has he taken you . . ." Her voice trailed off but her meaning was obvious. Wally nodded.

"A bit more than that." He wasn't sure he would be able to explain even if he'd wanted. "But I'm not sure. I—I take it you've been there, too, then?"

Carlotta nodded. "Since before there was *there,* if you know what I mean."

He wasn't surprised to hear that either. "So...are you...a member?"

She giggled and took a swallow of her beer, which was nearly empty. "Oh, you bet. I got the decoder ring and learned the secret handshake...and I play shortstop on the softball team."

"Really?" Jack hadn't mentioned any secret handshakes.

"No. That's not exactly how it works—no membership cards, no decoder rings. But yeah, I guess you could say I'm part of it."

Wally took a long gulp from his own glass in an effort to catch up. Setting the glass back, he asked, "If that's the case, how did you end up at BLAB? I thought everyone was getting away from all that."

She looked more serious than he expected. "Some of us—me, Faro Jack, a few others—work up here. A few of them have never been down there. It's a risk, like when you saw me on the corner. But it's necessary."

"So you were—"

"Undercover," she nodded. "That's why I had to ignore you. And again, I apologize."

"It's okay," Wally said.

He knew it was banal. He knew it was straight out of high school. But the fact that Carlotta was an Unplugger was more an enticement to move underground than the fact that he had a chubby ex-insurance investigator squatting in his rewired house. Only then did Wally remember that he'd left several thousand dollars in cash stuffed under the floorboards in Margie's old office. *Dammit.* For some ridiculous reason when he left the house with Bingham, he was under the impression he'd be returning a few hours later, and that Bingham would be going home.

Carlotta drained her glass and swung to face him. "If you're still having some doubts, there's someone I think you should meet."

As quietly as possible Wally sighed. It never seemed to end. This time at least he hoped it wouldn't involve jumping aboard any moving trains.

She hadn't asked him a thing about his background, his job, if he had a family, or what he'd been up to these past months. She hadn't asked him anything at all. It was as if his knowing Jack and hanging out at Seamus McWingWang's had told her all she needed to know.

Before they left the speakeasy, he saw her catch Ivan's eye, then tap her wrist with two fingers. Without a nod, without anything, Ivan picked up a tiny communitainer unit, flipped open the screen, and punched a few buttons, before closing it again and replacing it behind the bar, nestled between two unmarked bottles.

Without a clue where he might be headed this time, Wally followed Carlotta out the door, where the two of them stood waiting by the curb.

"Um," he began, then stopped.

Two anxious middle-aged men approached from the far corner, shouting at each other while pushing a third man in a rattling and unstable office chair. He seemed at first to be asleep, but when the wheels of the chair hit a crack in the sidewalk the man's head flopped backwards, both his mouth and his eyes open. With an unintelligible cry, one of the men pushing the chair knocked the head forward again, and the entire body slumped over heavy and limp, nearly spilling onto the pavement.

"Get him up! Get him up!" one of the men shouted as he stopped pushing.

Both Wally and Carlotta turned.

"Harvest Home'll find them soon enough," Carlotta said, before turning her attention back to the oncoming traffic.

"No doubt," Wally agreed. Corpses being pushed down the street in office chairs had become as commonplace in recent years as midgets. It usually took only a few minutes before Harvest Home, the mobile organ donation unit, arrived on the scene.

"Um... where are we going?" Wally finally asked.

"You'll see. Don't worry."

Wally frowned. He hadn't considered worrying until she told him not to.

Two minutes later an armor-plated black sedan with tinted windows pulled to a stop in front of them. Carlotta opened the back door and gestured that he should climb in. With raised eyebrows but no question he did, and Carlotta followed.

He hadn't been in an automobile in years. Oil prices, tolls, insurance, parking—as well as the increasingly outrageous prices for the vehicles themselves (especially the driverless models like this one)—had left automobiles a monopoly of the hyperwealthy. It still didn't help the traffic situation. The streets remained as clogged and loud as they had ever been. Traffic was particularly absurd in Manhattan, which was where they seemed to be headed.

As they crawled along, pinched between two modified tanks, the air growing thick and dark with exhaust, Carlotta told him about her brief stay at Habitat Seventeen—an Unmutual camp in western Nevada. That's where she'd been imprisoned for two weeks before being rescued by a crack team of Unpluggers from Reno.

"They're the same bunch who're trying to get Sid Powell back on the air in a regular time slot," she mentioned offhandedly.

"Really? I saw that show once, a couple months ago."

"That makes you one of the chosen few, but I guess they're getting closer." After a pause, she got back to her own story.

"If I hadn't been a terrorist when they threw me in there," she said, "I sure as shit would've been one by the time I got out—even without the thumbscrews and the stocks."

Hearing that there was actual medieval-era torture taking place in the camps didn't shock Wally. It had been on the news when the legislation was signed redefining "torture" as "an enhanced chat." It wasn't a secret, and he supposed it was one of the thousand reasons why he wanted to drop out of the whole production. But dropping out in an effort to preserve his own humanity was one thing. Joining a revolutionary movement intent on overthrowing the machine was something completely different.

He looked over at Carlotta again.

Or maybe it wasn't.

ELEVEN

Wally looked up at the imposing black facade. This sure wasn't what he was expecting from a bunch of revolutionary hippie kooks.

"There are two dozen vids between here and there," Carlotta instructed. "Once we're upstairs you have nothing to worry about. It's clean. But just play it cool until then and try to hide your face."

Wally began hunching his shoulders and tugging his shirt collar up.

"No," she said. "Just...just keep your head down. Look at your shoes."

She led him from the car to the front doors of the complex. Above the entrance, brushed steel letters read BILDERBERG

BUILDING. Carlotta took him casually by the arm and together they walked through the doors, which were held open by two smartly dressed Doorbots.

As Wally and Carlotta passed, both bots emitted an almost friendly "Good day... sir... ma'am" simultaneously.

"They recognize me," Carlotta explained. "Don't worry. You're my guest."

The guard at the security desk bowed silently, meekly waving them through.

"Don't keep your head *that* far down," Carlotta said quietly. "You look like you're either drunk or retarded. Just be casual. Everything's fine. You still might want to keep your head down until we get off the elevator and into the apartment. But not that far down."

She led him down a thickly carpeted hallway illuminated by two crystal chandeliers. When they reached the bank of elevators, Carlotta hit the button and Wally watched the glowing red numbers count down from fifty-seven.

When the elevator arrived and the door slid open, the two stepped inside. It was the largest elevator Wally had ever seen. It occurred to him that it was as large as some Manhattan apartments he'd visited.

While he looked around at the paneled walls and the artwork, Carlotta reached to her throat and began pulling a long, thin chain from inside her sweater. At the end of the chain was a triangular black key unlike anything he'd seen before. She inserted it into a lock near the bottom of the button panel, then punched a seven-digit code into a keypad on the wall.

There was a click and a hum as a foot-wide screen folded

out of the paneling. Staring at them from the screen was an impeccably dressed young man with a thin mustache.

"Why hello there, Ms. Bain," the man said with a delicate lisp. "*Such* a pleasure to see you again. And I see you've brought a friend. How lovely."

"Hey, Chuck," she replied to the image. "May we come up?"

"Why most certainly. Colonel B. is anxiously awaiting your arrival. See you in a jiff."

Chuck?

With that, the screen folded back into the wall. The only way Wally could tell they were ascending was the slight drop in his stomach. Apart from that, the elevator was still and silent.

There was no use in trying to make sense of what was happening anymore. Wally decided the only thing to do was see what happened next.

Carlotta turned to him. "That was Chuck, the Colonel's personal assistant."

"Uh-huh?"

"You'll like the Colonel," she assured him. "He's great."

"I can't wait," Wally said, forcing a small smile.

When the doors opened again, Wally was startled to find himself standing face to, well, chest, with the unusually tall personal assistant, Chuck. He was wearing a sharply tailored charcoal gray tunic.

"Carlotta, my sweet!" he grinned, leaning in to hug her. Then, pulling back, he held out a hand to Wally.

"And you must be Barry."

"Wally," Wally corrected, shaking Chuck's cool and soft hand.

Chuck's eyes shifted slightly. "Yes, of course. Please *do* come in."

He led them through a reception area richly furnished in dark woods and burgundy velvet, then through a sitting room whose walls sported several large surrealist paintings and framed photographs of a powerful-looking, barrel-chested man posing with people Wally half-recognized but would never be able to name.

When they came to a massive set of closed double doors, Chuck—who really was one of the tallest people Wally could recall seeing—knocked three times, loudly.

There was no response, and he turned to give Carlotta an apologetic grin. "He probably didn't hear," he said. "If you'll pardon me." To the right of the doors leaned a heavy oak cane with a gnarled fist of a handle. Chuck hefted the cane in one hand and banged it violently against the door. Only then did Wally notice the dozens of chips and divots dug into the otherwise gleaming walnut finish, obviously the result of earlier knockings.

"*Yes, yes, yes,*" came a muddy voice through the polished wood. "*No* need for all *that.*"

"There is, though," Chuck whispered over his shoulder before sliding the doors back and stepping aside to let Wally and Carlotta enter. Once they were inside, he slid the doors closed behind them.

A wide and imposing mahogany desk dominated the center of the room, its top buried beneath stacks of manila folders, loose papers, three-ring binders, and old spiral-bound notebooks, all of them red. Two walls were lined with overloaded bookshelves. To Wally's left, a picture window looked out over the Manhattan skyline; to his right another offered a panoramic view of the East River. A small fire crackled in a fireplace as wide as Wally's old (and now decimated) couch. Rolling across the carpeting toward them was an elderly gentleman in an antique, cane-backed wheelchair.

The Colonel's thick silver hair was brushed straight back from his high forehead and flowed down past his collar. His face was rocky, with an absurdly square jaw and a nose that had apparently been broken more than once. His eyes, however, were bright and sharp. He wore two cardigans, the top one evergreen, the one beneath a deep maroon. A rough, checkered flannel blanket lay folded in his lap. For a moment Wally let his eyes focus on the old man's hands. While the left hand seemed perfectly normal, the skin of his right was much darker—almost a grayish red. And the hand itself was distorted, the fingers thick and twisted. Not wanting to be impolite, he snapped his eyes away.

"Grandpa!" Carlotta chirped, as she bounded across the room to meet him.

Grandpa?

"Ah, sweet Carlotta," he growled, "so very good of you to come. You do my heart good." He squeezed both of her hands as she leaned in to kiss him on the cheek.

As she stood, he swung his wheelchair toward Wally. "And you, young man . . . you must be Billy."

"Wally," Wally said, extending his hand. He tried not to shriek or flinch as the old man raised his deformed right hand and grabbed Wally's in a grip that nearly brought tears to Wally's eyes. "It's very nice to meet you... um, sir." The old man's skin was cold and scaly.

"Ah, call me Colonel. Colonel B. That'll do. I've had enough *sirs* in my day."

"All... right," Wally said, gratefully extracting his hand from the Colonel's dreadful grasp. "I will."

"Let me first apologize for the chill," the old man said, sounding both contrite and fed up. "It seems the only thing I can't control in here is the thermostat, thanks to those chimps at the Agency for the Preservation of Energy. But the fire should help take the edge off."

Wally hadn't noticed a chill. Quite the opposite—the room was a sweat lodge. He put it down as an old man thing.

The Colonel rolled back a few feet and scrutinized Wally from top to bottom. "Maybe," he said quietly, reaching up to stroke the hard line of his chin with a distended red thumb. "I'm not sure I can see it yet... but it's still early."

In spite of his determination to go with the flow, to see what happens, all these people expecting something of Wally without bothering to explain to him what or why began to make him uneasy. It had been less than two hours since he'd run into Carlotta by happenstance at McWingWang's. What could this "Colonel" character possibly know about him, let alone expect from him? Maybe there had been something in the signal she'd flashed Ivan. Or maybe there'd been something in his beer. Maybe the Colonel had a touch of dementia.

"My granddaughter has not told me much about you... ah... ah..." For a moment Wally thought the Colonel was going to sneeze.

"Wally," Carlotta said.

"Yes, yes, Wally... She's not told me much, but she's told me some. Enough. And I'm presuming you know why she's brought you here today."

Wally looked helplessly to Carlotta, who was smiling and nodding in a way that did not help him at all. What had she told the Colonel, and when? *Ah, crap.* He turned to the Colonel. "Not in, ah, any great detail, no s— No. Except to say you could convince me that . . ." He realized he had no idea why he was there, or if he should bring up the Unpluggers. "I guess I don't really know, Colonel, no... sorry."

The Colonel frowned. This wasn't the answer he was expecting. His eyes drifted toward the ceiling, resigned. "Okay, then," he sighed. "That means we start from the beginning... *Again.*" He shot a look at Carlotta. "I trust, then, that my granddaughter hasn't told you much about me."

"Um...," Wally said, "that's correct, yes. I know nothing, in fact. All Carlotta said was that I would like you."

The Colonel again looked to his granddaughter. "Well, my Carlotta does like her surprises." It sounded less than lighthearted. He smacked his dry lips. "Okay. I suggest then that you take a seat." He pointed toward a couch near the fireplace. It was another antique, the thin cushions embroidered with coils of gold and crimson.

Wally, fearing another lecture was afoot, did as he was told. Carlotta followed, sitting next to him. The Colonel rolled to his desk and, with some difficulty, grabbed three folders and dropped them into his lap before pushing himself over to face them both. As Wally saw it, the old man was blocking his escape.

The Colonel tried to clear his throat, but to no obvious effect. "Now," he began, as Wally tried to keep his eyes off the red claw, "the story I am about to tell you took place several years before you were born, but its implications are only now coming to full bloom. I'm hoping that as I explain you'll . . . you'll come to understand why you're here."

It was early spring, 1963. Nestled on a narrow and shadowy Baltimore side street was a tavern called Sweaty's, which, given its proximity to Fort Meade, had become a favorite watering hole for three agents from the National Security Agency—Max Frost, Harry "Monster" McGee, and the Colonel, who had been known to friends and colleagues alike as the "Colonel" long before achieving that particular rank.

They had selected Sweaty's for two primary reasons. First, they found that they were much more productive as a team after they'd had a few. And second, though there were plenty of other bars in the vicinity to choose from, there was enough action at Sweaty's that three men with dark glasses, identical haircuts, and matching black suits could function there virtually unnoticed.

The three agents, as they did at least three nights a week, occupied a small round table against the back wall. The cacophonous blend of jukebox music, drunken hooting, and breaking furniture was loud enough most any given evening that no one in the bar, even if they cared to listen, would have been able to hear what the three men were saying. And if they could, they likely wouldn't remember it the next morning.

"You and your exploding cigars," Agent Frost was chiding Agent McGee. "We tried it once, remember? It was a bust."

"You aren't *listening* to me," McGee shot back, gesturing with his second vodka tonic. "I'm talking about one of those enormous cigars—one of those three-foot jobs you see at carnivals." He held his hands apart to illustrate. "He wouldn't be able to resist it. We'd be able to pack at least—at *least*—half a kilo of C-four in there. He wouldn't have a chance."

"What, you're Wile E. Coyote now?"

Even before Jack Kennedy was elected, the trio had been charged by the Joint Chiefs of Staff with the task of formulating a means to justify a military invasion of Cuba. Or, short of that, simply eliminating Castro. Pain in the ass, that guy.

To date, however, nothing had worked, and "Monster" McGee, as he usually did near the bottom of his second vodka tonic, reproposed the exploding-cigar routine.

"Gentlemen," the Colonel said, raising his own highball. "You're getting off point. Disposal of the target with some cartoon gimmickry is only a fallback plan. Our primary objective—in which the elimination of the target would play only a small secondary role—involves a justification for a military incursion that is at once plausible, moral, and . . ."—he paused, trying to think of the right word—"sexy."

The other two agents stared at him across the table, suspicious of the Colonel's knowing smirk.

"I began sketching out an idea today. And so gentlemen, for your consideration, I would like to hear your thoughts on Operation Castor Oil."

"*Castor* Oil?" spat McGee, who never liked anyone else's code names.

"What, don't you think it's funny? I think it's funny."

Over the next three minutes, and amid some tipsy giggling, the Colonel laid out the fundamentals of his plan. The details would come later, after they had agreed it was the only logical course left open to them.

When he was finished, he sat back and spread out his arms, waiting for a response.

After his raucous laughter had subsided, Frost was the first to pipe up. "So... in other words, you're saying we should burn down the Reichstag again."

"Well... in a manner of speaking, perhaps. It worked for Hitler, didn't it?" Then, considering it, "Though you may not want to use that particular analogy during the presentation."

"I think I saw something like this on *The Outer Limits* a few weeks ago," McGee said. "You see that one? The one with Robert Culp and Leonard Stone?"

"I know the episode you're talking about," Frost said. "The one with the alien, right? Yeah, I saw that. It was pretty good. You see it, Colonel? There's these scientists, see—?"

"*We all saw that episode,*" the Colonel snapped. "Okay? Yes, they used the same general principle as an *Outer Limits* plot. Big deal. They've used it in a lot of things. It's a common idea in dystopian literature. False flag operations have been a standby throughout history. That doesn't make it a bad idea. It's a standby because it works *every time.*"

"No one said it was a bad idea, Colonel," Frost offered.

"Yeah," the Colonel said derisively, "but you can't resist telling me you saw it on the *tee-vee.*"

"Good show is all I was saying," McGee tried to clarify.

"Sure, but," Frost asked, "who's gonna be the alien here?"

"Would you two just *shut up* about it? There *is* no alien. It doesn't matter."

"I'm just saying."

For a moment it seemed likely the furniture at the small table against the back wall would start breaking, but all three men regained their composure and more or less forgot about the show.

"Now. Then," the Colonel said, re-establishing control of the conversation. "If no actual Cuban terrorist groups are available or willing, we will simply need to supply one ourselves. Easy enough. We've done it before."

"Never on American soil," Frost cautioned. "Or with U.S. civilian casualties."

"All the more reason to provide our own. We can better control the timetable that way. Plus all the more reason it would be effective."

"Think they'll go for it?" McGee asked.

The Colonel shrugged. "I just want to see their faces when they read it."

"You know," Frost said, after briefly pondering the possibilities and implications of Operation Castor Oil, "the real beauty of the plan—now that I think about it—is its plasticity." He looked from one agent to the other. "It can be used for *anything,* really. You want to invade another country, fake an attack on your own people and blame it on them. You want to unify a divided populace, consolidate your power, whatever, fake an attack, blame it on some invisible enemy...*aliens,* even." The Colonel nearly reached across the table and smacked him, but Frost was caught up in the idea. "Present them with tangible evidence of an outside threat and the populace will overwhelmingly vote for whatever you want them to vote for. War, martial law, jailing Swedes, banning baseball and hamburgers... whatever you want, it's yours. I think it's a capital idea, Colonel." He raised his glass. "Now, who's up for another round? We need to toast this properly."

And so the three agents agreed that Operation Castor Oil was exactly what they were after, and two weeks later the final proposal was finished, complete with a list of potential civilian targets in Florida, Georgia, and Tennessee, estimated casualty rates, and probability of success, with "success" being measured in terms of public outrage and demands that swift retribution be taken against the perpetrators. Part of the mission's success also lay in its complete deniability. Better yet, invisibility. That the plan was even discussed by government officials could never, ever come to light. Therefore, even the tiniest task would be delegated on a need-to-know basis. Only the president, a few select members of the Joint Chiefs, and five NSA administrators would get the whole picture (along with Frost, McGee, and the Colonel).

The NSA brass signed off on the plan in a heartbeat, one even drawing a red smiley face at the top of the report's cover page. The Joint Chiefs were equally enthusiastic about the possibilities. Then it landed on Kennedy's desk.

"Kennedy, to put it mildly, wasn't too keen on the idea," the Colonel told Wally. "And Operation Castor Oil was unceremoniously shelved. Instead they went with some lame-brained, hamfisted military operation that was an utter disaster from the moment it was conceived. But at least I wasn't blamed for it. And even though Operation Castor Oil had been filed, it apparently struck a few chords along the way." He chuckled dryly, then began coughing. Carlotta hopped off the couch and began slapping him sharply between the shoulder blades until he raised his hand to indicate that he was okay.

"Ironic isn't it?" he wheezed, his chest rattling, "That a plan Kennedy rejected would first be used to take him out of the picture?" He looked at Wally with watery, amused eyes but saw no response. "Well, I think it's ironic. I was horrified at the same time. Part of me, I'll confess, never *really* thought anyone would take it seriously. It was a drunken joke, after all, a plan straight out of Machiavelli, Hitler, and *The Outer Limits.* Which doesn't mean it's a *bad* plan, mind you."

"Yes sir—Colonel," Wally began, "but you—"

The Colonel sat up suddenly and Wally was afraid that the old man was having a stroke. Then his eyes widened and he announced, "I want soup."

"Pardon?"

"*Soup.* I want some soup. Bean with bacon. Doesn't that sound good? You want some bean with bacon soup?"

Carlotta put her hand on Wally's knee. "We're fine, Grandpa, and you know your choices are limited these days. You can have soup, but not bean with bacon."

The Colonel scowled at her and Wally, to be honest, could've gone for a nice bowl of soup at that point. He hadn't had much of anything to eat all day.

"If you want some soup," she said, standing, "I'll have Chuck make you some."

She excused herself and left the room. Once the doors were

closed behind her, the Colonel turned to Wally. "Sweet girl. I love her with all my heart. But goddammit, I don't care how old I am—if I want some damn bean with bacon soup, I think I should have it, don't you?"

It didn't seem like a rhetorical question.

"I . . . I . . . yes," he said.

"I should think so," the Colonel agreed, satisfied.

The doors to the study opened and the Colonel turned to see Carlotta enter. As he turned, Wally noticed for the first time the shoulder holster beneath the two sweaters.

"Chuck says he needs a few things for soup," she announced. "He has to run to the store."

"Yeah, he would," the Colonel muttered. He took a ragged breath. "Well, then, while we wait . . ." He seemed to be getting out of breath, so Carlotta, who'd assumed her seat next to Wally, jumped in.

"After Kennedy," she said, clearly having heard the story several times before, "there was the Gulf of Tonkin and the Moscow bombings that led to the war in Chechnya—"

"How the Kremlin got their hands on my plan, I'd still like to know," the Colonel interjected.

For a moment, Wally considered reminding him that he himself had said the plan was an old one, but it didn't seem like the thing to bring up.

"So you see," the Colonel went on, "like Frost said, it was wonderfully plastic, my plan, applicable to almost any situation."

"So," Wally tried to extrapolate, "you're saying then that . . . the Horribleness . . . ? That it was Operation Castor Oil, too, that the president ordered it?" What shocked him more than the idea itself (which didn't) was that the idea had never occurred to him before—or much of anyone else, it seems. The precious few who expressed even the tiniest doubt that it had been the work of Australian terrorists found themselves in Terminal Five before they could tie their shoes.

"*President*?" the Colonel barked, banging the arms of his wheelchair. "C'mon, son, get with the program! Use your noodle! We're far beyond *presidents* at this point. Have been for an awfully long time. The closest thing we have to a president nowadays is PROTEUS X. That man you see on your vidscreens is nothing but a computer-generated image, a simulacrum, whose actions and reactions are preprogrammed. Even last year, remember, when he got sick at the press conference? All part of the show. Just there to keep the citizenry docile. But with PROTEUS X, you see, we are afforded coldly logical decision making based upon an almost infinite amount of stored data. For the first time, a nation is being ruled rationally." He paused. "At least that's what they've always said: rational decision making. In corporate terms, anyway." He picked up the files and straightened them.

"But," Wally said, "the president has said and done some incredibly stupid things. A lot of them—like that crack about Oregon last year. That wasn't very rational."

The Colonel shook his head. "It's part of the program. Doesn't get in the way, doesn't change anything, and gives him that air of believability." He smiled again, almost sadly. "PROTEUS determined that the populous prefers a stupid president. It makes them feel better about themselves. And if people demand that he step down, well, all we need to do is remodel the image, Give 'em whatever they want, simple as pie."

"Guess that would explain the elections," Wally said. It was somehow comforting to know the asshole was nothing more than a picture on a screen.

"Forgive me, it seems I got sidetracked." The Colonel regarded Wally with a sour expression. "In answer to your earlier question, yes, that—the Horribleness, as they call it—was Operation Castor Oil too," he said. "My baby. No offense, Carlotta. I recognized it immediately, all the earmarks. But it was all grown up now. Much bigger, much less subtle."

He exhaled through his nose. "And I never got my bonus."

"Bonus?" Wally asked.

The Colonel shook his head. "They activate your operation, you get a bonus. That was in my contract. Given the number of times they've used Castor Oil, I should be a very wealthy man now."

Wally nodded sympathetically, trying to imagine what "wealthy" meant to the old man. "Did...did you ask them for it?"

"Indeed I did. That afternoon, in fact." The Colonel closed his eyes, remembering the strained and brief exchange. "I was informed that there had been enough significant modifications to the original plan that it was no longer mine. They fired me the next day. Within a week, the NSA was subsumed along with all the other independent intelligence agencies—DIA, CID, Majestic. Some of the operations went to DOD, most to SPOOK, a few others—quite a few, actually—straight to BOO and the PROTEUS X project." He paused and took another deep and rattling breath.

"See, son, over a decade ago, PROTEUS X decided the masses needed . . . cultivation. They were too unruly. Too boisterous. They weren't buying the right products. If you'll remember, things were a mess. Drugs, violence, pornography, unemployment. Next thing you know, PROTEUS pulled up my plan and terrorists began falling from the sky onto grocery stores."

"I should probably be shocked," Wally glanced at the fire, which was almost out. Still, it was a nice thing, a fireplace. The world is run by an evil computer. Imagine. He looked over to Carlotta again, who was staring at her grandfather, enraptured.

"You ever read a book called *Player Piano,* son?"

Wally snapped back to attention. "No, sir—Colonel—I'm afraid . . . no, I haven't. Didn't have a chance before the ban." *This guy's all over the place,* Wally thought. *Must've forgotten his pills.*

"You should sometime. It might help. I'll tell you, people in the security and intelligence communities, they've always had a taste for dystopian literature. Treasure trove of ideas. And in this case, the case of PROTEUS, the Horribleness, the whole nine yards, it was almost as if a social engineer with a great deal of power, very little imagination, and no sense of irony had simply grabbed elements from a dozen dystopian novels and films and dropped them into his plan. Or fed them straight into PROTEUS." He was growing more agitated, gesturing with his ruined claw. "And even the name *PROTEUS,* for godsakes, was lifted—from either Kurt Vonnegut or a science fiction novel from the seventies." He looked to his lap, the corners of his mouth turning down sharply. "Terrible novel . . . just awful . . . I'm sure that must've been it. But nobody noticed. No one said a word, which just goes to show."

Wally was about to ask him what it showed when Carlotta jumped in.

"You're getting tired, Grandpa. Maybe we should—"

"I'm not *finished* yet!" he snapped with a ferocity that seemed to startle all three of them. Then, more gently, "And I'm still soupless."

It was nearing dusk when they left the building. They couldn't afford to stay on the streets much longer, especially in Manhattan.

"We couldn't risk taking Grandpa's car again," Carlotta explained quietly, scanning the darkening sky. "If we were stopped, not only would they trace it back to him, but you'd be caught with *that*." She tapped his belly. Before they'd left the Colonel's apartment, Wally had been handed a folder containing a printout of the original proposal for Operation Castor Oil, which he'd tucked beneath his shirt. Making things even more damning, the Colonel had insisted on inscribing the document for him: "To Willie—Go get 'em, tiger! Yours truly, Col. B."

"He sure can talk, can't he?" Wally asked, still dazed from the experience. They'd been in the apartment for nearly five hours. "I mean for an old—a man of his age."

"Grandpa's a remarkable character," Carlotta said. "Before he joined the NSA, he wanted to be a lawyer...wanted to be one ever since he was very young. But he wasn't the best student, so he ended up suing his way through grade school. Sued the teachers, sued the schools. Sued the school board, even, demanding that he be allowed to move on. Then he sued his way through high school and college, then law school. Sued every one of his professors first year."

"Wow," Wally said. "He must've been good."

"The best," Carlotta said. "Harvard opted to settle out of court and just gave him a damn degree. But after that he went straight into intelligence work. Never practiced law again."

"Maybe by then he was all sued out."

Carlotta was still keeping her eyes peeled up and down the streets for any potential trouble. "These days," she said, "he doesn't talk to many people—I guess for obvious reasons—so when he gets the chance . . . I'm sorry about that. He's still pretty upset about that commission."

"I—I guess that's understandable. It's okay," Wally said, stealing a secret glance at her from the corner of his eye.

"He liked you, though. I can tell."

Wally thought about using this opportunity to ask her about the rest of her family—what her parents were like and where they were now. He also thought about reaching out and putting his hand on her back as they walked. If she didn't cringe or pull away or slap him, maybe he could let it slide lower. And if she still didn't protest . . .

For the first time in years he felt a tingle in his loins and began looking around. It had been an awfully long time. They were passing a lot of alleyways. Most of them were equipped with crime-deterrent vids, he knew, but that didn't seem to stop anyone from sneaking in there. There were entire four-way channels devoted to alley sex, he'd heard, but you needed a special SMEG/MA permit to access them, and those were granted only to SMEG/MA employees.

He'd shoved his hands in his pockets when they hit the streets in a weak effort to conceal the file and now he kept them there. He knew it was useless, even tragic. It was the evening air getting to him, or maybe he wasn't thinking straight after being lectured all afternoon. To get his mind off what was happening just below the concealed folder, he said, "One thing I still don't get," as they turned the corner onto Second Avenue and began heading south. "Why did he meet with me, exactly? And whose side is he on?" Wally wasn't at all sure, even after all that.

He could sense Carlotta growing tense beside him as they walked. She remained silent, and he was about to rephrase the question when he saw the HappyCam on the next corner spin and redirect itself toward them.

Oh, hell.

"Should we cross the street?" he whispered, then added hopefully, "Duck down an alley?" But it was too late.

They stopped walking when the bot was still five or six yards away, hoping it might simply roll past, leaving them alone. Both Wally and Carlotta knew full well it wouldn't.

"Good evening, Good Citizens!" This one had a British accent—a first in Wally's experience.

"Good evening," they both replied, almost in unison.

"Are you in need of assistance, perchance?"

We're going to die, Wally thought. *It's going to ask to scan our cards and then it's going to kill us.* In a move he hoped didn't appear too desperate, he clasped his hands in front of himself and hunched his shoulders slightly in an effort to cover the obvious rectangular outgrowth on his belly. He would've folded his arms but knew the sensors would read that as a defensive posture, resulting in a search.

"No, thank you," Carlotta said, taking the lead and sounding assured. "We're just fine."

The HappyCam rotated a few degrees to face her more directly, much to Wally's relief.

"May I remind you then that this evening's curfew will be going into effect in twenty-three minutes, and that it might behoove the two of you to get home as quickly as possible."

"That's exactly where we're headed right now," Carlotta assured the machine, "as quickly as possible. But thank you for the reminder. It's a comfort."

"Merely performing my directives. And in so doing I might also suggest that you both consider a wardrobe upgrade in the near future. You would feel better for it. Having been privy to a preview of the upcoming spring lines, I must say they're quite fabulous."

"Thank you, we will."

The HappyCam rolled back a few inches, then pivoted and continued around them up the sidewalk.

Without daring to look back and make sure the HappyCam hadn't decided that Wally's posture was in need of comment as well, the two of them continued walking.

"Keep looking straight ahead," Carlotta whispered, taking his arm so they would appear to the vids like any regular couple on their way home from work or an early dinner.

"What was with that Ed Sullivan routine?" she asked.

"The what?"

"Nothing. Just someone Grandpa used to talk about." They

reached the corner and stopped, waiting for the pictogram. When it changed, she said, "Now's when you have to make a decision. You said earlier that you can't return to your house."

"Yeah, pretty much, I'm guessing," he said.

"So then what did you want to do? Join us or make a go of it on your own? Because if you're on your own, we'd better split right here."

Wally felt her warm hand on his arm and the soft bump of her hip against his as they walked. She wasn't making it easy for him to think.

It was turning into a cool but comfortable evening. He wished they could just walk a while, discuss his options. He also wished she'd said "join me" instead of "join us." It sounded so . . . official.

An open-topped DOD personnel carrier rumbled by, filled with armed curfew enforcement agents. In all likelihood it was headed to the deployment area at Eighty-sixth Street. A loudspeaker mounted atop the truck's cab announced the time in a metallic voice.

The decision was obvious. In fact, it was no decision at all. It was clear to him, and had been so for weeks now, that what he had attempted on his own was impossible. As the Colonel had laid it out, the forces he was up against were much more expansive and much more powerful than anything he could begin to imagine. He could try to duck them for the rest of his life, but how long would that be? Weeks at most. Hours, more likely. The world that had been created around him these past ten years could no longer be navigated or survived without a SUCKIE card, without allowing yourself to be scanned, without electronic implants. He wouldn't be able to buy food or new shoes or see a doctor. He couldn't earn an income, or travel, or report a fire. They'd made sure of all that. He'd be squashed like a roach. Being stopped by the HappyCam back there proved it. He didn't have a goddamned chance.

Things might have been different if he were a little smarter, if he had the slightest understanding of how these electronic doodads worked. But Margie had been right—he was an incompetent boob. He'd allowed himself to be trapped. His goal had been to make himself unscannable, but the only way to do that, he understood now, was to get rid of the scanners themselves. All of them. As much as everything inside him hated to admit it, the only way he could release himself was to do something that would release everyone, whether they wanted to be released or not. And the only way to do that would be to work with the Unpluggers. They might well fail, too, but they had a hell of a better chance than he did on his own. The way out at this point was to tear down the whole machine, like Jack said. It was, after all, the logical conclusion—and the only conclusion—to what he had started. And it was a job far too immense for one man to pull off on his own—especially one as dull-witted as he was. No, if he wanted to smash the machine, he'd need a little help. He didn't much relish the idea of living and working with other people again, but if that's what it took.

For the first time in his life, reluctant as he was to admit it, Wally Philco had something to believe in and fight for. Something bigger than himself. This wasn't just dodging strollers in the morning. This was something for all mankind—every last stinking one of the bastards. At least those who lived in New

York. This, for godsakes, was a life-or-death battle between good and evil.

Which was all mighty big of him, he felt, considering the way he'd been treated over the years.

Plus, it meant he'd be able to stay near Carlotta.

The last thing Jack had said to him came back again: "Just be sure you're right, then go ahead on."

But first things first. The adscreens were becoming brighter and louder. The deep shadows of approaching night were closing in on them. Another DOD truck rolled past. By now the enforcement agents were spreading out from Eighty-sixth Street, as well as south of them, at Allied Secretions Square. They had to get somewhere safe, and quickly.

When they reached the next corner, he looked up at the sign. They were only at Fifty-eighth Street. He turned to Carlotta, who was staring at him, waiting for an answer.

"Well," he said, "do we wanna run thirty-five blocks or take our chances with the C.H.U.D.s?"

TWELVE

"The days dwindle down!... To a precious few!"

At the sound of the unfamiliar shrill and distant voice bouncing off the tunnel walls, both Wally and Jack looked up.

"What the hell was that?" Wally asked.

"That's just ol' Pye again, a-hootin' an' a-hollerin'."

There didn't seem to be any rhyme or reason behind Jack's slipping into cowboy mode. Wally wondered if Jack himself had any control over it, or if he was even aware of it happening.

"Should we... um... go see what the trouble is?"

"Oh, no bother. I reckon I know what the trouble is already. And you will too in a sec."

Wally waited for an explosion, a crash, anything.

"Pye hollers something every time he crawls back outa the

subbasement. Usually Weill. He's like a cat that way—he shits, then he yowls. In Pye's case, though—" He stopped. "You might wanna hold your breath."

Before he had a chance to ask why, the thick, noxious stench wafted into the room.

"Oh *God*—"

"It'll pass," Jack gasped, still trying to hold his breath. It seems every time Pye returned from the subbasement, his shout had become a warning to all the other Unpluggers in the complex to take cover. Two years of accumulated human feces down there meant that breaking the seal even the tiniest crack brought work to a standstill and made life unbearable for the next few minutes.

Faro Jack, red-faced from the effort, finally allowed his breath to sputter out with a liquid rattle. He took a tentative sniff of the air, then nodded, his eyes watering. "Okay," he said. "It's 'bout gone."

"Whew," Wally said, relieved and a bit dizzy.

"It normally doesn't get this far down this wing. Sorry...we gotta do something about that. Get some quicklime, post a schedule, anything."

"Why haven't I heard him before?" Wally asked. "Or, y'know...noticed?"

"Well, ol' Pye, see," Jack said, leaning back in his wooden chair, "he has a way. Long before he ever found himself in these parts, he took up with this yogi, who filled his head with all sorta crazy fool notions about controlling the body with the mind. This was before he got so darn interested in the comings an' goings of his DNA. Well, wouldn't you know it, but some of that yogi gobbledygook actually stuck, so nowadays Pye there only needs to relieve himself once a month. Sometimes once every two, depending." After a pause he added, "But I'll tell ya, when it comes time for him to go down there, he's down there for a while."

"I see," Wally said, strangely impressed by this. "Come to think of it, for all the time I've been down here, I can't say as I've ever seen him eat. With that suit and mask, it can't be easy."

"You ever see how a fly eats?" Jack asked.

"No."

"It's something like that."

He removed a small notebook from the pocket of his slicker and jotted a quick line. "It's getting a little outa hand down there, but Pye won't let us clean it out."

"Maybe a few air fresheners?"

Jack shook his head. "Tried 'em. Don't last. And trust me, you do not wanna mix that with Springtime Meadow or Rose Garden Delights. Thousand times worse." He closed the notebook and replaced it in his pocket.

The two of them were sitting in what had been declared Wally's quarters. It was nearly as bare as Jack's—a small desk, a couple of mismatched chairs—but at least Wally's room came with a folding cot. It was, he thought, at least as comfortable as his house had been at the end.

The two men were at the desk, going through the Operation Castor Oil report, looking for clues, a weak spot, anything that might be useful.

Flipping idly through the crisp pages once again, Jack frowned. "The thing about this here is that it's almost fifty years old. They're talkin' about a damn island that don't exist no more, for godsakes. Lessen you count the amusement park."

Having known the enigmatic Colonel for some years now, Jack was well aware of Operation Castor Oil long before Wally showed up. It was apparently a story the Colonel told whenever he had the chance. But Jack had never seen the actual report itself and it consumed him for days. He was startled, not only by the Colonel's clear enthusiasm for the project but also by his freewheeling and excessive use of exclamation points in what would normally be considered a stony-faced official military proposal.

"This is 'bout as useful as a two-legged horse," Jack said, slapping the report down on the table. "You hungry?"

"Oh—um, yeah, getting there."

"Let's go rustle us up some vittles."

It had been nearly a month since that afternoon with Carlotta and the Colonel, and Wally had remained underground ever since. Of all the meals he'd eaten in that time, he had to admit he'd recognized only about one-third of them—but given what Jack had told him earlier about dumpster diving, he wasn't sure he wanted to know what the others were.

For some godforsaken reason, Wally's decision to work with the Unpluggers had galvanized the entire underground. What had previously been little more than idle chatter about "maybe, possibly sort of doing something kind of radical one of these days" had abruptly shifted toward some serious scheming for decisive action. What had been approximately fifty people each working on his or her own halfbaked revenge plot had become a surprisingly organized collection of fifty very different minds focused on a single, monumental goal.

All around him in the Hub people with an intense concentration in their eyes were tapping at keyboards, scratching out designs on paper with pencil nubs, and creating handheld devices to scramble GPS and communitainer signals. Friendly chitchat and unexpected outbursts had dwindled, and coffee consumption had increased eightfold.

Strolling through it all, Wally had little idea what to do with himself. He had no engineering or technical skills, nor was he much of a strategist. There were men and women down there who could glance at the blueprints of a power plant and see any microscopic vulnerability as easily as you could spot a tennis shoe in a goldfish bowl. Wally had trouble reading road maps.

It didn't seem to matter. The Unpluggers, buggy and nerdy as they were, were looking at him as if he knew exactly what he was doing, asking his advice—even offering him extra portions of, well, whatever it was they were having for lunch. All the weekly progress reports were delivered to him personally for his approval, and even John Pye, team biologist, waved at him from the corner.

Wally quickly grew accustomed to the treatment and, in spite of some initial obvious insecurity, soon evolved into his role as Unplugger Figurehead. Still, he knew he didn't dare make any decisions or proclamations without consulting Jack or Carlotta first.

He felt a soft hand grab his elbow and turned to find Carlotta.

"Hey there," he said.

"Hi. What goes on?"

As the pair headed toward a far corner, Wally said, "I was just thinking that Jack never told me where all this equipment comes from. It's probably something I should know."

"Did you ask him directly?"

"I did once," Wally admitted, "but I…I couldn't understand his answer. Something about doggies, I think, or cutting someone off at the pass."

"Well, there you go then. It's no secret, really." She stopped and looked back at all the people hunched over desks. "Some brought their own when they decided to come down here. You know these renegade techies. Latch on to their machines the way they would a cocker spaniel. Especially when they know they're gonna have to let go soon."

Once again Wally wondered whatever became of Miguel.

"Some of the other equipment was . . ." She paused. "Acquired in one way or another. And Grandpa offered a little backing of his own when it came to the initial setup."

"You mean he's behind all this?" It was something he had suspected from the moment he met the long-winded old man, but no one had come right out and told him as much.

"Not *behind* it so much," Carlotta corrected. "Let's just say he's a booster."

"That's very generous of him."

"Yes, it is," she said, pulling him closer and giving his arm a squeeze. Odd, Wally thought, that he still knew so little about her background, except for her time in the camps. He'd asked, but something had always come up to deflect an answer.

"You sign off on those progress updates yet?" she asked.

He pulled himself back to the present. "Oh, um,

yeah... Didn't understand a word of most of them, but so long as things are moving along."

"Don't worry, I'll take a look at them. They're in your room?"

"On the table, yeah. But hey—" He stopped her before she hustled off down the tunnel. "What does 'low yield' refer to, anyway? I keep seeing that term."

"I'll explain tonight. See you later."

As he watched her go he wondered again, as he did every night and in his quieter moments, what life with Carlotta would be like after the revolution.

At a small desk located as far away as possible from the four-way (and everyone else), a small, round figure was staring at the stone wall. Angelika Titters was a squat, dense woman with square spectacles, graying hair pulled into a frayed bun, and an air about her that alerted all trespassers that she had very little time or patience for their bullshit. For as much as he'd spoken with the others, Wally and Angelika had shared only the briefest of greetings.

With the others, Wally had discussed their collective situation in mostly abstract terms—how, instead of the future they'd all been promised, full of flying cars and domed vacation colonies on the moon, they'd ended up with dictatorial computers, armed security units in the streets, unfathomable bureaucracies, and endless, mind-corroding commercials. That they were in deep shit was a given. The specifics of what was to be done to rectify the problem, however, was Angelika's ball game. You wouldn't guess it by looking at her, but Angelika Titters was the Unpluggers' chief strategist. Problem was, she rarely talked to anybody.

Wally, deciding it was about time he changed all that, headed over to Angelika's desk. Her computer screen was glowing with mathematical incantations far beyond anything Wally would ever likely comprehend.

If she was aware of his approach, she didn't make it evident.

"Angelika?" he inquired tentatively.

She continued to stare at the wall. "Sit *down,*" she said. "You make me uncomfortable standing there staring down at me like some needy bird."

"Oh," Wally said, making a monkey face at the back of her head. "Of course."

He looked around for a free chair, but nothing in the vicinity seemed to be available. With a huff, Angelika pushed herself away from the desk and stood.

"Here," she said. "Sit here. And I'll look down at you. That'll be better."

With a nod he lowered himself into the seat, which was still quite warm.

"Yes?" she asked, folding her stubby arms as well as she could across her ample bosom. Wally knew there was no need to be nervous given his newfound status, but Angelika made everybody nervous.

"Well, uh... Angelika... it's just that we haven't spoken much and, uh... I was just wondering what you were up to."

"At the moment?" She was no less brusque. "At the moment it seems my work is being interrupted by a ninny."

He nodded. "That's just it, see. Everything we're trying to accomplish down here begins with you. So I'm just wondering, um...what sort of strategy did you, you know, have in mind?" He spoke the word "strategy" slowly to ensure it didn't come out "stragety." He couldn't imagine what she'd call him if he let that slip. "Is it some sort of a computer virus or something?" For all the progress reports he'd read, he honestly had no idea.

Angelika nearly spat. "A *virus*? Where the hell have you been—bowling? You do realize what we're up against here, don't you? It ain't kid stuff. They have their systems keyed up so tight the most we'd ever be able to do with a virus is cause some mild inconvenience for a few minutes, an hour or two at most. A mosquito bite. And with the kind of digital reverse transcription they've been developing, they'd track us down about five minutes after that, no matter where we launched or how we routed. So in answer to your witless question, no." From behind her square lenses, her eyes burned through him. "Haven't you been reading my reports?"

Wally fidgeted in the chair. "Well, yeah, I have. Sure. But I—some of the math is a bit—"

Angelika shook her head and sighed. She obviously hadn't accepted him as her personal savior quite yet. "No, screwhead, I had something a little bigger in mind." She turned her head away and mumbled a snide "*virus.*"

"Look, I'm sorry," Wally said, growing irritated with Miss Attitude here. "I need to understand. That's all. Like Jack said, we're all in this together, right? If nobody—and by *nobody* I mean me—understands what you're doing, then what the hell good is it?"

As he watched, something about Angelika began to melt a little—just a little—like an ice sculpture on an unexpectedly mild December afternoon. She unfolded her arms and leaned back against the desk.

"Can I have my chair back?"

"Pardon?"

"My chair. I'd feel better talking to you sitting down. Knees."

"Oh," Wally said, thinking at first that she'd just ordered him to kneel. "Sure. Knees I understand." He stood and held the chair for her, then moved around to lean against the desk.

"Now, I imagine in your case the place to start with all this is with the basics, am I right?" She didn't wait for an answer, knowing she was right. "So what are we facing?"

Before he had a chance to make a guess, she cut him off. "It's not the ninnies and the twits, it's their weapons themselves. It's the computers, it's the sensors, the vids, the scanners, the . . . the communitainers, the—"

"Ads?" he offered. It sounded like she'd been talking to Matthias, one of the more militant Unpluggers.

"Yes, the ads—all those things that enslaved us up there." She pointed toward the ceiling. Wally was simply relieved to have been right about the ads. "And all those things are small branches of the entire fucking electrodigital dynamic. It's that grid, you see, that feeds our enemy. Get rid of the grid, you get rid of the machines, you get rid of the enemy. The Greeks knew it. The Carthaginians knew it. Cut off the food supply."

Wally nodded but didn't interrupt. The more she spoke, the more spirited she was becoming, and he was afraid if he interrupted and said the wrong thing now she'd bite him.

"What will happen, do you suppose, when *all* the electricity goes out? Think about it. You've been through blackouts in this city, you know what those are like. But I'm talking something much *bigger.* I can't believe you haven't been following these reports." She shook her head again. "It's not just no lights and no four-way. It's no computers, no GPS signal, no SUCKIE scanners, no communication, no refrigeration, no databases, no cars, no *nothing.*" She clapped her hands and clasped her fingers together. "Oh, it'll be *glorious.*"

"What about PROTEUS X?"

"*Nothing.*" Angelika's eyes were sparkling now. "And that," she went on, "is the only way we can win. Anything else we do—signal jamming, whatever some of the techs are up to—would only be a half-assed measure, and they'd crush us. Because, face it, they have the superior manpower, firepower, and technology. The only way to win is to take the technology away from them, and take it away from them for good."

John Drake suddenly leaped from his chair for the first time that week.

"*I will not be pushed, filed, stamped, indexed, briefed, debriefed, or numbered! My life is my own!*"

Angelika half swiveled in her chair and shouted over her shoulder, "Yeah, that's sort of the whole *idea,* there, Drake, ya *mo-ron!*"

The entire Hub fell silent as every head turned to look at her. Few of them had ever heard Angelika speak before, let alone call someone a "mo-ron."

She turned her attention back to Wally, who was a bit startled himself.

"I... um... yeah, I see what you're saying, Angelika," he said, trying to get back on point. "But how are you proposing we do this? There are . . ." He looked around the Hub at the handful of people present and thought once again that he was stuck down here with a bunch of delusional pencilnecks, some of whom even *he* could beat up.

"Not as hard as you might think," she said as she began hitting a few keys. A new window blinked open on the screen, and it too was filled with equations.

"I really, um," Wally said, holding up a hand, "I wouldn't bother with that. Could you just give me the gist of it?"

"Sure, I'll just go get my hand puppets," she said. With mild disappointment, she pulled herself away from the screen. "Let me ask you, Philco. Do you remember back in the old days, when everyone was scared to death of a full-scale nuclear war?"

"Vaguely," he shrugged.

"*Well,*" she said brightly, as if she were about to give him the secret to making the perfect angel food cake, "in any nuclear burst, before the shock wave, before the radiation, before the firestorm or the mushroom cloud, there's a little something called the electromagnetic pulse. Are you following me?"

"I think so."

"It knocked out electricity, car batteries, radios, everything." She paused, frowning. "I guess I won't be explaining exactly how it works. If you can't even make sense of this"—she nodded toward the screen—"you'll just have to take my word for it."

"I'm perfectly willing to do that, but wait," Wally said. He was beginning to get worried. "Are... are you saying the plan is to set off a nuclear bomb?"

Angelika laughed harshly, then reached out and slapped his leg. "No, dumbass—that would be pretty stupid, wouldn't it?

We'd be right down here again with the damn C.H.U.D.s for the next forty years." She stopped and took a breath. "I'm talking about something a little cleaner. EMP alone, without all that pesky radiation and what have you... not much, anyway. Very low yield." She seemed to fade away then, into a private wonderland. "Imagine it, knocking everyone back to the preindustrial age in a matter of *seconds*... The entire monstrous economy straight down the crapper... We'd have a second chance. All of us. We could rebuild the world from scratch, maybe even end up with a world that isn't ruled by ninnies and twits."

Wally couldn't see for sure behind the glasses, but he could swear she was almost misting up.

"Can you see it?" she said, as if asking him to step into her reverie. "People would be forced to start reading again. Sitting quietly someplace with a book, reading? Imagining things for themselves? Lord knows what would happen to the world then. People might—all by themselves—think of a different way of doing things, on account of some words someone wrote in a book five hundred years ago. Isn't that something?"

He wasn't sure how to respond to that. "That's really beautiful, Angelika. Really. But I still don't understand... If you're not planning on setting off a nuclear device, how do you, y'know, intend to do all this?"

"Oh," she said, "that's all taken care of."

He waited.

"You didn't know about this?" she sounded disturbed. "I was sure Faro Jack would've taken you to the storeroom already. Listen, you *really* gotta start reading those reports. What the hell have you been doing all this time?"

"Christ, Angelika," he said, frowning, "I'm still learning everyone's name."

She sighed. "Okay. Well then." She pushed herself to her feet. "It's time we took a little walk."

Angelika lied about at least one thing—it wasn't a "little walk." But unlike Wally she had the good sense to use a motorized three-wheel personal mobility scooter. Printed on one of the saddlebags was the brand name GoGo Gopher. A plastic American flag on a stick sprouted from the back of the wide leather seat.

Angelika jabbered the entire slow trip down the long and shadowy corridor. Along the way, Wally learned more about her than he knew about Jack and Carlotta combined. He learned about her childhood on the Jersey shore, her years at Hopkins studying physics and engineering, her gaming, her countless affairs, and, much to Wally's discomfort, her pre-Horribleness career as a high-priced dominatrix.

"There was one client," she was telling him. "He was about ninety. Now, mind you, the older they are, the rougher they want it. That's *always* the case. And this guy insisted that I hang him from fishhooks. Now, an old man's skin, believe you me, is not the kind of thing you want to go— Oh, here we are."

The sharp hum of the scooter shifted to a low sputter as they slowed to a stop in front of an unmarked door identical to all the others they'd passed. Wally had no idea how anyone could keep track of these things, unless there were landmarks of some kind along the way that simply hadn't been pointed out to him yet.

Reaching into one of the saddlebags, Angelika withdrew a metal key not unlike the one Carlotta wore around her neck. Handing it to Wally she asked, "Could you open the door, please?" It was the first time he'd encountered a lock anyplace down there.

He inserted the key, pushed the door open against the darkness, then slapped the wall beside him in search of a light switch.

When the banks of cool overhead panels blinked on, he saw a neat stack of long wooden crates resting in the middle of the cement floor. There were, by his initial count, fifteen of them, each approximately six feet long by two feet square. Stenciled in black on the side of each were the letters RAWDEAL.

Against the wall to his right stood twenty or thirty smaller wooden boxes, each similarly stenciled.

"Raw deal?" he asked, as Angelika rolled into the room and came to a stop beside him. "That doesn't sound very good."

She slapped his leg again. "Not 'raw deal,' ninny—*RAW-DEAL.*"

"Oh," he said. "My mistake."

Angelika sighed, then translated. "Research into Advance Weapons Design, Engineering and Logistics." She waited for some hint of recognition in his face. When none arrived, she said, "It's DOD's experimental weapons division."

"Oh," Wally said again. "Okay... I guess I won't ask you how we got DOD property down here, so why don't you just tell me what's in the boxes?"

"Glad to." Angelika revved the accelerator and whirred toward the longer boxes. Reaching over, she began sliding the lid off one. She looked at Wally. "You gonna help me here or are you just gonna stand there like a stump?"

Wally grabbed the other end of the wooden lid and lifted. Not yet knowing what he was dealing with, he gently leaned the lid against the side of the crate.

Nestled inside, half buried in a lake of fluffy pink Styrofoam shells, lay a device of burnished black steel, five feet long—tubular, though flaring slightly at both ends. Visual and data screens sprang from various points along the shaft and a padded ergonomic handgrip curved away from the bottom.

"What's new, Bazooka Joe?" he said reflexively, suddenly ashamed to have quoted a comic strip from some distant and smoggy memory. Trying to cover the faux pas, he asked, "Is that right? Are these bazookas?"—shocked that he remembered the name.

Angelika shook her head. She was stroking the device tenderly. "Better than that. Shoulder-launched EMP mortars." She looked up at Wally. "It's not as crude as it sounds. A single shell"— she pointed to the boxes against the wall—"that's what's in those. And that will shut down everything in a one-mile radius—electrical power, batteries, wi-fi signals, satellite signals, everything. And shut it down for good too. Completely fry the boards. Operational databases flushed, computer memories erased. Launched at carefully selected strategic locations, we could make all of Manhattan a free zone. Maybe even more—" She stopped short. "But that'll take a little more research and calculation. Plus a little luck."

She continued stroking the weapon with loving care. Behind her thick lenses, he could sense a wonder and gentleness in the eyes, as if she were petting the warm, plump belly of a dozing cat.

"These are fresh off the assembly line—second-generation prototypes. Well oiled and ready to go. That's why we keep them down here."

Rubbing his fingertips together, Wally saw she was right about the "well oiled" part. Wiping his hands on his pants, he asked, "So how *did* you get your hands on these?"

She began trying to heave the lid back onto the box with one hand, and again Wally helped her. "Believe it or not," she said, "we have some sympathizers in some unexpected places. It wasn't exactly legal, but then again neither are we."

Wally was uneasy. He knew this was what it came down to, but the leap from whacking apart a VidLog to advanced experimental weaponry was a big one. He lowered himself onto the box to give his legs a rest, but then promptly stood again, afraid it might go off somehow.

"I dunno, Angelika. I gotta be honest. Don't you think this is kind of an... extreme approach?" He was trying to keep the unease out of his voice. "If you're right about these things, you'll shut down hospitals, respirators . . ." He wracked his brain for other things. ". . . cardio implants, airplanes, umm... restaurants."

"Maybe," she agreed. "Probably. But as the man said, you gotta break a few eggs. *They* did." She pointed to the ceiling again. "Still are. But in our case, as another man said, 'extremism in the defense of liberty is no vice.'"

"Who said that?"

She revved the throttle again and rolled toward the door.

"Most people think it was a politician by the name of Barry Goldwater, who said it in 1964. He was actually misquoting somebody else. It's irrelevant. Anyway, point being this is all about reclaiming what was taken from us."

Apparently they were finished in here. Wally followed her back into the tunnel, still not completely convinced. "But don't you think this goes a little beyond that? I mean, you're talking, ultimately, about the end of civilization. At least in New York."

She stopped and half-spun in the chair as he locked the door behind them and replaced the key in her saddlebag. "More than that if I can help it. What, exactly, do you think's worth saving up there? Robot soccer? *That's* civilization... Look, Wally, if it bothers you, don't think of it as the end of civilization. Think of it as giving civilization another chance to get it right."

He had to admit, she may have a point.

"Besides," she added as they began to make their way back toward the Hub. "Civilization ended a long time ago. It's just that nobody noticed."

She had a point there too.

"But what about backlash? Have you thought of that? They could say it's another terrorist attack. It could make things a lot worse."

"And who, exactly," she asked, "is going to be saying that? And how? With no computer bulletins, no four-ways, no communitainers? Somebody gonna send a letter to the newspapers? Hey, guess what—there *are* no newspapers anymore! We're all gonna be going back to square one together."

Wally looked down at her as she puttered along beside him. She seemed quite content.

"Lemme ask you, then. If these...EMP mortars work the way they're supposed to, will it have any effect on strollers?"

She glanced up at him, both curious and understanding. "No, I'm sorry, unless of course they're the motorized kind. Or unless the strollers themselves are caught in the immediate blast zone, which is entirely possible."

He thought about this for a moment.

"Good," he said.

THIRTEEN

The designer skirt she was wearing had been cut from black leather and stopped at a point just above the knee. She wore black four-inch stiletto heels, and the top two buttons of her cream silk blouse remained undone. A fake Vid-Log (much more realistic than Wally's) was clipped to her collar and fake chip scars had been reapplied on her wrist and above her ear. Her normally loose curls had been pulled back to make sure the communitainer scar wouldn't go unnoticed.

Carlotta waited while Wally climbed the ladder and carefully pushed aside the rusted iron grating leading into the warehouse.

Gray early summer light was filtering through the smeared and broken windows, together with the sounds of the usual congested, impatient traffic on the FDR.

He slithered out of the hole and, trying to stay below the windows, checked the front door. It was still locked. A cursory glance around the warehouse revealed nothing out of the ordinary. He pressed his back against the cracked wall and leaned his head around carefully, just enough to peek out one of the front windows to the sidewalk. It was crowded but everyone seemed preoccupied. They'd pay no attention when Wally and Carlotta stepped out the door. More importantly the Colonel's sedan was idling by the curb. Everything seemed to be a go.

He returned to the hole and gave Carlotta the all-clear. When she reached the top of the ladder, he extended his hand to help pull her up, trying to keep her from dragging her blouse or skirt against the soot-blackened opening or the generally grimy floor. Stained clothes would blow her cover.

"Car there?" she asked quietly. He nodded as, grunting, he shoved the heavy grate back into position. To the uninformed eye it was nothing but another large drain in the floor, indistinguishable from the other three.

They crept to the front door and once again Wally peered outside to check for any approaching HappyCams or DOD agents. He saw nothing apart from Good Citizens in usual mode—heads down, eyes glued to small screens, their steps brisk, their paths random. As they waited for the right moment, Wally and Carlotta heard one citizen bounce hard off the front door before the sharp click and scrape of his polished shoes carried him farther down the sidewalk.

Once he was gone Wally nodded. They straightened themselves and tried to look normal. Carlotta punched in the code unlocking the front door then pulled it open as casually as possible. They stepped outside onto the crowded, bleary sidewalk as if they were leaving a business meeting together. She pulled the door closed behind them and reset the lock.

Heads down, they stepped across the sidewalk to the waiting car. Neither said a word until they were safely inside and the car began moving toward the expressway entrance.

"So it's Wall Street first?" Wally confirmed.

"Uh-huh, then north from there."

They were getting down to the nitty-gritty reconnaissance work, scouting out which locations would make the best targets—not just in terms of shutting down the city but also symbolically, in the hopes that anyone paying attention might recognize what had motivated such outrageous Luddite carnage. Given the limitations of their resources, they had to choose carefully, in terms of both direct and poetic effect. Resident Control was an obvious target, as were the CIALIS and DOD headquarters. PROTEUS X itself was the ultimate target, but that was in Maryland, buried in bedrock a reputed thirteen stories under the earth's surface. That would have to come later.

Discussions had been going on for weeks beneath Twenty-third Street. A list of suggested targets had been maintained on an old blackboard someone, somehow, had smuggled out of the rubble of CeDell Davis High School in the Bronx.

Everyone involved fully realized that a simultaneous (or close to it) attack on fifteen targets around Manhattan would be touted as another heinous act of external terrorists, and that if it didn't work it would lead to even more steel-fisted security measures. That was the risk. That was also why they had no choice but to ensure it worked.

They'd dubbed the plan Operation Fluffy. Nobody was really sure why or how that happened, other than that in a choice between "Operation Fluffy" and "Operation Hezbollapalooza," the former was just, well, funnier. Plus it was easier to spell.

No date had been chosen yet but there was a general, unspoken sense among the Unpluggers that it would have to be soon.

Wally always grew uneasy in lower Manhattan, mostly because he always got lost down there. The tangled narrow streets careened off one another at unexpected angles, and the aging buildings jutted from the pavement like corroded teeth. Everything felt darker and more ominous.

Wally watched the pedestrians through the tinted black windows and sighed. It would certainly be interesting to see what they did when those lifelines they had implanted in their heads were disconnected.

Suicide rate'll probably quadruple, he thought. *That might not be such an awful thing.*

The car pulled over near the corner of Nassau and Pine, roughly two blocks from the Stock Exchange.

Sliding across the seat to follow Carlotta, Wally slammed the door closed behind him and the car hummed its way back into traffic.

"It'll circle the block until you signal," Carlotta said, scanning the area. "Here." She handed Wally a black plastic disc an inch across. In the center of the disc was an orange button. "Put that in your pocket. If you need the car, hit the button. It'll find you." She gave him a serious look. "And if anything should happen—security-wise, I mean—lose the disc."

Uncomfortable as he was having any such tracking device on his person—he'd much rather chase the car into traffic and leap on the hood—he nodded and slid it into his pocket.

She looked up at the massive digital clock on the side of the Ban-Rol Investment Corp building. It was 11:23.

"Okay," she said, "you can take it from here, right?"

Wally, who had been absently staring at her legs, looked up. "Hm?"

"You can take it from here. You know what you're looking for." Then, more uncertainly, "Right?"

Wally's face belied his confusion. "I'm not sure what you're saying. Are you gonna go grab us lunch or something?"

Carlotta looked around impatiently, then grabbed his arm and pulled him out of the flow of oncoming unpredictable foot traffic. In so doing, she also pulled him close enough to talk quietly. "You mean Jack didn't tell you?"

He shook his head, having no idea what she was talking about. "Jack didn't tell me anything except that we were—" he began before she cut him off.

Realizing that two people having a normal conversation on the street might appear suspicious, she began walking. "Keep your head down *and* your voice down," she said. "Try to blend in." Glancing quickly at his clothes, she added, "Pretend you're a tourist...but don't be too obnoxious about it."

As insulting as that could've been, Wally let it slide. Together they began walking down Nassau toward Wall Street. They both saw two armed DOD agents approaching, a dog between them, and dropped their heads. When the men passed without incident Carlotta spoke again.

"Look," she said with a sigh, clearly both uneasy and unprepared. "I just needed a ride downtown. Now I have to go someplace...but you still need to continue scouting. You'll be fine. I'll see you back at the Hub later."

Trying to keep his head down, Wally found himself looking over at her every few steps, trying to gauge her expression. Every time he did, though, he collided with a stock broker or an investment analyst and lost a few steps.

"I don't get it—where are you going?"

"God, this is not good," she said, then took a deep breath. He'd never seen her agitated like this before. "Wally, I'm sorry, but I told you that I'm kind of a recruiter."

"I thought you said you did reconnaissance work."

They reached the corner and found themselves standing in a crowd of thirty people waiting for the pictogram. They stopped talking.

Once across the street, she continued. "Yeah, that's true, but part of that is recruiting."

"Recruiting who?"

"Right now, someone who works down here. That's all I can say."

"I still don't get what the big deal is," he said. "It would be great to have someone who knows the Stock Exchange layout."

She wasn't listening.

"It doesn't mean anything to me," she said. "But we could use another source of funding. That's all this is about."

It seemed like a non sequitur until he began piecing it together. The short skirt, the high heels, the sheer blouse. She never dressed that way around the Hub. And out here it was more than just a simple disguise. Something began to itch inside his skull.

"Aw, *Christ,*" he said. "You're not telling me—"

"It's not that big a deal."

He knew she was some kind of hippie but "not a big deal"? No, being a gardener or an insurance cog is not a big deal. Being a shameless hussy for the revolution, though? That's a big deal.

He stopped walking and a financial counselor slammed into his back, bounced toward the street, then veered back into the stream of pedestrians.

"You've gotta be kidding me," he said. In spite of the numbness creeping through his body, the anger was beginning to swell. "We've known each other how long? We all but live together. But you don't tell me until now—and *here*—and you say it's nothing? What kind of bul—" He swallowed the word, aware of his surroundings. "What's *that* all about?"

"Jack was supposed to tell you," she said, looking away.

"Jack." Wally snarled. "*Jack*? What does *Jack* know about... man alone?"

"What are you even saying?"

His eyes were almost wild. "I'm saying, why couldn't *you* tell me? Cut out the middleman. That would make more sense, wouldn't you think?"

Carlotta shook her head. "Oh, this is not good," she mumbled, half to herself. She looked around for a HappyCam, fully expecting to see three closing in on them. "It's all just part of the deal, okay? It doesn't change how I feel about you. But what might is if you go all caveman on me about it."

"Cave—?" Wally sputtered. "*Look* at me!"

Three people who were passing did, and Carlotta whispered, "Wally, you gotta get out of here. People are beginning to notice. We've got to talk about this later. Make one pass by the Exchange—and for godsakes keep your head down. Then call the car." She looked up helplessly at another clock on the side of the Bank of Eritrea building. "I have to go—I'm sorry." She turned quickly and vanished into the crowd.

Wally stood silently, not sure what to think.

Then he knew perfectly well what to think, and he was pissed. It wasn't just Wally Philco she was messing with—she was jeopardizing Operation Fluffy itself.

With a snarl and a skull full of glass shards and broken cinder blocks, he lowered his head and began stomping down the sidewalk, grinding his teeth, mumbling and slamming into pedestrians. For once, he actually fit in. Unlike the rest of them, however, he had no idea where he was going, and within minutes he found himself lost on a tiny side street.

He looked up hoping to spot some recognizable landmark, but his view in all directions was blocked by decaying gray and brown buildings. Not caring, he lowered his head and continued walking. The street seemed to grow narrower with each step.

Behind him he heard a rhythmic clicking. He refused to look back.

It was quite distinct from the high heels and patent leather you generally heard clicking around Manhattan. It was accompanied by the soft scrape of metal on metal.

As he listened, still walking lord knows where, the tempo began to accelerate. He both hoped and dreaded it would be Carlotta. Mostly dreaded. He wasn't in the mood right now to hear her apology, especially if she was going to turn around again and run off to meet some accountant for a few hours.

But maybe she wouldn't turn back around. Maybe she'd changed her mind.

His steps slowed. It wasn't like she'd lied after all. Not exactly. She simply neglected to tell him the truth. She'd recruited him, hadn't she? Like she said, it was part of her job. But of course in his case there hadn't been any... Ah, Christ, he loved her, the silly harlot. He just didn't like imagining her like that.

He whirled, ready to shout her name and catch her in his arms, when all visions of Carlotta splashed from his mind and he screamed.

Bearing down on him was a jackbooted Stroller Brigadoon, her teeth bared.

"*Jesus Christ!*" He jumped aside, slamming into a solid brick wall as the oversized stroller's momentum carried it past him.

Through his pain and his tear-filled eyes, he recognized the face. All that heavy makeup. It was Ingrid Ogami herself, founder and president of the Brigade. Wally had no idea she was that tall.

Ms. Ogami nimbly whirled the massive stroller and began closing in again. It had been tricked out like a chopper, the single front fork angling down to the street from the double-wide basket. The basket itself, which cradled a pair of sleeping infants, was hooded, perched waist high and encased in polished steel painted an intense candy apple red. Airbrushed on one side of the basket was the Brigade logo, on the other a leering wolf's head.

Wally looked up and down the street in a panic. He was trapped.

As Ms. Ogami charged toward him, a row of six thin and deadly blades sprang from the bottom of the carriage and clicked into place, poised to tear through the average human crotch. Above them he saw the circular cuts in the red metal that hid the recessed gun turrets.

Ms. Ogami paused in her charge, clutching the handle with the typical blend of moral fury and self-satisfaction. The crumbling makeup flaked lightly from her face and dotted her black leather blazer. Her dark hair was piled high atop her head, making her seem even taller. She was wearing dark wraparound shades.

Oh, this is a terrible day, Wally thought, as he tried again to press himself backward against the brick wall.

He noticed for the first time the double row of razor blades attached along the extended fork. A careful strike could easily slice an artery.

"*Whatever... it... takes!*" Ms. Ogami growled.

The fire in Wally's skull—the rage at Carlotta, which had admittedly been fading—was reignited and redirected. He could feel his facial muscles twist his features into a nauseous mask of disgust. This was madness, being chased by smug homicidal people with strollers. Why had he lived so long like this? Why did other people?

Wally, much to his own astonishment, stood his ground. Of course there wasn't much of anywhere for him to run, but that was beside the point. He stopped trying to push through the wall. He did not cower and weep.

"I see you've forgotten your VidLog too," Ms. Ogami said with an arrogant curl of the lip. "Bad form, Citizen." Without warning, she began to howl in a voice that at any other time would've made Wally's shoulders twitch. "*Unmutual! Unmutual!*"

As she made a final, lethal lunge at him with the stroller, Wally lashed out with his foot, catching the fork low, just above the wheel but below the razors, holding it at bay just long enough to bend over and grab both sides of the carriage. Tearing it from her hands with an unexpected burst of adrenaline, he sent it crashing to its side, firing two of the spring-loaded blades into the wall behind him. Trailing pink blankets stitched with the Brigade logo, the two sleeping infants flew from the basket and hit the pavement, each bouncing once and skidding briefly, facedown, toward the street. Both were silent. Neither moved. For just an instant, there was an unnatural stillness in the air as if the whole universe had blinked, like that lidless eyeball in his dream.

A crowd was already gathering around them, raised minivids capturing the action.

Wally and Ms. Ogami stood in a shocked hush, staring at the small still bodies.

"I knew it," Wally whispered to himself. Then he looked at the proud mother. "I *knew* it. Lady, you're a phony. A goddamn *phony!*"

On the ground a few feet away lay two SidsCo Brand Ultra-Real vinyl dolls. ("Fool your friends!")

"Your whole fucking *program* is a fraud from the bottom up, isn't it . . . *lady*?" Ms. Ogami continued glaring, dumbfounded, at the dolls. "But everyone believes it, and that's the only reason it works!"

He wiped the spittle from the corner of his mouth. He wasn't used to shouting like that.

Out of the corner of his eye he spotted the HappyCam turning the corner, heading toward the public disruption. Realizing that the whole thing was being filmed from eighteen different angles, he spun and began running, pausing to snatch up one of the blankets to cover his face. Stumbling briefly, his foot caught the head of one of the dolls, booting it nearly fifteen feet through the air into the middle of the noon traffic.

He didn't stop or look back. He ran, his face half covered, crashing his way through the crowd, knocking one senior vice president type off his feet and nearly flipping over a garbage can before dodging a coffee cart. He didn't care. He had to get away. He reached into his pocket and felt for the disc. At least with all that footage, everyone would see that big fat phony for what she really was.

Miracle of miracles, the Colonel's sedan was waiting when he turned the next corner. He dropped the blanket in the gutter and leaped into the backseat, slamming the door as the car pulled away.

He looked out the window at the people. Such ridiculous awful creatures. It was a madhouse up here.

This had to be done. Carlotta or no Carlotta. They were going to get the war they deserved.

FOURTEEN

FELTCH officials announced today what we've all been fearing for the past year—the first reported case of the Golden Orb SuperVirus in this country. According to her parents, ten-year-old Clorox Cardiban of Boston complained about a case of the sniffles two weeks ago... However, when they rushed her to the emergency room, it was discovered that she had in fact been infected with the SuperVirus and was subsequently quarantined... After ravaging Africa and northern Europe with six thousand reported cases and almost twenty deaths, the SuperVirus is poised to have an even more devastating effect on our nation... While FELTCH researchers continue to scramble for a vaccine, BOO administrators have stated that they believe this outbreak to be the result of, quote, the most sinister terrorist plot in history...

He'd paused only briefly by the Hub's four-way on his way to his quarters and now he'd seen all he needed.

... the Golden Orb SuperVirus, all rights to which were recently acquired by the Bilderberg International Corporation...

He shook his head and began the long walk to his room.

Lying back on his cot half an hour later, Wally plucked the top book off the stack next to him and opened it. The Unpluggers had a surprisingly well-stocked library. Most of the volumes had been donated from the private libraries of various Unpluggers, many of whom began hoarding books long before widespread bannings began. A number of them had grown a little moldy after spending years beneath floorboards and in subbasements, but you could still read the words, even if the pages themselves were musty.

Along with several volumes of military history, the stack next to his cot included works by Caesar, Lao-tzu, and General George S. Patton. A collection of inspirational essays reputedly written by Sid Powell, *Stop and Think, Shithead,* was a big help too. Elementary physics and engineering textbooks. Wilderness survival handbooks. Since everyone else down there seemed to own it, he borrowed Angelika's copy of *Capital of Pain,* but quickly realized that French surrealist poetry from the 1920s wasn't something his brain was willing to digest. And since the Colonel had mentioned it, he'd also grabbed a tattered paperback edition of *Player Piano.* It would probably be a while before he got to it, but he would.

Picking up a book for the first time in so many years was odd. Its structure seemed so alien and yet so perfect. It wasn't just the structure—though reading something you didn't scroll through took some getting used to—it was the amount of information crammed onto the pages. Digital Information Dispensaries (DIDs) had reduced the answer to any question to a sentence or two, composed in a vocabulary easily understood by any six-year-old and always accompanied by lots of pictures and animation. None of these books next to him now contained any pictures at all, and it sometimes took several pages to explain something. Plus there were all those old words. It threw him at first, the amount of work it took. He'd read a few books as a kid, but the effects of the past decade were undeniable. After he started reading, he realized that he did know a lot of those words—it's just that no one used them anymore, for fear of offending the simpleminded.

As Angelika had suggested, he even found himself forming a few ideas of his own based on the things he'd been reading. During his biweekly meetings with her, he discovered that he could now do more than listen and nod. He could hold his own with her, and she no longer referred to him as a "ninny." Not as often, anyway.

The coordinated attacks should take place late at night—sometime between midnight and four, the way the FALN and IRA had done it. That way they could reduce the potential for any civilian casualties. Even though the Unpluggers would be more vulnerable up there at that hour, it also meant there would be fewer troops around, and fewer Good Citizens looking to earn themselves a T-shirt. Each of them would carry a jammer to block the vids (if the new jammers were operational at that point). And even if the jammers didn't work they'd all wear masks.

It was no surprise that masks of any kind had been banned

in the city post-Horribleness, but as it happened one of the Unpluggers had been collecting Halloween masks most of her life and couldn't bear to part with them when she made the move underground. She had everything from monsters and old political figures to popular celebrities such as Whit Bissell. She had Martin Van Buren, Pat Paulsen, Jack Elam—even a rare William E. Miller mask. In many cases the years had not been kind, neither to memory nor to the latex, but they would do just fine.

With only fifteen EMP launchers at their disposal, they were stretching their capabilities mighty thin. The engineers were working on the plans to design more, but that could take months, even years, and they didn't have that kind of time. They'd spent too much time talking about it already.

If Operation Fluffy went according to plan, there would be no need for the Unpluggers to return to the Hub (except possibly to avoid the inevitable riots that would ensue). That would be the exact moment to start spreading the word to Unpluggers in other cities and other grids—even other countries, though Wally had no idea how that might happen, or if it would be worth anything. Most of them had problems of their own.

"If my calculations are correct," Angelika had said at their last meeting as the two of them examined a map of the city, "knocking out the substations on Rivington and Thirty-third simultaneously will cause a cascade effect, wiping out the power up and down the eastern seaboard. We won't get everything," she clarified. "Just the electricity outside the immediate EDG, and it won't be forever but at least as they scramble to get the power back on in Philly and Washington, we'll have a chance to move south toward Fort Meade."

Everything depended, however, on Operation Fluffy working in Manhattan. If it failed, or was only half successful, they were all royally screwed.

He heard the sound of bare feet padding up the tunnel toward his room. Only one person down there ever went barefoot, and only one person ever ran. He marked his page, closed the book, replaced it atop the stack, and waited.

A moment later Carlotta appeared in his doorway, out of breath, obviously having run the nearly half-mile from the Hub.

"Wally—I think you might want to see this."

He looked at her for a moment. "See what?" he asked. She didn't seem to be holding anything.

"The news. They just showed it, but they'll be showing it again in a few minutes—you'd better run."

He rolled from his cot and headed for the door. "What is it?"

"I think you should see it for yourself." There was worry and urgency in her eyes like he'd never seen before. Few things ever seemed to worry her.

Things between them had, needless to say, been a little tense and uncomfortable in the weeks after he learned about her true role within the movement. There had been long, painful silences interrupted by short bursts of cruel rage. She could understand his pain, she said, but she also had a job to do. They all did. It was the movement that mattered now. Continually sniping at each other and casting reproachful looks across the Hub would be bad for morale. It was upon that agreement that they had been able to forge a truce, even begin to take a few tentative steps toward rekindling what they once had. As the preparations for the assault intensified, all that emotional hoo-hah would need to take a back seat for a while.

She began trotting toward the Hub. Realizing that Wally wasn't keeping up, she stopped and turned. "Run!" she commanded. He removed his hands from his pockets and reluctantly began jogging with thick, heavy steps.

When they reached the Hub, both of them out of breath now, a half dozen Unpluggers had gathered around the four-way, including Jack and Angelika. They were all silent, staring at the screen, waiting for the commercials to end and whatever it was Wally was supposed to see to return.

Down one of the unused wings, Wally could hear the distant, muffled blasts of Unpluggers training with the EMP launchers. They weren't firing live rounds, of course, just getting a feel for the weapons.

"*. . . will be returning in just a moment to our live coverage of Ambien McCorkle's brave struggle to recover from that sprained ankle,*" the newscaster was saying, "*but first a follow-up to something we reported here fifteen minutes ago. New Yorkers were stunned today by a brazen and deadly daylight attack upon beloved Stroller Brigade founder Ingrid Ogami and her two helpless children . . .*"

"*Thank God,*" Wally sneered.

"Shhh," Carlotta insisted, nodding at the screen.

"*. . . spite of her brave efforts to battle the creature, her children—both infants—did not survive. The creature is believed to be a C.H.U.D.—or cannibalistic humanoid underground dweller, long rumored to be living in the sewers and subway tunnels beneath Manhattan. The attack took place shortly before noon to-*

day in the Financial District and was captured by over a dozen professional and citizen vids. We do warn you, the footage we are about to air is shocking and graphic, so we suggest that some of you might want to go make a sandwich or use the bathroom at this point."

The first thing Wally noticed when they cut to the footage was the unmistakable stroller—the red chopper with the wolf's-head insignia. Ogami's back was to the screen and it had been shot at such an angle that you couldn't see the knives.

The focus, however, was on the creature Ogami had pinned against a brick wall with the stroller. Wally had never seen anything like it before—a squat, lumpy beast, its flesh warty and dark, its skull flat, with red eyes and a wide, dripping mouth filled with curved fangs. The arms ended in wicked talons, but swing them as it might they were too stubby to reach her.

"That's a C.H.U.D.?" Wally asked, never having seen one before.

"Yup," Jack said.

"Guess so," added Angelika.

On the screen, you could hear Ogami screaming "*Unmutual! Unmutual!*" She pulled the stroller back a few feet to make a fresh run at the monster's belly, but as she began her new thrust the C.H.U.D. grabbed the stroller in its claws, tore it from Ogami's hands, and threw it savagely to the ground, spilling the two children onto the pavement.

"Oh my God," Wally whispered, only then recognizing exactly what he was seeing.

"Now you know why I wanted you to see this?" Carlotta asked.

As several of the Unpluggers turned away from the screen,

Wally watched as the monster scooped up one of the infants, shoved its bobbing, howling head into its ugly maw, and bit down. Blood sprayed from between its lips as it shook its head from side to side, at last tearing the headless body away and casting the lifeless, tattered hunk of meat to the sidewalk.

Then, in a final insult to all that is decent in the world, the C.H.U.D. reared back and spit the infant's severed head into the air. It flew fifteen feet, the vids following in slow motion, until, with a sickening wet crunch, it splattered in the street before being run over by a passing Mini Fort.

With a hissing roar, the creature bounded down the street and around the corner with a speed improbable for something of that size and shape. Stranger yet, its feet never seemed to make solid contact with the sidewalk. The image cut back to the newscaster.

"*DOD agents are currently searching for the heinous beast, and patrols have been stepped up in the Financial District. Half an hour ago, city officials announced that they plan to prevent any such horror from happening again by flooding the subways and sewers throughout the city with cyanide gas. No date has been set yet, but officials say it will be within the week and assure all Good Citizens they will be given at least half an hour's warning before the gassing begins... Meanwhile, for her heroic efforts to protect the city from this terrible creature, Ingrid Ogami will be presented with the city's highest honor, the Medal of Superness, at a ceremony in the Resident Control building tomorrow. And tonight she'll be a guest on* The Roland Rollin Show, *where she will recount her harrowing experience. Now back to our live coverage of poor Ambien—*"

Wally leaned over and turned down the volume, still stunned.

"But that happened two weeks ago," he said, looking around at the gathered Unpluggers. "And the babies were fakes."

"Guess it took them that long to work up the CGI inserts," Faro Jack suggested.

"Two weeks, really? I wouldn't've guessed that long."

"Well, if you think about it—"

"Gentlemen?" a voice asked.

"—they'd have to come up with some designs first. They don't have any C.H.U.D. photos to work from that I'm aware of, so they'd be starting from scratch. Then comes the modeling. If you look close, it seems they were rushing there at the end—the movement was—"

"*Gentlemen*?"

Both Wally and Jack stopped and turned to find Angelika glaring at them, arms folded.

"I think we have bigger concerns right now than the workings of the city's News Enhancement Bureau."

"And what might those be?" Jack asked.

"Weren't you listening?"

The term "cyanide gas" finally began seeping into Wally's brain. He grabbed a chair from the nearest desk and dropped himself into it. He was awfully pooped from all that running, and now this. "Holy *crap,*" he said. "We've got less than a week before they're down here."

"So what do we do?" Suddenly every set of eyes in the room was on him. Even people who hadn't watched the C.H.U.D. spectacle had since wandered over after it became apparent something was up. Wally could feel his armpits growing damp. It was a little late at this point, he supposed, to run back to Brooklyn and hide in his almost empty house. He had to be what they needed him to be.

"Only one thing to do," he announced, leaning forward and letting his eyes drift across the gathered faces. "We've all been talking about late October, but that clearly ain't gonna happen, is it? What's the date today?"

"August third," Carlotta offered.

"And we've got a week or less," Angelika added.

Wally was silent, considering. "Well...we're together here, after all, right? We've got the equipment, we've got the plan. At this point it's simply a matter of arranging teams and getting a little more training time in—" He stopped and looked at Carlotta. "You said it was the third today?"

"Saturday the third, yeah."

"So that would make Thursday the eighth." It wasn't a question; he was merely thinking aloud. Then he began to smile for the first time in days. He glanced around the room at the Unpluggers, *his* Unpluggers, in a way. Such odd, odd faces staring back at him, waiting.

"Horribleness Day," he said at last.

There was a long silence before the gathered Unpluggers erupted into hooting laughter and applause. Wally, for the first time in his life, felt justified in rising from his chair and taking a bow.

FIFTEEN

Over the next three days the lights in the Hub never dimmed. Everyone worked in shifts, and at a pace Wally had never witnessed before, either aboveground or down here. The crazy outbursts were stilled, and even Pye took part in the EMP training (though he found it hard to fire the weapon while wearing six layers of latex gloves).

An oversized map of Manhattan had been hung from the chalkboard, delineated into fifteen zones, the target within each zone marked clearly with a red X. The Unpluggers—including Wally, Carlotta, Jack, and Angelika (who wouldn't have missed her chance to fire an EMP mortar at Resident Control for anything)—were divided into teams of three.

The synchronized assault was scheduled for two-thirty a.m.

on the morning of August eighth—the twelfth anniversary of the Horribleness. With luck, no one would be hurt, no one would be captured, and the city would be free for the first time in over a decade.

Taped to the wall to the right of the city map hung a schematic of the sewer system. The Unpluggers would be using the sewers to travel as inconspicuously as possible to their assigned targets, and so each needed to know the route blindfolded. "What do they do if they're stopped along the way?" Wally asked Jack as they examined both maps for any logistical problems they might have overlooked.

"They won't be."

It was shortly after seven on Tuesday morning and Wally was at a desk in the Hub, once again poring over the team list, trying to make certain for the last time there were no potential personality conflicts. The last thing they needed was someone screwing up because he couldn't stand the way someone else cracked his gum or snorted when she laughed.

Faro Jack slapped him on the shoulder. "Hey, *amigo*, c'mon, we gotta hit the trail."

He looked up from the sheets in front of him. "What?"

"There's some hombre up yonder, says he's finagled us three more EMPs and a dozen more shells."

"You're kidding. That's great. A little last minute, maybe, but still great."

"We'll need 'em for backup, but we gotta go wait for the wagon. Can't exactly load all that into the old man's trunk. So go get your gear. We can't afford to let this varmint vamoose on us."

Wally had learned to stop questioning things like this. Jack and a few of the other scavengers simply had a way of coming into some impossible things. New washers and dryers, real meat, a black Maneki Neko, anything. Drake had even found a complete set of blueprints for the Resident Control building stuffed in a trash can on Thirty-eighth Street. Whatever an Unplugger needed, they provided it, somehow—including a new pair of comfortable shoes.

"I'm set," Wally said, putting down the papers and rising from the desk. "Where are we going?"

"To a place where there is no darkness," Jack said.

"Where, now?"

"Never mind. Let's get a move on."

They never bothered hiding on the Lexington platform. No other trains ever came by. Just the work train, and it was always empty, and always on time.

They'd been waiting five or six minutes when Wally heard a sound from the shadowed end of the platform—a pebble being lobbed gently against a tiled wall.

He turned to Jack. "What was that?"

"Nothing. A gonk from outside." He was humming to himself again and wasn't much interested in distractions. Wally decided against going to investigate. Down there you never knew when it might be a C.H.U.D.

In the distance, he saw the lights appear from around the bend and heard the echoed squeal of the slow approaching train. After all this time underground, jumping aboard moving trains had become almost second nature to him. He'd learned what cars to look for, where to aim his body, and how to stop his momentum once he hit. Most important, he'd learned how to stay out of sight while they were passing through an active station.

"Thar she blows," he said.

"Mm-hmm," Jack replied, working it effortlessly into the tune.

As the three cars of the grimy yellow train groaned into the station, Wally poised to make his jump. But then the train hissed to a painful stop.

"Climb aboard," Jack said.

Wally paused. "I don't get it. It's never stopped before."

"Did this time. Let's just hope it stops later, too, otherwise it'll be a bitch to load."

Wally gingerly stepped onto the flatbed, praying the train didn't jerk to life again before he had both feet down.

Jack followed, and the moment he'd lowered himself against a wooden crate with a grunt the train began moving up the tracks.

"That was convenient."

"Weren't it, though?"

Once they were moving, Jack stopped humming and began singing. He sang slowly, almost mournfully, his adopted drawl more pronounced than ever.

> *Just as the moon was peepin' over the hill*
> *after the work was through*
> *There sat a cowboy and his partner Bill*
> *Cowboy was feelin' bluuee*

Then the tempo picked up suddenly. Even with the upbeat tempo, Wally thought he could detect a strange undercurrent of menace in the song. Strange for a cowboy song, anyway. He couldn't tell if it was the song itself or the performance. No matter, really. He'd be content to sit back and enjoy the ride, still unsure where they were supposed to meet this arms dealer.

If Margie could only see me now, he thought. *I'm going to meet an arms dealer.*

As the tracks rattled and strained beneath them on their slow journey, Wally tried to remember how long it had been since he'd filed a daily report with CIALIS, or had had an abrasive ad blast aimed directly and unexpectedly into his cerebral cortex, or had received an unwanted call, or showed his SUCKIE card to some overweight corporate slug, or stood still for an iris scan, or had his bag searched by a man with a gun. It felt like years. But it couldn't be—it had been just a year ago that he'd been sent to BLAB for language modification and a good haranguing. *I was modified, all right,* he thought.

As important and necessary as all of those things were made to seem aboveground, he could honestly tell himself that he didn't feel any more vulnerable in their absence. Quite the opposite. For all the endless and epic weirdness of the past months, his life, he felt no shame in admitting, had become exciting and interesting and *fun.* Illegal, maybe, but still. Here he was, an outlaw, riding atop a mystery train through forgotten tunnels beneath New York, on his way to pick up some extremely powerful weapons to help the revolution. A revolution he was leading (sort of).

Who's the boob now? he thought.

They might fail. There was always that possibility. All the Unpluggers could end up either dead or in Terminal Five. But even if that did happen—and he didn't think it would—at least they'd have given it an honest shot. Nobody could take that away from them.

He glanced over at Jack, leaning back against the crate, eyes upward toward the passing overhead lights, still humming.

Twenty-five minutes later the train groaned to a stop along the darkened platform of another desolate and forgotten station. Wally tried to read the name of the stop on the wall, but the mosaics had been chipped and scraped to illegibility.

"Where are we?" he asked.

Jack looked around the platform. "Somewhere in the seventies," he said. "Upper East Side. This is it. C'mon."

He pushed himself to his feet and stepped lightly onto the platform. Wally followed, brushing his hands on his already stained pants. He wasn't sure if there'd be time to do a load of laundry before the attack, but it sure would be nice to enter the new world with clean pants.

Jack made his way toward a black metal door upon which "Employees Only" had been stenciled in red and white. He grabbed the broad silver handle and twisted it. With a hollow click and a wheeze, the door was pulled open. The darkness inside was impenetrable. No matter how much Wally squinted, he couldn't make anything out.

"Careful," Jack warned. "There are steps here. They're steep, and there's no railing. Move slow and feel your way…and try not to run into me."

Wally put his hands out to either side until he found the cool cement wall to his right. Lowering his left foot gently until he found the first step, he realized Jack wasn't kidding—the steps were only six or eight inches wide, and of drastically varying heights.

Once he'd worked himself into something akin to a rhythm on what was beginning to feel like an endless staircase plunging him deeper into the earth than he'd ever been before, he asked, "I probably should've asked this earlier, but who is this guy we're meeting?"

From the blackness a few feet in front of him, Jack said, "Dunno. He's one of Carlotta's contacts. Can't give you a name. All I know is that this is where we're supposed to meet him, so this is where we are."

Getting the impression it would be wise not to ask too many more questions, Wally merely grunted. He was beginning to grow nervous at the prospect of hauling all that weaponry—however much there was of it—back up these stairs. How many trips were they going to have to make? His knees were getting rubbery as it was.

At last, he heard Jack's feet reach the bottom—or at least what he prayed was the bottom. With one hand in front of him and one still on the wall to his right, he took the last step and felt his hand touch the smooth vinyl of Jack's slicker.

"This it?"

"Yup, I suppose it is. Now hold on."

Wally heard three knocks—two short, then a third—on what sounded like another solid metal door.

Jack took a step back and the two of them stood side by side as the sound of sliding deadbolts and snapped locks leaked through the door. Then came the click of a latch and the door began to creak open.

Squeezing his eyes shut against what, in contrast, seemed a blinding white glare, Wally heard Jack say to whoever opened the door, "We're expected."

Feeling Jack brush past him to step inside, Wally slowly opened his eyes and found himself looking down into the dark and dour face of the midget in the black suit.

"Good day, Mr. Philco," the midget said, holding out a black-gloved hand. "I'm so glad to meet you properly at last—my name's Sid Powell."

Oh, this was all way too much. With nearly overwhelming trepidation, Wally reached out and took the gloved hand. "I've seen you on the four-way," he said, deciding it best to put the elbow incident behind him, considering. "I must say, the resemblance is less than . . . um."

The small man shook his head. "I get that a lot. Now won't you come in? There's some business to attend to."

Finally stepping through the doorway, Wally's first thought was that it looked like the last place anyone would be making a black market arms deal. He expected cracked, smoke-stained concrete walls, a single bare incandescent bulb dangling from the ceiling, rats rustling in the corner, and a wiry, wild-eyed loner in fatigues—not oriental rugs, track lighting, plush, leather-upholstered easy chairs, and an obscenely large semi-circular polished oak desk.

As Jack, seeming quite at home here, dropped himself into one of the easy chairs, Wally—still trying to grasp it all—turned back to Sid Powell. "So this . . . this is where you hide out? I thought you were in Nevada." Then, hoping he wouldn't sound like too much of a fanboy, added, "I, um . . . I really liked your book."

Powell offered a flicker of a smile—more a facial twitch, really—but it was the closest Wally had come to seeing him express any emotion. "Thank you, yes. But hide out? Not exactly. I work here."

Before Wally could ask anything further, a bell *ting*'ed twice behind him, on the far side of the room. With a hiss an elevator door opened.

"So good to see you again, my boy. I'm so pleased you could make it." The Colonel rolled his wheelchair out of the elevator toward the desk. "Won't you take a seat next to Jack, there? We'll get down to work."

"Oh," Wally said. "Hello." *There's that hand again,* he thought as his eyes fixed on the malformed reddish claw. The old man was wearing the same two cardigans, and the blanket was still folded on his lap.

Sid Powell stepped around Wally and marched briskly over to the Colonel.

"Will you be needing anything else at the moment, sir?" he asked.

"Oh, no, Sid," the Colonel said as he eased the chair in behind the desk. "I believe we're quite all right. If we need anything, I'll call."

With a bow but not another word, Powell stepped into the elevator and punched a button. The doors hissed shut again.

In spite of his surprise at the surroundings and learning that the midget who had elbowed him in the park was in fact Sid Powell, professional rabble-rouser, media legend, and manservant, Wally couldn't say he was all that surprised to learn the Colonel was the shadowy weapons dealer. Given his background and Carlotta's admission that he was a major backer of the Unplugger movement, it only made sense. Jack's behavior, however, suddenly struck him as very odd, given that they all knew the Colonel.

With both Jack and the Colonel looking at him, Wally took a seat. "It's... good to see you, too, Colonel. So... you're the one who's supplying the EMPs?"

The Colonel coughed out a dry laugh. "Oh, no, my boy, perish the thought. Well, those you saw, yes, of course I arranged for their delivery, but . . ." He stopped, his eyes shifting. "Perhaps I should apologize initially. You see, you were summoned up here on pretenses that weren't, shall we say, exactly truthful."

Wally turned to Jack, who was trying to look innocent beneath the cowboy hat.

"It's—" Wally began, but he didn't know where to go after that.

"Yes, Mr. Philco, I'm sorry—I have no more weapons for you today. But I needed some plausible pretext for pulling you away from the Hub on the eve of such a momentous event."

"There's still a bit to do, yes," Wally began.

The Colonel looked around his bare desktop, trying to find something he knew had to be there. "Perhaps it's best I cut to the chase... You, Mr. Philco, have been the subject of a little experiment. And while I'm sorry to inform you of that, I am happy to report that the experiment—from our point of view—was an outstanding and complete success."

Suddenly, Wally's mouth went dry, as if someone had tucked a wad of cotton beneath his tongue.

"Experiment?" He was beginning to feel nauseous.

" 'Fraid so, *amigo,*" Jack said. There was no sheepishness or hint of apology in his voice. Now he was all business.

The Colonel nodded. "I must say, this has always been my favorite part of the movies, don't you agree? The part where the villain gets to outline the details of his fiendish plot before dispatching the hero? Though," he qualified, "I don't consider myself a villain, and I can assure you that you are in no danger."

It struck Wally that somehow, apart from the hand and the attire, the Colonel seemed twenty years younger than he had during their previous meeting. "You see, Mr. Philco, it's like this... The boffins at SPOOK decided—just for fun, really—to see if it was possible to take an average Good Citizen like yourself, say, and transform him without any kind of torture or coercion into a terrorist. Simply through the art of conversation. So much cheaper and cleaner than torture or mind control drugs, you see."

Wally half rose and whirled on Jack. "You said I was a freedom fighter!"

Jack shrugged. "That I did."

The Colonel waved Wally back into the chair with his good hand. "Yes, yes, yes—you say to-mah-to, I say to-may-to. I've worked with people who've made that distinction. So has Jack here, for that matter. But it's all semantics, really. Doesn't change a thing."

They were both so calm, it was infuriating. Wally sat back down.

"We chose you, you see," the old man went on. "Completely at random. It could've been anybody, granted. Your neighbor Mr. Chambers, for instance, which would have been amusing, or perhaps your wife. But here we all are." He stopped and peered at Wally. "Would you care for a glass of water? You're looking a touch green."

Before Wally could tell him to go fuck himself, the Colonel tapped a button beneath the desktop, then resumed. "As I was saying, we chose you, a typical Good Citizen, and just a few months later you were perfectly willing to go so far as to kill *children* in the fight for an insane and hopeless cause."

"*But not many!*" Wally erupted.

"Yes, well, in short, the experiment was a complete success. Isn't that a stitch?" He considered Wally's face again. "Well, yes, I can perhaps understand why you might not see it that way at this particular moment in time, but trust me it is. A stitch, I mean. You'll come around."

Wally looked to Jack for something, anything.

"Think of it this way," the Colonel said amiably. "If we hadn't chosen you, and you had opted to follow the same path? Doubtful, of course, but say you did. You wouldn't've lasted a week. Do you realize how many times we could've picked you up had we wanted to?"

"I have some idea, yes," Wally admitted sullenly.

"If we hadn't selected you for this program, you'd presently be serving life at Terminal Five. Nine times over, in fact, by my count. Do you honestly think DOD lets citizens *walk away* after using hate words on Stroller Brigadoons? Heavens, no. And that scene in the bank? That, I must say, was priceless. I play that for everyone who stops by." He chuckled gently to himself. "Ah, but we were keeping an eye on you."

Wally's head was spinning and the cramps were hitting his stomach in waves. This was a sick nightmare.

"So you're government agents?" he forced out in spite of himself, looking from one to the other. "You told me you were fired."

The Colonel made a face. "It wasn't a *complete* lie, I suppose...I was rehired a few days later. And in answer to your government agents question, no, not quite. Unless you want to consider PROTEUS X the government, which perhaps you should. I still don't care for the name, though I guess we could call ourselves Proteans."

"Hey, I like that, Colonel B.," Jack said.

"Yes...yes, now that I hear it, I must say I'm rather fond of it myself." Then for good measure, he repeated it. "Proteans, yes. A nice ring to it."

The elevator door opened again, and into the room stepped that goddamn troll in his stupid black suit, pushing an ornate silver tea cart that held a crystal carafe of water, three glasses, three porcelain bowls, and a covered pot, which, by the smell of it, contained bean with bacon soup.

Still struggling to hack through the insanity, Wally, his voice increasingly strangled, asked, "But what about all the other Unpluggers? Angelika, and...and Pye and that abductee? We were all working on this. They believed as much as I did."

The Colonel lifted the lid to the pot and took a mighty whiff. He smiled sadly and looked back to Wally. "Oh, my boy, do you honestly believe, in this day and age, that *that* many people—especially in New York—would give up everything to fight back against their oppressors? Nonsense. They voted for their own oppression."

"Not all of us did."

"No, but most of you did, and would again. That's democracy." He paused. "Think of it this way, Mr. Philco. Even if my Operation Castor Oil was a touch unorthodox for the time, perhaps a little extreme, I gave the people what they wanted. They want to feel safe. They don't give a hoot in hell for what you think liberty is. If you don't believe me, take a survey. There were plenty taken in the years after the Horribleness, and they all reported the same thing. The citizens wanted security, not freedom, and that's what they were given." He spread his hands apart as if to illustrate his innocence. "*You,* on the other hand, were going to take all that away from them by means that were just as unorthodox and extreme. More so, even. So who's the villain here?"

As much as he hated to admit it, Wally knew it was finished. Operation Fluffy wasn't going to happen. He knew that now. The cramps in his stomach subsided, replaced with something solid and cold and dead. He accepted the glass of water Sid Powell offered him and took a swallow. "So all of this has been an elaborate hoax, like the Horribleness?"

The Colonel paused while ladling some soup into a shallow bowl. "Mr. Philco, every civilization in the world is held together by hoaxes. Religion, politics, terrorism. Take your pick. It's how we stay together."

"But—" Wally started.

"*But,*" the Colonel interrupted, still ladling, "in this case everything you were told was true. Everything I told you was true, everything Jack told you, and my granddaughter—well, I don't know *everything* she told you, but she's an honest girl, makes an honest living." He put the ladle in the pot and replaced the lid. "There was no reason to lie. We simply presented the truth to you couched in a certain attitude and perspective, spoken with a certain tone of voice, you see. All those people down there are really working on the things they said they were working on. Only difference is that they're working for us, not against us."

Now it was Wally's turn to shake his head. "I don't believe you. The ultimate goal... the goal we were all talking about after New York... was PROTEUS."

The Colonel raised his hands slightly, "Oh, well, yes, that part wasn't exactly true. Something has to happen in New York and other places, yes. Reinforcement is central to the program, and I still have every intention of collecting that commission, after all. But only in order to protect PROTEUS. Everything leading up to that, though, yes. Yes, all the rest was true, I assure you." He picked up his spoon, then set it down again, placing both hands on the desk. "PROTEUS has so many plans. So many glorious plans. We really haven't seen anything yet. Citizens won't be able to think an unmutual thought or clip an unmutual hangnail without PROTEUS knowing about it instantaneously. Not that those things will even be an issue five years from now."

Wally tried snarling at him, "We're not your slaves," but it came out all wrong.

"Weren't you listening? Yes you are."

"No we aren't."

"*Yes,*" the Colonel insisted firmly, "you are. Come now, my boy, wouldn't you rather be on the winning side, for once?"

The room fell silent. Then something occurred to Wally.

"I don't understand," he said. "If this is your plan, why would you put someone like Sid Powell on the air? If I saw it, other people saw it and they'll get ideas, too."

The Colonel's smile was condescending. "Do you honestly believe anyone saw him but *you*? We were in a van across the street from your house. Directional antenna, you see."

"But why—?"

"Because. My granddaughter was one seed. We needed to plant another. You were very susceptible, I must say, albeit in a way we like."

As the Colonel resumed calmly eating his soup, Wally's mind was racing backward to the beginning, through everyone he knew and everyone he'd dealt with. Were they all part of it? And where had it begun?

"That woman with the stroller," he finally said, mostly to himself. He looked to Jack. "That Brigade cow on Horribleness Day—that's where this all started. I *knew* she'd targeted me. I saw the film and I knew it."

"Oh, no, actually," Jack said, surprised. "No, she has nothing to do with us. I'd never seen her before. She just rammed you because she wanted to, I guess. That was just a happy accident."

Wally's heart sank. Margie had been right all along.

"And now, Mr. Philco," the Colonel said, pushing the bowl aside and sliding open a drawer. He removed a sheaf of official-looking papers. "That being settled, we can get down to the business of why you're here today." He paused a moment and examined the papers more closely, making sure they were the ones he wanted. Satisfied, he set them down again. "You see, we have a job in San Antonio that calls for someone with your unique qualifications. Jack will explain the details on the way."

Wally glared across the desk with the transparent, fearful defiance of a man who knows damn well he's been beaten.

"Oh, no need to look so glum, there, chummy," the Colonel said. "It's just *history,* after all, and you're about to play a very important role. You'll be the new Guy Fawkes. My goodness, you may even get your own holiday out of it."

With a last, dying ember of hope, Wally said, "Couldn't I—?" but the Colonel was already shaking his head with what appeared to be melancholy understanding.

"No, I'm sorry, Mr. Philco. It's too late. As the trite saying goes, you know too much." He paused. "You see, think of it this way. The organism has priority over the cell. You understand? You isolate a cell, take it away from all the other cells and put it on a slide, you know what happens? Without that input from the other cells, it's programmed to destroy itself. So that's the point. We can use you, and you need us, but we can also live without you quite easily. No offense."

"None taken."

"It's true, though. Simple biology. The integration of the whole is dependent upon the death of many of its parts. Now, whether one of those parts is you or several thousand Texans, well . . ." He raised his eyebrows. "At this point you have but two destinations from which to choose: San Antonio or Terminal Five. I'd suggest San Antonio, myself. It's nicer." He chuckled softly. "For the time being, anyway. Now, chop chop—" He clapped his hands together sharply. "Plane's waiting."

Wally couldn't have said anything if he'd wanted to. He continued to stare, seeing neither man, feeling nothing.

Well, he thought, as an expectant and deathly silence settled over the room, *I tried.*

ABOUT THE AUTHOR

Jim Knipfel lives in Brooklyn, where the hunt for the blind spot rolls on.

ACKNOWLEDGMENTS

I would like to extend my deepest gratitude to the following people, whose contributions to this book were invaluable.

Special thanks are due my tireless agent, Melanie Jackson, who continues to pull off the impossible, and to my remarkable editor, Sarah Hochman, who showed me once again what good editing is all about. Working with both is nothing short of a pleasure and an honor.

Special thanks are also due my good friend Don Kennison, one of the finest copy editors on earth, as well as a man of rare insight.

I would also like to thank Germ Books and Gallery; Daniel Riccuito and Marilyn Palmeri; Violet Turner; Brian Berger;

Brian Slattery; Richard Dellifraine; Jerome Deppe; Tito Perdue; Ryan Knighton; Erik Horn and Brad Parrett of Super!Alright! Media; Homer Flynn; TRP; J. R. Taylor; Mike at Loki; Magister Peter Gilmore; Shep Abbot and Douglas Cheek (who together unleashed C.H.U.D.s on the world); Philip Harris of Electron-Press.com; Dave Read; Mom and Dad; Bob, Mary, McKenzie, and Jordan Adrians; Derek Davis; John Strausbaugh; Ken Swezey and Laura Lindgren; Bill Monahan; Alex Zaitchik; Leif Solem; Reid Paley; Luca Dipierro; and finally Philip Glass and the inimitable Tex Johnson and His Six Shooters for providing the sound track.

My deep and endless gratitude goes to Morgan Intrieri, with my love. Her sharp intelligence, twisted humor, infallible eye, and profound wisdom continue to inspire and challenge me. Her contribution to this book (and so much else) has been immeasurable. She makes it all worthwhile.